THE
RUNAWAY

Hollie Overton is a television writer who has written for ABC Family, CBS and Lifetime.

Overton's father was a member of Austin, Texas notorious Overton gang, and spent several years in prison for manslaughter.

Raised by her single mother, Hollie draws on her unique childhood experiences to lend realism and compassion to her depictions of violence and complicated family dynamics.

THE RUNAWAY

HOLLIE OVERTON

arrow books

Road
London SW1V 2SA

Arrow Books is part of the Penguin Random House group of companies
whose addresses can be found at global.penguinrandomhouse.com.

Copyright © Hollie Overton 2019

Hollie Overton has asserted her right to be identified
as the author of this Work in accordance with the Copyright,
Designs and Patents Act 1988.

First published in paperback by Arrow Books in 2019

www.penguin.co.uk

A CIP catalogue record for this book is available from the British Library.

ISBN 9781787460744

Printed and bound in Great Britain by Clays Ltd, Elcograf S.p.A.

MIX
Paper from
responsible sources
FSC
www.fsc.org   FSC® C018179

Penguin Random House is committed to a
sustainable future for our business, our readers
and our planet. This book is made from Forest
Stewardship Council® certified paper.

THE
RUNAWAY

ASH

It's a work of art, thought sixteen-year-old Ash as she gazed down at her forearm at the delicately inked tattoo. This wasn't Ash's first tattoo, she had four others, but this one, with its lifelike image of a human eye, an elaborate sword piercing through it, was special.

"Now you're one of us," her boyfriend, Nate, said, smiling at her, his blue-gray eyes sparkling. She watched as Nate's family huddled around, inspecting the final product. Ash had always been an outsider, afraid to get close to people. Nate had changed all of that.

Leslie, the sweet-faced seventeen-year-old from Padre Island with dimples and streaks of purple through her brown hair, smiled and high-fived Ash.

"Nate's right. You're so badass. You didn't even flinch," she said approvingly, holding her wrist up to show off her matching tattoo. Ash smiled back at her, watching as Leslie flitted away toward the center of camp.

Kelsey and Andrea, the hipster couple from Portland, weren't the chatty types, but even they seemed pleased, patting Ash on the back before they moved away. Eli, the youngest of the group at fifteen, giggled, pushing his platinum-blond hair out of his eyes as he held up his own forearm to Ash to reveal his matching tattoo, like he was a superhero and they were activating their powers. "It's awesome, Ash. We're lucky to have you here."

"Thanks, E," Ash said, squeezing his hand. He blushed, and hurried over to the center of camp.

"That kid's got it bad," Nate said teasingly.

Ash shrugged, offering up an exaggerated hair flip. "What can I say? I'm irresistible."

Nate laughed. "Agreed." He pulled her onto his lap and kissed her. A groan interrupted the moment. Until now Vic, the family's resident tattoo artist, had been silent, but he was shaking his head, with a mock look of disgust. "Can we cool it with the PDAs? Mo's here with dinner and I'm about to lose my appetite," he said as he carefully packed his needles into a small black bag.

Ash laughed. Nineteen-year-old Vic was the most serious of the group. At first, Ash had found him a bit unnerving. He was a mountain of a man at six foot five, with arms the size of tree trunks, and his entire face was covered in tattoos, not an inch to spare. The others had warned her it would be impossible to win Vic over, but Ash always loved a challenge.

"Sorry, Vic. Can't stop. Won't stop," Ash said, planting

another kiss on Nate, who laughed. Vic rolled his eyes, but Ash clocked the hint of a smile. She was finally making progress.

"Hey, Vic, mind giving me and my girl a few minutes alone?" Nate asked.

Vic nodded, glancing down once more at his handiwork. "It really is amazing," Ash replied.

This time she got an honest-to-goodness smile as Vic shuffled away to join the others. Mo, the family's matriarch, had arrived and was handing out sandwiches. She offered Ash a friendly wave. Ash waved back. "The food is here, and I know you're hungry." Nate was always hungry. "We should join the others," she said.

"Let them wait," Nate said, staring back at her with those worshipful eyes. Sometimes his intensity made Ash uneasy, as though she weren't quite worthy of his devotion. He pulled Ash closer, wrapping his arms tightly around her waist. The folding camp chair sagged under their weight. She didn't care. She loved being here in his arms, watching as the sun disappeared into the horizon, light bouncing off the downtown city skyline.

Moments like this, Ash could almost forget where she was. Then a rat the size of a housecat would scurry by in search of food, or a junkie would let out a bloodcurdling scream, or a sharp, pungent odor would invade her nose and Ash would be reminded that none of this was normal. Nate was homeless, living here on the streets of Skid Row. They all lived here, Leslie, Eli, Vic, Mo, and the others, joining thousands of homeless men, women, and children. They called themselves the Tribe, a makeshift family that looked after one another. It wasn't an ideal situation, but Ash was glad he'd found people to look out for him. Nate deserved that.

"You're too quiet. What's going on up there?" Nate asked, his finger lightly tapping her temple.

"Just thinking about us," she said with a kiss. Her phone buzzed, the familiar text alert. It was her foster mother. *Got stuck on a case. Running late. You order the pizza. I'll pick it up. Home by eight thirty. Xoxo*

Ash's eyes flitted back to her newly inked tattoo. She was so caught up in the moment, everyone cheering her on and encouraging her to get the tattoo, that she hadn't thought about Becca. Not her smartest move. Her foster mother was going to be pissed.

Ash blamed Nate. He made her careless. All the promises she'd given to Becca, her probation officer—even her therapist—went out the window once he came along. When she wasn't hanging out with him, she was thinking about when she could see him again.

Not wanting Becca to worry, Ash quickly responded. *Can't wait. I'm starving. Hope you had a good day. See ya soon.* She hit send and turned back to Nate. "I have to go," Ash said softly.

"Can't you stay a little longer?"

4

"No. She would worry." Ash wound her arms around Nate's neck. "You could always come with me."

His entire body tensed. "I can't and you know it," he said.

Ash couldn't hide her annoyance. "Are you serious? Jesus, Nate, I've been sneaking around for three months. Lying to Becca about us for three months."

Nate's carefree demeanor vanished, his grip loosening on her. "Please don't do this, Ash. Not now. Not tonight."

That's what he always said. *Not now. Not tonight. This isn't a good time. Don't ruin it.*

"All I'm asking is for you to come to dinner, so Becca knows you exist. One night. That's all."

"Then what? She welcomes me with open arms, no questions asked? Nothing about how we met? Where we met? No questions about my parents? Or where I live and go to school?"

They'd had this discussion before. Ash understood Nate's concern. He was a minor—as were many of the others. If Becca found out they were living on the streets, she would be legally obligated to report it.

"I'll run interference. Keep the interrogation to a minimum. I'm good at that," Ash said, trying to keep her voice light.

Nate wasn't having it. His hands were clenched tightly into fists. "I can't do it, Ash. It's not just me. I can't put the family at risk."

Ash stepped away from him, pushing her dark hair out

of her face. What about what Ash was risking? "So I do all of this lying and sneaking around behind Becca's back. I even get this damn tattoo for you..."

"For me? I didn't force you to do anything. You said it was cool. You said it would bring us closer together," Nate said, frustration clouding his face.

Ash sighed. "I know, and I wanted to do it. I just don't understand why you can't do this for me," Ash said. She hated how weak and needy she sounded.

"And I don't understand why you want to screw up what we have," Nate said, his voice rising.

"You okay, Ash?" Ash turned to see Eli eyeing Nate warily. He'd puffed his chest out as though he was attempting to make himself larger. A surge of appreciation flooded through her.

"We're fine, Eli," Nate snapped before Ash could speak.

"I wasn't talking to you," Eli said, not backing down. Ash was surprised. Eli looked up to Nate, always following him around, asking him to teach him a new chord on his guitar. He was such a sweet kid. Crush or no crush, she appreciated his support. But she could handle Nate.

"I'm fine, E. Go finish your food. We'll be over in a minute." Eli hesitated. He didn't leave, standing his ground.

"Jesus, Eli, give us some fucking space," Nate shouted. Eli flinched just as Mo appeared.

"Okay, what is going on here and how can we resolve it?" she asked. Mo was the oldest of the Tribe, mid-forties,

6

with ruddy sunburnt skin and gray-streaked brownish hair that she always wore in a ponytail with a tie-dyed scarf. She was regarding them curiously, as though they were some kind of sociological experiment she was documenting.

Eli startled, eyes cast downward. "Nothing, Mo. It's nothing," Eli said as he hurried away. Nate didn't say a word, staring down at his scuffed sneakers. As far as Nate and the others were concerned, Mo could do no wrong. Ash wasn't so sure. There was something about Mo's excessive cheerfulness, always wearing this slightly off-kilter smile. She reminded Ash of a puppet she once saw at the local library, the puppet master pulling its strings tighter and tighter until it was impossible to distinguish a smile from a grimace. Mo placed a gentle hand on Nate's shoulder. "Relationships are complicated. I understand and value that. I'm happy to offer some insight if you'd like."

Ash wasn't sure why this rubbed her the wrong way. It wasn't like Mo had made such great life choices. "What I'd like is to talk to Nate in private," Ash said.

Nate stiffened, but Mo didn't react at all, her smile unwavering. "Didn't mean to intrude. If either of you change your mind and need my counsel, you know where to find me."

Mo slipped away, leaving Ash alone with Nate. He kept his voice low, speaking through gritted teeth, his eyes flashing. "How could you talk to her like that? You know what Mo means to me. What she's done for me."

"You know what Becca means to me. What she's done for me. You just don't care."

Nate didn't speak. A long, awkward silence lingered. The last thing Ash wanted was to pick a fight. There was a simple solution to all of this. She reached out, taking Nate's hand in hers, keeping her voice low. "Mo and the others don't need to know. I won't say a word. Just say you'll come to dinner." She stared at him with pleading eyes. *Come with me. Come with me.*

He shook free from her. "Damn it, Ash, I said no. Don't ask me again," Nate snapped.

This time he was practically shouting. Stunned, Ash took a step back. She turned and saw the others, now eyeing her with suspicion, all their goodwill seeming to vanish.

"Guess you better get back to your family," she said. She turned and headed down the street, expecting Nate to follow her, begging her to come back. He didn't. It wasn't until Ash rounded the corner that tears began to fall. She glanced down at her arm, a stinging sensation setting in, as if the tattoo were suddenly mocking her. All of Ash's excitement, that sense of belonging and closeness, vanished. She wasn't Nate's and she certainly wasn't part of this family. Not even close.

ASH

An hour later, Ash unlocked the door and slipped inside the elaborate two-story Silver Lake craftsman, lovingly remodeled and filled with handmade furnishings and dozens of scented candles. After the grit and grime of Skid Row, being back in this well-lit, perfectly maintained home was a jolt to the system.

Freud, Becca's raucous pit bull mix, burst into the hall, barking loudly, his tail wagging furiously, demanding to be petted. Ash bent down and hugged Freud tightly, allowing him to lick her face, his tail thumping loudly in excitement. She knew things were bad when even Freud's presence wasn't enough to cheer her up. "Come on, buddy. I've gotta clean up."

She hurried up the stairs to her bedroom and peered into the mirror, her eyes bloodshot, cheeks tearstained. She splashed cold water over her face, grabbed her concealer, and went to work. The last thing she wanted was for Becca to start asking questions. She eyed her phone, willing Nate to call or text. All she wanted was for him to say he was sorry and that they'd figure things out together. She wanted to know there was some kind of plan.

Downstairs, Freud began furiously barking, signaling Becca's arrival. Ash couldn't think about Nate now. She had to survive this dinner. She caught sight of the tattoo in the mirror, bright red and raw, and quickly reached for her favorite oversized Dodgers hoodie. She would have to explain the tattoo eventually, but she didn't have the energy. Not tonight.

Ash hurried downstairs and found Becca in the kitchen, dressed in her standard uniform of khakis, button-down, and her LAPD windbreaker. "Sensible clothes for a sensible lady," Ash liked to tease.

"Sorry I'm late. I swear to God they must have gone to Sicily for this pie," Becca said with a rueful smile as she placed the pizza on the counter. She kicked off her shoes and hurried over to the fridge, pulling out the salad fixings. "How was the mission today?" Becca asked.

There it was. Another one of Ash's lies. She used to volunteer three times a week at the Downtown Mission, teaching photography classes and helping out in the soup kitchen. Since she met Nate, those evenings were spent with him and the Tribe.

"It was fine," Ash said. "Nothing new to report."

Usually, Becca wanted more details, requiring Ash to come up with elaborate stories about her volunteer work.

Tonight though, Becca seemed tired, not at all her usually inquisitive self.

Ash watched as Becca began pulling china and cutlery from the cabinet. Before Ash moved in, she'd never even seen china, except on TV. Growing up with her birth mom, Faye, Ash learned to scrounge for food. Usually it was straight out of a can, her mother passed out in another room or off on one of her dates. Not Becca. The entire Ortiz family took food very seriously. Each night they'd sit down at the dining table for dinner, even the nights Becca worked late, even if it was only takeout.

"Are you okay?" Ash asked Becca as she began setting the table.

"Kind of a terrible day," Becca said, sighing heavily as she pushed her long black hair out of her eyes. "We lost a jumper. Married, two kids. I don't think we could've done anything to stop him, but…" Becca trailed off.

Ash could see Becca's hands were trembling, her eyes ringed red. Becca was a shrink who worked with the LAPD. Her unit was dispatched to all kinds of calls involving crazy people, which meant she saw a lot of terrible shit. Ash hadn't even thought about what Becca might be dealing with. Here she was moping around about a fight with her boyfriend, while Becca was watching someone end their life.

"Wanna talk about it?" Ash asked, working hard not to seem distracted.

"Actually, I thought we could eat and then I might take a bath, get to bed early."

Ash's shoulders sagged with relief. "Sure. That sounds good."

They dished up the pizza and salad, settling at the dining table to eat. They discussed Ash's latest photography project and upcoming spring break. Eventually, the conversation waned, Ash and Becca caught up in their own thoughts, and they ate in silence.

Half an hour later, Ash was back in her room, sprawled out on her king-sized bed, Freud curled up at her feet. When Ash first moved in, she couldn't believe this giant bed was all hers. She'd never seen anything so luxurious in her entire life. The blankets were so soft that she used to say it was like lying on clouds.

The first few weeks Ash slept on the floor. One morning Becca found her there, shook Ash awake, and sank down onto the floor beside her, Freud joining them. "Sweet girl, what in the world are you doing down here?"

Ash's face flushed as she thought about all the excuses she could give. She opted for the truth. "It's so nice here, but I don't want to get used to all of this in case you change your mind and send me away." She could still remember Becca's shocked expression. "This bed is yours. This home is yours. You're not going anywhere."

Sometimes though, Ash wanted to go back to when she didn't care about Becca. She'd gotten good at not caring.

Her birth mother taught her that. Faye wasn't much of a talker, but her hands were quite expressive. The palm strike across the face when Ash was four. The quick jab to the ribs when she was five. By the time Ash turned six, she learned to manage the pain, but the betrayal never got easier. How could her mother, the woman she loved most in the world, want to see her suffer?

Ash gave up on answering that question. She was thirteen the last time it happened. Faye lunged at her, hatred burning in her eyes. Ash finally had enough. She smashed the woman in the head with her algebra textbook and grabbed the three hundred bucks she had saved from under her mattress. Two hours later Ash was on a Greyhound bus, bound for LA.

Growing up in a shitty trailer park on the outskirts of Macon, Georgia, Ash spent years daydreaming about where she'd go if she had the courage to run away. TV always made it seem like breaking into show business was easy. Ash figured why not. She thought once she arrived in LA, some hotshot agent would make her famous. Or maybe she'd get on one of those reality shows. She had a decent voice, better than most of the singers she saw. She envisioned shopping on Rodeo Drive and lounging at the Beverly Hills Hotel while waiters attended to her every need.

The second Ash stepped off the bus, she was confronted with a much different reality. The ugliness wasn't just lurking beneath the glittering lights, it was front and center. The city streets were covered with discarded beer bottles, fast-food wrappers, and used condoms. The Hollywood Walk of Fame was teeming with emotionally unstable vagrants jostling for space alongside desperate wannabe actors in superhero costumes, all of them trying to make a quick buck from the horde of selfie-obsessed tourists.

Ash worked hard to keep a low profile, steering clear of the cops. She'd heard plenty of stories about how shitty foster care was. She'd already survived a hellish existence with Faye. No way was she going back to another. Which was how Ash ended up living on the streets.

Her first year had been a special kind of hell. Ash had created a system: sleep during the day, keep it moving at night, and always be on the lookout for potential threats. She had done her best to stay clean, washing up in park bathrooms and in shelters. People were always eager to offer a few dollars to a cute kid, and she had learned to pick pockets so she hadn't starved. She'd done her best to avoid the pervs, and had learned to fight back when she had to. A chance encounter with Becca had changed everything. Together they'd built a home. The last thing Ash wanted was to ruin it. It was selfish though, because she didn't want to lose Nate either. She wanted them both.

Exhausted from the stress of the day, Ash felt her eyes flutter closed. Her phone buzzed. She jolted upright, reaching for it. *Please be Nate. Please be Nate.* She held her breath.

It was.

Relieved, Ash clicked on the message. A grainy video appeared on-screen. Nate sat alone in his tent, guitar in hand, strumming lightly. "This song goes out to my girl," he said with an overexaggerated twang. He began to sing, belting out Billy Ray Cyrus's "Achy Breaky Heart." Nate wasn't big on country music, not like Ash, but he sang the hell out of the song. Ash laughed, watching the video two more times. No one could make her laugh like Nate.

Another message appeared on-screen. *I'm a total fucking idiot. Of course the Tribe is important to me but so are you. Name the time and place and I'll meet Becca. Dinner. Lunch. Brunch. Whatever you want, I'll do it.*

Ash blinked back tears, her heart soaring. She wondered if the last few hours were as miserable for him as they were for her. She glanced at the time. It was almost midnight. If she left now, she could see Nate and make it home before Becca ever woke up. Ash texted back a heart emoji, wanting to surprise him, and hurried out of bed, quietly slipping on her jeans and sneakers.

Becca monitored Ash's Uber usage, so Ash Googled the number of a cab company and scheduled a pickup. She pulled her hoodie back on and grabbed a fifty-dollar bill from her drawer, part of the money she'd received from Becca for her sixteenth birthday. She smoothed out the comforter, a force of habit, and tiptoed downstairs. Freud trailed after her, nudging Ash with his wet nose. She plied

15

him with treats to keep him quiet, and slipped out of the house undetected. Ash rushed down the street, relieved to see the cab already waiting for her.

She sank back into the seat, anxiously staring out the window, the empty streets zipping by. Fifteen minutes later, the driver pulled onto Alameda Street, a block from Nate's campsite. Ash never came down here this late, knowing the dangers lurking in the shadows. Her stomach fluttered as she eyed the dozens of bodies lined up alongside the sidewalk, some in tents, others sleeping on the sidewalk. She quickened her pace. She would be safe with Nate. She always was.

She rounded the corner and spotted the Tribe's camp. Despite the late hour, everyone was gathered in a semicircle outside Mo's tent. She found Nate, standing on the outer edge of the group, his hands tucked in the pockets of his pants, his shoulders slightly hunched as he stood beside Leslie. Ash stepped off the curb. She was so focused on Nate she didn't even see the first punch land. Eli's guttural scream got her attention. She turned her head and watched as his nose shattered, blood pouring down his face. Eli gazed back at his attacker. Ash couldn't believe what she was seeing. Vic towered over Eli, a sneering scowl on his face. She stood frozen, watching in horror as the others descended. Ash recognized Kelsey and Andrea, but the rest were a blur of fists and legs. A mob on speed.

The shock wore off and Ash knew she had to act. She

broke free and raced across the street. "Stop. Fucking stop it," she shouted at them.

As if on cue, they all whirled around, eyes widened in disbelief. Vic took a menacing step forward. "Stay out of it, Ash," he barked. A terrified Eli used this distraction as his opportunity to attempt an escape, crawling toward Ash, blood streaming down his face, staining his gray T-shirt.

"Help me. Please," he begged. Ash saw it then—that familiar look of betrayal, and she was transported back to her childhood, cowering in her room, her mother wielding a belt. No mercy. No escape. People knew what Faye was doing to her. The bruises, the cuts. Neighbors, teachers, the church ladies. No one intervened. No one said a word. They'd all turned their backs on her. Ash couldn't do that to Eli.

"Stop! Get away from him," she said again, this time with more force. It was useless. Vic grabbed Eli by the hair and he was swallowed up by the mob. They unleashed more punches and kicks as Eli curled into himself.

Helpless, Ash spun around to see Nate and Leslie looking on in silence. They were in shock. That was the only explanation. Ash grabbed Nate's arm and shook him. "You have to make them stop." He stayed completely still. Leslie blinked furiously as though she couldn't believe what was unfolding, but she did nothing.

The old Ash would've stayed out of this—no, the old Ash would have run away and never looked back. Running was what she did best, but things had changed. Ash had changed.

She took a few steps forward, ready to throw herself into the fight. A second later, she felt Nate's arms around her as he lifted her off the ground. "We have to go. *Now*," Nate said, each word punctuated. Ash struggled against him, but it was futile. Nate had at least three inches and thirty pounds on her.

"We can't just leave him," Ash screamed.

Nate tightened his grip, silently half dragging, half carrying Ash away. She caught a glimpse of Mo. Her arms were crossed.

"Mo, you can end this," Ash yelled. They'd listen to Mo. They always listened to her. She was their leader. The guru of the streets.

Everything was happening so quickly, but Ash could have sworn she saw a smile on Mo's face. It was as if she was actually enjoying this.

"Nate, goddamn it, let me go," Ash shouted, struggling against him. He didn't stop, carrying her farther and farther away from the brawl. There were dozens of people camped out on the street, men and women in dirty clothes, and tents and sleeping bags, but no one paid them any attention. It was as though Ash were completely invisible, her distress unremarkable in this vast sea of despair.

Nate carried her another two blocks before stopping in a vacant alley. His breathing labored, he finally set her down.

"We're good, Ash. We're okay," Nate insisted over and over, his arms still wrapped around her.

"Okay? You think we're okay?" Ash asked, shoving Nate hard. She wanted to jolt him free from whatever stupor he was in.

"It's...it was nothing," he said.

Ash shook her head. This wasn't nothing. Nate swore these people were good and kind. She believed him. Fuck, she even got a tattoo for him. That stupid Tribe tattoo. She couldn't think about that now. She had to help Eli. A million thoughts flickered through her brain. Ash didn't trust cops. In her experience, they were generally useless. There was only one person she trusted. Ash fumbled for her phone.

"What are you doing?" Nate demanded.

"I'm calling Becca," she said. Before Ash could press her number on speed dial, Nate grabbed her wrists, pinning them and the phone together. From the start, Nate swore that he would always protect her. Ash winced. "Ow. Nate, you're hurting me."

Nate instantly released her, regret clouding his expression. "I'm sorry, Ash. I'm so sorry, but you can't tell anyone what happened."

"Screw that. Eli's hurt. We have to tell someone. He needs help."

"No, stay out of it. This is family business," Nate said.

"Family business? What does that mean?"

"Mo said Eli violated the code. We have to send a message," Nate said.

She couldn't believe this was happening. The more Nate said, the worse things got. Code? What code? What kind of a message? She didn't know what the hell he was talking about.

Tears pricked at Ash's eyes. She could feel the panic building. She rubbed her hands on her faded blue jeans. Becca always said, "When things get hard, most people panic. The ones who survive remember to breathe."

"I can't...I can't stay here. I have to go," Ash said. She needed to get away from him; she needed to think about what she was going to do.

Nate went to stop her. This time his touch was gentle, his voice urgent. "Ash, promise you won't tell anyone. Promise me?"

Ash hesitated. "Ash, please," he said.

"I promise," she whispered, but she couldn't shake the feeling that after today nothing between them would ever be the same. Ignoring Nate's pleas to stay, Ash summoned a page from her old playbook, and she ran.

BECCA

An explosion of sound jolted Becca Ortiz from the depths of sleep. Her entire body tensed, her breath catching. *Please let it just be the wind. Please.* She held her breath, waiting. It wasn't the wind. She heard it—the unmistakable sound of footsteps and the crunching of glass. Shaking off the last remnants of sleep, Becca bolted out of bed. Someone was breaking in.

Her next thought was of Ash. Becca grabbed her phone and raced down the hall toward her daughter's bedroom. "Ash, wake up. Someone's in the house," she whispered urgently.

No response. "Ash, you have to wake up." Only silence greeted her. God, teenagers really could sleep through anything. Becca fumbled around in the dark until she located the nearby lamp, a gentle white light illuminating the room. It took a moment to register what she was seeing. Ash was gone, her bed still neatly made.

Working in law enforcement, Becca was well versed in what to do in the event of a burglary or kidnapping.

21

Stay put.

Call the police.

Remain calm.

Do not confront the intruders.

Unfortunately, rules didn't take into account love and maternal instincts. Becca headed back down the hall, taking the stairs two at a time, pausing at the bottom landing, her breathing ragged. Where was Ash? Did someone take her? Were they still in the house? Becca's thoughts drifted to the old service revolver her ex-husband left behind, remembered with regret how she stored it away in a lockbox on a shelf in the garage. A lot of good that would do her now.

Breathe. Just breathe. Becca always told her clients that when panic set in. She rounded the corner and saw Ash, illuminated by moonlight, down on her hands and knees, frantically sweeping up the remnants of one of Becca's flowerpots. Freud sat on his hind legs near Ash, eyeing her warily. As much as she loved Freud, he really was a worthless guard dog. "Ash? Are you okay?"

Ash let out a startled gasp. "Jesus, Becca, you scared me."

Becca let out a shaky laugh. "The feeling is mutual. I thought someone was breaking in. I was this close to calling the cops."

"Okay, talk about overreacting. I took Freud for a walk and accidentally knocked over the pot... I didn't mean to wake you."

Becca studied Ash, searching for signs she was lying.

"Here, let me help," Becca said, bending down to gather up the larger pieces of glass, hoping to get a better look at Ash. She scanned the young girl's face, searching for the thin sheen of sweat beading on her upper lip, the bloodshot eyes, and the unfocused gaze, all the telltale signs of a relapse. Instead she saw Ash's cheeks, a little flushed from the crisp night air, her eyes bright and clear. She sagged a bit with relief. "You sure everything's okay?" Becca asked.

"I thought you were off the clock," Ash said pointedly.

For years Becca's family insisted she stop therapizing them, which was easier said than done. Being a therapist wasn't something she could shut off, an inescapable occupational hazard. Today had been hard. She was still reeling from the loss at work, the man's tortured expression right before he leapt off the freeway to his death etched on her brain. Was she projecting, looking for a problem where there wasn't one? Becca knew Ash used before she took her in, but things got worse before they got better. It seemed Ash was constantly pushing boundaries, ditching school to score drugs, stealing pills from Becca's medicine cabinet. They'd worked hard to reach this point. Once again, Becca took in Ash's bright eyes and clear speech, and her heart rate slowed. This was nothing more than an accident. Accidents happen. Ash was fine.

Becca intercepted the broom and dustpan and finished cleanup duty. "We should get back to bed. We both have an early day tomorrow."

Ash's posture relaxed ever so slightly as she headed upstairs. Becca closed and locked the back door and checked the front door for good measure. She was headed back up the stairs when she heard Ash call down. "Okay if I crash with you and Freud tonight?"

There it was. Something was wrong. There was a time when Ash first moved in when she'd crawl into Becca's bed. She'd mumble something about a bad dream and then drift off to sleep. Becca couldn't remember the last time she'd done that. She wanted to say something, but she didn't want to make it a thing, didn't want to see Ash roll her eyes and stomp upstairs.

"Of course. There's always room for you," Becca said. They settled into Becca's king-sized bed, Ash on one side, Becca on the other, Freud in the middle. Becca switched off the lights but couldn't sleep, all her anxiousness and uneasiness whirling around. She lay there for what seemed like hours, listening to Ash's steady breathing. Becca turned to watch her, seeing the easy rise and fall of her chest. Ash stirred and turned over, the sleeve of her hoodie slipping off to reveal her tattooed forearm.

Becca let out a quiet gasp, clocking a new tattoo, an intricately drawn eyeball, a sword piercing the center. She wasn't sure what was worse, the disturbing image or the fact that Ash got this tattoo on her own without asking permission. Becca stifled the urge to shake Ash awake and demand to know when and where she got this.

It's only a tattoo, she told herself. In the beginning when Ash first came to live with Becca, this tattoo would have been serious cause for concern. That was before rehab and countless hours of therapy. That was ancient history, she told herself. Ash wasn't the angry, sullen kid she had been before. She was clean and sober. There was no reason to think anything was wrong. In fact, Becca could already hear her therapist's gentle reminder.

"Sometimes things are as good as they seem. Don't go borrowing trouble."

Yet that nagging voice in Becca's head said there was something going on. Becca wouldn't ignore that voice. She'd done that before and it ruined her family, cost her brother his life. Becca shook away any thoughts of Robbie. This wasn't about him. This was about Ash. Whatever was happening, Becca was confident they would find a way through. She squeezed Ash's hand. *Whatever's going on, sweet girl, we'll fix it together. You have my word.*

MO

Mo's mantra from the start was hard and fast: "No outsiders." That was the only way to maintain the family's integrity. She never should have forgotten the rules. Not for anyone. Not even Nate.

She stretched her legs against the fabric of her tent, her muscles tightening. She needed to walk and contemplate next steps. She pulled on a pair of old tan chinos and a faded black T-shirt and tied her hair back with her favorite tie-dyed scarf. There was a time in her life, years ago, when Mo obsessed over every article of clothing, dedicating hours toward skin care and makeup, working tirelessly to achieve perfection. Thankfully all of that was behind her. At forty-two, she was no longer a prisoner of Botox and waxing and five a.m. gym sessions. She hadn't even looked at a mirror in years.

She climbed out of her tent and slipped past the giant blue tarp that protected her from the elements, LA's glittering night skyline greeting her. Mo listened to the hum of cars whizzing by, the frenzied tone of two junkies arguing in the distance. Most people were unsettled by Skid Row's soundtrack, but Mo found the chaos comforting.

"You okay?" a voice asked. Mo turned to see Vic standing by his tent, a few feet from hers, sucking on a Marlboro. Despite the late hour, Vic always sensed when Mo needed his counsel.

"You're such a sweet boy. I'm doing much better now that I've seen you," Mo said. He half smiled, which Mo considered a win. Vic was massive, almost six foot six, barrel-chested, with tribal tattoos covering his entire upper body and all of his face. His appearance was so off-putting that most people wouldn't even get close to him. This isolation made Vic sullen and angry. With time and patience, Mo had gained his trust and Vic had blossomed. He was her most treasured confidant.

"Want to walk?" she asked. He nodded, and wordlessly led her across the street and down an alley. They fell in step, dodging heaping piles of trash, dog shit, and hypodermic needles as they did a loop around the block.

The situation that had occurred was unfortunate. Ash was never supposed to be there tonight. Eli's punishment wasn't any of Ash's business. From what Mo had gathered when Nate returned, they were dealing with a potential crisis. She didn't need some hysterical child ruining what she'd built. Nate assured Mo that everything would be okay. The last thing she wanted to do was to question his loyalty. He was a newer addition to the family, a sweet kid. She tried not to play favorites, but over the course of the last year, Mo had developed a real fondness for him. He was so thoughtful and caring, a substantial, unwavering presence, always eager to read and debate, and a talented musician. When he had come to Mo and said he'd met someone, she wanted to be supportive. "Tell me all about her."

Ordinarily effusive, Nate had hunched his shoulders ever so slightly. He leaned in closer as if he were confessing a shameful secret. "She's not one of us," he said.

Mo had gone quiet, surprised he would find someone who hadn't embraced their home-free lifestyle. "Where does she live?" Mo had asked.

"In Silver Lake. With her foster mother. We met when Ash was living on the streets, but we got separated. We just ran into each other again a few months ago. I care about her... a lot. Of course I want your blessing to keep seeing her."

Nate was smart enough to know that bringing someone around and allowing them to be a part of the group was a decision that required a great deal of care and concern. If anyone told the cops about them, they might start asking questions or making inquiries about their living situation. "As long as you're careful. Not everyone will understand what we've built here."

Nate had taken Mo's words to heart. He'd introduced Ash to the family, one by one. They were all charmed by her. Mo wanted to like her, but something about this girl rubbed her the wrong way. She was a little too quiet and introspective, always deflecting Mo's questions as though they were beneath her.

Mo had remained quiet about her misgivings. As the days and weeks wore on, Ash had become a constant presence around their campsite. Most afternoons she would stop by, draping herself all over Nate, the two of them unable to keep their hands off each other. It was slightly distasteful, but still Mo had kept quiet. A few nights a week, Ash would sneak away from her own home and spend her evenings sitting with the Tribe, listening as Nate played music, the others singing along. Through it all, the voice inside Mo's head had been practically screaming, *Don't trust her.*

She hadn't been consulted about Ash's tattoo either, arriving too late to put a stop to it. She'd been disappointed that Vic allowed this to occur without consulting her. Mo should have intervened sooner. Now she had no choice.

As they walked, Mo looked at Vic, his shoulders hunched up, cigarette dangling from his lips. Mo regarded him more carefully, noticing the slight tremor under his left eye. A dead giveaway he was concealing something. "I'm disappointed in you, Vic."

Her words startled him. "I don't…why?" he stammered.

"You're not being truthful. What is it?"

He looked down again, kicking at the broken glass. "Vic, I asked you a question."

30

Vic's eyes instantly met Mo's. "I made a promise to Nate," he said.

Mo flinched. This was worse than she'd thought. First Nate getting caught up with Ash. Now Vic was keeping secrets from her.

"You made a promise to me. To the family. Is what you're not telling me something that could harm us? Endanger our future?"

His eyes widened, and Mo gave herself a mental high five. She knew Vic even better than he knew himself. She touched Vic's arm. "Whatever it is, you can tell me, sweetheart."

He sighed. "Did you know Ash's foster mom works for the five-oh?"

Mo went still, fighting the rising tide of fury. No, she did not know the girl's mother worked for law enforcement. If she did, she never would have allowed her into their sanctuary. The police were never to be trusted. They'd destroy everything Mo had worked to build.

"Far as I know she hasn't said shit to her mom. Nate said she wouldn't. Said he swore her to secrecy," Vic said.

They both grew silent, considering the possibility that Ash couldn't be trusted. It would be easy to lose control. Mo needed to be swift in her decision making. This was the only solution.

"When Nate wakes up, I want to have a chat with him, and then once I get a better sense of how he's doing, I'll speak to Ash. I'm sure I can smooth things over," Mo said confidently.

"What happens if you can't?" Vic asked, his tattooed brow furrowing.

She gently patted his arm. "Let's hope for the best but prepare for the worst, my dear boy. Just like we always do."

ASH

The image of Eli's battered face and desperate cries haunted Ash's dreams. She startled awake, her breathing ragged and heavy, blinking at the bright sunlight streaming in through the curtains. She'd gone to sleep without saying a word to Becca about what happened to Eli, and the guilt gnawed at her. She wondered where he was now, what they'd done to him after she left. She was such a coward, leaving Skid Row, Nate, and Eli behind. To make matters worse, she'd been so careless, waking Becca up and asking to sleep in her room like she was some kind of scared little kid. So much for keeping it together.

Ash stilled, as the smell of bacon and eggs began wafting up the stairs. She grimaced, knowing that she was officially in trouble. Becca wasn't a morning person. The only time she ever stepped foot in the kitchen before ten was when she wanted to talk. Then she was like Martha Stewart on acid.

Ash grabbed her phone off the nightstand and saw a flurry of missed calls and texts from Nate.

We need to talk.

Please Ash call me back!

I'm freaking out. CALL ME!!!

Her finger hovered over his number. She didn't know what to say. Her phone buzzed again. *Ash?*

Shit, he saw she'd read his message. Ash switched off her phone, unsure of what to say, whether there was anything to say. She'd always seen Nate as a protector. Someone who looked out for the underdogs. Now she wasn't so sure.

Ash sat up in bed. The last thing she wanted was to go to school. She considered telling Becca she was sick, but she could already imagine the interrogation that would follow. She took a quick shower, dressed, and made her way downstairs.

She watched as Becca bustled around the kitchen, a stack of vegetables and fruits piled up in front of her. Things kept getting worse. Becca was actually using the juicer. Ash hadn't even known it worked.

"There you are," Becca said, her smile a little too wide. She held out a glass of fresh-squeezed OJ. "Hope you got some rest." Her words came out in a flurry, her tone too cheerful for the hour. Ash sank down at the table, the plate of eggs, bacon, and toast turning her stomach.

"So, I know something is going on and I want you to know whatever it is, you can tell me."

Becca regarded Ash with those Bambi-esque eyes, her

head cocked in that calculated manner they had to teach in therapist school.

Ash didn't answer, pushing her eggs around the plate.

"Okay, how about we start with the new tattoo? Wanna tell me about that?" Becca asked.

That goddamn tattoo. Ash's eyes darted down to her wrist, covered by the hoodie. She wondered when Becca had seen it. God, she should have been more careful, made sure she kept it hidden. Actually, that was wrong. She never should've gotten it in the first place. Ash shrugged, trying to keep her expression neutral. "It's just a tattoo."

"Really? Is that the best you can do? Where did you get it? When did you get it?" Becca demanded.

Ash winced, hating Becca's accusatory tone. She couldn't remember the last time Becca spoke to her this way, doubt and suspicion tingeing her every word.

"The other day, all right? It was some random place downtown. Jesus, Becca, it's just a tattoo," Ash snapped. Hurt flickered across Becca's face.

Damn it. This wasn't Becca's fault. Why was Ash acting like a total bitch? *Old habits die hard*. For a split second, she considered telling Becca everything. Spilling it all about Nate and Eli, how she'd been sneaking around behind Becca's back and lying for months. She wanted to tell her, but all she could hear was Nate's desperate plea: "Promise you won't tell anyone. You have to promise."

She needed to be smart. She didn't want to get Nate in

any trouble, and she definitely didn't want to violate Becca's trust. Not after everything they'd been through. She would figure this out. She had been in terrible situations, and always found a solution.

"I'm sorry. I'm just tired, and this chem final is going to be a real bitch. I'm fine. I swear to you." Ash gave Becca her most winning smile and dug into the eggs, eating heartily. After what seemed like forever, Becca cleared her throat and offered Ash a small smile of her own.

"All right, finish up and I'll drop you at school," Becca said. There was something in her tone that said this wasn't over.

Half an hour later, Becca pulled up in front of Silver Lake Academy, the small private arts high school Ash attended, and put the car into park. "Ash, I know it goes without saying but I'm saying it again. I'm here for you. Whatever is going on, you can tell me."

Becca's green eyes were so sincere and genuine; Ash could feel tears pricking at the corners of her eyes. If she stayed in this car any longer, she might lose it. "Too bad you suck at chemistry."

"Ash..."

"Becca, I'm going to be late. I'll see you later," Ash said, grabbing her backpack and practically leaping out of the car.

Most days, Ash despised school. The classes were fine. In the beginning she had struggled to keep up, but the teachers were patient. You could tell they actually liked what they were doing. No, it was the other students that Ash disliked. Most of them were shallow, brain-dead idiots. They'd never been through anything real, and Ash lacked the energy to educate them. She chose to keep to herself, ignoring the gossip and the judgmental looks. She was used to being alone. At least that's what she told herself. Once Nate came along, she realized what she'd been missing. She thought she'd found someone to fill the void, someone who understood her completely. Now she wasn't sure what to think.

Ash endured an endless morning of classes, barely hearing a word the teachers said. Nate dominated her every thought. She eyed her phone, knowing that if she turned it on, there would be more messages.

At lunch, Ash grabbed a green juice from the cafeteria and headed straight for the quad. That's when she spotted him. She should have known Nate wouldn't give up. He was standing near the football field, leaning against the fence, staring back at her. Ash wondered how long he had been there, whether he'd been waiting all morning just in case he might catch a glimpse. Nate caught her gaze and waved tentatively, as though he were worried she might not wave back.

Even from this distance Ash could see Nate looked terrible. His clothes were rumpled, and his hair was greasy and hanging limply in his eyes. Her first thought was to run to him, wrap her arms around him. Then she saw Eli, bloodied and pleading for help. She remembered Nate carrying her away from him, away from the desperate cries. She balled her hands up in fists. *Don't lose your nerve, Ash. Stay strong.*

"What are you doing here?" Ash asked, careful to keep a safe distance.

"I needed to . . . I needed to make sure you were okay."

"I'm not okay. Is that what you wanted to hear? Not even a little bit. What happened to Eli was fucked up, Nate," Ash said softly.

"It looked worse than it was . . ."

"Hold up. That's your defense? It wasn't as bad as it looked? You can't mean that."

Frustrated, Nate ran a hand through his hair. "Okay, it was bad. I know that, and I'm sorry you had to see it. I swear it's all been handled now. Vic took Eli to the hospital. They patched him up, and he's moving down to Venice."

"Smart move on his part," Ash said sarcastically.

"Mo and Vic and the others . . . they're not bad people. You know that, don't you?" His voice cracked.

"All I know is what I saw, and what I saw was fucking brutal," Ash said. She wouldn't cry. The last thing she wanted was to give her classmates ammunition to use against her. She met Nate's gaze. "I want to know what happened. I want to know why they hurt Eli. Why Mo allowed them to hurt him," Ash said, knowing that nothing happened without Mo's approval.

"It's...it's a sensitive subject. Mo asked if she could explain," Nate said. "She wants to explain."

Ash was ready to tell Nate that she didn't give a shit what Mo wanted. He went to hold her hand, his eyes brimming with tears. "If Mo hadn't found me, if the Tribe hadn't taken me in, I wouldn't have made it. All I'm asking is for you to hear Mo out. That's it. If you don't like what she has to say..." His voice cracked. "Then I'll leave you alone."

There was something so terribly broken about the way he was looking at her. She should have said hell no. That was what she missed about the old Ash. The old Ash didn't let sentiment and emotion cloud her judgment. Not this Ash. She couldn't walk away from him, not until she understood what went down. More than anything she wanted to make sure Nate would be safe. That Mo and the others wouldn't take out their anger on him next time.

Ash said to hell with her last two classes, and an hour later she was back downtown sitting across from Mo at the McDonald's just a few feet from the Tribe's campsite.

"Hope you like strawberry," Mo said, pushing a gooey, whipped-cream-covered sundae toward Ash. The gesture was kind, but it didn't comfort Ash. This woman made her uneasy. She blamed some of that on Becca's talks about energy and auras. Becca always said you should trust the energy coming from another person. "It'll tell you whether they're good people or not." She definitely didn't get the "good people" vibe from Mo.

For a split second, Ash considered leaving. *Stand up and go. Do it now.* Her gaze landed on Nate outside the windows, sitting in his camp. What was she going to say to him if she walked away without hearing Mo out? "Sorry, Nate. Her vibe was off."

Ash grabbed a spoon, took a small bite, and offered Mo a smile. "Strawberry is my favorite."

"Isn't that interesting? I've always known what people want and need," Mo said.

Ash raised her eyebrows. "Is that why you let the others beat up Eli? Because it's what he needed?"

"Sarcasm is your default, isn't it?" Mo said.

Ash shrugged.

"It's okay. We all have them. Defaults. Ways of coping with life's challenges," Mo said.

Ash resisted the urge to roll her eyes. She could hang out with Becca if she wanted to be psychoanalyzed. "I'm only here because Nate said you wanted to discuss what happened to Eli."

"Can I ask you a question first?"

"I guess," Ash said, already regretting coming here.

"Nate said you lived on the streets for a while. Were you on your own the whole time?"

Unable to hide her irritation, Ash's face flushed. Being a young girl alone on the streets, and small for her age, made Ash a target. People tried to fuck with her. Some succeeded. Some didn't.

40

"Yeah, until I found Nate. After we got separated, I went into foster care..." She trailed off. Ash's relationship with Becca was none of Mo's business.

"And your foster mother...she's been good to you?"

"Yes."

"See, you're lucky. Not everyone finds that, but we're searching, constantly searching. We all want that connection. We crave it. The connection makes the world go round. I know what we have here may not make much sense to you, but we're a family. When I saw Nate a year ago, something spoke to me. I knew he belonged with us. It took time to earn Nate's trust. I'd fill his guitar case with dollar bills, wanting to help him, wanting him to understand that we could provide him with a safe place to stay. I wanted him to know that there would always be someone to watch his back and keep his belongings safe. I promised him he would always have enough food to eat and there would be laughter and love. He resisted. I didn't give up. None of us did. We kept showing up until he agreed to come here and see things for himself. He saw what we'd built. It's unconventional, but it works."

Ash couldn't contain her annoyance. "Mo, are you going to tell me what happened with Eli or not?" Ash said. That's why she was here. That was the only reason she was here.

Mo sighed. "He went into Leslie's tent and made sexual advances. She fought him off, but he said he would 'fuck her up' if she told anyone. Of course, Leslie trusted I would

41

know what to do. When I confronted Eli last night and told him he was no longer welcome here, and was no longer part of the Tribe, he refused to leave . . ." Mo paused, taking a sip of her soda. "He threatened me. That's why Vic and the others were so ruthless. It was a warning to Eli and to anyone who might try and hurt one of us."

Ash's stomach churned. She regretted eating the ice cream, the liquid now settling like cement in her stomach. Hearing Mo's explanation about Eli cast him in an entirely new light. Out here on the streets things were positively primal. Consent was bullshit that therapists spouted. On the streets no one cared if you said no. They took what they wanted. Ash didn't want to believe that Eli was capable of something like that, but guys like that were everywhere. All smiles and kindness until you dropped your guard, and then they were on you. It wasn't as if Leslie could go to the cops and report him. They barely cared what happened to regular citizens. Sometimes street justice was the only justice available.

"I didn't know," Ash said, trailing off.

"I wanted to respect Leslie's privacy. When Nate told me how concerned you were about what happened last night, I knew you needed to hear the whole story. The last thing we want is for you to be afraid of us."

Ash's freak-out suddenly seemed extreme. These past few years living in her comfortable Silver Lake bubble, she'd forgotten the ugliness that existed out here.

"I care about Nate, and he cares about you," Ash said.

This time Mo's smile grew wider. "I'm lucky to have found him when I did. He was in a bad way. He says I saved him. I like to think we saved each other."

Ash understood. It's what she found with Becca. A home and a family that looked after her. "I know you two don't get to spend a lot of time together and the last thing you want is to hang out with some old lady. Just know that if anything is bothering you, we can talk. I'm always here. Not many places I have to be," Mo said with a chuckle.

Yeah, it was a hard pass on future heart-to-hearts. She wasn't joining Mo's fan club or buying into any of the Tribe's bullshit anytime soon. The thing was, this made sense. At least she could understand why they'd done that to Eli. Hopefully, Eli would think twice the next time he tried to mess with some girl.

It was getting late, and Ash had to hurry if she wanted to beat Becca home. She said good-bye to Mo, Vic, and the others, wanting to make sure everything was cool. A visibly relieved Nate walked Ash to the nearest Metro station, holding her hand, and pulling her in for kisses every few feet.

"I told you it would all be okay," Nate said with a smile. His relief was palpable.

"Yes, you did," Ash said. She gave him a kiss, trying to convince herself everything was okay. The truth was, Nate still lived on the streets, and Ash wasn't sure what to do about it. She wanted to help him, wanted him to have all the things she had. A roof over her head, clothes, school, and plenty of food to eat. She wanted him to always feel safe and not to have to confront sexual predators or any of the millions of other dangers lurking out here.

They said good-bye, Ash finally pulling away after a final kiss, racing to make it to the train. She could still remember her first meeting with Nate almost three years ago. By then Ash had been living on the streets for almost five months. One day she'd started talking to some chick she met on the Santa Monica Pier who'd told her about a guy who had a spare room where Ash could crash for a few days. She weighed all the possibilities. What if this place was shady? What if this girl was setting her up? In the end the promise of a shower and sleeping in a real bed had won out.

Ash had arrived at the West LA three-bedroom apartment, complete with air-conditioning, a shower, and a fully stocked fridge. It had seemed too good to be true, and the second she met Justin, the owner, she knew that it was. He was pushing forty, balding, wearing a too-tight Batman T-shirt, designer jeans, and Gucci sneakers. Ash's perv meter was instantly activated.

"Make yourself at home," he'd told Ash, offering her a drag of his joint. She'd declined, feeling his eyes scanning her up and down. She'd seen the other kids, mostly girls, ranging in age from eleven to sixteen, flitting around him, like he was some kind of god. She'd smiled at him and made her way into the kitchen. No fucking way was she spending the night here. She figured she'd come all this way; the least she could do was grab a bite. Ash had gone into the kitchen and begun searching through the fridge. It was filled to the brim. She'd snatched a few beers, a couple of cans of soda, and some yogurts and a granola bar and stuffed them in her backpack. She suddenly froze. Someone was watching her. Ash had whirled around to find a gangly teenage boy leaning against the counter, eyeballing her. "What the fuck?" she'd said.

He'd smiled good-naturedly. "Actually, my first name is Nate. 'What the Fuck' is my middle name."

Ash had snorted. "Hello, Nate What the Fuck, and good-bye," she'd said, closing her backpack as she prepared to leave.

"You know you can crash here. Justin's got room."

"Yeah, I don't think so. This shit doesn't feel right."

"Listen, Justin is a total pussy. He only targets weaker girls. All you have to do is make sure he doesn't think you're one of them. And if he tries anything, you've got this." Nate had handed Ash a small white switchblade.

"You're just going to give me this?" The knife handle was made of ivory with tiny flecks of gold embedded in it. Handcrafted and expensive. No one gave anyone anything, especially something this nice, without wanting something in return.

Nate had shrugged. "It was my granddad's. Consider it good karma. C'mon, you really got anyplace better to go?"

Ash was still starving, and the idea of getting real sleep that night was tempting. She'd tucked the knife in her pocket and watched as Nate moved around the kitchen like it was his own.

"How long have you been crashing here?"

"A few weeks. I'm not Justin's type, but he likes my friend. We're kicking it here until he realizes she's never going to fuck him. Sure as shit beats sleeping on the street. You should give it a few nights," Nate said. "We'll look out for each other."

She wasn't sure why she'd agreed. There was something so sincere about Nate; this innate goodness emanated from him. They'd hung out at Justin's, fake laughing at his jokes and eating his food. Nate's friend had taken off a few days later, but Nate stayed behind. She told herself it wasn't because of her, but deep down, she knew differently. He was already looking out for her.

For six weeks Nate and Ash had stayed, playing house. During the day, they'd head to Venice Beach or Santa Monica. Nate would play music for the tourists, and at night, they'd eat Justin's food while Justin got high and told terribly unfunny stories. When another girl left, Ash and Nate had called dibs on the bedroom. Nate would sleep on an air mattress on the floor beside her. Sometimes when the nightmares startled her awake, he would climb in bed and hold her until she drifted off. Nothing creepy or kinky. It was never like that. He never even tried to kiss her. Some nights they'd grab a slice of pizza and sit on the beach, side by side, imagining what life could be like.

"We'll have a house in the mountains," Nate joked. "And a summer home in the Vineyard."

"I prefer Cape Cod," Ash said, using her best posh upper-class accent.

"Of course, darling. We'll summer on the Cape," he said with a smile. But he would always grow serious. "It could happen, right?" She hated when he got serious.

"Of course," Ash said confidently. "We're in this thing together," Ash said.

"You said it. That's a binding verbal contract. Now you'll never get rid of me."

Ash laughed, surprised by how much she cared about him. Deep down she knew it was too good to last. Good things never did. Two weeks later, while Nate was out picking up burgers, the cops had raided Justin's place and hauled the pervert back to jail for violating his parole and fraternizing with underage kids. Ash went into foster care, and Nate disappeared onto the streets of LA.

Ash had never stopped thinking about Nate. When she could sneak away from whatever shitty foster home they'd put her in, she would return to their old neighborhood, searching everywhere they used to go, praying she would find him. Once she went to live with Becca, she was sure she'd be able to find him. Becca spent months trying to track him down, but she finally told that Ash it was no use—Nate had vanished.

Ash sometimes wondered if Nate was even real. Maybe she'd conjured him, creating someone to help her through those darkest days.

Then three months ago, just as she had finished her volunteer shift at the mission, she heard someone calling her name. Ash spun around to find a teenage boy jogging toward her. He was at least six feet tall, slender, with faded jeans, a blue polo shirt, and white sneakers.

There was something about him, an energy that radiated off of him, something kinetic and uncontained yet familiar. He was taller now, his hair longer, almost shaggy in the front. The second he reached her, Ash knew. She would never forget his blue eyes, his kind smile, or the guitar slung across his chest. It was Nate. She'd finally found him.

"I can't...I mean, I don't believe it. It's you," Ash said, practically throwing herself at him. He held on to her, the two of them standing in the middle of downtown, reunited at last.

Without saying a word, they were back together. This time things were different. They weren't little kids anymore. There was something more, a deeper connection neither one of them could explain.

That first day, Nate insisting on escorting Ash back to Silver Lake, the two of them walking the reservoir and talking for hours. When he kissed her, it seemed like the most natural thing in the world. She agreed to keep their relationship a secret, knowing that it might not even last. But as the weeks passed, Ash knew that this was something real. It was important that they tell Becca so they could start thinking about their future. It wasn't as if Nate could stay on the streets forever. Ash swore to herself that the next time she saw Nate they would talk about it. They would make a plan.

"What the fuck is wrong with you?" Ash swiveled around to find Leslie standing in the center of the subway car, glaring at her. A young mother with a baby stroller across the aisle shook her head disapprovingly and put in her earbuds, drowning out their conversation.

"Excuse me?" Ash said, startled by Leslie's harsh tone.

"Why did you come back down here? Why the hell didn't you stay away?"

"Mo wanted to explain what happened last night. I'm sorry about Eli…what he did to you," Ash said.

The tough-girl facade wasn't a natural fit, and just like that it vanished. Leslie sank onto the subway seat, holding her head in her hands, her shoulders shaking, sobs racking her body. The train made two stops before she finally spoke. "Mo's lying," Leslie whispered.

"Leslie, it's okay. I know what happened with Eli. I know all about guys like that."

"Would you shut up and fucking listen to me? Eli didn't do shit. Not to me or anyone else."

That glimmer of doubt she'd felt about Mo and what they'd done came roaring back. "I don't understand. Why would Mo want him hurt?"

"I don't fucking know. Vic wouldn't tell me exactly what happened. All he said was that Mo ordered the beatdown. Don't you see how things work? Mo makes the rules and if she thinks you violated them, bad things happen," Leslie said.

Ash took this in. "What about Eli? What happened to him?"

"He was in bad shape last night. Vic said he dumped him at the hospital, but he's gone, Ash. Like fucking vanished."

Ash shook her head. "Yeah, I know. Nate said he was moving down to Venice."

"I went to every hospital. No sign of him. I even went down to Venice where he used to crash. I asked all over. No one's seen him."

"Then where is he?"

Leslie shook her head. "I don't know. I don't…" She let out a shaky sigh. "What I do know is you showing up last night was a fucking mistake. Now you're on Mo's shit list. Also maybe you should have mentioned your foster mom is a fucking cop."

Ash went pale. Nate knew, but they'd both agreed not to mention it to the Tribe. Most street people hated law enforcement, and Nate didn't want them to see her as an outsider.

"Becca's not a cop. She's a shrink."

"If she works with the cops, she's a fucking cop," Leslie snapped.

"I don't understand what's happening. Nate said Mo wanted to talk. To explain what happened. Why else would she have me come down here?"

"It's a test."

"What kind of test?" Ash asked.

"To see how loyal you are."

Ash's eyes lingered on her tattooed wrist. She thought about Nate's promise. Were they really in this together? Was she wrong to trust him?

Leslie was still talking. "In Mo's mind, you're bad news, a narc messing with Nate's head. She's planning something. I shouldn't be telling you this, but I couldn't... I mean, I don't want anything to happen to you."

"What is she planning?"

"I don't know." The train rounded the corner, the next stop fast approaching. Leslie stood. "You want my advice? Stay the fuck away. From the Tribe. From Nate. That's the only way to be safe."

The train slowed to a stop. Leslie hurried toward the doors. Ash jumped up, grabbing her sleeve to try to stop her. "Wait! You can't go back there," Ash said.

Leslie offered Ash a sad smile. "Where else am I supposed to go?"

The train doors opened, and Leslie raced out, leaving

a stunned Ash behind. She thought about following, but Leslie's warning haunted her.

Ash sank back onto the bench. Was it possible they'd killed Eli? Were they capable of that? She couldn't believe Nate would allow that to happen. She couldn't believe he wouldn't tell her. Ash's heart ached as she considered the possibility that Nate might have betrayed her. Her entire body was trembling. The woman with the stroller was staring at her. "Are you okay?" she asked gently. Ash nodded, but she wasn't okay. She hadn't been this afraid in so long. Ash needed to think, but her mind was a jumble. A flicker of an idea appeared.

No, don't do this, she told herself. The more Ash thought about it, the more she wanted something to numb the fear, something to help her think. She quickly grabbed her phone and texted, holding her breath, hoping her dealer hadn't changed his number.

A few minutes later, he texted back. *Hey stranger. What do you need?*

Ash wasn't going to use any of the hard stuff. All she wanted were a few pills, something to ease her nerves and make things a bit clearer. She confirmed their meeting place near the reservoir and closed her eyes, remembering Eli's desperate cries for help, Leslie's warning, Mo's cartoonish smile, and Nate's possible deception. There was no denying it, Ash was totally and utterly fucked.

BECCA

The sun was slowly setting, slivers of pink and orange peeking through the crown of palm and eucalyptus trees, bringing the purple bougainvillea to life. All of nature's efforts couldn't disguise the run-down housing project on the south side of Los Angeles. The LAPD cruiser's sirens wailed as it turned onto a cul-de-sac. From the passenger's seat, Becca watched as neighbors milled around, eyeing the first officers on the scene with the usual amount of suspicion and disdain.

"Dispatch said you know this family?" Sergeant Nina Stanton asked, pulling up beside another cruiser, their ambers still flashing.

"Mother's name is Yvette Parsons. Daughter is Raya. Twenty. Diagnosed with schizophrenia last year. Since then, Mom's called us out on three separate occasions. Each time, Raya was hospitalized."

"History of violence?" Nina asked.

"Self-harm. No history of hurting others."

"That's good news," Nina said. "You know this call will probably take hours."

"Guess I'll have to cancel the facials," Becca teased.

"Reschedule the mani-pedis," Nina said.

Becca laughed, the two of them relying on humor to see them through the darker nature of their job. For the past eight years, Becca had worked alongside the LAPD in conjunction with the Department of Mental Health. As a licensed clinical psychologist, Becca was part of the Mental Evaluation Unit. In this unit, a clinician like Becca was partnered with an armed patrol officer. They were dispatched to mental health crises involving a range of issues, including suicide, domestic violence, barricades, stalking, or any situation that required de-escalating. In more severe cases, Becca and Nina were responsible for transporting people who posed a risk to themselves or others to the hospital. Though Becca wasn't a police officer, she underwent tactical training when she was hired to ensure she knew what to do in case she was mistaken for an officer. This job wasn't for the fainthearted. It was high stress and high pressure, but that was something Becca thrived on. She steeled herself. This job didn't allow for distractions.

As she went to climb out of the car, Nina grabbed her arm, eyeing Becca with concern. "You okay?" Nina asked softly. "Your vibe is off."

"Don't go stealing my lingo," Becca said. She was big on reading people's energy, assessing their "vibe," as she liked to call it. This opened her up to her share of teasing, but Becca didn't care. After riding with Nina off and on for eight years, she was more than used to it.

"I'm serious. What's going on with you? You're not your usual annoyingly upbeat self. You've barely said a word since we left the station."

Becca wasn't interested in discussing Ash. "I didn't sleep well, that's all."

"I know yesterday was rough. But we did everything we could. Sometimes we can control the outcome. Other times it's out of our hands."

"I know, Nina. It's just…"

Nina winced. "Shit…you heard about Christian?"

Becca froze. "What about Christian?" she asked, hating the high-pitched timbre of her voice. Even two years later the mere mention of her ex-husband could throw her off-balance completely. Christian was a police officer but they worked in different divisions, and after the divorce they rarely crossed paths. Becca hadn't seen or spoken to him in almost a year. "What is it?" she asked, trying to sound casual.

Nina shrugged. "It's nothing. Forget it."

"Okay, now you know you have to tell me," Becca insisted.

Nina shrugged, trying and failing to act nonchalant. "I'm not even sure it's true. I heard one of the guys at roll call saying he got engaged. I could be wrong though. I mean, I didn't even know he was dating anyone, did you?"

Momentarily stunned by the news, Becca felt her stomach twist. Eleven years together, eight of them married, and now he was someone else's, and she didn't even know. She forced a smile, refusing to let this news rattle her.

"No, I didn't know. And it's not like this is a bad thing. Whoever this woman is, he's her problem now." This time she almost believed what she was saying. Nina cocked her head. "It's something else? Is it Ash?"

Ordinarily, Nina's probing would have annoyed her. Becca was the therapist. It was her job to ask the questions and assess when someone was struggling. There was a reason Nina had worked in this unit longer than any other officer. She was innately intuitive, profoundly compassionate, and spot-on. Becca's vibe was off and it *was* because of Ash.

Becca couldn't shake the feeling something more was going on, though Nina was the last person she wanted to discuss it with. As much as she loved Nina, her friend thrived on drama. Becca often thought it was because Nina's life was so drama-free. She was married to her husband of fifteen years, a history professor at UCLA who loved good wine and impromptu romantic getaways. She was the mother to sixteen-year-old twins, a boy and a girl. The minute Becca voiced her concerns, Nina would rattle off all the things that could be wrong.

Maybe Ash was pregnant?

Or working for the cartels?

Or wanted to pursue a career in acting?

Becca's imagination was active enough without Nina adding to her worries.

"You're talking nonsense. No more discussing Christian

or Ash. Let's focus on the call," Becca said. They both climbed out of the car and headed across the street.

"All right, Ortiz, but this isn't over. I'm going to get to the bottom of whatever is bothering you. I always do," Nina said knowingly. She gave Becca a quick smile and focused her attention on the first officers on the scene. "Hey, guys, we're with the Mental Evaluation Unit. Sergeant Stanton. Dr. Ortiz," Nina said, all semblance of teasing and joking vanished. Each and every call they responded to required ultimate vigilance and a laser-like focus.

After a quick briefing, it was decided that Nina and Becca would take point, and the other two officers would back them up. Nina motioned for Becca to follow her. Standing on the porch, Mrs. Parsons stood motionless, still angrily clutching a baseball bat. Becca's heart ached for this woman, pain etched on her well-lined face. As they grew closer, the woman's body tensed, raising the bat higher.

"Ms. Parsons, we understand you've asked your daughter to vacate the premises and she refused. I want to confirm that you'd like us to remove your daughter from your residence," Nina said, her tone compassionate yet firm.

"I don't want her hurt," Mrs. Parsons said. Becca could tell the woman was having second thoughts now that they were here.

"We're not going to hurt her, Mrs. Parsons, but you called us. I need you to put down the bat. We're not the enemy."

Mrs. Parsons snorted. "Tell that shit to someone who doesn't watch the news."

Standing a few feet behind Nina, Becca quietly assessed Mrs. Parsons. She was rail thin, her hair graying, eyes bloodshot; the strain of the situation was weighing on her. Fortunately, Nina's words resonated. Mrs. Parsons held the bat out and Nina reached for it, setting it down out of reach.

"Thank you. My colleague Dr. Ortiz is a psychologist with LAPD's Mental Evaluation Unit. She's here to assess your daughter and make sure she's not a danger to herself or others," Nina said, gesturing to Becca.

"Mrs. Parsons, I'm not sure if you remember me."

Mrs. Parsons's eyes narrowed. "Oh yeah, I know you. You're a goddamn liar. You're the one who said my girl would be okay," Mrs. Parsons spat out.

Becca winced, remembering her last visit almost six months ago. She'd been partnered with a different officer when they got the call that Raya was in the throes of a massive schizophrenic episode. They arrived and found Raya, her hand bleeding from a self-inflicted knife wound. She was convinced aliens were invading her body. The only solution, she told Becca, was to cut them out with a butcher knife.

After an intense negotiation, Becca was able to convince Raya that the hospital would have proper tools for alien extractions, and she finally relinquished the knife. Raya was taken to a psychiatric hospital and kept on a 5150, what they called a seventy-two-hour hold, so doctors could evaluate her. Throughout the ordeal, Becca never made any promises about Raya's condition to Mrs. Parsons or Raya. A cure wasn't something she would ever promise. There was no cure. Raya's illness was a life sentence filled with trial and error, trying to find the right combination of pills, struggling to remember all the medicines, battling the terrible side effects. She promised Mrs. Parsons that the doctors would do everything they could to control and monitor Raya's condition. The trouble was people heard what they wanted to, which often made Becca's job difficult.

"You ain't going to say nothing? My girl never came home." Her eyes flitted toward the inside of the house, her voice a tortured whisper. "I don't know who that girl is, but it isn't my Raya."

She took a threatening step forward. Nina blocked Mrs. Parsons's path, shielding Becca from her rage. "Ma'am, I'm going to have to ask you to stay where you are," Nina said. Becca was reasonably confident Mrs. Parsons wasn't a threat, but that wasn't her call. She'd learned long ago to trust her partner.

"I never meant to deceive you. Like I said before, Raya's condition is complicated," Becca said.

"No shit."

"What I need to know is how is Raya doing? Does she have a weapon? Anything that might harm Officer Stanton or myself once we're inside?"

"No. She ain't got no weapon. Least none I know of."

"That's good. Is Raya in a clear state of mind? Does she know who she is and where she is?"

"She did at first. That's why I told her she could come by for a visit. Told her I'd make her lunch. Next thing I know she's refusing to leave. There's no telling when she'll start spouting off that nonsense. That's why she's got to go."

There was a harshness in her voice that didn't match the ravaged, hollowed-out expression in her eyes. She wasn't unfeeling. She simply lacked the tools necessary to manage her daughter's illness.

"Ma'am, before we can remove your daughter, we need to go inside and evaluate her. Please let us help Raya."

Mrs. Parsons's shoulders sagged as if she was giving something up. "Just don't hurt her," she said. Nina motioned for another officer, and he led her toward the sidewalk.

Nina gestured to a second uniformed officer hovering nearby, and the two of them made entry into the home, Becca trailing behind them both.

Inside, the house was pitch-black and reeked of stale cigarette smoke. Becca spotted Raya at the dining table. She was twenty years old, African American, with jet-black hair she wore in neat braids. A gray Caltech T-shirt hung from her gaunt body. She could have been a college student home on break, before this disease stole her future. Raya didn't react when they entered, her attention focused on a picture frame she was tightly clutching. Becca couldn't make out the image, but judging by Raya's grip on the photo, it was significant.

Nina cleared her throat, her soft, reassuring voice filling the space, but they kept their distance. It was all part of the training. One must remain at least twenty-one feet from a suspect. Getting too close could put the officers at a disadvantage, giving the victim an opportunity to attack.

"Ma'am, I'm Officer Nina Stanton with the LAPD. Your mother called us and said—"

"She wants y'all to get rid of me, don't she?" Raya said.

"She's accusing you of trespassing and asked us to remove you from the premises," Nina replied.

"This is my home. How can I be trespassing?"

Nina looked at Becca and raised her eyes as if to say, "You're up."

"Hey, Raya, you remember me. It's Dr. Ortiz—"

Raya rolled her eyes. "Shit, Doc, just 'cuz I'm nuts don't mean I got memory problems. I remember you."

Raya's sarcasm wasn't enough to hide how terrified she was. "Can you tell me how you're doing? Are you thinking of hurting yourself? Having bad thoughts like before?" she asked.

"No. I've been taking my meds. It's just I don't get my check 'til the end of the month, which means I got no money and no place to stay."

Raya gnawed at her fingernails, all of them bitten to the quick. "I asked Mama if I could shower here, maybe rest for a few hours. She said no. She said I'm not welcome anymore." Raya's voice cracked, her hands gripping the picture frame even tighter.

Becca eyed Nina, the two of them in agreement. Raya wasn't having a mental breakdown. She was articulate about her situation. She wasn't in danger, and neither was anyone else. At least not today.

"Raya, I'm afraid if your mother doesn't want you here, you can't stay," Nina said.

Raya's eyes darted back and forth from Becca to Nina. "Where the hell am I supposed to go?" Raya asked.

There was no easy answer. The city was bursting at the seams with people who needed assistance. Addicts, the mentally ill, veterans struggling with joblessness and PTSD, even paroled inmates, were all vying for space in shelters and public housing. The lack of resources forced people to make difficult decisions. Tents were sprouting up all over the city as Los Angeles rents continued to climb. Becca was already racking her brain, trying to think of where they might take her.

"Raya, if you come with us, Officer Stanton and I will do everything in our power to find you a place to stay for tonight. After that, you and I can work toward finding you more permanent housing."

Becca held her breath, praying they wouldn't have to physically remove this young woman. She understood the trauma that would cause, her mind working out all the possible scenarios. Raya seemed to sense she was out of options. She took a longing look around and stood, setting the picture frame on the dining table. Now Becca could clearly see the photo, a Sears-style portrait, taken when Raya was a toddler, sitting on her mother's lap, the two of them wearing matching red blouses and cheesy grins.

Her heart ached for this family. In the very next instant Ash flashed through Becca's head, a family torn apart by things out of their control. *This won't be us*, she promised herself. *It can't be.*

"I'm ready. Can I get my bag?" Raya asked, pointing to a worn-out backpack lying near the door. Becca forced herself to focus, turning to Nina.

"I have to inspect the contents to make sure you don't have any weapons or anything you might harm yourself with. Do I have your permission?" Nina asked.

"Do what you've gotta do," Raya said.

"I'm also going to search you for weapons, and cuff you. You're not under arrest. This is just a safety precaution while we remove you from the premises. Okay?"

"Yeah. I know how this all works. Doc, you can tell this broad I'm not some kind of a troublemaker," Raya said. Becca gave Nina an encouraging nod, watching as she patted Raya down and cuffed her.

Mental illness had stolen so much from this young woman. Even now the law was treating her like a criminal, though she'd never committed a crime. She understood why this was necessary and respected the rules, even if she didn't always agree with them.

Once Raya was properly secured, Nina and the officer led Raya out, Becca by her side. As they headed down the sidewalk toward the cruiser, Raya spotted her mother. She strained against Nina and the cuffs.

"Mama, don't do this," Raya pleaded.

Mrs. Parsons's mind was made up. She turned her back on Raya and slipped inside the house, shutting her daughter out with the slam of the door. Becca patted Raya's arm. "If it's okay with you, we'd like to place you in the squad car while I search for a shelter that can take you."

Raya shrugged, the fight drained from her. She allowed Nina to place her in the back of the cruiser and leaned her head against the headrest, her eyes closing as exhaustion overtook her.

The other cruiser was already speeding off, the officers heading to another crisis unfolding in the city. Nina resumed her spot in the driver's seat, already radioing dispatch with a status report. Becca leaned against the hood of the car, feverishly texting her contacts. Securing housing for the mentally ill required charm and a whole lot of luck. Fortunately, the Fates were with her today. Within a few seconds, her phone buzzed. Andrew from St. Paul's Mission, one of Becca's contacts, was the first to text back. *Got a bed for you.*

Becca smiled. This was what she loved most about the

job. She understood that this was a short-term solution for Raya's long-term problem. At least for tonight, this young woman would have a warm, safe place to stay. Becca knocked on Nina's window. In response, Nina stepped out of the car.

"Victory is mine," Becca said. Her smile faded with one glance at Nina. On the job, Nina's poker face was the best in the department. Outside of work, it was total crap.

"There's been...an incident," Nina said.

It was Ash. "What happened? Is she okay?"

"I received a call from Northeast. An undercover busted Ash in the Silver Lake Reservoir. Said she was trying to score."

Nina's words landed like a grenade. *Trying to score. Trying to score.* Becca's knees wobbled, and she leaned against the car to steady herself. Nina reached out and placed a reassuring hand on Becca's shoulder.

"I talked to the arresting officer. He said he'd meet us at the station. I know this guy. He's kind of a dick, but a real company man. He said he would hold off on booking 'til we get there. Good news is I'm so charming and persuasive, we'll get him to drop the charges. No problem."

No problem. Nina lived and died by that theory. On a good day so did Becca. Right now all she could think about were the weeks and months it took for Ash to get clean. Not to mention the other sacrifices Becca made: her marriage, the fights with her mother, the endless worry that kept her awake most nights. It was all worth it to see Ash thriving. Two years clean and sober. Two years.

Becca wanted to shake her. Why throw it all away? Why? Yet she understood there were so many reasons why addicts relapsed. Coping with an addict was like riding a wave. If Becca allowed herself to get pulled into the undertow, they'd both be swept up. No, she had to stay calm and focused. She darted a glance at Raya still sitting in the back of the cruiser. Nina was one step ahead.

"I'll drop you at the station and talk to the officer. Then I can take Raya to the mission and make sure she's good."

Becca nodded gratefully. The sooner she could see Ash the better. First, though, she had to brief Raya on what to expect. The hardest part for mental health patients who found themselves in the system was the lack of control. Becca always tried to provide as much information as she could. Restoring the balance of power, she liked to say. She opened the car door, and Raya sat up straighter, tears in her eyes. Becca knelt down so they were face-to-face.

"Hey, Raya, we got you a bed over at St. Paul's Mission. We need to drop by the station, and then my partner will take you and get you settled, and I'll check back in tomorrow. We'll schedule a meeting with a social worker, discuss long-term housing options. Okay?" Becca said.

"Sure. Sounds swell," Raya said flatly. This was where Becca was supposed to say something encouraging and consoling, but all she could think about was Ash. She patted Raya's leg and gently shut the door. Becca climbed into the passenger's seat and Nina sped away, lights flashing and sirens blaring. As she drove, Nina reached out and squeezed Becca's hand. "Ash is a good kid. Whatever happened, you'll get through it," she said encouragingly. Becca nodded, wanting to believe that was true. Her phone buzzed. She reached into her bag and unearthed it, a text message appearing on-screen. Becca gasped, staring back at the text in disbelief.

"Are you okay?" Nina asked.

"I'm fine," Becca said, though that wasn't true at all. The text was from Louise, Ash's social worker. *BIG NEWS! Ash's birth mother relinquished all parental rights. We can finally proceed with the adoption process. Congratulations to you both!*

Becca might have laughed if it weren't so goddamn ironic. She could feel the panic rising. *Deep breaths. Deep, calming breaths.* It would be easy to start thinking the worst. That her mother was right and Ash was nothing but trouble. That she'd gambled her future on a lost cause. That, despite all her efforts, she had failed Ash somehow. Becca shook her head. She couldn't let those thoughts consume her. She certainly couldn't give up now. Not after they'd come so far. From the start, Becca had promised Ash she would never stop fighting for her. Nothing was going to change that. Nothing at all.

ASH

Since Ash's arrival at the Northeast Community police station, a meth head proposed marriage, a USC frat boy vomited on her shoes, and an elderly woman thrust a Bible into her hands, terrified Ash's soul would "perish for all eternity unless you repent."

Ash couldn't believe how stupid she'd been. On the list of what not to do when you're trying to score, getting busted by an undercover cop was number one. Sweat dripped down her back, and yet she couldn't stop trembling. She wasn't sure what was worse, sitting in this disgusting smelly room with all these freaks, or knowing she would have to face Becca.

She heard her voice before she saw her. "Ash, let's go," Becca said though clenched teeth. Ash spotted Becca standing in the center of the bull pen. She leapt to her feet and reached for her bag, catching Nina's woeful gaze from across the room. Nina offered a half-hearted wave and mouthed, "Hang in there."

Ash would need all of Nina's encouragement to get through this. Becca's green eyes were staring back at Ash with such fury, they could have been weaponized. "Becca," Ash said softly. "I want to . . ."

"Not here. We're not doing this here," Becca replied impatiently, her voice low. Becca wasn't one to cause a scene, always so calm and self-contained. Ash couldn't remember ever seeing her this angry.

She hesitated, not moving, her eyes scanning the room. "The officer, the one who busted me, he said he didn't give a shit who I was related to..."

"Yeah, well, you're lucky that Nina has connections and is willing to use them to vouch for you. So move it. Unless you'd rather stay here?" Becca snapped, her patience wearing thin.

Ash grabbed her backpack and followed Becca out. She slumped down in the front seat of Becca's SUV. The drive to Silver Lake was less than four miles, but the traffic had slowed to a crawl, an accident turning the roads into a parking lot. Normally, Becca never stopped talking. Ash couldn't stand this punishing silence. "I didn't mean to, I wasn't trying to hurt you," Ash said.

Becca's eyes never left the road, her hands gripping the steering wheel so tightly her knuckles appeared translucent. "Hurt me? Hurt me? What about *you*, Ash? Why would you want to hurt yourself? Please enlighten me."

Ash didn't answer. What was she going to say? "I fucked up and wanted to forget."

"I swear I don't even know what to say right now. I'm just so disappointed in you."

Ash's eyes filled with tears and she sank even lower in her seat. She closed her eyes, and the next thing she knew

Becca was shaking her awake. "Ash, wake up. We're home," Becca said.

Home. This *was* Ash's home. The first time she saw the elegant craftsman, she thought Becca was fucking with her.

"There's no way you live here," Ash said. She didn't know what kind of money shrinks made, but they definitely couldn't afford a house like this.

Becca laughed. "This house used to belong to my parents. They gave it to me as a wedding gift."

"Most people get toasters. They must be loaded."

"They bought it a long time ago before it was worth anything. We put a lot of work into making it special. It's your home now. For as long as you want to live here."

Ash thought about those early days, before Christian moved out, when Ash would do everything she could to push Becca's buttons, getting fucked up all the time, coming in late, acting like a total shithead. She thought about all the fights between Christian and Becca, the hushed tones and his insistence that Ash was going to ruin things. She remembered when he'd packed his bags and Becca shrugged. "It's not about you," she'd promised. Ash knew that wasn't entirely true, but she'd been thrilled. At last someone wanted Ash. Becca picked Ash. She wondered if Becca was regretting that decision. She wouldn't blame her if she did.

Ash followed Becca inside, where they were given a heroes' welcome by Freud. Ash gave him a pat on the head, dreading what came next.

"Kitchen table. Now," Becca ordered. Ash shuffled over and sank into one of the dining chairs. Becca settled down across from her. The only sound was the steady hum of the refrigerator.

"I want you to answer yes or no to my question," Becca began. "Do you still want to be my daughter?"

Ash's mouth quivered, her hands furiously patting Freud's head. "I know I screwed up. It's cool. I'll go anywhere you want to send me."

"Damn it, Ash, answer the question. Do you still want me to adopt you?" Becca said.

"Yes. Of course I do. You know I do."

"I thought so. After what occurred today and you almost relapsing, I'm not so sure. Maybe being here, being with me, isn't what's best for you."

Ash could see how much this pained Becca, and it killed her. "That's not it. I swear to you . . ."

"That's not how it looks," Becca replied.

"Why are you asking me this?" Ash said softly.

Becca pushed her phone across the table. "I received this text today."

Ash scanned the text message, her eyes narrowing. "Faye signed the papers?" Ash asked in disbelief. For months Faye had put them both through hell, sending Ash all kinds of shitty e-mails, alternating between begging for forgiveness for the years of abuse and telling Ash she was a worthless brat. When Ash didn't respond to her messages, she started harassing Becca, demanding money in exchange for signing over her parental rights. Ash wasn't sure why Faye gave in. Probably something to do with a guy, but the reason didn't matter. Ash was finally free.

"So I'm going to ask you again. Do you want to be an Ortiz? The decision is yours."

Ash couldn't believe this. "I thought you were going to freak out and lose your shit. I know I screwed up today."

"That's like saying the *Titanic* experienced some engine trouble. This is the screwup to end all screwups. Ash, I don't know what's going on with you, but we're going to figure it out together. I've made an appointment with Dr. Garrett tomorrow, and we're all going to sit down and discuss what's going on. You're going to start a new treatment plan, which will include returning to Narcotics Anonymous. Four meetings a week. Not to mention you're grounded for a month to start. Yes, you screwed up today. That doesn't mean I love you any less. All today tells me is we have to work a bit harder to make sure we're okay."

Ash shook her head. This was too much. It was all too much. "No. I don't deserve you. I don't deserve any of this."

"That's not true. You know that's not true. You deserve all good things."

Ash went quiet, her eyes lingering on the floor. When she looked up, there were tears in her eyes. "Becca. I want this. I want you to be my mom," Ash said. Becca reached out and grabbed Ash, hugging her tightly.

In the early days, Ash wasn't used to physical expressions of love. Faye had a firm "no hugging" policy. It didn't matter the situation. Skinned knees, monsters camped out under the bed, the neighbor's terrifying Great Dane, her mother deemed Ash unworthy. "Shitheads don't get rewarded for bad behavior," she liked to say.

Becca was different. At first, Ash thought it was phony, the enthusiasm with which Becca approached absolutely everything. The more time she spent with her, the more she saw that everything Becca did was a hundred percent authentic. Even today, even after Ash's giant fuckup, she wasn't letting go of Ash, holding on to her tightly.

Tell her. Do it now. The steady drumbeat in Ash's head continued. It would be a relief in so many ways to unburden herself. Becca would leap into action the way she always did when something or someone needed to be fixed. She would figure out what really happened to Eli, and she would make sure Nate was safe and that Mo and the others couldn't hurt him or anyone else. She would protect Ash. That's what Becca did best.

"Are you hungry? I'm thinking burgers on the grill? We can eat outside?" Becca said.

Ash was shocked. She expected the silent treatment or nonstop lectures. The fact that Becca was willing to forgive her meant everything. Since she'd found out about Eli and

Mo, Ash's stomach had been tied up in knots, her insides twisting and churning. Suddenly her appetite came roaring back.

"I'm starving. I'll prep the grill," Ash said, slipping out the back door into the garden, willing herself not to cry. If she told Becca the truth now, she could ruin this. *I'll tell her tomorrow. I'll tell her everything.*

Ash reached into the pocket of her hoodie for her phone, staring at Nate's name on the screen. All Ash ever wanted was a family, someone to look after her, and now she finally had one. As much as she loved Nate, she couldn't screw this up.

I can't do this anymore. I'm sorry. I'm telling Becca everything. Ash hit send before she could change her mind, and switched off her phone. The relief she felt told her she'd made the right decision.

Together, Becca and Ash made dinner, chopping the veggies and potatoes and settling in at the picnic table in the backyard, the jacarandas in full bloom, Freud lingering at their feet, begging for scraps. Bound by confidentiality laws, Becca wasn't allowed to discuss the specifics of her day, though she gave Ash a vague rundown, telling her about the schizophrenic young woman she'd managed to help. They talked around today's events, both accepting that hard conversations loomed in their future. After dinner, Ash allowed Becca to choose the movie.

"There's a first time for everything," Becca joked. While they watched the movie, they devoured a pint of

McConnell's Salted Caramel Chip. Becca sneaked sips of her favorite J. Lohr cab from a coffee mug. Ash always thought it was funny that Becca felt the need to sneak the wine. Alcohol wasn't Ash's preferred substance and she didn't care at all if Becca had a glass or two at dinner. Ash didn't say anything, snuggling under the blanket on the sofa beside Becca, soothed by the warmth and love filling the room.

Sometime between Molly Ringwald going on a date with the smug rich guy and the short-haired redhead making an incredibly ugly pink dress, the stress of the day caught up to Ash and she drifted off to sleep. The next thing she knew Becca was shaking her.

"Hey, it's late. You should go up to bed," Becca said, her voice barely a whisper, the faint smell of wine on her breath. Ash didn't argue, heading upstairs and crawling into bed, Freud snuggling up next to her. She wrapped her arms around the giant dog.

Ash wasn't sure how much time passed. She stirred, a shiver running through her. She did a quick scan, taking in her surroundings. Freud sat at the foot of the bed, his tail wagging. The curtains fluttered in the breeze. Ash froze. The window was open. She never slept with it open, Becca's lectures about home safety ringing in her head. Ash sensed an energy shift, an awareness that she wasn't alone. Someone was here—in her room. Before Ash could move, a hand clamped down over her mouth.

"Shh...it's me," Nate whispered. Ash's entire body tensed. Nate had walked her home dozens of times, but he would never come inside. That was his choice. "It's too risky if Becca comes home." But here he was. In her bedroom. In the middle of the night. Ash squinted in the dark, straining to get a better look at him. Beads of sweat covered Nate's upper lip, his pupils wide and dilated. There was something unhinged in his appearance and in the timbre of his voice. "Ash, I need you to be quiet and listen. You're not going to say a word. Do you understand? Not one word."

ASH

When Ash was little, whenever her mother was on the warpath and a beating was on the horizon, Ash would race to her room and grab her favorite stuffed animal. Moosey, as she so cleverly named the stuffed gray moose, gave Ash strength. Holding on to him, she could almost convince herself everything would be okay. After the beating was over, she'd cling tightly to him until the pain subsided. When she left home, Moosey stayed behind. Time to grow up, she told herself.

A year later Ash found something that offered the same sense of security as her stuffed moose—a small and very sharp switchblade. The blade Nate gave her. Becca had tried to take it away once and they'd had one of their biggest fights ever. It soothed Ash knowing she had it, knowing she could protect herself. Ash agreed not to take it to school, but she kept it with her whenever she went out. At the end of every night, she tucked it under her pillow, always within arm's reach.

She couldn't imagine Nate hurting her, but Ash knew firsthand that people did terrible things to those they loved.

She couldn't escape Leslie's words echoing in her head. "Mo's testing us. It's a loyalty test." If she could just grab her knife, she would be okay. She could protect herself.

Nate must have seen the fear reflected in her gaze, because he instantly released her, sinking down onto the bed, his hands raised in surrender. "Ash, I won't hurt you," he said softly. "Is that what you thought?"

She didn't answer, scrambling for the knife, clutching it in her hands, feeling the weight of it and knowing she was protected.

"What the hell are you doing, sneaking into my bedroom like some kind of psycho?" Ash snapped.

"Shh…keep your voice down," Nate said, darting nervous glances at the door. "Things are fucked up. We have to leave, Ash. We have to go right now," Nate said.

Ash pushed the covers away and sat up. "I'm not going anywhere. I told you in my text it's over," Ash said, casting her eyes downward, not wanting to see the hurt in his eyes.

He reached out and gently lifted her head to meet his gaze.

"You have to listen to me. Something's fucking seriously wrong. Last night I went to my tent and I found Leslie waiting for me. She was crying so hard I could barely understand her. She said that Mo's told the others that you're a threat. She said Mo called it the reckoning. That you've corrupted me and can't be trusted. Don't you understand, Ash? Leslie's warning us. We're not safe here. Not anymore."

Ash sank back against the covers, her body trembling uncontrollably. "Eli isn't okay, is he?"

"No," Nate whispered. "I don't think he is." Ash saw it now. It wasn't anger or aggression that transformed Nate. It was fear.

"How the hell did this happen? How could you have trusted them? Trusted her?" It wasn't fair to blame Nate. Hell, Ash had almost bought Mo's stupid bullshit about Eli too, but she needed someone to blame, and Nate was an easy target.

"Mo said they were going to teach him a lesson for messing with Leslie. I swear to you that's all I knew. I don't know how Leslie found out, but she said they've done this before. She said that they've hurt people...not just Eli." He trailed off. "I can't let anything happen to you, Ash. That's why we have to go."

Ash's entire body vibrated with fear. She didn't want to leave Becca. There had to be another way. "Fuck Mo. Let's come clean. I'll wake Becca up. We'll tell her everything."

Nate leaned back, crossing his arms, his eyes flashing. "And then what?"

"I don't know. Becca's partner, Nina, is cool. She's helped me out. Between the two of them, they'll know what to do."

"Oh yeah, Nina's cool? Think she'll be cool with my arrests? The assault charges and my running from the cops?"

She knew Nate had been arrested for assault. Some guy was trying to get rough with him and he fought back. It wasn't his fault. "We'll explain that the guy was lying. That you were defending yourself."

Nate shifted on the bed, his annoyance growing. "Think about it, Ash. We've both got records. You think the cops are going to take our word for it when we say bad things happened? We don't even have Eli's last fucking name or proof of what they did to him. Shit, you know as well as I do, even when you have proof, people don't do shit," Nate said.

Ash still remembered her first-grade teacher, Mrs. Boyles. She was magical, with her multicolored cardigans and gardenia-scented perfume. Her classroom was Ash's escape, her only respite from her mother's brutality. Each day she would try to find the right way to say the words out loud. "My mother hurts me."

On the last day of school, Ash summoned all her courage and confessed that her mother beat her. The woman's pale pink lips pursed, her eyes narrowing into small slits. "Now, Ashley, I've met your mother, and she's a lovely woman. Why would you make up such horrible lies?"

Ash imagined sitting across from the police and telling them about Eli. "They were beating him, and we left. We just left." She imagined their questions, tinged with accusation.

"Why didn't you do anything to stop them? Why didn't you call for help? You waited a whole day to come forward? Why is that?" She imagined sitting across from Becca, her face etched with disappointment.

"I don't know what to do," Ash said softly.

"Have you ever been to Taos?"

"New Mexico?"

"Yeah, it's amazing. When I was seven, my mom and I went there on our way to the Grand Canyon. It's like this funky town with a bunch of artist types. You could take photos, and I could play music. We could get jobs, find a place to live." He glanced over at Freud. "We could even get a dog of our own."

"So we go to Taos and what—hide out?" Ash asked.

"No. We move there. Start fresh. Start over. Our new life together."

Ash's eyes darted toward the giant framed photo hanging on the wall. It was taken right after Ash got her Leica camera. It wasn't a perfect shot, a little off-center, and a bit blown out. But Ash loved it. She'd captured the joy on Becca's face as she splashed about with Freud in the Malibu waters.

"What about Becca?" Ash whispered.

"What about her?" Nate said. She flinched, the harshness in his voice startling her.

"I'm sorry. It's just…it's not like Becca's your real mother."

83

Ash didn't say anything, thinking about today's big news. All it would require was a trip to the courthouse and a judge's signature. Then it would be official. Becca would be her mother. Ash would be her daughter. Her silence lingered.

"So that's it? You've got Becca, and now I'm out on my own." She could hear the betrayal in his voice.

"No, it's just..."

"If I stay here, I don't know what will happen to me, Ash. You're all I have left. And I...I don't know if I can leave without you."

Ash thought about all those months she spent on the streets, alone, searching for someone who cared about her, who would look after her. She imagined Nate back out there on his own, without anyone. Or worse, Nate forced to go back to Mo and the others.

The last thing Ash wanted to do was leave Becca. She knew that she would be devastated, but Becca had her family and Nina and her job. Nate was all alone.

Her decision was made. Ash told herself this wasn't good-bye forever. One day, once they were away from Mo and things calmed down, she would find a way to explain everything to Becca. Right now though, she owed Nate. She reached for his hands, holding them tight against her heart. "We've got this, Nate. You and me together."

ASH

They ran—through the back alleys and side streets of Silver Lake, Ash leading the way with Freud trailing after them, Nate following as they headed east toward Hollywood. Together, their combined net worth was two hundred dollars. They still needed money for bus tickets and a place to crash when they got to Taos. It was Nate's idea to steal Becca's jewelry. "No way. That's a shithead move," Ash said.

"C'mon, Ash, what other options do we have?" Nate asked.

She ran through their options. If she told Becca the truth, Ash could end up in a group home or worse, juvenile detention. Not to mention Nate's record. The charges were bullshit, but it didn't matter. They'd wind up where they started, alone and prisoners of the system. Ash couldn't imagine that life again. It was unbearable.

Ash steeled herself, tiptoeing into Becca's bedroom while she slept downstairs. *One day I'll make this right*, she silently promised.

She didn't have a good reason for taking Freud. She saw

him staring up at her with those giant doe eyes, his tail wagging excitedly.

"I'm bringing him," Ash said, almost hoping Nate would stop her or tell her to stay. He didn't, patting Freud on the head. "C'mon, buddy, you ready for an adventure?"

In some ways having Freud with her made Ash feel closer to Becca, or maybe that was just her shitty justification. She tossed a few changes of clothes into a duffel bag, and an album of her favorite photos along with the insanely expensive digital camera Becca bought her for Christmas. She took one last look at her beautiful room with the teal bedding and matching curtains, the framed photos and scented candles Becca filled every room with, wishing that things were different. That she hadn't screwed it all up.

It was nearing dawn when they finally reached Sunset Boulevard near Hollywood.

"I need to stop," Ash said, her breathing labored, her sides aching.

"Let's rest here," Nate said, crouching beside an old gray Honda Accord, breathing heavily, clearly weighed down by his backpack and guitar case. He was uneasy, as though they were under surveillance, his eyes scanning the empty streets, on high alert, searching for an unseen enemy. A wet nose nudged Ash and she saw Freud anxiously awaiting instructions.

"We're okay. We'll be okay," Ash said, trying to reassure Freud, and herself.

Nate reached for Ash's hand. "Hey, we're gonna be okay. You know that, right?"

"Yeah. Of course," Ash said. Previous experience taught her things were usually the opposite of okay, but Nate *was* trying. Ash needed to do the same. "I'm good. Let's keep going," she said.

They made their way to a grimy Internet café in a run-down strip mall a few blocks from Grauman's Chinese Theatre. Before she met Becca, this was one of Ash's favorite spots. She came for the cheap coffee, free air-conditioning, and unlimited Wi-Fi. She told herself the odds were slim that the Tribe would find them here. She told herself they probably weren't even looking. Nate took a seat at a table, Freud sinking down onto the floor beside him while Ash went to order.

"Two black coffees and the Wi-Fi code," Ash said to the barista.

The strung-out clerk glanced at Freud. "Not supposed to have animals in here," she said half-heartedly.

"He's a therapy dog," Ash said, preparing to launch into an explanation of the legalities of service animals. The girl just shrugged and handed Ash her order.

She delivered Nate's coffee and set up camp at one of the computer stations. She'd already turned off her phone in case Becca tried to track her. She logged on to the Internet and did a search for the Greyhound bus schedules and departure times. There were two buses leaving LA and arriving in Las Cruces. One at nine thirty, which they wouldn't make if they were going to pawn the jewelry, and another at six o'clock. The first half of their journey would take thirteen hours. They'd transfer in Santa Fe and travel twenty-one hours before finally reaching Taos. Now that Ash knew when they were leaving, she focused on the pawnshop plan, printing out a list of the closest pawnshops. The plan was simple. Sell their shit and get the hell out of town.

Ash's pawnshop knowledge ran deep. Keeping the whiskey flowing was a costly endeavor and made it difficult for her mother to hold down a job, so Faye was always pawning something. Along the way Ash learned some valuable tips. Avoid corporate shops at all costs. They were much more selective and wouldn't sell to anyone without an ID. The twenty-four-hour pawnshops were also a no-go. They paid much less than the others because they understood you were in a hurry. The smaller, less regulated shops were where they needed to go. If they waited another hour or two until they opened, they could hit up several at a time. The only problem was getting Nate to agree with her plan.

"No way. We're not separating. I'm not letting you out of my sight."

Ash appreciated the chivalry but she wasn't going to let it get in the way of making a better profit. "Nate, I'm telling you, if we try to sell this stuff together, these assholes are gonna offer us a bulk rate for everything. We want them to give us a price for each item. You can head downtown, hit up some shops near the bus station, while I go to the ones in this area. We'll cover more ground that way."

Ash patted the switchblade she had tucked in the pocket of her jeans. "And you know I can handle myself and so can Freud."

He shifted in his seat, staring down at his coffee. "If something happened to you, I mean, I got you into all this."

"Fuck that. This isn't your fault. How could you know Mo was a total psycho?"

Nate winced. "I should've known. I should've seen it. I was just so lost after we got separated. I thought Mo cared about us. I really thought she did."

"And then I came along and wrecked it?" Ash said.

"No. You made me see who she really was, who they all were."

"We know now. We'll get out before it's too late. But I need you to trust me."

Nate leaned forward and kissed her. "We'll do things your way, then," he said.

Ash wanted to stay right here with him, but the clock was ticking. They had to make that bus, and they needed money. Ash pulled away, and she downed the last of her coffee.

"You've got your list of shops, and I've got mine. We'll meet at the bus station downtown when we're done. The last bus to Taos leaves at four o'clock. Don't be late," she said, giving him one last kiss.

"I love you," he said.

"I love you too." Ash led Freud out before she could change her mind. Ash's first shop was a bust. Tucked into a back street behind Hollywood Boulevard, the first pawnshop owner was a nosy bitch, staring at Ash's tattoos with disapproval, wanting to know why she was selling all this jewelry, asking how old she was and where her parents were. Of all the days Ash encountered someone who actually gave a shit, it had to be today.

"It's none of your damn business," she told her before storming out.

Ash crossed McCadden and located another pawnshop, nestled between a CrossFit studio and a porn theater with a sign advertising GIRLS GIRLS GIRLS. The clerk, a gaunt, skinny man in his thirties with a lazy eye, a nervous laugh, and a toothpick between his teeth, surveyed the jewelry with practiced indifference. "I'll give you twelve hundred," he said. His eyes narrowed, inspecting Ash up and down. "Unless you're interested in coming to the back room? We could have a little fun, double your profits," he said.

"Yeah, I'm not interested in anything little," she said, glad the days when things like this happened were behind her.

The man's smile turned to a sneer. "On second thought, this shit's only worth nine hundred. Take it or leave it," he grunted. Ash gritted her teeth, annoyed she'd given this dickhead the power to lowball her. She gazed down at Becca's jewelry. God, she didn't want to be the kind of person who stole from the people she loved. She was doing this for Nate though. That's what she had to remember.

"Fine. Whatever," she told Pencil Dick. She grabbed the cash, flipping him the bird on her way out. Ash hurried down Hollywood Boulevard, darting nervous glances, searching for any sign of the Tribe, when she spotted Hopper. He was an old Gulf War vet she befriended while hanging on the boulevard with Nate. The first time she saw his HOMELESS VET NEEDS HAND UP, NOT HAND OUT sign, she lost her shit. Ash's grandpa and Becca's dad were both veterans. She hated anyone who lied about their service. She marched right over and told him what she thought about his bullshit, while Nate looked on in surprise.

Hopper quickly set Ash straight. "Girly, I served in Desert Storm and got my leg blown to shit. So save that shit for someone else." She'd felt like a total jerk and made it a point to give him some cash for food. After that, Ash would visit with him, listening to his old war stories. Sometimes she stopped by with a Double-Double and a chocolate shake from In-N-Out, always insisting Hopper tell a story in exchange for the food. His stories about his war days and life on the streets were hilarious and heartbreaking.

Hopper had seen her hanging out with Nate and the others and tried to warn her. "Them folks ain't right in the head, I know it," he said once. She ignored him, telling herself it was just the ramblings of a sad old man. She wished she could go back in time, wished she could listen, really hear what he was trying to tell her. Hopper wasn't exactly warm and fuzzy, but he was a decent person. She figured for the right price, she could count on him to help her out. She knelt down beside Freud and wrapped her arms around him. He happily licked her face.

"You are the best dog in the whole world. You know that, don't you?" Ash said. "Promise you'll look after Becca, okay?"

He wagged his tail even harder. Ash hugged him one last time and grabbed Freud's leash. She hurried across the street, calling out to Hopper. Taking Freud was a mistake, but she could at least make that right. Once she was done, she would finish her round of pawnshops and meet Nate. In a few short hours they would board a bus together and head off toward a brand-new future. Just a few more hours.

BECCA

Becca opened her eyes, wincing as the light burst through the downstairs curtains. She blinked furiously, trying to orient herself. She must have fallen asleep on the sofa. Becca remembered with instant regret the bottle of cabernet she opened after dinner. She rarely drank, but as the night wore on, Becca's uneasiness grew, and she told herself one glass would take the edge off. Once Ash went to bed, Becca kept refilling her glass again and again, until the bottle was empty. She fell into a heavy, dreamless sleep. Her skull ached, and her mouth was dry. She would definitely regret her carelessness today. Becca sat up, fumbling around on the coffee table for her cell phone, stunned to find that it was almost seven thirty. Damn it, Becca wanted to talk to Ash about her new recovery plan and now there was no time. They were both going to be late.

Becca eased herself off the couch. "Ash! Freud! We overslept," she called out, waiting for Freud to come bounding down the hall. She was met with an overwhelming silence. Becca headed upstairs and back down the hall. "Hey, Ash, rise and shine. It's time to wake," Becca called out.

No one responded. Becca pushed open Ash's door and

gasped. The bedspread was lying in a heap on the floor. The drawers were half-open, clothing and papers strewn about the room. Becca's heart dropped. Ash always kept everything spotless, her bed neatly made, clothes hung in tidy rows, organized by style and color. This was common with foster kids. Keep everything neat and tidy, don't make any messes, and maybe they'll let you stay. If you don't, it's easy to pack it all up again. Becca swallowed hard, trying to remain calm. She could imagine Ash teasing her about overreacting. "Becca, you really need to chill," she would say. *Don't panic yet.*

She turned on her heels, doing another loop around the house. "Ash! Freud!" Becca shouted, unable to control the frenzied tone. She searched the guest room and her bedroom. No sign of them. Becca grabbed her cell phone and dialed. Ash's voice mail picked up on the first ring. "This is Ash. Leave a message. Or better yet text me."

"Ash, it's Becca. Where are you? Please call me back. I'm worried," Becca said. She hung up and sent a quick text. *Please call me. I woke up and you weren't here. I'm very worried!*

They probably just went on a walk. That's all, Becca told herself. She threw on her sneakers and ran outside, doing a loop around the neighborhood. She knocked on neighbors' doors asking if they'd seen Ash or Freud, to no avail.

Her heart was pounding, dread settling in her stomach. Becca returned home and made her way back to Ash's room. She needed to focus, make sure she wasn't overreacting before she sounded the alarm bells. If she contacted the police and

Ash's social worker, she might jeopardize the adoption. She scanned the room, her heart pounding as she caught sight of a note on Ash's bedside table, Becca's name written in Ash's neat cursive script. Her hands trembled as she read.

Becca, I'm so sorry. I can't stay here anymore. It's nothing you did. You've been amazing and so good to me. I hope one day I can explain everything. I love you.

PS Don't be mad about Freud. I'll take good care of him.

Becca studied Ash's note, reading it over and over again, trying to understand what was happening. This was a nightmare, an honest-to-goodness nightmare. Ash and Freud both gone. It didn't make sense. Ash wanted to be hers. She said so a few hours ago. What could possibly have changed her mind? Her hands trembling, Becca stopped herself. Once Ash was home, she could figure out the whys. Right now she needed to focus on finding her.

Becca understood runaways were low priority. Generally, an officer wouldn't even file a missing persons report unless the person was missing for twenty-four hours. At that point the police would issue a missing persons bulletin, which would inevitably get lost in the sea of murders, rapes, and robberies. There was also the issue of Ash's age. She wasn't a child. She was a teenager with a troubled past and a long history of running away. She could imagine an officer shrugging his shoulders with a casual "she'll turn up," or offering Becca a party line like "searching for her would be a waste of resources."

This was when working for the police came in handy. Becca used to look down on nepotism. Today she didn't care. If it meant finding Ash, she would call in every favor in the book. She dialed Nina.

Pick up. Pick up. The voice mail clicked in. "Hi, you've reached Nina Stanton. I'm not available, but leave a message. If this is an emergency and you need assistance, please hang up and call 911."

Becca closed her eyes. Today was Nina's day off. She rarely answered phone calls or e-mails, valuing quality time with her family. Becca usually admired Nina's ability to disconnect. Not today. She could drive to Nina's home in Culver City, but she didn't want to waste any time. The sooner Becca began her search for Ash, the better her odds were of finding her.

Becca flipped through her phone contacts, trying to decide whom to call. She worked with other officers. There wasn't anyone she trusted as much as Nina. Becca paused, her finger hovering over Christian's name. That wasn't true. There was a time when she trusted him more than anything.

The last time Becca spoke to Christian was almost a year ago, the day their divorce was finalized. But, despite their rocky past, he was a fifteen-year veteran of the LAPD. There was no doubt in her mind that he would treat this situation with the seriousness it deserved. Becca said to hell with it and dialed his number. He picked up on the first ring.

"Becs? Is that you?" Christian asked, not bothering to hide his surprise.

"Yes...I know it's been a while but..." Becca faltered for a moment, her face flushing, wondering if she'd made a mistake in calling. What if he didn't want to help her?

"Are you okay, Becs?" he asked. Becs. Only Christian called her that. Never Becca or Rebecca. Just Becs. She swallowed hard. She couldn't believe she was asking the man who broke her heart to help her. The world was a cruel and mixed-up place, but she wasn't going to back out now.

"It's Ash. She's gone, Chris."

"Someone took her?" he interrupted, his voice stern, already switching into cop mode.

She wanted to say yes. The only way Ash would ever leave was if someone took her against her will. "No. She ran away. Left a note and everything."

She braced herself for more questions, but Christian didn't ask a single one. "Send me all of Ash's pertinent details, height, weight, date of birth, and a current photo. I'll put out a missing persons report ASAP and I'll be there in fifteen minutes. Maybe less."

She wasn't sure why she was surprised. That he would be willing to drop everything and help her. That's who he was. She wondered whether his fiancée was there, if he'd tell her where he was going, if he'd told her all about how their marriage crumbled. Those thoughts were eclipsed by memories of Ash. There was something comforting in his take-charge demeanor. She needed that. "I can't lose her, Christian," Becca whispered.

"You won't. We'll find her, just hang in there, Becs. I'm on my way."

Heartbroken, Becca sank down onto Ash's bed, gazing at the framed black-and-white photos covering the walls. The first summer Ash came to live with them, Becca insisted that she take a class, something to keep her busy and out of trouble while Becca and Christian were at work. Ash reluctantly enrolled in a photography workshop, and to both their surprise, a passion was born.

Becca lingered on one of Ash's photos, her favorite, an artsy portrait of Becca and Freud, one of those magical Southern California days, a perfect seventy-five degrees, no traffic, and a gentle surf. A few days after it was taken, Ash relapsed, returning home high off her ass and crying. It was Christian's breaking point. She could still see him now, glaring at Becca, the bitterness and resentment seeping out. "You want to pretend Ash will fix everything broken inside you, but you're kidding yourself. No matter how much you try to make it so, she will never be yours." She'd done her best to prove him wrong, but here she was, sitting in Ash's room, Christian's words echoing over and over in Becca's head like a terrifying prophecy. *She will never be yours. She will never be yours . . .*

MO

Trouble comes in threes. That's what they always said. Mo sure as hell hoped that was true, because she wasn't sure she could handle any more troublemakers. A few hours earlier she woke to Vic frantically shaking her. "Nate took off," he said, his voice thick with betrayal.

"He'll be back," Mo said confidently. No way he would leave her. One look at Vic's face told Mo she was wrong.

"His shit's gone. All of it."

Mo pushed past Vic, surveying his tent. Clothes, books, even Nate's prized Rickenbacker guitar were gone. She realized now that someone should have been watching him. They would have to discuss that error later.

Mo was profoundly disappointed, but none of this was Nate's fault. He wasn't thinking rationally. It was that girl. She poisoned him. They had to do something about her.

"Find out what happened. Someone must have heard him packing up or saw him leaving," Mo said.

"Mo, I already know what happened. It's my fault," Vic said.

"What is it?"

Vic didn't hesitate, his words spilling out as though he needed to unburden himself. "Leslie tricked me. Made me think she wanted...that she was interested in me again. She started asking all these questions, saying she wanted to get closer. Mo...I told her things...about Eli, and Ash, and the reckonings."

She rarely lost her temper, but Mo couldn't help herself. "What the hell were you thinking?" Mo snapped.

Vic hung his head. "I'm sorry, Mo. I'm so sorry."

Mo went quiet, hating the hangdog look on Vic's face. The stress of these past few days was getting to her, but that didn't mean she had to take it out on Vic. She could handle this. She was always good in a crisis.

"At least we know where to start. I want to speak with Leslie and find out why she did what she did. Do you know where she is?"

"She went to get food with Kelsey. She'll be back soon," Vic said.

"She needs to know that we mean business. Can you make that clear?"

"Of course, Mo. Of course," Vic promised. She watched as he lumbered off in search of Leslie.

She watched him go, her annoyance fading. He was one of the best parts about this life she was living. She slipped into her tent, knowing that tonight would be emotionally taxing, and needing to rest. She thought about Vic, loving

100

how trusting and good-hearted he was, and hating how people used that goodness against him. Mo and Vic were an unlikely pair. She understood that. They met two years ago at the beginning of Mo's home-free journey. When she found herself out on the streets in her forties, Mo wasn't sure what to do or where life would take her.

At first, she simply roamed up and down the vast stretch of beaches, moving from Santa Monica to Venice and back again, camping out, panhandling, scrounging in dumpsters for food, sleeping on benches and beaches. At night, she unfurled her sleeping bag, lying awake, contemplating all the possible ways she could kill herself. Drowning. Drugs. One sure-footed step in front of a bus. As the days wore on, she grew closer and closer to surrendering for good until the divine powers intervened.

The spirits were guiding her the day she spotted Vic panhandling on the Venice Pier. Tourists were terrified of him, that much was clear. He was only seventeen, and an intimidating presence. Everyone who passed him averted their eyes, rushing past, hoping not to attract his attention. Some people shouted, threatening to call the police, though Vic never raised his voice in return. In an instant, Mo saw the depth of this boy's suffering, the hopelessness that surrounded him. Mo recognized a kindred spirit. She bought two Subway sandwiches and cautiously approached him. The poor boy was starving. He devoured his sandwich and then he scarfed down hers. For the next week, Mo would return with food for Vic. Before long, they were inseparable.

At first, it was just the two of them, camping on the beach, relocating anytime the cops got close. Mo was skilled at appealing to tourists and earned a bit of money. After witnessing how careless most people were with their belongings, Mo and Vic began stealing wallets and purses, which meant they never went hungry. Sometimes they even had enough to spend a night or two in a motel, though as time went by Mo preferred being outdoors. In exchange for Mo's monetary support, Vic provided protection from addicts, the crazies, or anyone else looking to screw with them. The girls were next to join their ranks. Kelsey and Andrea were sixteen, a couple from Portland. Mo and Vic were grabbing a slice on the pier when they saw two frat boys hassling them. She almost intervened, until she saw the girls were more than able to handle themselves. It didn't take much to send the frat bros running. She had this sense that they were all meant to find one another. Impressed by their toughness, Mo approached the girls and asked if they were hungry.

"Famished," Kelsey said. Mo bought slices of pizza for everyone, listening as Kelsey and Andrea explained that they'd fallen in love at one of those "pray the gay away" camps and ended up on the streets. After conferring with Vic, who gave his blessing, Mo asked the girls if they wanted to join them, and that was that. They'd bought a few tents and set up wherever they could find space on the beach. Eli came next. Then Leslie. After their numbers reached six, Mo swore she wouldn't take on any more. Until she saw Nate.

"Leslie's ready to talk when you are," Vic said, peeking his head into Mo's tent. She nodded and followed him outside, offering the others who were gathered outside their tents an encouraging smile. This was a minor hiccup, and it would be business as usual before long. She slipped inside Leslie's tent, studying the young girl's busted lip and blackened eyes, both hands and feet bound. Mo understood this might seem harsh to outsiders. When someone violated their code, extreme measures were required.

She lowered herself beside Leslie. "Hello, my darling."

Leslie whimpered, tears streaming down her face. Mo reached out and gently patted her leg. "I know you're hurting, and that's unfortunate. The thing is, Vic says you've been deceitful. Is there something you want to tell me? About Nate and Ash?" Mo asked, her voice soft.

"I didn't mean to hurt you, or the Tribe. All I wanted was to protect us. That's why I told Ash to stay away. I just wanted her to leave us alone," Leslie whispered.

"You don't think you should have discussed that with me? Or with the rest of your family first?" Mo asked. Leslie nodded tearfully. "Instead, you try to handle things on your own, and now Nate is gone. I need to know what you said to him."

Leslie was crying harder now, her shoulders convulsing.

Mo scooted a bit closer, gently taking Leslie's face into her hands. "Remember when Vic and I found you, all strung out, hooked up with that low-life pimp who was whoring you out for dime bags?"

Leslie whimpered in agreement, blood and tears streaming down her face. Mo reached into her pocket for a tissue. She wiped away excess blood, recalling how sickly Leslie was when she first joined them, nothing but skin and bones. Mo oversaw Leslie's healing, watched as she grew stronger and more confident. Hours upon hours she invested in this girl's rehabilitation, spending the Tribe's hard-earned money feeding her, nourishing her mind. "Remember what I said to you when you joined us?"

"You said as long as I was loyal to the Tribe, I always had a home."

"I also said we didn't tolerate liars," Mo said, doing her best to stifle her anger. Losing control would not get her what she wanted. She needed all the facts. It would dictate how she handled Nate and Ash.

Mo reached out and took Leslie's hands. "All I want is for you to tell me the truth about Nate. Tell me what you said to him, and we might have a chance at restoring things to the proper order."

She saw a hopeful flicker on Leslie's face. "I said you were upset with Ash. I just wanted him to know so he'd stay away from her."

"And what was Nate's response to that?"

"He said they were gonna leave town together."

Mo's heart physically ached, hearing this news. She couldn't believe it was that easy for Nate to leave. That he would just walk away without any consideration for her or the family. There was no way. This wasn't his idea. It had to be that girl's.

"Did he say where they were going? How they planned to get there?" Mo asked.

"He said they were gonna take a bus...somewhere in New Mexico." Leslie's tears were making it difficult for her to speak.

Mo patted her leg again. "It's okay. This is all very useful. Now I need you to do me a favor. Does Nate still have his phone? The one he talks to Ash on?"

Leslie couldn't hide her shock. God, this girl must think she was a total idiot. There was a reason Mo was in charge. She knew everything that went on with the family. As a rule, the Tribe rejected technology, though Mo kept a phone for emergencies. She reached into her pocket and pulled out the cheap burner phone she'd purchased from the corner store.

"I need you to do something for me," Mo said.

"Whatever you want, Mo. I'll do anything."

"I want you to call Nate. You have his number, don't you?"

Leslie nodded, her head bobbing up and down. "Good. Tell him you want to go with him and Ash. Ask him if you can meet him and what time. Can you do that?"

"Of course, Mo. I'll do anything to make things right."

Mo leaned over and gently untied Leslie's hands and handed over the phone. She gestured for Leslie to dial, and the girl obeyed.

"Nate, it's Les . . . please don't hang up. I need your help." Leslie paused, listening carefully. "Nate, I don't know what to do. I'm scared. Of Mo and the others," she said, her voice quivering.

Deceptive little bitch, Mo thought.

Leslie's head bobbed enthusiastically as she listened. "Yes, I can do that. I'll meet you there. Okay. I will. Be careful," Leslie said.

She hung up and returned the phone to Mo, who offered Leslie a bright smile. "My dear, you've missed your calling. It appears that we have a star in our midst."

Leslie laughed nervously. "Nate said he's meeting Ash at the Greyhound bus station later today. They're going to Taos. Bus leaves at four o'clock."

"That's excellent news. You've done a wonderful job." Mo was starting to relax, confident she would be able to readjust. She leaned over and hugged Leslie, the young woman's body sinking into hers, her breathing slowing. Mo truly loved this child, just like she'd loved Eli. That's what made all of this so disappointing.

"You did well. I'll send Kelsey in; we'll clean you up and get you something to eat. You can rest for a bit before we go and meet Nate."

"You won't hurt him, right?" Leslie asked.

There was no way Mo would harm Nate. At least not yet. He deserved a chance to prove his loyalty. Leslie didn't need to know that. "Of course not. You know that boy is precious to me. I would never lay a hand on him."

Leslie's relief was instantaneous. "I screwed up, Mo. I see that now. But I swear nothing like this will ever happen again."

"I know, darling girl," Mo said as she stepped out of the tent. She spotted Vic nearby, inhaling deeply on a Marlboro, his dark eyes heavy and tired. This was taking a toll on all of them. She hoped they could all get some rest soon.

"What's the story?" Vic asked.

"The good news is I know where to find Nate."

"I can't believe he left us. It's fucking wrong, Mo."

Poor, sweet Vic. Such a loyal, caring soul. "I understand you're upset."

"We should take a vote. For Nate's reckoning," he said.

Mo bristled. That wasn't Vic's decision to make. She was the one who made that call. "I understand the depth of emotions you're feeling. You care about Nate. You feel wounded. I see things a bit differently. I believe negative forces have unduly influenced Nate. I'm optimistic he will

107

see the value in returning once Ash is no longer part of the equation."

"You really believe that?"

Mo nodded. "I do," Mo said.

Vic glanced toward Leslie's tent. "What about her?" he asked.

"Leslie's another story. I'm afraid she can no longer be trusted."

"I figured as much. What should we do with her?" Vic asked.

"Kill her. And make sure she suffers."

BECCA

Don't panic, Becs. You're not panicking, right?" Christian asked as he barreled past her and headed inside. Becca was always amazed by the sheer force with which Christian moved through the world.

"Panic was half an hour ago. I've moved on to full-blown freak-out," she said. The statistics flashed through her head like a news crawl. Almost eighty thousand runaways vanish every year in LA. Some were lured into sex trafficking by pimps; others were victims of drug overdoses, taken in and strung out, and still others were beaten, raped, and left for dead, their bodies never recovered. What if Ash were one of them? What if Becca never found her? What if? What if?

"How long do you think she's been gone?" Christian asked, interrupting Becca's terrible train of thought. At six foot four, he towered over her, his upper body ripped from countless hours in the gym, though Becca noticed with a bit of satisfaction the hint of a potbelly pushing through beneath his shirt. It seemed his love of beer and pizza outweighed his quest for the perfect LA physique.

Becca hesitated, a deep crimson staining her cheeks.

"I'm not sure. I had a few glasses of wine and fell asleep on the couch. I didn't hear anything. Not a sound. I shouldn't have…" She couldn't even look at Christian. What a disaster she was.

"Hey, don't do that. None of this is your fault." He stopped, his eyes scanning the room. "Where's Freud?" he asked.

The lump in Becca's throat made it difficult to speak. She swallowed hard, her words taking on a strangled quality. "Ash took him."

She held out the note. Christian held on to it, reading it carefully. "Fucking hell. Talk about kicking someone when they're down."

Becca didn't disagree. "Chris, I don't understand. Ash knows how much Freud means to me," Becca said. She wasn't even a dog person. At least not until Freud showed up. Her mother was a neat freak, always said animals were too dirty. As she got older, she told herself they required too much time and attention. It wasn't until four years ago, right after the second miscarriage, when Christian came home, carrying a malnourished pit bull puppy he found hiding under the porch of a meth den in North Hollywood. He assumed, mistakenly, that it might cheer Becca up.

"A puppy?" she said scornfully. "You brought me a puppy?" As if a dog were some substitute for having a child of their own. Furious, Becca retreated to the bedroom, locking Christian and the dog out. She was no match for

Freud and his full-court press. He was relentless, brushing his wet nose against Becca's hand, demanding to be petted, whimpering until she invited him up on the bed or the couch, following her everywhere she went. She didn't know it, but the second Christian carried that puppy through her front door, Becca was a goner. Of course she endured an endless amount of teasing from her colleagues. "You have a dog named Freud," they said, amused she'd named her dog after one of the world's most famous analysts.

Even Ash had laughed when Becca first made introductions. "A bit on the nose, don't you think?" She was right. It was totally on the nose, but Becca didn't care. Once you got to know Freud, you could see how well suited he was to his name. He was uniquely attuned to people's emotions. It was like a sixth sense, understanding intuitively what Becca needed. On nights when Christian worked late and Becca was home alone, Freud would leap onto the bed and press his massive furry body next to hers. Sometimes he would lay his head on her belly as if he understood the emptiness. Other times, he would sit on her foot, acknowledging she was the leader of his pack and he was there for her no matter what. When Ash moved in, she instantly bonded with Freud. She loved how much he cared about Ash.

"I thought things between you and Ash were good," Christian said. She wondered how he knew, if he'd asked around or talked to friends of theirs.

"They were good," Becca replied, not wanting to mention

yesterday and the drugs and the tattoo, everything else she ignored.

"Becs, there's something I need to tell you. I should've told you earlier," Christian said with a heavy sigh. She looked at him and saw the negative energy practically emanating from him. She didn't say anything. Christian hated when she talked about auras and energies and reading people's vibes. He was raised by a family of academics, which meant he was all about logic and facts. She appreciated those things too, but you could tell a lot by a person if you paid attention.

She sank down into one of the dining chairs, remembering how she'd sat here with Ash, agreeing to make the adoption official. "What is it, Chris?"

"I need you to understand everything I did was because I still care about you."

"Okay, now you're scaring me. What is it?"

"About two months ago, I got a call from Ash. She was at school and she couldn't get ahold of you. She was crying and begging me to come to her school. When I got there I found out she got caught trying to skip class. She was supposed to call a parent or guardian, but…"

"She called you? Where the hell was I?" Becca asked in disbelief.

"Palm Springs," Christian said. Becca remembered a mandatory training course she'd attended, required for one of her certifications. Ash stayed with Becca's parents, the three of them taking a trip to Universal Studios. Nothing else stood out about that weekend. Ash seemed perfectly happy when Becca returned.

"I'm afraid I'm confused, because the man I used to know, the one I married, doesn't break the rules. He's Mr. Goddamn Law and Order," Becca snapped.

"I know that. Ash begged me not to tell you. She said if I talked to the principal, he would let it go with a warning. I told myself it was wrong to keep you in the dark, but the kid I saw that day wasn't the same kid I knew."

Becca wiped away her tears. He was right. Ash wasn't the same kid. She had changed.

Christian continued. "I barely recognized her; she looked so good. She told me all about her photography, and she said you were doing well at work and that you were both really happy. I told her you would understand. Ash was insistent. She kept saying if you found out, it would 'ruin everything,' I pulled the principal aside, and he confirmed Ash was thriving. He kept saying, 'She's done remarkably well. I couldn't be more impressed.' After all you guys went through, you think I wanted to be the one responsible for that?"

When Ash first came to live with Becca, this was a textbook move. Ash could play people off each other better than anyone. Becca thought that was something Ash had grown out of. Apparently not.

"Ash was busted yesterday trying to score. An undercover cop caught her in the reservoir," Becca said.

"I thought Ash was clean."

"I did too. Guess we're both in for a shock. Why the hell did they let you take her out of school without my permission?"

"I was still listed as her emergency contact. They knew I was a police officer, so..." Christian trailed off.

Becca shook her head, understanding a badge wielded instant authority. "Did Ash say why she was ditching school?"

"Something about wanting to see her boyfriend."

Becca leaned back in her seat. There was so much new information coming at her that she could barely keep up. "What are you talking about? What boyfriend?"

"You didn't know?"

"No. I didn't know. You think I wouldn't mention a boyfriend if I knew about him? Jesus, of all the times you decide to keep me in the dark. What the hell were you thinking?"

There was a flicker of contrition on his face, a rare occurrence for a man who never admitted he was wrong. "I fucked up, Becs. Ash told me she met this kid while she was volunteering downtown. She swore it was a stupid impulse decision to skip school and see him, and if I covered for her, she wouldn't do it again."

"Guess what, Chris? She fucking did."

He absorbed her rage. "I get you're pissed. We can sit here and you can keep chewing me out, or we can focus on figuring out who the boyfriend is, where Ash went, and how to bring her home."

Becca wanted to lash out at Christian, but he was right. They couldn't waste any time. "Tell me what to do, and I'll do it," she said.

"I need to look around," he said, standing and heading toward the stairs. A part of Becca wanted to stop him and tell him she was calling the shots, but she was too overwhelmed. She trailed after him. "Did you check and see if anything was missing?" he asked.

"No. There's no way she would take anything."

"You really sure about that?" Christian asked.

Becca went silent. She wasn't sure about anything anymore. She followed Christian, wondering how he felt about all the changes she'd made to their home. He was the one in the relationship who loved decorating. Every piece in their home had been labored over, hours spent searching for the perfect lamps and rugs and artwork. She used to joke that if Christian ever cheated, she would react appropriately by burning every single thing he loved. In the end though, she lacked the courage. She gave him everything, watching him pack it all away, and she started over entirely, redecorating from top to bottom. Nina called it Becca's exorcism, which wasn't far off. Her plan was to erase every last trace of him. A futile effort. Christian's essence was as much a part of this house as the crown moldings and high ceilings.

He headed straight for Becca's room at the top of the

stairs. She joined him, her eyes zeroing in on her armoire, tucked into the corner of the room. One of the drawers was slightly ajar. Becca pushed past Christian, rushing to inspect the contents. His well-honed instincts were spot-on. Her pearls, her grandmother's collection of turquoise jewelry she brought over from Mexico, even Becca's wedding ring—all of it was gone. Ash had cleaned her out.

"Best guess is she plans to pawn it," Christian said.

Hurt danced across Becca's face. She turned away, not wanting Christian to see as she slammed the drawers shut. "It doesn't matter. They're just things," Becca said dismissively.

"Bullshit. You have a right to be upset." He reached out and squeezed her hand. "From an investigative standpoint this could be a good thing."

"Oh, really? Ash stealing my jewelry is a good thing?" He ignored her sharp tone.

"It's a starting point. I'll put in some calls to my buddies at the local precinct. "They'll know the pawnshops in the area. Places most likely to buy from a minor. We'll canvass those shops. See if anyone saw her or might know where she was heading."

This was good. This was a plan. Clear steps they could take. That's what Becca needed to focus on.

"Can I see Ash's room?" Christian asked. She led him down the hall. For a brief period of time, this was the nursery. If Becca blinked, she could see the two of them in here together, Christian covered in yellow paint, Becca camped out on the floor, morning sickness making her immobile and useless. She clocked a slight hesitation on his part as he headed for the window, carefully studying the framing. She wondered if Christian's fiancée wanted children. What would their nursery look like? She ignored the deep pang of jealousy and forced herself to focus.

"Do you see anything?" she asked Christian, who was studying the windowsill.

"The lock was jimmied. Looks like someone climbed in. I'd like to take a look outside," he said. He didn't wait for Becca to answer, turning on his heels and heading back down the stairs.

She followed, watching as Christian made his way toward the back patio. The sprinklers were on an evening timer, the ground outside Ash's room wet beneath his feet.

"There's one set of footprints here. Which meant some-one went in the window, but it doesn't look like that's how they left. Considering they had Freud with them, they probably went out the front door."

Becca shook her head, hating herself for the wine and for not knowing what was happening with Ash. There was a part of Becca that wanted to believe this kid forced Ash to leave, that she hadn't left of her own free will. The facts wouldn't allow it.

"Do you have any idea who this kid she is seeing might be?" Christian asked.

"No, but you said she met him at the mission, so we should head downtown. We can talk to Patrick, Ash's volunteer coordinator."

"Good. We should also—"

We. That was one of the things Becca missed most. She was no longer part of a "we." Everything was on Becca, all the decisions, good and bad, all the responsibilities. She hated to admit it, but she was comforted knowing she wasn't alone in this.

"Oh my God, is she still missing?" a shrill voice called from inside the house.

Becca froze. Of all the people she wasn't emotionally prepared to deal with, her mother was at the top of the list. She shot an accusatory look at Christian.

"You called my mother?" she said, contemplating whether she should strangle Christian now or wait until there were no witnesses.

"I knew you wouldn't do it, and I wanted to see if your parents knew anything. I specifically told Virginia not to come unless she heard from me."

Becca seethed. "Did you suddenly black out and forget who my mother is? She's never listened to anyone about anything in her entire life," she said.

"Rebecca, where are you?" Virginia Ortiz shouted.

She glared at Christian. "Don't mention the jewelry. I'll never hear the end of it," she said. She also didn't want to give her mother another reason to dislike Ash when she came home. Becca and Christian headed back inside, where her mother and father were inspecting the living room as though they were *CSI* lab techs. Virginia Ortiz spotted Becca and strode across the living room, managing to appear both concerned and judgmental with one sharp hawklike look.

"Seriously, Rebecca, I cannot believe this is happening. Rafi, isn't it terrible?" she said.

If there was one skill her mother possessed, it was stating the obvious. Tiny, five foot three, with dark hair styled in a pixie cut, she wore a hot-pink pantsuit from Chico's and a face full of makeup in similar shades, a look Becca dubbed "LA telenovela."

People often underestimated Virginia because of her diminutive size. She didn't mind. Growing up, Virginia always told Becca and her brother, Robbie, that her personality was what allowed her to escape poverty. "People think coming to America is the dream, and it is, but once you're here, you've got to show this country what you're made of."

Later, after Becca's brother died, Virginia said her entire life had prepared her for a tragedy of that magnitude. "I'm strong because I decided to be strong," Virginia liked to say. "Because if you let it, the world will break you."

Sometimes her mother's strength overpowered everything, like a solar eclipse blocking out the sun. All Becca wanted was to focus on Ash. Now that Virginia was here, she would have to endure her mother's steady stream of questions, each one tinged with her patented brand of disapproval. Becca saw her father hovering in the background. Raphael "Rafi" Ortiz remained the quiet anchor of the family, a successful real estate investor. He was wearing his usual uniform—a lovingly worn Dodgers T-shirt, and jeans. He reached out for Becca and kissed her on the forehead.

"*Mija*, we're so sorry...," Rafi began.

Virginia cut him off. "I guess Ash hasn't come home?" her mother said, surveying the house.

"Actually, Mom, she's right here. It's difficult to see her because of her powers of invisibility," Becca said.

"Becca." Her father sighed his "don't start" sigh. Her mother didn't bat an eye at Becca's sarcasm.

"It's okay, Rafi. I know Rebecca's just upset. We're here because we wanted to help," she said.

Now her mother wanted to help? She thought about all the times over the past few years when she could've used her mother's support. Someone to offer advice and encouragement. Someone who would tell her even on the hardest days when Ash was angry and ungrateful that this was normal teenage stuff and it would pass. She wanted her mother to say, "You're doing a good job." None of that happened. As it was, Becca could still recall the dinner where Virginia revealed her true colors. It was almost two years ago, when Ash was still struggling. She was supposed to be at a friend's doing schoolwork. Instead, Ash stumbled in, strung out and emotional, making a total scene.

Becca knew that in Ash's condition a lecture was useless. She helped Ash up to bed, giving her water, Advil, and a promise that they'd fix whatever was troubling her. When Becca came back downstairs, Virginia was livid, grabbing Becca by the shoulders and shaking her. "You have to stop this right now. After all that you've done for that child, this is how she repays you?"

Becca tried to explain yet again the depth of trauma Ash endured, the suffering she'd experienced in her life. Virginia wouldn't hear it. "She's ungrateful. That's all there is to it. She's not worth the heartache, Rebecca. Send her back where she came from."

Send her back... like she was a puppy Becca rescued from the pound, not a child. Becca understood it wasn't just about Ash; it was history bubbling up. Resentment and blame for the things they couldn't change. But Ash was at the heart of the matter. No matter how solid Becca's argument, Virginia refused to accept that Ash was capable of change.

In the end, Becca's only solution was to keep her distance. She still saw her father every few weeks for brunch or dinner or the occasional Dodgers game. But Becca made it clear that until Virginia apologized and accepted Ash as part of the family, she had nothing to say to her. Her mother was equally stubborn. Now she wanted to show up and act like no time had passed at all.

"And what about Freud? Where is he?" Virginia said. Becca hated that her mother seemed more concerned about her dog than about Ash. She recalled how annoyed Virginia was when Becca decided to keep him, listing all the reasons having a dog was a bad idea. "You and Christian are so busy. A neglected dog, especially a neglected pit bull, is bound to hurt someone. Think about it. Their jaws lock, Rebecca. What about when you have a baby?"

If anything, her mother's disapproval made Becca want to keep Freud even more. In the beginning, Virginia barely acknowledged Freud. Of course he wore her down too. Before long Virginia was volunteering to dog sit, making him gourmet dishes of rice and ground beef, and sneaking him treats. Becca was certain her mother would eventually warm up to Ash just like she'd done with Freud. She was mistaken.

"Ash took him with her. She ran away sometime early this morning," Becca said. "That's all we know right now."

"Poor girl," Virginia said, tsking in between words. "I said a prayer on the way over, and I'll go to Mass later tonight and light a candle." She reached out and tenderly touched Becca's cheek. The gesture startled her. When Becca was little, Virginia smothered Becca and her brother with kisses and hugs. After Robbie died, everything changed. Becca could count on one hand how many times they even hugged. It was why she was so vigilant about hugging Ash, doing everything possible to make her feel loved.

"This is just too much. Eventually, you have to draw a

line in the sand. Kids need boundaries, and as much as you want to believe she's fixed, the damage is done."

It didn't shock Becca that her mother would discount all of Ash's progress over the past twenty-four months. She wasn't there for any of the hundreds of victories they'd shared. The holidays and birthdays, the movie nights and Disney vacations, Ash's continued progress in school and her newfound love of photography. Virginia didn't care. She never really accepted Ash. She wasn't flesh and blood and therefore she didn't really count.

"Virg, this isn't the time," Christian said, his voice soft, but Becca could hear the edge. It took a lot to push Christian's buttons, but her mother always seemed to know just how to do it.

"Christian, you know what I'm saying is true or you wouldn't have called me."

Becca seethed. Since when was Virginia on Team Christian? What happened to all those times she told Becca she was making a mistake marrying a cop? Her constant monologue about how they were power hungry and cruel and didn't really care about people?

"Virginia, don't do this. Not now," Christian said sharply.

"I'm not saying anything we don't all know. Ash is a damaged young woman, and eventually you have to reconcile you've done everything you can to save her," Virginia insisted.

"Mama, stop talking. Please," Becca said.

"You think this isn't hard on me, or your father? After everything we've been through."

After Robbie's death, all her mother's warmth and softness vanished, replaced by an icy indifference to everything and everyone. Most days she acted as if Robbie's death were some singular event that only affected her, like Becca's brother dying hadn't ravaged the entire family. Becca dug her nails into her palms, doing her best not to say something she might regret.

"Virginia, that's enough!" Rafi snapped. Everyone turned toward him, his brown eyes dark slits. By nature, Rafi was as quiet and reserved as Virginia was outspoken and brash. To hear him shout, especially at her mother, was entirely unprecedented.

"Rafi, she can't keep—"

"Virginia, shut up. Do not say another word," Rafi said again. Virginia stood with her mouth hanging open, staring back at him in stunned silence.

He regarded Becca with his wise, knowing eyes. "Becca, what do you need from us?" he said.

Until that very moment, Becca wasn't sure what she needed. She wasn't sure of anything. Suddenly it all came into focus. "Christian and I are going to look for Ash. Can you stay here in case she comes home?" Becca said.

"Of course, *mija*. As long as you need us to."

Becca glanced over at Christian. "Can we please go?"

"I don't know. I forgot how entertaining the Ortiz family could be," he said.

Becca spent her entire marriage ignoring Christian's ill-timed attempts at humor. Today was no exception. She hurried into the kitchen, grabbed a plastic Baggie and a handful of Freud's treats. Freud was such a big baby, he would likely be uneasy when she found him. The treats would calm him. She tucked them into her pocket and headed for the front door. She told herself to keep going, but something stopped her. She had spent so long staying quiet, allowing her mother to say whatever she wanted about Ash. It seemed disloyal now. She spun around, all her anger and frustration directed at Virginia. "Mama, I want you to listen to me carefully. I will not allow anyone, especially you, to disparage Ash. She's a child who has been through hell and is clearly dealing with something now. If you can't accept that, if you can't respect me and Ash, I don't want you in my home," Becca said angrily. She didn't bother to wait for her mother's reaction. She was almost out the front door when Rafi stopped her.

"Becca, wait."

"Papa, I have to go."

"I know, *mija*." He reached out and pulled her in close, holding her tight, the same way she hugged Ash. "Good for you for standing up for Ash."

Tears welled in her eyes. Rafi never spoke up, always giving Virginia a pass, knowing how much she'd suffered losing her only son, allowing her to wear the grief loudly while he suffered in silence. "Now, go on. But please be careful and bring our girl home."

"I will," Becca promised, turning away, desperate to escape the confines of this house, her mother's judgment, and her nagging worry that she was never meant to be a mother.

BECCA

I've always said searching for an addict is like searching for a World War Two submarine. When they go underwater, you're never going to find them. Eventually though, they have to come back up for air," Christian said as he navigated the unmarked sedan down the steep incline of Coronado and into the strange middle ground that ran between Silver Lake and Echo Park, yet somehow belonged to both.

"We have got to work on your pep talks," Becca said with a withering glare. He was always the less optimistic of the two of them, and she was annoyed to see that hadn't changed. When they first began dating, this particular personality trait caused numerous fights. "I'm just telling it like it is," he often said. Becca insisted that "telling it like it is" usually made you an asshole, not a pragmatist.

Christian shook his head. "I'm trying, Becs. I really am." She could see he *was* trying, *Ease up, Becca. He's not the enemy.*

"You have to remember Ash isn't Robbie," Christian said.

Becca startled at the mention of her brother's name. "What does Robbie have to do with any of this?"

"I know how you are, always anticipating worst-case

scenarios, expecting every situation will end the way Robbie's ended. And I know it was—"

"You don't know anything," Becca interrupted. That wasn't true though. Christian knew exactly what she was thinking. Of course Robbie's death affected how Becca saw the world. No one would've believed Becca's brother, an outgoing sophomore at Stanford University, would be capable of hurting anyone, or taking his own life, but that's what happened. Some days Becca still didn't believe that it was almost twenty years since he died. The raw ache and blame she felt over losing her brother never faded, and the thought that Ash would suffer the same fate... No. She couldn't think about that.

"Can we please not discuss Robbie right now?" Becca said, sinking back into her seat. Christian opened his mouth to say something just as Becca's phone began to ring. She reached into her purse, praying Ash was calling to say she was sorry and that this whole thing this was a stupid mistake.

Becca's heart sank when she saw Nina's number flashing across the caller ID. She couldn't leave her hanging. "Nina," Becca said.

"Holy shit, Becca, the kids and I went to church and when I got out, I turned my phone on and got your message, and the missing persons bulletin. I'm sure Ash is just embarrassed about yesterday and acting out. We'll find her. I'm on my way to your place right now," Nina said without taking a single breath.

"Actually, I'm already out looking for her. My parents are at the house if you want to head over."

"Your mother's there? Glad I brought my Taser," Nina said. If Becca weren't so worried, she would have laughed.

"Why don't I meet you? You shouldn't be alone," Nina said.

Becca braced herself for Nina's reaction. "I'm not alone. I'm with . . . I'm here with Christian," Becca said.

"You're fucking joking. That's a joke, right?"

She could sense Christian eyeing her. "Nina, you didn't answer. I needed someone I trusted to file a missing persons report and look for Ash without any bullshit bureaucratic rules and regulations," Becca said.

"Makes sense. I'll focus on the big picture, and once you find Ash and bring her home, we really have to discuss your decision-making skills," Nina said. Becca understood Nina's dislike for Christian. Once he broke Becca's heart, he became persona non grata. On more than one occasion, she suggested to Becca that, if she wanted to, they could plan the perfect murder. Becca wasn't entirely sure Nina was joking.

"I appreciate that. Will you let Elena know I'm going to be out of the office for a few days?" she said, refusing to worry about work and her high-maintenance boss. Even if Becca found Ash today, she would need time off to figure out why Ash felt the need to run and deal with all the fallout from that decision.

"I'll handle the old nag. Just focus on Ash. Whatever

you do, don't take any shit from that man. And tell him if he fucks things up, he's going to have to answer to me."

Becca ended the call. "I assume Nina is thrilled to hear I'm on the case?" Christian said wryly.

"Ecstatic. Over the moon. Couldn't be happier. Thinks I'm in excellent hands."

"That's what they call overkill," Christian said. "Hey, I may be a cheater, but even Nina knows I'm a good cop."

Becca held her tongue. The last thing she wanted right now was to rehash Christian's infidelity. It didn't matter that he swore nothing had happened. It took Becca months and months to stop reliving the awful moment when she'd logged on to his computer and saw the stream of text messages and sexy pictures. A trainer at Gold's Gym for God's sake. He'd turned them both into a goddamn cliché.

She often wondered what life would be like if they hadn't lost their babies. Would their marriage have survived? Their friendship? After that last miscarriage, once Becca fully recovered, she told Christian it was time to discuss other options. "We can still be parents. Fostering. Adoption. There are plenty of children that need homes," she said. Christian agreed. "We'll build a family of our own."

Fostering a teenager wasn't something they discussed. It wasn't something Becca had even considered. Ash was one of life's unexpected surprises. She'd done her best to reassure him. "I promise you, she's special. All she needs is someone to believe in her. To fight for her and make her feel safe."

He agreed. She didn't bully him into it. They sat down over dinner and a bottle of rosé and made the decision together. Like every decision that came before it. Then things got too hard. His infidelity was a betrayal she could never forgive. She blinked, the humiliation as fresh today as it was two years ago.

Christian made a right and headed east, Skid Row coming into focus. This Los Angeles neighborhood stretched from the area east of Main Street, south of Third Street, west of Alameda Street, and north of Seventh Street, spanning almost fifty city blocks, a homeless population ranging from eight to eleven thousand.

It was almost impossible to prepare someone for the sheer magnitude of suffering you witnessed when you arrived on Skid Row. Becca had been here hundreds of times and yet she still braced herself as her car sped past rows and rows of tents and tarps, homeless encampments. Outside the tent cities dozens upon dozens of people, lost souls, hungry, high, or craving a fix, lurched and shuffled down the streets.

If you somehow found yourself dropped into this neighborhood without any explanation or understanding of where you were, you could realistically believe the world you once inhabited no longer existed; maybe a zombie apocalypse or the fallout from a nuclear war was to blame. There had to be some explanation for this massive sea of human suffering. Unfortunately, this homeless crisis wasn't a cinematic creation. It was a combination of human error and hubris, a political battle that resulted in creating what was now one of the biggest homeless encampments in the country. Every time Becca came to Skid Row, she recalled the George Bernard Shaw quote she'd read in her freshman comp class: "The worst sin towards our fellow creatures is not to hate them, but to be indifferent to them; that's the essence of inhumanity."

She was relieved that Christian didn't feel the need to fill every silence, something Becca often failed at. He parked at a meter, and together they headed toward the Downtown Mission a half a block away. The sidewalks reeked of rotting garbage, the stench of urine filling the air. Every now and then, they'd encounter an unknown stink so sharp, they'd have to plug their noses. Rats skittered about, undeterred by their presence. They crossed the street, passing a young mother and her daughter, a toddler no more than three years old, fast asleep on a flattened box in the middle of the sidewalk.

"Fucking disgrace," Christian said under his breath. Becca agreed. When she saw things like that, her job seemed like an exercise in futility. She would have to remind herself again and again of all the people whose lives she influenced: the teenage girl with the eating disorder she convinced to seek treatment; the family of five she relocated to an apartment; even Raya, whom she managed to get off the streets. This work was her calling, her salvation.

Becca's parents never spoke about their feelings, never

acknowledged their own pain. They locked it away, pretending it didn't exist. After Robbie died, Becca spent years floundering, forced to suffer in silence. An Intro to Psych class in college turned that all around, and she became obsessed with reading about and studying trauma and PTSD and various mental disorders. She realized that she wanted to connect with people who had experienced trauma, to aid the emotional wounds others couldn't see. Becca earned her BA in psychology at USC and then a master's and PhD at UCLA. During all those years of study, she survived on financial aid and student loans, working in clinics counseling troubled girls, working for an organization that found housing and jobs for battered women, teaching life skills to youth offenders. She studied her ass off, writing papers late into the night after working all day.

After gaining enough hours to earn her license, she made the decision to open her own private practice. She would earn two to three times more, not to mention she could make her own schedule. She told herself it would give her time to volunteer for causes that were important to her. Having her own business would also give Becca time to raise a family, something she naively assumed would happen when she was ready. With Christian's encouragement, she rented office space in Beverly Hills, and her private practice took off.

She received referrals from high school friends who were now climbing their respective career ladders in finance and film. There were TV stars and fitness personalities, athletes and plastic surgeons. Before long Becca built a thriving practice, even having to turn clients away. After a year and a half, she found herself growing disenchanted. Her job was to listen and offer guidance, to stay impartial. Some days her high-functioning neurotic clients left Becca resentful and annoyed.

She understood the TV writer's annoyance that his boss gave a script to some "less qualified woman" or that his college buddy got a two-picture deal and he didn't. She understood the young housewives who'd grown frustrated by their husbands' demanding schedules, feeling neglected and unseen, how bored they were by their yoga/boot camp/Pilates schedules, their lives a Groundhog Day of privilege. She understood it. She did her best to see them through each and every one of these struggles. As time wore on, she began to resent them all. Not a good quality in a therapist, but she was only human. Sometimes she wanted to say, "Get over yourself. Take a step back and look beyond you. See what's happening in the world."

She hated feeling this way. People's problems were relative. Her clients deserved someone who was totally and completely invested in her work. She didn't talk about any of these feelings, not even with Christian. She could imagine his teasing, "Guess only poor people can have problems."

Eventually, she had to make a change. She'd been on the receiving end of bad police officers, watched in shock at the callous way they dealt with her family, how they ignored

Robbie's mental illness, choosing to treat him like a criminal instead of a person in the midst of true suffering. It wasn't until Becca met Christian, and saw the kind and compassionate way in which he did his job, that her feelings about law enforcement changed. There were lots of good cops out there, and lots of smart and well-meaning people like her trying to change the way law enforcement handled mental health situations. She thought about how different things would've been if the officers who arrested Robbie treated him with kindness, if they'd understood his fragile mental condition.

The more time passed, the more Becca began to search for a new way to serve those in need. She was looking at job boards when she saw the posting for the Mental Evaluation Unit.

She didn't even tell Christian she was applying. She figured the odds of landing the job were slim, especially considering her brother's criminal record. Two weeks later, she received the news that she'd been hired. A month after that she terminated the majority of her private clients, keeping only a handful as she began her new career.

Christian later regretted Becca's career change, frustrated by how much time and energy the work required. "You're like an addict and this job is your drug," he often said. She couldn't deny it. There was a cost when forced to deal with the endless merry-go-round of suffering. Many people in the unit burned out, got divorced, suffered mental breakdowns. Becca understood how challenging it was, but she couldn't imagine doing anything else. In many ways, this job healed her.

It was almost ten thirty when Christian and Becca arrived at the Downtown Mission, a private Christian homeless shelter. Hundreds of people were queued up, waiting in line as volunteers piled heaping servings of scrambled eggs and bacon onto their plates. Becca led Christian into the depths of the mission, zigzagging through a maze of hallways toward a back office tucked in the recesses of the building. She knocked on the door and heard a muffled "come in."

Becca opened the door and found Patrick sitting at his desk. Late fifties, he was never without his LA Kings cap perched on his head, a perpetually frazzled scowl on his face. Upon seeing Becca, the scowl was replaced by a smile. He waved her in. "Hey, Becca, good to see you. Please have a seat. I'm going through these budget reports, so you're saving me from a nervous breakdown."

Becca and Christian settled across from him, the two of them practically knocking knees in the cramped space. "Pat, this is my . . . this is Sergeant Christian Stevens."

Patrick nodded, the furrow in his brow returning as he studied Becca. "How's Ash doing? We really miss her around here. She's such a great kid. Clients loved her. Staff too."

Becca leaned forward, rubbing her hands against her

jeans. "What do you mean you miss her? She's been volunteering here three times a week."

An awkward silence lingered. Patrick leaned back and took off his glasses, tiredly wiping his eyes. "I'm afraid that's not true. A few months ago Ash came to me and said, between school and her photography, she was too busy to continue volunteering with us. We were really sorry to lose her."

Jesus, Ash, more lies? How was it possible that Becca didn't know about this? How could she have been so blind to what Ash was doing? Teenagers were adept liars, she knew that, though it wasn't much comfort right now.

"You could've called me . . . I wish you would have," Becca said, trying to keep the accusation out of her voice.

"I didn't think anything about it. Ash's court-ordered community service ended almost a year ago. She wasn't obligated to continue volunteering. I'm so sorry, Becca. I really am."

Christian seemed to sense that Becca was struggling to process this news and stepped in. "We think Ash has been seeing someone she met down here and that she may have run away with him. Do you know anything about that?"

"No. Once the volunteers are trained, we send them on their way. It's so chaotic around here, I'm usually putting out some kind of fire. You might want to talk to the clients, ask around and see if they know anything. She was very popular with everyone. They loved her pictures."

Ash's pictures. Becca didn't know why she hadn't thought about them. "Hey, Pat, did you keep any of Ash's photos?" Becca asked. There was a good chance that if Ash took photos here, Becca might be able to locate the boyfriend.

"Oh yeah, Ash uploaded all of them to the cloud before she left. You're welcome to go through them." He pressed a few buttons on his keyboard and stood, gesturing for Becca to take his seat.

"Are you sure it's okay?"

"Of course. I'll check with the other staff and volunteers, see if anyone might have any insights or know anything about who she was seeing. Please let me know if you need anything," Patrick said.

"Thanks, Pat," Becca said, her voice wavering.

"We appreciate your time and cooperation," Christian said, shaking Patrick's hand.

Patrick nodded, but directed his attention to Becca. "I know this isn't easy. When Maddie, my youngest, was a teenager, she was a total hellion. We made it through. You'll do the same with Ash. I mean, that kid adores you. Everyone can see that," he said.

Becca's eyes welled with tears. She appreciated Patrick's kindness. If it were true though, if Ash really adored her, she wouldn't have left. He closed the door behind him, leaving Becca and Christian alone with thousands of Ash's photos. She hurried over to Patrick's desk and sank into the seat, scrolling through the massive file of photos. Christian stood behind her, his breath on her neck, the closeness unsettling. Becca forced herself to focus as she made her way through the massive selection. The images were of the residents captured in and around the mission, illustrating the beauty and sadness of street life. There was a photo of a group of wrinkled men and women seated at folding tables, happily eating ice cream cones, their smiles a stark contrast to their surroundings. Another photo showed a homeless mother and her infant son on a cot, wrapped in a loving embrace, surrounded by dozens of other families asleep on their cots, their faces slightly out of focus.

"Ash took all of those?" Christian asked. Becca could hear the amazement in his voice.

"She's really good, isn't she? I used to think I was biased, but her talent is undeniable. I keep telling her if she keeps it up, her work could be in a gallery one day."

Maybe that was part of it. Maybe Becca was too pushy, expected too much. She insisted Ash take her studies seriously, insisted she take the photography classes and continue her volunteer work. Virginia was the same, always pushing Becca and Robbie. Be better. Do better. Work harder. Maybe this was Becca's fault. She kept clicking through photos, hundreds zipping by.

"Wait, Becs, go back. That's her," Christian said.

Becca swiped back and saw Ash. She usually preferred to be on the other side of the camera, always refusing to allow Becca to take pictures. This time she made an exception.

The image was taken at dusk, against the backdrop of a brick wall. Ash's eyes were sparkling, a radiant smile on her face as she looked up at a tall, gangly teenage boy. Their fingers were intertwined, the two of them regarding one another with expressions of pure, unabashed love.

Becca's hand trembled as she leaned forward for a closer look. She saw the tattoo on the inside of his wrist, the same tattoo she'd seen on Ash's wrist. She studied the boy's face, and gasped. Becca knew this boy.

No. No. No. This isn't happening. This can't be happening. Becca's face flushed, her breathing taking on a strangled quality.

"Becs, what is it? What's wrong?" Christian asked.

She couldn't seem to speak, her words catching in her throat. Becca couldn't remember when she had her last panic attack, but she recognized its anatomy instantly, the dizziness, the tightness building in her chest, her limbs going numb. She couldn't breathe in this cramped, airless room, and she couldn't stare at these goddamn photos any longer. Becca leapt to her feet and raced toward the door, desperate for air, desperate to escape the reality of what was happening. Ash was in danger, and it was all Becca's fault.

BECCA

Becca dodged the mission residents as she raced down the long corridor. She burst through the front door, gasping for fresh air. Instead she was met by the overpowering scent of garbage. Waves of nausea gripped her. She leaned forward, hands on her knees, trying to calm herself. "Breathe in and out. Breathe in and out."

It didn't work, her breath short and choppy. In her teens and early twenties, Becca's struggle with PTSD was her own shameful secret, the panic attacks coming at all times of the day or night. It wasn't until her first year of grad school that her advisor, a wonderfully kind professor, got to the root of Becca's problems.

"This is your body's way of processing trauma because you refuse to do it yourself. These physical symptoms will only continue. Once you're armed with the tools and you tap into all of that, you'll be free."

He was right. For years Becca avoided talking about Robbie or addressing anything related to her brother's breakdown, telling herself that she was okay. The panic attacks told a different story, and it took years of therapy to learn how to cope with them. She knew all the tricks of the trade, but right now her mind was blank. Her breath came out in short, harsh gasps, as though someone were sitting on her chest.

She heard Christian calling her, felt his arms wrap around her waist. He held on to Becca tightly. "You're okay. I'm right here. You're safe. You're in control. Nothing is so bad you can't find your way out," he kept repeating in a calm and soothing manner.

Becca wanted to believe him, but it was almost impossible. She knew too much. She'd seen the victims of sexual assault, watched how the light vanished from their eyes. For so long, Ash's eyes lacked their brightness and sparkle. She'd finally gotten it back and now...Becca leaned forward, straining against Christian, her breath still coming out in short, rapid spurts.

"Close your eyes. Remember that trip to Idyllwild at Christmas. You, me, Freud, and Ash. Remember how we all woke up early to go on a hike. How clear the sky was. The crisp air filling our lungs. There was still snow on the ground, and Ash couldn't stop giggling."

Becca stilled in Christian's arms, remembering that gorgeous winter day. Ash, bundled up in Rafi's old army jacket, letting out a squeal as she launched herself over and over again into a mound of snow. As they wound up the trail, Christian and Becca held hands, occasionally stealing a kiss, then soaking up the silence and the possibility that maybe this unlikely family could work. It was one of her favorite memories of the three of them, and Christian remembered it too.

After a few minutes, Becca's breathing normalized, the feeling in her hands and feet returning. "You good, Becs?" Christian asked.

Becca's cheeks flushed, suddenly aware of how close they were. She slipped from his embrace. "I'm okay now. I'm fine," she said, though the tremor in her voice told another story.

"Come on. Let's go back inside. You should sit for a minute. I'll get you some water."

She wanted to resist, but she was still shaky, slightly unsteady on her feet, and the overpowering scent of urine was making her nauseated.

Becca followed Christian back into the mission and they returned to Patrick's office. She sank down into the chair, her body still feeling the aftereffects. Christian disappeared and returned a few minutes later with a bottle of water. "Drink it all," he said. She drank thirstily, giving him a grateful nod when she was finished.

"Your visualization techniques are really impressive."

"I learned from the best," he replied. She gave him a half smile. Early on in their relationship, Becca urged Christian to consider mindfulness training. Every time she tried to get him on board, Christian dismissed it as too hippie-dippie. "You do your things your way. My way is working."

The nightmares and sleepless nights and the occasional angry outbursts told a different story. She made him a bet.

"Meditate once a day for six months, and if your sleep isn't better and you don't feel more grounded and at ease, I'll do the dishes and the cooking for the next six months. If you do feel better, then you'll wait on me hand and foot."

Never one to walk away from a challenge, Christian agreed. At the end of the six months, he was a convert, and Becca enjoyed six glorious months free from kitchen duty. He even implemented a mindfulness component when training new officers.

"What's going on, Becs? Do you know that kid?"

She nodded, her stomaching churning. "He was living on the streets with Ash when I found her."

"So he's the boyfriend?" Christian asked.

"I would bet my life on it. His name is Nate Sutton. They were living together with a bunch of other kids in this pedophile's house when we found Ash. Nate went out to get food and wasn't there when the cops were called. They were separated that day."

Becca remembered Ash's single-minded obsession—find Nate. It was all she talked about. "We promised we would always be there for each other. He has to be freaking out now that I'm gone," Ash said. Becca empathized. Ash had no one until she met Nate. It made sense that she wanted to find him again.

"I said I'd try and track him down, and I kept my word. I made hundreds of calls, followed up with social workers all over the city, made the rounds at local shelters, asking them to call if a kid that matched Nate's description turned up. Got nowhere. A year after Ash moved in, I get a call from a social worker. She said the cops arrested a minor by the name of Nate Sutton. Charged him with assaulting the owner of a liquor store. I couldn't believe it. I'd finally found him. I decided not to tell Ash right away. I wanted to see him first. I drove to Riverside to the juvenile facility where Nate was being held. I met his social worker. The picture she painted about this kid was ugly. Violent family. History of abuse. Mom murdered by his father, who took his own life, and Nate had a front-row seat to this whole thing."

"And the assault... what did he say about that?" Christian asked.

"Claimed the assault was self-defense, that the man at the store was trying to screw with him, and he was just defending himself. I didn't doubt his story. It sounded credible. My heart broke for this kid. All the cards were stacked against him. The social worker agreed to arrange a meeting."

"I'm taking it the visit didn't go well," Christian said.

"It wasn't bad," Becca said, every detail of the day rushing back. The giant open area with half a dozen round ceramic tables, and ugly white tile floors. The posters on the wall with bland inspirational sayings like "Mind-set is everything."

Across from Becca, Nate glared at her, the angriest fourteen-year-old she'd ever met. "Did your caseworker tell you why I'm here?" she asked. He grunted no, crossing his arms defensively.

"I wanted to see if you were okay, and if there was anything you needed?" she said.

"Getting out of this fucking place would be a start," Nate said.

"I'm afraid I don't have that kind of authority. I was thinking money for snacks or toiletries..."

He leaned forward. "Why would you do that? Who are you?"

"We have a mutual friend in common. Her name is Ash," Becca said. All the walls Nate put up, the crossed arms, the scowl, all of it vanished. He sat up straight, leaning forward, his eyes no longer flat and dull. "You know Ash? Is she okay? That pervert didn't hurt her, did he?"

"Ash is good. She's safe and doing well."

He relaxed, his shoulders loosening. "Can I see her? Or talk to her?"

"I don't know."

"You asked if I needed anything, I'm asking for this. I just want to hear her voice and tell her I'm sorry I left her. Please can't you try and make that happen?"

Becca winced, remembering the sincerity in this kid's eyes. "I didn't know what else to say. I told him yes."

"You lied?" There was no judgment. Christian was simply stating a fact.

"I didn't plan to. I wanted to help Nate, but Ash was struggling. I was so worried if this boy came back into Ash's life, he might—"

"Drag her down?"

Becca wanted to deny it. She couldn't. "I wanted Ash to have a chance, Christian. A real chance."

"I know, Becs. Everyone knows how hard you've tried with Ash."

"I have to try harder," Becca said forcefully. Ash was her responsibility.

Christian sensed that his opinion wasn't necessary. "What can I do, Becs?"

"See if Nate is in the system? Was he ever sentenced for that assault, and if he was, when was he was released? I need to know everything about him," Becca said.

"Okay. Okay. Just take a breath. I'll drop you back at home and I'll go to the station and see if anything's come up with the missing report and what I can find on Nate."

Becca shook her head. "I'm not ready to go yet. Maybe someone will recognize Nate and lead us to them."

"Okay. I'll put in a call about Nate and then we'll canvass," Christian said.

She cocked her head. "Hold on. You're not going to push back and insist we're wasting our time, or force me to argue with you until you finally give in and let me have my way?" Becca asked.

The corners of Christian's mouth turned up ever so slightly. His "almost smile," she used to call it. "Sorry to disappoint you. I know you enjoy a good debate, but I'll follow your lead on this."

They tracked down Patrick, but he had no luck. For the next hour, they talked to everyone at the mission, from regulars to staff members who had interacted with Ash on a regular basis. It was clear she'd made an impression. Everyone loved Ash, but no one had any information about Nate.

Exhausted, Becca wiped away beads of sweat, surveying the crowd. They'd talked to everyone here. There was no one left to ask.

"Becca, you know we've done all we can here. We need to go," Christian said gently.

"We should do a loop around the area. See if anyone around the mission may have seen Nate or Ash," Becca said.

"There's a haystack and needle reference to be made."

"I can't go home. Not yet," she pleaded. Christian's expression signaled his frustration, but he relented. "Let's go," he said. Becca's gaze landed on the bodega across the street.

"Give me one second," she said, ignoring his annoyed expression. She raced inside the store and purchased three cartons of cigarettes. Law enforcement relied on cigarettes as bargaining tools. Cigarettes were often used to get a suspect to talk or console a grief-stricken victim. Once, after hours spent trying to talk a suicidal man off the Seventh Street Bridge, all it took to get him to come down was the promise of a carton of Newports.

"I see you've learned some things on the job as well," Christian said.

Becca shrugged and kept walking. "Apparently not

enough, or we wouldn't be here. Ash and I would be finishing our walk around the reservoir and arguing over where to go to brunch, and you, you would be hanging out with your fiancée," Becca said. The words were out of her mouth before she could stop herself. It wasn't necessary, but stress often made people petty and small. Christian's surprise was obvious. She regretted it instantly. "Forget it. What you do in your personal life is none of my business."

"I planned on telling you. It's a recent development."

She didn't wait for a response, not actually wanting the details about the woman he planned to marry. It was easier to block it all out. Becca picked up the pace as she hurried toward Seventh Street. She couldn't get caught up in the past. It was all about forward motion and finding Ash.

Thankfully, Christian followed silently as they made their way down San Pedro and over to Fourth Street and toward Alameda. Becca was focused on talking to as many people as possible, but they had to be strategic. In her time working with the LAPD, Becca created a system in which to categorize the various people she encountered on the streets.

First, there were those on the streets who were simply looking to make a quick buck. They hustled and panhandled, hoping to appeal to people's altruistic nature or simply guilt them into giving up their cash. These types weren't exclusive to Skid Row. In fact, they often spent more time and attention in the touristy areas like Hollywood and Venice Beach.

In the second category were people seeking drugs and

alcohol, people consumed by their addictions. Perhaps they wound up homeless because of their disease or some other life-altering circumstance. For the most part they were purely motivated by the quest to get more money to fund their addiction.

The third group were people with criminal records, unable to get work or stable housing. In the fourth and final category were people with serious mental health issues, people like Raya, whom the system and their families had failed. Many were discharged from psychiatric hospitals or jails with no follow-up care or support system and found themselves with nowhere else to go. Becca could usually assess a person within thirty seconds. As they began their canvass, Becca stopped anyone who seemed even remotely coherent, showing them her phone with the photo and asking, "Have you seen these kids? Please look at this picture. Please can you look closer?"

When people refused to even look at the photos, Becca offered up cigarettes, which proved effective in that they would speak to her. But all they got were more noes.

They avoided the haphazardly constructed encampments, unsure of who or what they might find lurking under the tarps and blankets, nor did it seem wise to disrupt what were well-constructed walls made from found objects: handbaskets from ninety-nine-cent stores, discarded office chairs, and beach umbrellas. Becca did her best not to make eye contact with anyone talking to themselves or anyone naked, which proved more difficult than one might imagine.

Christian didn't help matters. Most people they encountered wanted nothing to do with the cops, and despite Christian's civilian clothes, his crew cut and macho swagger screamed law enforcement. One middle-aged man with no teeth and a T-shirt covered in dirt, and what Becca assumed was blood, followed them for a full city block, screaming over and over, "I ain't trusting no pigs."

But once word got out that they had cigarettes, she and Christian suddenly became the most popular people on Skid Row. People began approaching them with all kinds of elaborate tales about where and when they'd seen Ash.

"Think I saw her turning tricks over on Fourth Street."

"Heard some girl OD'd the other day. Not sure if it was a white chick. She was definitely dead."

"They're taking folks off the street for government experiments. The boy's one of them. I'm sure of it. They're gonna experiment on all of us."

Other people would take a cigarette or two, offer up a cursory glance at Ash and Nate's photo, shrug, and scurry away. A middle-aged woman who reeked of whiskey took three cigarettes, shaking her head in disapproval. "Pretty girl like that don't belong out here."

Thanks for stating the obvious, Becca thought. She was tired and frustrated and they weren't getting anywhere. It wasn't long before Becca was down to her last pack of cigarettes, which coincided with Christian reaching his breaking point.

"That's it. Enough is enough. We're done. I'm taking you home," he said.

The thought of returning home without Ash, of having to face her mother, was almost too much to bear. Unfortunately, Becca was out of ideas. They weren't any closer to finding Ash than they'd been a few hours before. Which meant Becca would need to come up with another plan.

She followed Christian back down the trash-covered streets toward San Pedro. They were almost at his car when she heard shouting. "Hey, Doc. Hey, Doc, hold up. Hold up."

She spun around to find Raya jogging toward her. Christian instinctively stepped forward, his jaw clenched, eyes narrowed, hand raised as though he were a bodyguard and she were his assignment. "Easy, Chris. She's one of my clients."

Raya reached Becca, her breath coming out in short spurts. She noticed the young woman was wearing the same clothes from yesterday, a sharp odor emanating from her. Her eyes were heavy as though she hadn't slept. "Raya, why aren't you at the mission? You should have been able to shower and get some rest."

"I was going to. Then I caught a couple of bitches going through my stuff. I didn't start any shit, but I sure as hell finished it."

There was no way to know if these women were really trying to steal from Raya, or if this was the reality she created in her mind. It didn't matter though. Fighting was prohibited in the shelters, so in all likelihood she'd been asked to leave.

"You got a second to talk?" Raya asked. She gave Christian a dismissive glare. "Without the cop."

"It's okay, Raya. He's a friend," Becca said.

"Not my friend. I don't do cops. Especially pretty-boy cops."

"Christian, do you mind giving us a few minutes?" Becca said.

"At least she called me pretty," he said, forcing a smile. "I'll go make some calls, but I'm right across the street if you need anything," Christian said.

"Don't worry, handsome. Your lady is safe with me," Raya said. Christian shot Becca a pointed look, one that said "watch yourself," and jogged across the street.

"I'm sorry the mission didn't work out, Raya. If you don't mind waiting, I can make some more calls. Try and get you in somewhere else," Becca said. This would take time away from her search for Ash, but Becca couldn't ignore this young woman. She had a professional obligation.

"Nah, I'm cool. Gonna crash with a friend when he gets back to town tomorrow. I'll make do 'til then."

Becca was consistently amazed at people's ability to adapt. "Make do" likely meant Raya would spend tonight sleeping on the streets.

"Are you sure? We can drive you someplace safe," Becca said.

"Yeah, that's not why I came looking for you. My boy Otis said that some crazy broad was out here on the streets looking for her missing kid. I saw you and I was like, 'Oh shit, I know that crazy broad.'"

Raya shifted nervously back and forth on her heels, waiting. She probably heard about the cigarettes and wanted payment up front. Becca reached into her pocket and pulled out the last pack of cigarettes and the hundred-dollar bill she kept in her wallet in case of an emergency. "I'm afraid this is all I have," Becca said.

Raya's eyes flashed. "You think that's why I came here? Because I was looking for a handout?"

That was exactly what Becca thought. She regretted it instantly, her instincts operating at a deficit. She needed to be more careful, especially with someone as vulnerable as Raya. "I didn't mean anything by it."

"You think I'm like these fucking pathetic people out here? Is that what you think?" she said. Becca shook her head, but Raya wasn't waiting. She turned to go.

"Raya, wait! Please. I didn't mean to upset you. I wasn't… I'm trying to find my daughter. I just want to find my girl."

Becca fumbled for her phone and pulled up the photo of Ash and Nate. Divulging personal information was against protocol. Sharing too much could cause trouble. Clients could form unhealthy attachments, and if they were resourceful they might even track you down. Becca understood the rules; she just didn't care. Not today.

"This is Ash. She's sixteen. I believe she took off with this kid. His name is Nate Sutton. He's got a record, history of violence."

"Shit, Doc, did you and your girl have a fight or something?"

Becca could feel her eyes watering. "No. I don't know why she ran away. I'm desperate...I have to find her," Becca said.

Raya paused, studying the photo intently. "Your girl... is she sick like me?" Raya asked, her demeanor softening.

"I don't think so. I think she's in trouble, and needs help."

Raya eyed the photo. "I've seen this kid," Raya said.

Becca froze, the first bit of good news she'd heard. "Really? Around here? At the mission?"

Raya leaned in closer. "I don't know where. I know that face." She squinted, leaning even closer to the photo.

"Where, Raya? Where did you see him? Think, please."

"Doc, it's somewhere up there," Raya said, tapping her head. "You know there's all sorts of messed-up shit floating around in there. But it'll surface. It always does. I've got your card. I'll call you the second I remember," Raya said.

"Thank you, Raya. I mean it." The young woman reached out and impulsively hugged Becca.

"Your girl is lucky to have you. So damn lucky," she said. She spun around fast and walked away, before Becca had a chance to say anything else.

Becca was grateful to Raya for trying, but she wasn't holding her breath that this lead would pan out. She raced across the street to Christian, who was leaning against the black SUV.

"We gotta roll. One of my buddies, a patrolman in Hollywood, said that a girl matching Ash's description with a dog came into one of the shops a few hours ago. Pawned some pearls and a wedding ring."

Becca let out a ragged sigh. This was the break they needed. Hopefully by dinner Ash would be home. She closed her eyes, thinking about Ash and Freud curled up on the sofa, binge watching *The Voice* and eating McConnell's Salted Caramel Chip ice cream. Getting her second wind, Becca climbed into the passenger's seat. Christian drove, speeding toward the freeway.

"That girl…is she okay?" Christian asked.

This was another thing she'd always loved about Christian. He really cared.

"She's schizophrenic with no support system so she's definitely not okay," Becca said, knowing confidentiality rules prevented her from saying more. Christian understood, already changing the subject. "I got a hit back on Nate Sutton. He managed to escape custody before his trial. It's been almost a year and a half. Cops have a warrant for his arrest. I put out a BOLO on both Nate and Ash." BOLO meant "be on the lookout."

Becca let out a ragged sigh. In response, Christian

squeezed Becca's hand. The gesture was so familiar and natural, and somehow made her feel lonelier than ever. She quickly pulled away, unable to tolerate the silence, but lacking the energy for small talk. She grabbed her phone and scrolled through it, searching for the playlist Ash made her. When Ash first talked about her love of country music, Becca thought she was kidding. Ash wasn't. She took her love of country music seriously. "My grandpa listened to it. He was real old-school. Educated me on all the greats: George Jones, Patsy Cline, Waylon Jennings, Johnny Cash."

Becca was an LA girl. She grew up on rock and roll, going to shows at the Viper Room and Whisky a Go Go. She'd always avoided listening to country. Under Ash's tutelage, Becca's appreciation for this music grew. Patsy Cline's "Walkin' after Midnight" began to play and Becca smiled, remembering last Christmas when Becca surprised Ash with a karaoke machine, the two of them singing this song at the top of their lungs. She wanted more than anything to be back there.

Twenty minutes later, Christian exited at Vine Street and made a right onto Hollywood Boulevard, or "Fanny Pack Boulevard," as Ash liked to call it. Every major brand name had a storefront here, commerce alive and well. The traffic slowed to a standstill, the streets teeming with sightseers, street performers, and protesters warning eternal damnation was near.

Becca anxiously scanned the streets, hoping luck would

be on her side and she would see Ash in the throng of people. Underneath the pink-and-white Victoria's Secret sign, she spotted two giggling teenage girls snapping photos with an Edward Scissorhands look-alike, while a rumpled Elmo chatted with a slightly paunchy Superman.

Christian glanced over at Becca. "Parking's going to be a nightmare. Let's find a spot and we'll walk to the shop. It's just a few blocks up," he said. Becca focused on the passersby, still anxiously scanning all the faces.

The light turned green and the car lurched forward two inches. Out of the corner of her eye, Becca saw something, her heart dropping. She blinked, not quite believing what she was seeing. Freud! Her boy was here, dozing at the feet of a weathered homeless man in a folding chair, a sign propped up in front of him that read HOMELESS VET NEEDS HAND UP, NOT HAND OUT.

"Christian, over there. There's Freud. Pull over. Please pull over."

Christian's gaze followed hers. "Hold up. Let me find a spot," he said.

"Chris, he could be gone by then," Becca said. If Freud was here, Ash might be close by. She couldn't wait. She couldn't let her slip away. Becca flung open the car door.

"Becs, don't," Christian said, reaching out to grab her. The light turned red. Behind them drivers laid on their horns, shouting obscenities. Becca slipped free from his grasp, shooting him an apologetic look. She darted across the street, zigzagging around a TMZ tour bus and the throng of Uber drivers.

Becca was trying to assess the best course of action on how to approach when she heard Freud's excited, frenzied bark. He had spotted her, and now his only goal was reuniting with Becca. The man looked over, clocking Becca, and he visibly startled. She wasn't sure what caused his sudden freak-out. He tossed his sign, grabbed Freud's leash, and began to run. Freud seemed spooked and followed after him. The last thing Becca wanted to do was scare this man, but she couldn't let him go. Right now he was her only connection to Ash.

"Wait...don't run. I just want to talk to you," Becca called out. But he wasn't listening. Becca began to follow, picking up her pace. The man tried running, his pronounced limp slowing him down. Less than half a block later, Becca closed the gap between them, reaching out and touching his arm. The man stopped short, breeching the distance between them in seconds, until they were so close they were almost dancing. The smell of sour whiskey emanated from him.

"I just want to talk to you about Ash," Becca said gently. A second later, she felt the pressure. Her breath caught as she glanced down at the barrel of a pistol pressing against her abdomen.

The man was smart too. He clearly knew his way around a firearm, holding the gun in such a way no one even noticed, the steady hum of tourist activity continuing all around them.

Becca could let him take charge and pray he didn't lose his cool, or she could do her best to shift the power dynamic. She took an unsteady breath, knowing if this was the wrong play, she was gambling with her life. "Put the gun down," Becca said, her voice loud and clear, cutting through the noise of the bustling city street. The man hesitated, lifting the gun away for a fraction of a second. She took this opportunity to step back a few feet, eager to put some space between them before he pointed it back at her. She was still in the line of fire though. Freud was barking and whimpering, straining to get closer to Becca. She hated seeing him in distress, but Becca didn't move. She stood frozen as a costumed Wonder Woman spotted the standoff and let out a Hitchcock-worthy scream.

"Oh my God, he's got a gun," she shouted, before racing down the street, away from danger. More screams rang out, dozens of people following her.

"Now, why the fuck you gotta go and do something that stupid?" the man whispered, whiskey on his breath. Becca knew the rules. Always keep your distance. Twenty-one feet or more. It was too late now. The man's eyes narrowed, his finger hovering over the trigger. One wrong move, one miscalculation, and Becca was dead.

BECCA

The autonomic nervous system has two components, the sympathetic nervous system and the parasympathetic nervous system. The sympathetic nervous system functions like a gas pedal in a car, revving the engine and triggering the fight-or-flight response, a burst of energy that courses through the body so it can respond to perceived dangers.

Becca had been in numerous situations where the instinct was to flee. A schizophrenic grad student once held a knife to her throat. A Goth teen, high on PCP, once threw acid, narrowly missing Becca's face. In her line of work, high-risk situations were part of everyday life. She remembered the panic attack today, and she willed herself to stay calm. This would be a very dangerous situation if she lost control.

In the distance, a small crowd formed, three uniformed LAPD patrolmen, what Becca assumed were two plain-clothes detectives, and Christian in the center of the huddle, likely providing a rundown of what was happening. Becca's stomach dropped. She wasn't the only one in harm's way. This man, whoever he was, was now in the LAPD's crosshairs. They were likely making their own assessments.

Isolate the threat.

Secure the area.

Protect innocent life at all costs.

Becca bladed her body, turning it to ensure that if they tried, the officers couldn't get a clean shot of this man without hitting her. The last thing she wanted was for anyone to get hurt. Becca didn't know anything about this man. All she knew was that he was terrified and was in his mind protecting himself. She was the one who had acted carelessly.

"Please put the gun down. I don't want you getting hurt," Becca said calmly, trying to keep the tremor from her voice.

"You dumb bitch, you've got me in big trouble now," he spat out.

"Sir, I'm the one with the gun pointed at me, so I'd say we're both in big trouble."

The man darted nervous glances at the chaotic scene unfolding around him. Becca could see dozens and dozens of people leaning down from the balconies of the mall's numerous restaurants and shops, watching and filming with camera phones. An image of her body lying on the ground, blood pooling from a gunshot wound, flashed through Becca's head, her murder going viral. As if he sensed her worry, Freud let out a low growl, straining against the leash.

"Calm that fucking dog down. He's making me nervous," the man grunted, tightening his grip on Freud's leash.

"The dog is a rescue dog, and you're the one who's

making him nervous. Loosen your grip on the leash," she said gently. The man loosened his grip. Freud was still at attention. "Freud, sit," Becca ordered. There was a fifty-fifty chance he would actually obey her command, but he must have sensed the importance of this moment because he sank down beside Becca and the man, a few whimpers still escaping.

Becca focused her attention back on the man with the gun, noticing he had removed his finger from the trigger. He understood trigger discipline, the sign of a man with military or weapons training. You only put your finger on the trigger if you intended to fire. She wasn't sure whether to be comforted by this fact, or terrified.

She knew that if she reacted suddenly, Freud could lunge or cause a reaction. She stayed still, waiting for him to speak.

"I ain't no dog thief. I told Ash I didn't want trouble, but the damn girl begged and pleaded for me to return this damn dog to her mom. Gave me fifty dollars to make it happen."

Becca wasn't sure what was more upsetting, that Ash took Freud or that she left him behind with this stranger. She could worry about the why later. Right now she needed to earn this man's trust.

"What's your name?" Becca asked, hoping to build a rapport. Her question caught him off guard.

"Why the fuck does that matter?" he asked.

She ignored his cursing. "I'm Becca Ortiz. Ash's foster mother."

He looked startled. "You're the one Ash said to call. I ain't no liar. I was giving the damn dog back. I just needed to locate a phone."

"I believe you. I really didn't mean to scare you. This is all a misunderstanding," Becca said.

The man tensed, his hand already trembling under the weight of the pistol.

"I ain't scared. Been on these streets for damn near twenty years. That's why I keep my good friend with me at all times," the man said, gesturing to the gun. "You gotta protect yourself out here. Didn't used to be like that. Folks used to leave you alone, especially if they knew you'd served your country. Not anymore. There's no honor. People are always trying to fuck with you."

"I'm not trying to do anything to you. I swear to you. If you put the gun down now, we can figure this out together."

"I don't know you. Why would your word mean jack shit to me?"

"Because I don't want anything to happen to you."

He shrugged. "Shit, everyone's gotta go sometime. If this is my time, so be it," the man said, shifting his stance ever so slightly to take the pressure off his foot. Becca made a quick mental note.

"I'm a psychologist."

"Then you're just as fucking crazy as I am," he said.

"Listen, I work with the police, and so far you've done nothing here you can't come back from. Just put down the gun."

"You asking me to trust the five-oh? You're a real fucking riot, lady."

"Becs, your friend's name is Hopper Jenkins," she heard Christian calling out. The man flinched.

"How the fuck does he know my name?"

"I'm sure there's an officer around here who knows you and he passed that information along."

The man grunted. Christian called out to her. "Becs, why don't you ask Mr. Jenkins to put the gun down?"

"That's what we're currently discussing," Becca called out pointedly.

"Who the fuck is that guy?" Hopper said.

"He's LAPD...and my ex-husband," Becca said.

He snickered. "Maybe I should give you the gun."

Becca let out a shaky laugh. "Mr. Hopper."

"Shut up. I need a minute. It's so loud I can't think," he snapped.

Helicopters buzzed overhead, the shrieking of sirens sounding in the distance as more officers descended. Becca was sure snipers were being deployed, and it wouldn't be long before this entire area was on lockdown. All she wanted was to ask this man a few questions. Did he know Nate? Did he trust him? Why did Ash leave Freud with him? Where did she go?

Out of the corner of her eye, Becca could see Christian eyeing her. Twelve years together taught you how to communicate without saying a word, his gaze confirming what Becca was thinking. *You need to handle this.*

Self-defense wasn't something Becca ever intended to learn. Before she dated Christian, her idea of a tough workout was hot yoga. But Christian's own experiences, watching his girlfriend suffer after her assault, made him hypervigilant. "Every woman, especially one who works in law enforcement, should know how to handle herself," he always said.

The second Becca stepped inside the gym for her first Krav Maga class, she was hooked. Her entire life she'd always felt slightly out of control. In the gym, she was in charge. The rush of power she felt, taking her opponent down with one strategic, well-placed blow to the arm or a single well-aimed kick. The difference was that if a defensive move went wrong in the gym, there were no real consequences. A bruise or bump, nothing a little ice and rest couldn't fix. If it went wrong out here in the real world, it could be fatal.

Shooting a gun was also something she had never intended to do. Until she fell in love with a cop. Christian kept weapons for home protection, and that was something nonnegotiable. Becca decided that if there were going to be guns in her home, she would force herself to learn how they worked. In many ways it was a fear she had to overcome. On weekends Christian and Becca would spend hours at the gun range. She fully loved shooting, but she respected what guns could do and the power they wielded.

Becca knew that the longer she waited to make her move, the more likely it was that the police would take him out. She did a quick assessment of the risks involved in making this decision. From the whiskey on his breath and the slight tremble in his hands, she could tell he was inebriated. The limp she saw when he was running and the way he favored one leg suggested an old injury, which meant his reaction time would be slower. Becca also had the added advantage of being a woman. Most men underestimated a woman's ability to fight. She ran through her mental checklist of disarming techniques.

Redirect the line of fire.

Control the weapon.

Counterattack and disarm.

She eyed Freud. He was an unknown quantity. *Please cooperate. Please.* Becca counted to ten, then fumbled in her pocket for one of Freud's treats. She tossed one at him and he strained against the leash, startling Hopper. For a split second, his attention was diverted. Becca wasn't the threat in that moment; Freud was. Becca took this opportunity to reach out and grab Hopper's hand and the gun, pinning them in her fist to ensure the gun couldn't be fired.

Hopper's natural reaction was to pull away, which gave Becca the opportunity to step in closer, twisting the gun and his hand back in one swift motion. He let out a cry as Becca literally twisted the gun out of his hand. Once she had the gun, she took a step back, pointing it at him. "It's over, Hopper," Becca shouted. He staggered back, stunned at the sudden reversal of roles. There wasn't time for him to react. Six LAPD officers descended on him and took him down.

"Stay down. Stay down on the ground. Do not move. You are under arrest. Do you hear me? You're under arrest."

Hopper was shouting, calling Becca all kinds of names. An officer reached out and took the gun from her. Becca began to tremble uncontrollably, a surge of adrenaline flooding her body. Becca stepped back, watching as officers cuffed Hopper and hauled him to his feet.

"He needs a psychiatric evaluation," Becca said.

"No shit," one of the officers barked. "We're taking him to Hollywood Pres."

Becca blinked, her eyes suddenly blurring. She squinted, struggling to keep her focus on Hopper.

"I need to know what Ash said to you. Did she tell you where she was going?" Becca asked.

"Go fuck yourself," he spat at her.

Her eyes were burning now. "Please, I need to know where..." She stopped, a pain in her head so fierce it nearly sent her to her knees. Christian appeared by her side. "C'mon, Becs, this is ridiculous. I'm taking you home before you get yourself killed."

She shrugged free from his grasp. "I need to talk to

him. He knows Ash. He might be able to tell us where she went," Becca said. Her words slurred, her tongue becoming heavy against her mouth. The pounding in her head was growing stronger. She blinked again. In the distance, she saw her. She saw Ash.

"There she is. Ash," Becca shouted. No words came out. She could see her girl standing in the middle of the street, cars whizzing past. She would get hit if she didn't move. Becca tried to scream Ash's name to warn her. She couldn't speak. It felt as though her throat were closing up.

"Becs, what's wrong? Can you hear me?" Christian's words were muffled, as though they'd been put through a filter. "We need a medic over here," she heard him shout.

Becca fought to speak, every word a struggle. "Keep... looking... find... Ash," she gasped as Christian's face blurred, the roaring in her head growing louder and louder until, mercifully, her world went black.

ASH

The yellow taxi lurched toward Seventh Street, the sky a ghoulish shade of gray, black storm clouds looming in the distance. Horns blared, LA drivers already preparing for the impending deluge, their manic, kamikaze driving in full effect.

She'd planned to take the train, but something was going on in Hollywood and they weren't running. Ash waited for almost forty minutes and then said to hell with it. She rushed back up the stairs and flagged down a taxi. Traffic in LA was always out of control. Today it was next level. Ash wasn't sure what was going on until she heard the driver muttering about the president's visits and wasting taxpayer dollars.

Ash could hardly sit still, anxiously eyeing the meter, watching as the bill crept toward fifty bucks. She let out a sigh of relief when she spotted the bus station in the distance.

"I'll get out here," she said, knowing she could get there faster if she walked. She tossed the driver a fifty and jogged the rest of the way, reaching the entrance of the bus station, the giant blue Greyhound sign greeting her. The station was located in an industrial, run-down area of LA; there were no trees or flowers, nothing, only car repair shops, liquor stores, and abandoned buildings. Ash anxiously looked around, searching for Mo and the others, knowing they were only a few blocks from Skid Row.

The air smelled of gasoline and there was a hint of despair as she made her way toward the entrance. Ash hurried inside, searching for Nate. Her stomach churned, thinking about what might happen if he didn't show. That was silly. The minutes passed, Ash anxiously staring at the clock. The door finally opened and she saw him searching for her. He was here. They'd done it. They were so close.

"Nate!" Ash shouted. He spotted her, a smile lighting up his face. Ash raced toward him, launching herself into his arms. He squeezed her tightly.

"We made it," Nate said. Ash smiled and kissed him again.

"I'll get the tickets," Ash said, scanning the times on the board, searching for their departure time.

"Okay, we have to get a ticket for Leslie too."

"Leslie?" Ash said. "She's coming here?"

"She called and said she was afraid and didn't want to stay with Mo and the Tribe anymore. She sounded so scared. I didn't know what to do. I said she could come with us."

There were moments in Ash's life when she saw things so clearly. That day she left her mother's house, knowing if she didn't she would wind up dead; her first meeting with Nate, when she knew he would be important; her meeting with Becca at the West Hollywood police department. Those moments altered the course of her life. She saw it again now, what Nate couldn't, Leslie's parting words, "The Tribe's my family. I could never leave them," echoing in her head.

Ash grabbed Nate's hand. "We can't stay here. We have to go right now," Ash said.

"But the bus will be here soon."

"It's a trap, Nate. Mo's trap."

Nate's eyes met hers. He shook his head emphatically. "No way. Leslie wouldn't do that," he said.

She loved Nate's innate goodness but felt a surge of anger. How could he be so trusting?

"Leslie's got nowhere to go. She has no one. She told me herself she couldn't lose the Tribe."

Nate's eyes widened, his mistake registering. He didn't move, seemingly paralyzed by his mistake. Ash grabbed Nate's hand. "Let's go, Nate. Now!" she said, leading him toward the exit.

As if on cue, the doors opened and Mo and Kelsey entered, scanning the premises with laser-like focus. Ash stopped short, Nate almost bumping into her. Mo zeroed in on them, shaking her head in dismay, her eyes angry slits.

The two of them changed directions, rushing toward the back of the station. Ash spotted Vic at the back entrance.

He hadn't seen Ash and Nate yet. She didn't have to look around to know the others were here somewhere.

Nate stopped and kissed Ash again, his lips pressing hard against hers. This kiss was different. None of the hope and promise and passion of before. This was a good-bye and an apology all rolled into one.

"Run! Do it now. Don't stop running until you get somewhere safe. Call Becca. Do whatever you have to do. I'll handle Mo and the others," Nate said. He shoved her hard, and she stumbled backward. "Go! You have to go!"

Ash didn't think about anything. She just ran, sprinting toward the back of the bus station, passing the bathroom and a row of vending machines. She wondered how it was possible that no one saw her terror, how not a single person stopped to ask if she was okay. She spotted a door with a sign reading DO NOT EXIT, and she burst through it, ignoring the blaring alarms that began to sound.

Outside a steady rain was falling, Ash's tears mingling with thick, fat raindrops. She continued running, racing across the parking lot, turning onto Seventh Street, and zigzagging through a maze of streets. The rain had sent everyone scurrying inside, the streets completely deserted. Ash kept going, her sides aching. She rounded a corner and heard the sound of a coyote howling in the distance. Ash's science teacher, Mr. Neth, once said coyotes howl to let the pack know they've captured their prey. The unmistakable wail is an invitation to share the kill. Today their ritual began early, reminding Ash that as much as LA was known for its glitz and glamour, it was still an untamed wilderness.

Her legs were aching, and she was trembling violently, waging an internal war with herself. Keep going or stop and catch her breath. She told herself just a few more blocks. She rounded a corner and literally slammed into a man, the force of the impact stunning her. She blinked and saw Vic towering over her, his tattooed face twisted in a grotesque snarl, his hands balled up into fists, already spoiling for a fight. Ash spun around and saw Kelsey and Andrea moving toward her. There was nowhere left to run. In an instant, they were on her. Punching. Kicking. A full-blown assault.

"Liar."

"Bitch."

"Whore."

Ash was knocked to the ground, her face and head slamming into wet concrete. She remembered what Nate and Leslie said, how Mo decided who needed to be punished, and the Tribe followed those orders. She remembered what Nate told her and Ash realized with growing horror that this was her reckoning.

Ash thought about Eli. How she left him behind, then kept his beating a secret, allowing these people to go unpunished. Paybacks really were a bitch.

"I'm sorry," Ash said over and over again. She was sorry that she'd lied to Becca. That she hadn't told her what was happening. She was so damn sorry. There were more punches and kicks; these people, the ones she considered friends, were unleashing holy hell on her.

"Enough," Mo called out.

The attackers retreated. Ash grunted, trying to breathe, waves of pain coursing through her body, the metallic smell of blood filling her nose. She squinted, Mo's silhouette coming into focus. She was kneeling over Ash.

"You know you brought this on yourself. Got Leslie caught up in it too. You're responsible for everything that's happened. I hope you know that."

Ash's eyes welled with tears. She was so tired and scared, but she couldn't let this awful woman win. She had to fight back. She fumbled in her pocket, the cold steel of the switchblade instantly comforting. "My mom is coming for me. She won't stop until she finds me," Ash said, blood filling her mouth. Wishful thinking, but she needed to buy time.

Mo leaned in close enough so Ash could make out her twisted smile. "I look forward to meeting her," Mo said, her breath hot and stale.

This was Ash's chance. She understood it wouldn't save her, but she wanted to hurt Mo, the way Mo hurt Eli and Nate and God knows who else. She slashed at her, but Ash's grip was too weak. The knife clattered to the ground. She heard a collective gasp of outrage and, within seconds, Vic and the Tribe surrounded her. More kicks and punches. There was no mercy. None at all.

A white-hot heat radiated through Ash's body. She tried to scream. No words came out. In the distance, she heard shouting and the sound of sirens. It sounded as though the coyote's howls were growing louder. She prayed they'd find her and finish her off. Anything to escape this pain.

Ash's final thought was of Becca. She wanted more than anything to see her one last time. She wanted to tell her how much she loved their pancake brunches, and walks around the reservoir with Freud. She wanted to thank Becca for forcing her to sign up for that first photography class and for spending hundreds of dollars on equipment. She wanted to tell her how much she loved that she'd framed Ash's photos, even the terrible ones, hanging them on her bedroom walls and oversharing them on Facebook, with the world's dorkiest captions. She wanted to tell her she was sorry for being such a bitch to Christian, and for playing a part in their relationship crumbling.

If she could do it all over again, she would tell Becca how grateful she was, but it was too late now. Mo plunged the knife into her gut. The last thing she saw before the pain consumed her was Becca's face. *I love you*, she thought, her screams drowned out by the roaring rain and wind.

BECCA

C'mon, Becca, don't be an asshole. Wake up already."
Becca heard Nina's voice, felt the gentle touch of her hand.
Becca lifted her head, slowly opening her eyes. She squinted,
the glare of the fluorescent lights causing the pounding in
her head to intensify. A quick glance around the room told
her she was in the emergency room.

"Your bedside manner is shit," Becca croaked.

"And you are a total attention whore," Nina said, a smile
creeping across her face, though Becca clocked the worry.
Nina leaned down and gave Becca a hug.

"Seriously, you know you scared the hell out of all of
us," Nina said.

"I'm sorry," Becca said softly. "Any news? Did you find
Ash?" Becca asked hopefully.

Nina shook her head. "Not yet."

Disappointment flooded Becca. She sat up gingerly,
doing a quick scan of her body, searching for any potential injuries. Nothing visible. Only the pounding inside her
head, a steady drumbeat she couldn't escape.

"What happened?" Becca asked, rubbing her temples in the hope that it might ease the pressure behind her eyes.

"Do you mean before you were nearly shot and killed on live TV or after?" Nina said.

"Let's go with after," Becca replied.

"Apparently, the guy you went toe-to-toe with fancies himself an amateur chemist. Spends his free time cooking up homemade narcotics, and cuts his dope with embalming fluid. Somehow in your interactions, you must have gotten it on your skin. That's all it took. Boom. Lights out."

"And Freud? Is he okay?"

"Your mom picked him up. He's probably halfway through his second T-bone."

"My mother was here?"

"Once the doctors reassured her that your condition wasn't serious, she took Freud home. From what I hear Virginia's set up quite a command center at Casa Ortiz."

"Command center?" Becca said, feeling like she was ten steps behind and struggling to catch up.

Nina reached into her purse and handed Becca a flyer. On it was a candid photo of Ash, her smile bright and hopeful, the words "Have You Seen This Girl?" in jet-black ink. "Your mother is rallying the whole neighborhood. Got her friends and half the church canvassing the city."

Tears pricked at Becca's eyes. "My mother made this?"

"I know she's not the easiest person to deal with, but

she's trying. We're all trying to find Ash if you'd let us help," Nina said. Becca ignored the dig.

"Do you know where Christian is?" Becca asked. She owed him an apology, for not listening, for putting herself in such a reckless situation.

"I kicked his ass and told him to stay far away."

"Nina…"

"He went back out to canvass the pawnshops. I told him everything was under control here. He said he would be back later," Nina said, squeezing Becca's hand. She remembered her plea for Christian to keep looking. A surge of gratitude flooded her. He was always a man of his word. There was no reason this would be any different.

"What about Hopper?"

"You mean your new best friend? He's fine. Waiting on a psych eval. The ER is backed up so it could be quite a while before they're able to assess him."

"What do we know about him?" Becca asked.

Nina sighed. "Are you sure you don't want to rest a bit?"

Becca gave her a pointed look. Nina relented. "Fine. Name's Hopper Jenkins. Fifty-eight years old. Served in the army for eight years. Did a tour in Iraq during Desert Storm. Honorably discharged in 2004. History of drug abuse. Been in and out of rehab and jail for the last ten years."

"I need to talk to him, Nina. Find out what he knows about Ash."

Nina snorted. "After everything tonight, you're lucky you aren't in cuffs. No way in hell anyone is letting you get near that man."

"I won't give them a choice," Becca said, spotting her clothes wrapped in plastic on a nearby chair. She stood up, wobbling ever so slightly, and ripped open the bag. "I only need a few minutes. He might have crucial information," Becca said. She reached for her pants.

"Becca, stop it," Nina said, grabbing them from her.

"I can't sit here and do nothing. Not while Ash is out there. Not when I don't know if she's safe or scared or..." Becca said, trailing off. She could hear the panic in her voice, the desperation. Nina placed a calming hand on Becca's shoulder.

"You know I'm always on your side, but you're scaring me, Becca. I've seen this before. I know what happens when you lose control."

Becca snatched her clothes back from Nina and began dressing. "You swore we'd never talk about that. What happened back then is different. I'm different."

"You can pretend all you want that it was some kind of blip in your operating system. It wasn't. I was the one who found you and that empty bottle of pills. I was the one that made you vomit them up and kept watch over you. I thought you were fine, and then I see you on the goddamn news today, acting like some kind of..."

"Nut job?" Becca said.

Nina's face fell. "No. That's not what I was going to say."

"You sure about that? They say crazy runs in the family," Becca said as she slipped on her T-shirt, her face burning with shame. She used to think those feelings would fade. Two years later, it was hovering right there on the surface. When she thought about what happened, Becca could see every action and reaction, all her decisions leading to that terrible day and the bottle of pills.

It was easy to blame it all on Robbie's death. His death took everything from her, her sense of self, her understanding of how the world worked. After he died, she was forced to rebuild entirely, forced to reorient herself in the world. She threw herself into her career, then focused all her attention on being the best wife possible to Christian. She tried everything humanly possible to have a baby. When that didn't happen, she took in Ash, convinced she could outrun the bad thoughts. She did everything she could to keep it together. Then Christian moved out and a few days later, Ash was busted with a bottle of Vicodin at school and the courts sent her to a mandatory treatment center.

Becca found herself all alone. No Robbie. No Christian. No Ash. She sat in her empty home, mentally tallying all the things that had gone wrong in her life. From a therapeutic standpoint this pity party was a definite no-no. Becca wasn't thinking like a therapist. Not that day. She wasn't thinking at all. Her sadness seemed to grow with each passing second until she did something so terribly stupid, downing a bottle of Ambien. As she drifted off to sleep, she realized what she'd done. She tried to make herself vomit up the pills, but she was so tired, and that's when she called Nina. That's what mattered—that Becca asked for help. "I reached out to you. You know I didn't really want to die," Becca said.

"That's what I told myself. That's why I kept your secret. I also knew what was at stake. Your status with the department. Ash's status living with you. I didn't want to jeopardize everything you'd worked for. That was then. I'm telling you this now, if I think you're putting yourself in danger, I won't be silent again. I love you too much to do that."

Becca owed Nina so much. She understood what would have happened if the department found out. All the gossip and whispers, the sideways glances. She avoided the closed-door meetings with the administration. This job took its toll and there were some clinicians who suffered mental health breakdowns and were never allowed to come back.

"You have my word. If things get bad, I'll reach out to Dr. Atterman," she said. He was the therapist Becca saw after the "Ambien incident." She hoped this would allay Nina's fears. The last thing Becca wanted right now was to rehash the past. She had to keep focused on Ash. Becca sank back onto the gurney. "I just want Ash back, Nina," Becca said.

"I know. That doesn't mean you get to break all the rules

and put yourself in danger. You need to remember that," Nina said.

Becca offered a tight smile. "I will. I swear to you. Right now I just want to go home. Can you find the doctor? Make sure I'm cleared for discharge?" Becca said.

Nina eyed Becca warily like a scientist observing a newly discovered life-form she didn't quite trust. Becca met her gaze, steady and unyielding. After a few seconds, Nina relented.

"I'll track him down. I also promised to call your mom when you were awake," she said, giving Becca's hand a final squeeze. "I'll be back in just a few."

Becca let out a giant exhale, relieved that Nina was gone. She slowly stood, her legs wobbling slightly as she leaned against the railing of the bed, steadying herself. Becca hated lying to Nina, but she was doing what any mother would do to find her child. Becca dug through her purse and pocketed her LAPD badge. As she stepped into the hall, she saw that Hollywood Presbyterian hospital was practically bursting at the seams. Becca watched as a frantic, bloodstained surgeon wheeled a gunshot victim past her. She dodged several firefighters, heading down a hall where a young mother was shouting in Spanish that her baby was in pain. Becca was often a witness to this kind of suffering, though it never got any easier.

The smell was almost unbearable. No matter how hard the hospital was cleaned and mopped, nothing could erase the scent of death. It clung to the walls and ceilings, invaded every crevice and surface. Non–medical professionals weren't attuned to the nuances of smell. Becca's senses, on the other hand, were well honed. She often chalked it up to her earliest experiences, being exposed to death at such a young age.

She made her way down the hallway, going room to room until she spotted Hopper, all alone in a cold, sterile examination cubicle. He lay splayed out on a gurney, his hands cuffed to the bed, his eyes closed. She was about to step inside Hopper's room when a wide-eyed trainee nurse stopped her. "Excuse me, can I help you?" she asked.

Becca offered her most professional smile, knowing she must look like an absolute disaster, and hoping her confidence would distract from it. "I'm with the Department of Mental Health. I need to speak with the patient for a few minutes."

"I thought he already saw the doctor and they were processing his admission."

Becca didn't miss a beat. "It's a secondary screening."

The nurse shrugged and waved Becca in. "Fine by me. Not sure how much you'll get out of him. The drugs have probably kicked in already."

Becca forced a smile, her heart sinking. She understood that it was standard protocol to sedate Hopper if he was agitated or combative. The drugs would significantly diminish Hopper's ability to talk and even focus. That didn't mean she was going to walk away without trying. She just needed to keep her expectations low. Becca entered the room, knocking gently on the door.

"Hopper," she said softly. The man's eyes popped open.

"What the fuck do you want?" he mumbled. The Haldol numbed him, made him looser, though there was a bit of fight left in him.

"Hopper, I need to find Ash. If you have any idea where she's gone?"

He blinked again, shifting in bed, straining against the cuffs. "Girl's probably long gone. Said she was catching a bus. Leaving this godforsaken city."

"Taking a bus? Did she say to where?"

He shook his head, his wild gray mane trembling in response. "Ain't said, and I didn't ask."

"She asked you to take the dog. Did she say why?" Becca asked.

Hopper didn't respond, his eyes wandering around the room aimlessly as if he were struggling to focus. Becca gently shook him. "Mr. Jenkins, why did Ash leave my dog with you?"

"I told that girl she was crazy. Ain't no reason to be hanging out on the streets. Especially with that group of hoodlums. I tried to warn her. Told her to stay away from them. Stay the fuck away. She wouldn't listen."

Becca didn't understand. "What group of hoodlums? What are you talking about?"

"She was too smitten to see those people are fucking crazy," Hopper said.

"Nate? Is this one of the hoodlums? Is this who you're talking about?" Becca asked, fumbling in her bag for her phone. She pulled up the photo and showed it to him. Hopper blinked and then nodded, waving the phone away.

"That's him. That's him. I told that girl he was bad news, but he ain't the one you need to watch out for. That tattooed freak was dangerous. But it was the old broad I kept clear of. She's the devil. Sure as I sit here that woman is as evil as they come. I told your girl to watch out for her and the entire Tribe. They're bad fucking news."

"The Tribe? Who is the Tribe?"

"No one's paying attention to what happens out there. No one gives a shit. All I know is if your girl crossed them, it's all over for her."

Becca tried to tell herself Hopper was just a rambling, sick old man, but what if he wasn't? "Do you know where these people are? Where I can find them? Please, Hopper."

"I ain't no snitch. I start running my mouth, and they'll come for me," he said. He turned his head, the bravado fading. Now he seemed tired, a man who had run out of fight.

"Hopper, please...tell me what you know." She reached out to shake him.

"Becca, what the hell are you doing?" Nina's sharp-edged voice startled Becca. She grimaced as she swung around to find Nina, her mouth open wide, her nostrils flaring, her irritation bubbling over.

"Have you lost your goddamn mind? You can't be in here."

She took Becca by the elbow and led her out into the hall, away from Hopper. Becca tried to explain. "Nina, he said Ash was hanging with dangerous people."

"He's medicated up the wazoo. He could have said Ash was the long-lost daughter of Elvis Presley or that she'd been abducted by aliens. I swear, Becca, did you not hear a damn word I said earlier?" Nina practically shouted, a passing orderly eyeing her with concern. She stopped herself. "I'm not here to scold you. Christian's waiting. He needs to talk to you."

Nina's voice was sharp and shrill, her tone leaving no room for argument. Becca darted another glance at Hopper and followed Nina back to the exam room where Christian was waiting.

"Any news on Ash? Or from the pawnshop?"

"He confirmed that he saw Ash earlier today. She sold him a few pieces, your wedding ring and some turquoise jewelry." Becca wasn't going to get emotional over this news.

"What else, Chris? Nina said you needed to speak with me."

He nodded. "I got a call from a friend... a homicide detective in Venice."

She studied Christian, the rote way he spoke to her, the kind yet slightly vacant expression. Becca called it his LAPD pose, honed from years of delivering terrible news to family members.

"They found a body near the pier," he said.

A body. They found a body. The roaring in Becca's head returned. Christian continued. "It's too soon to get an ID and it's . . . it could be difficult because the girl suffered serious injuries to her face and neck, but she's a brunette and the size and weight are a match."

Becca couldn't quite process what Christian was saying. "A match? A match for what?"

"Becca, we're not sure . . ." Nina's voice wavered, but she continued. "You need to prepare yourself for the possibility that this girl . . . that this might be Ash."

BECCA

Images surged forward, flickering through Becca's brain like a kind of twisted horror movie: the baby girl she miscarried at twenty-two weeks, her heart and lungs too small and misshapen to sustain her; the other two babies she lost, nothing more than cells and molecules, all her hopes and dreams disappearing into nothingness with the flush of a toilet. She survived all of that. She made it through. Those losses, as painful as they were, led her to Ash, this vibrant, headstrong, stubborn young woman. There was no way she was dead. No way. It simply wasn't possible.

"We don't know it's her," Becca said, jerking free from Nina's grasp. She needed to compose herself. They would expect her to fall apart. She couldn't let that happen.

Christian and Nina exchanged concerned expressions. She glared back at them. "Don't act like I'm not standing right here! You said you're not sure. Did you get an official ID? Fingerprints? Anything that confirmed it might be her?" Becca asked.

"No, Becs. I got the call that they'd found the body and I came straight here," Christian said.

She nodded. She wasn't going to wait around for answers. "I want to see her. If it's Ash, I'll know," Becca said.

Christian shook his head. "They're processing the scene. I can call and find out where they're taking the body...where they're taking her. Or they can send us a photo to ID," he said delicately.

That was the last thing Becca wanted. If Ash was dead, she needed to face it head-on.

"I'm not going to stand here and argue about this. I'm going, even if I have to go by myself," Becca said, knowing that she sounded slightly irrational. She fumbled in her purse for her phone to call a car, ignoring their pitying looks.

"Becca, I'm telling you now this is a mistake. If this is Ash, that's not how you want to remember her."

A wave of exhaustion gripped Becca, her body still suffering from the aftereffects of the drug. She shook free from it, refusing to give them an excuse to stop her. "I have to know. You understand that, don't you, Nina? If it were one of the twins? If it were Trevor or Ava?"

Becca hadn't mentioned Nina's children before. She wanted Nina to think about it, really consider what Becca was going through. Nina took this in, understanding that if the roles were reversed, she would want answers. "I picked up a shift tonight. Give me a few minutes to see if someone can cover it and I'll drive you," she said.

"I need to go now," Becca insisted, already thinking that she'd call an Uber. Whatever it took, she needed answers.

"I'll take her," Christian said.

Ordinarily, Becca would have been annoyed, the two of them talking like she wasn't even there. Those disagreements seemed pointless now. Becca hugged Nina. "I'll be okay," she said, wanting to believe that.

"I know you will," Nina said. "Call me, okay? No matter what time. No matter what...what happens." Becca pulled away, hating the tears that were staining Nina's cheeks. Eight years riding side by side, witnessing the worst humanity could inflict on one another, eight years celebrating Thanksgiving and New Years and birthdays together, and this was the first time she'd ever seen her partner cry. This was bad, Becca thought. This was really bad. For a second, she wanted nothing more than to crawl back under the covers. She could stay here in this hospital, go back to bed and pretend this wasn't happening.

"You ready?" Christian asked gently. There was no hiding from the truth. If this was Ash, Becca would find out sooner or later. She had to see this through. She steeled herself.

"Let's go," Becca said. She didn't look back at Nina, afraid she might lose her nerve.

Ten minutes later, they were speeding down the 101 when Becca's phone buzzed. *Your Mama's got your room ready and Freud is waiting for you. We're here whenever you need us. Stay strong, mija. We're praying for you and our girl.*

Becca bit back her tears. No doubt Nina had phoned her parents the second Becca left the hospital. That's what she loved about her friend—she could always count on Nina to handle things.

Christian cleared his throat. "Becs, there's something else I have to tell you," he began.

She glanced over at him. "Is it going to make any of this easier?" she asked.

"No. But it's something you should know…"

"If it's not urgent, can it wait? I'm barely hanging on as it is and my head is pounding. I just need…I need quiet right now."

Christian didn't hesitate. "Not talking it is," he said. This time Becca took his hand. She needed this now, the familiarity of his touch. The déjà vu was overpowering, the sense of total loss engulfing her. Sometimes, Becca couldn't believe Christian wasn't part of her life anymore. For so long he was her everything. Even now, some mornings she woke up and reached for him. She was a kid when they met, barely twenty-one. She'd been so pissed the night he pulled her over. Becca had spent hours cramming for finals, and she was heading home from the library in the early morning hours when she saw police lights in her rear-view mirror. Exhausted, she couldn't help herself, unleashing her frustration on the baby-faced policeman.

"What the hell is wrong? I wasn't speeding. I didn't change lanes or do anything illegal. I'm just going home."

Becca's hostility didn't faze him. "You have a flat tire. I didn't want you getting on the freeway."

"Am I getting a ticket?" Becca asked.

"No. I thought you might need assistance."

"I know how to change a tire," Becca said.

From the time she was old enough to understand simple instructions, her father insisted she learn life skills. "You cannot rely on a man. You have to make your own way in the world." Because of Rafi, Becca was capable of doing most basic automotive repairs and light plumbing.

"I have a spare in the trunk. Is it okay if I get out of the car?" Becca said.

"Of course," he'd said, stepping aside while she opened the door and climbed out. Christian stood there, watching as she grabbed the jack from her trunk and lifted the car to the appropriate height.

"It's late, and there have been several assaults in this neighborhood. Mind if my partner and I stick around while you change it?"

"Whatever. That's fine," Becca said, expertly removing the damaged tire and replacing the spare. Christian tried to make chitchat, but Becca wasn't interested. Her brother's illness and the aftermath of his breakdown gave Becca a perspective on law enforcement that wasn't exactly positive. The police treated her family like they were criminals, like they'd done something wrong. Once the tire was changed, Becca thanked him, gave a half-hearted wave, and drove away. She didn't think twice about the incident, focusing on her upcoming final exams.

A month later, Becca graduated from USC with honors. After a family dinner, her roommates dragged her out to the Short Stop to celebrate. The strange black box dive bar in Echo Park used to be a cop hangout, but by then it was just another brick-and-wood bar college students and neighborhood locals flocked to. That night Becca decided to let loose. She wanted to slip off the burden of responsibility. For the first time in her life there were no deadlines looming over her. Nothing until she started grad school in the fall. The freedom was simultaneously exhilarating and disconcerting.

At some point in the evening, she saw a familiar face drinking at the bar. She recognized him instantly. He was a few years older than Becca, maybe twenty-five, tan, with jet-black hair, and the kind of build that suggested long hours spent in the gym. He had an innate confidence, one of those guys who coasted by on good looks, the type of man who'd embraced his privilege at every turn. She imagined the badge only made things easier. He caught her staring and smiled, raising his shot glass in a mock toast.

Becca smiled back and jostled through the crowd until she was by his side. He grinned down at her. "I'd offer to buy you a drink, but a single independent woman like yourself, you'd probably be opposed," Christian said. She smiled even bigger, remembering what an asshole she had been to him that night.

"Actually, I'm a broke college student so I'll have a vodka

soda," she told him. He'd bought her a drink and two more after that.

She couldn't remember much of what they talked about, the evening taking on a glowing sheen; she'd been unable to take her eyes off him. Becca hadn't experienced that kind of instant attraction before. She hadn't even dated that much. Her life was consumed with school and looking after her parents and trying to survive losing Robbie. That night was the first time in years she'd managed to forget about all of it. She spent the entire evening flirting, deciding after two drinks that she was going home with him. She went to the bathroom with her roommates, who were shocked when she told them. "Since when are you into civil servants?" they teased.

She laughed it off. This was a one-night thing. A fun story to tell about how she celebrated her college graduation. She went back to Christian's bachelor pad, a sparsely furnished apartment in Koreatown. It was only supposed to be a one-night thing. Somehow though, Becca found herself drawn to him. It wasn't just the physical attraction. He was the most interesting person she'd ever met. It seemed as if he'd read every book, and he seemed to know as much about psychology as she did, something she found moderately annoying. He also appeared truly interested in her, asking so many questions that Becca couldn't help but laugh. "I think you missed your calling. You should be a therapist."

She remembered how he leaned in and kissed her that

first night. "I like your stories," he'd said. It wasn't just some line he fed her. Christian was innately curious. He wanted to hear about Becca's classwork, her family, her dreams for the future. She'd been so isolated and alone, never letting anyone get close. She sensed Christian was someone who wouldn't judge her. After three dates, she told him about Robbie. She wanted him to understand what her brother meant to her, the void he'd left in her life, the guilt she felt over not being able to save him. He understood that feeling of helplessness that gripped you when someone you loved was hurt. Originally from San Diego, Christian went to UCLA on a soccer scholarship. His junior year in college, his girlfriend Annie was assaulted on her way home from working a late shift at a Brentwood bar. The police never caught the guy, and after a few months she ended the relationship and moved back home to Michigan. Christian saw how the officers treated her, their harsh and dismissive questions, the lack of compassion they displayed. His guilt and helplessness fueled his desire to join the LAPD. He vowed that he would do better. Violence had touched both of their lives, and they grew even closer. A bond formed, and after a while, Becca believed that Christian would always be a part of her life.

She was still holding his hand, relieved that he was here and at the same time wishing she was alone. She was used to that, used to doing these things herself. Surviving by herself. Becca gently withdrew from his grasp, leaning her head against the window, the glass cold against her cheek. Somehow, in spite of all the thoughts swirling around in her head, Becca drifted off. The next thing she knew, Christian was gently shaking her awake.

"We're here," he said. She jolted up. They'd arrived in Venice Beach, the entire area lit up by the flashing red and blue lights of half a dozen squad cars. Floodlights illuminated the crime scene in the distance. A nearby ambulance sat parked alongside the coroner's van. The parking lot was cordoned off with police tape, and lookie-loos and reporters huddled together, separated from the scene by two officers and a barricade.

Christian and Becca's silent pact continued. He led her across the parking lot toward the beach, an innocuous stretch of Venice, away from the bustle of the boardwalk, set apart from the bars and the overpriced memorabilia shops, their gates pulled down for the night. In a few hours, shop owners would raise the barriers to welcome a steady stream of tourists. Nobody would ever know that a few short feet away a life had been extinguished.

Looming in the distance was a gray concrete structure, the public bathrooms, where officers and crime scene personnel had gathered. How terrible to die in this place, she thought, your life snuffed out, your body discarded like garbage. They approached the barricade, too far away to make out the body. Becca stood waiting, scanning the area.

"All this fuss and for what?" Becca heard one of the cops

grumble. She glanced over and saw a beefy patrolman. In another life, he could've been a Gap model. Who knows, she thought, he might even be one, moonlighting until he got his big break. "A hundred bucks says this chick was just some dumb runaway who got careless, pissed off some john..."

"Just some dumb runaway?" Becca asked angrily, pushing her way to the front of the barricade.

The officer looked flustered, puffing out his chest out to overcompensate. "Ma'am, this area is restricted."

"You don't know anything thing about her. Who she is. Where she's from. How she ended up here. Do you?"

"Becs," Christian said softly, placing his arm on her to calm her. She shook it free. All she could focus on was this officer, this stupid, callous man.

"What the hell is wrong with you? She's someone's kid. She was a person, and now she's gone." Becca's voice was rising.

Christian held out his badge. "We're here to see Detective Wishard. Want to make that happen?"

"Yeah. Sure thing," the officer said. As he moved away, Becca broke through the barricade and raced across the sand, ignoring Christian's and the officer's shouts for her to stop. The crowd of people gathered around the body seemed to sense something was unfolding, and they parted to let her through.

Becca could hear the waves of the ocean roaring in the

distance; she could make out the glittering lights of the pier. Her chest tightened as she looked down at the girl's body, half on the sand, half on the concrete. The first thing Becca saw was the girl's wrist and the tattoo.

She bit back a sob, scanning the young woman's battered body and up to her face, her brown hair splayed out, her mouth opened in a tortured cry. Becca crouched down, spotting a large widow's peak; the girl's complexion was slightly more porcelain than ivory. She looked down again, searching for the ladybug tattoo on Ash's ankle. It wasn't there. It wasn't . . .

She could feel bile rising in her throat. "It's not her," Becca whispered, the words taking on a strangled quality. "It's not Ash."

Relief flooded her, then a rush of guilt. It wouldn't be long before this nameless girl was carted away, her body tossed in a cold freezer, another lost and anonymous soul in the City of Angels. Becca clamored to her feet. She couldn't look at this broken girl anymore.

"Dr. Ortiz?" Becca saw Detective Joanne Wishard heading her way. Half-Japanese, half-Caucasian, Joanne was five feet tall and dressed in slacks and a button-down blouse, her polished demeanor a stark contrast to the rumpled detectives Becca usually encountered. Wishard wore a pleasant expression, something she used to her advantage, counting on the fact that most people, including the men in the department, would underestimate her.

Becca wasn't a fan, remembering their one and only encounter several years ago when she was called to the scene of a home invasion gone very wrong. The entire family was gunned down except for the youngest member, a five-year-old girl, who locked herself in a closet. Becca was called in to soothe the child and remove her from the home without subjecting her to any additional trauma. At the station, Becca and Wishard disagreed about protocol, the officer pushing the young girl to make a statement despite Becca's insistence that she wasn't ready. Things got heated when Wishard accused Becca of interfering with the investigation and asked her to leave. If Wishard remembered this tense encounter, she didn't show it.

"Dr. Ortiz, I'm so sorry we have to meet under these circumstances. We're doing everything we can to track down your foster daughter. I'm hoping we can talk about Ashley so I can get a little clarity."

Becca stiffened. God, she hated the qualifier. "Foster" daughter, as if Becca didn't really count as Ash's mother. Becca told herself that in a few short weeks, none of that would matter. She would bring Ash home and make things official.

"She goes by Ash," Becca said sharply. The least this woman could do was get Ash's name right.

"Of course. I want to assure you we're doing everything in our power to locate Ash and get her home safely."

Becca had heard cops say versions of this before. In fact,

she spoke platitudes like these as well to hundreds of clients. They were just words. Becca wanted action. She motioned to the victim's forearm, the medical examiner snapping photos.

"Ash had the same tattoo. So did this boy. I'm pretty sure that's her boyfriend," Becca said while pulling up the photo on her phone.

"Mind if I…?" Wishard asked. Becca shrugged, watching as Wishard took the phone, typed in her number, and texted Nate's picture to herself in less than thirty seconds. "Christian briefed me on your findings, Dr. Ortiz, but I'd love to hear more from you. It's going to take my guys some time to process the scene. Why don't the three of us head over to the IHOP? Talk over some coffee?" Wishard said.

"Fantastic. A crappy cup of diner coffee will make everything better," Becca said, the words out of her mouth before she could stop them. Wishard smiled and placed a reassuring hand on Becca's arm.

"It's actually the best coffee in town. Listen, I know this is difficult, but as Ash's mother, you may know more than you even realize."

Now she was buttering Becca up, making her feel comforted and supported. Becca recognized that trick as well, but Wishard didn't wait for Becca to answer, turning her attention to Christian. "I need a few more minutes here. I'll meet you both there in ten," she said.

Becca numbly followed Christian back across the sand

toward the parking lot. "Joanne's good police, Becs. You want her on this case," Christian said reassuringly. She didn't answer, already dreading all the questions about Ash, second-guessing every decision she made, wondering what she could have done differently.

They arrived at the IHOP ten minutes later. The place was bustling, the bar crowd filling their bellies with grease and coffee before sleeping off their hangovers.

"I'll be right back," Becca said, hurrying toward the bathroom. She leaned against the porcelain sink and closed her eyes, trying to erase the image of the young girl from her memory. She was so relieved that it wasn't Ash on the beach. And yet she couldn't stop thinking about the girl's mother out there somewhere, waiting for a phone call, praying one day her daughter would walk through the door. Becca sighed and splashed cold water on her face, knowing she couldn't hide in here forever.

She headed back toward the dining area, scanning the tables for Wishard and Christian. She rounded the corner and stopped short. Tucked into a corner booth, she saw Wishard leaning across the table. Wishard's ordinarily stern demeanor was transformed by the warm smile on her face. They weren't touching. To an outsider, it wouldn't even register, but Becca understood body language. She thought about the conversation in the car. "There's something you should know."

This was the woman Christian was going to marry. The fiancée.

It all seemed real now. He had truly moved on. She stood there, swallowing, trying to manage the rush of sorrow that overwhelmed her.

As if she sensed she was being watched, Wishard looked up and locked eyes with Becca. If she saw the stunned expression on Becca's face, she didn't show it. Christian, on the other hand, looked stricken. Becca steeled herself, hurrying across the restaurant to join them at the table. She slipped into the booth next to Christian. Wishard sat directly across from Becca.

"Dr. Ortiz, I don't know if you heard about my relationship with Christian...I want to assure you—"

"I'm here to talk about Ash. That's all," Becca said, cutting Wishard off.

Christian cleared this throat, a nervous tic that used to drive her crazy. It was important to remember those things, she thought. The annoying ones. "We just want you to know—"

"I told you I don't care. What you do in your personal life is none of my business. I'm here because you said it's important. Because I'll do anything to help you locate Ash. Anything else is wasting my time," Becca said.

Beside her Christian tensed, then nodded at Wishard to continue. She opened her notebook, visibly relieved that the personal discussion was over. She gestured for the waiter in that take-charge manner detectives always possessed, as if the entire world were at their beck and call.

"Three coffees with milk," Wishard said. "Anyone else hungry?"

Christian mumbled no. Becca shook her head. She could still see that poor girl's face lying on the ground. She wasn't sure she would ever be hungry.

"Hope it's okay if I eat." She didn't wait for them to answer. "I'll have an egg white omelet, whole wheat toast, and a side of fruit."

She shot Becca a wry smile. "Low blood sugar. I have to eat every few hours, or it's not pretty," she said. This always amazed Becca, the detachment of detectives, how they could compartmentalize. A necessary function of the job, she'd learned. Those officers who couldn't do that didn't last. "Now, Dr. Ortiz, can you tell me the last time you saw your foster daughter?" Wishard asked, her pen poised and at the ready.

There it was again. *Foster daughter.* "I saw Ash yesterday evening. We watched TV after dinner and she went up to bed around midnight. I don't know what time she left. I woke up around seven thirty, and she was gone."

"Was there anything bothering her? Any problems you two were having?" Wishard asked.

Becca hesitated. "Dr. Ortiz, I've read Ash's file, so I already know about her history of drug abuse. Anything else you can tell me that might help us fill in the pieces?"

Ash's file. Becca read it too. Her file said nothing about who Ash was, only the laws she broke. Shoplifting. Theft.

Excessive drug use. They talked about the abuse she'd endured, the reports sent from Georgia from social workers who came to visit and did nothing to help this child. A file that told you nothing about how sweet and resilient Ash really was. Wishard didn't want that. She wanted things related to the investigation. "Ash got picked up yesterday by an undercover for trying to score at the reservoir."

"Were charges filed?"

Becca looked down at her hands, knowing how bad this sounded. "My partner, Officer Stanton, spoke with the officer. It was just a few pills. He agreed to drop the charges if we sought counseling. Which I planned to do," Becca said defensively.

"So just to be clear you asked the officer to bury the arrest?" Wishard asked.

Was that judgmental tone real or imagined? She eyed Christian. He didn't seem to notice. "I thought I could fix things with Ash. We were doing so well. Or at least that's how it seemed. We'd just gotten word that we could proceed with Ash's adoption. It meant so much to the both of us. I didn't want to do anything to jeopardize it."

"So you put the adoption above everything, including Ashley's safety and mental health?"

Becca flinched. Now she knew she wasn't imagining this woman's disdain. Even Christian seemed surprised. "Come on, Joanne, that's not necessary," Christian said.

"I screwed up. I should have allowed the officer to

process Ash's arrest and then called her social worker. I know that now," Becca said.

Wishard nodded dismissively. "Let's talk about Ash's boyfriend, Nate Sutton. Christian said you know him." This was sounding more and more like an interrogation.

"I met him a few years ago. I didn't know that he was back in Ash's life," Becca said, her frustration bubbling over. Why was she sitting here grilling Becca when she should be out there hunting for Ash? She fought the urge to lash out. She needed this woman on her side.

"What about the tattoo? Ash and Nate both have one. So does the victim. There's a connection there. There has to be."

Wishard's face revealed nothing. Becca continued. "I also spoke to a man who knows Ash. His name is Hopper Jenkins."

"Ah, yes, the man from your show on Hollywood Boulevard," Wishard said dismissively. Becca forced herself to ignore what seemed liked pointed attacks.

"Hopper said Ash might be caught up with some bad people. He called them the Tribe."

Becca clocked the flicker of recognition on Wishard's face at the mention of the Tribe. "You know something about them, don't you?"

"I'm afraid I can't discuss case specifics," Wishard said regretfully.

"I'm part of this department. I've dedicated the last eight

years of my life to the LAPD. Aren't I owed a little professional courtesy?" Becca demanded.

Christian gave Wishard a pointed look. "Joanne, it's going to come out sooner or later. Becca deserves to know."

Joanne shot Christian an annoyed look. She sighed and closed her notebook, her words careful and measured. "What I'm about to tell you is confidential."

What did this woman think Becca was going to do? Instagram their convo? Snapchat it out to her followers? She bit back her sarcastic response. "I understand. I won't say a word."

Wishard leaned in closer, lowering her voice. "A few days ago homicide caught a case. They'd found the badly beaten and dismembered body of a teenage boy in an abandoned alley about a mile from Skid Row. A runaway named Eli Naylor. Eighteen months before, another body, this time of a young girl, Rachel Whiteman, only sixteen, was discovered, beaten and stabbed to death in a warehouse down there. Both victims had this same tattoo. All three were runaways. Which means..." Wishard hesitated.

Becca didn't need her to finish. She'd already put the pieces together. "These are serial killings," Becca whispered.

"That's the working theory," Wishard said.

Becca sat back in her seat. It seemed impossible that out of four million people in Los Angeles, Ash could wind up in the same orbit as a goddamn serial killer. It was truly unfair, but luck had never been on Ash's side.

"I understand how difficult this is . . . ," Wishard began.

Now she was going to play the sympathy card. Becca wasn't having it. She wanted action, not empty words.

"What's being done now? What are you doing to ensure that whoever is doing this, whoever this Tribe is, doesn't hurt anyone else?"

"There's an investigation underway."

"What does that even mean? Whoever is doing this appears to be targeting homeless runaways. You have the tattoo and a name. Why not go public with this information? This should be all over the news, all over the Internet. You should be notifying the shelters and social services agencies, getting the word out."

"Oh, I'm sorry. I didn't realize you were a police officer now."

"Joanne, please, Becca's concerned . . ."

"I don't need you to speak for me, Chris," Becca snapped.

"The last thing we want to do is create widespread panic. You really want people in this city to have more of a reason to go after the homeless? Because that will only make them more vulnerable. We have neighborhoods across the city in crisis because they can't move the tent cities out. Is that what you want?" Wishard demanded.

Becca shook her head.

"Joanne, ease up."

"I'm not going to ease up. Becca wants to sit here and act like she knows how to do our jobs better than we do. We

don't have any solid evidence or witnesses or anything link-
ing these crimes to anyone. The Bloods and Crips are now
hiding out in Skid Row, robbing, committing rapes and
assaults and God knows what else. Whoever these people
are, they're smart, they've stayed under our radar, the gang
units haven't heard of them. We're forming a task force to
deal with these crimes, uniforms are canvassing the streets,
searching for suspects. You know those people don't trust us."

Becca sat back in her seat. *Those people.* "That's what this
is really about, isn't it? *Those people* like Ash and Nate. I
mean, if a bunch of Malibu kids wound up murdered, this
story would be front-page news. What does it matter if
they're just a bunch of homeless runaways?" Becca said.

Wishard's eyes flashed with anger. "Dr. Ortiz, I'll remind
you again the information I provided was confidential, so
lower your voice. I know you're upset. You may not think
I understand, but I do. But I'm only going to say this once.
Please do not interfere in this investigation. What I suggest
that you do now is go home. Be with your family."

All the noise in the diner, the clanging forks, the endless
drone of the conversation, faded, Becca's anger building.
"Ash is my family. I thought you were serious about wanting to find her."

"Becs, Joanne's trying…"

"No, Joanne is sitting there judging me, doing her best
to make me feel small and worthless. I don't know if it's
because you think I give a shit that you're marrying my

211

ex-husband or if it's because you're the same coldhearted bitch who intimidated a terrified five-year-old so you could make an arrest. I don't know, and I don't care." She stood up quickly. Her vision blurred and she grabbed onto the table to steady herself, willing the dizziness to pass.

"Becs," Christian said in warning.

She ignored him, shooting daggers at Wishard. "All that matters is Ash. Not Ashley. Not my *foster daughter*. My daughter. And if you think I'm going to stop looking for her or trying to find who did this to her, you are the crazy one."

Becca turned and rushed out of the diner, refusing to give Wishard the satisfaction of seeing her fall apart. As long as Ash was still out there, Becca was going to do everything she could to bring her girl home.

MO

People rarely surprised Mo. They were actually quite predictable. Take Ash. From the beginning, Mo believed that she was a selfish little bitch. Everything Ash did supported Mo's hypothesis. Even in the end, that girl refused to acknowledge that it was her own actions that forced Mo's hand. Perhaps if Ash had been able to step outside of herself, perhaps if she had offered up an apology for sowing discord or tried to make amends, things could have been different. She tried to steal Nate from them, and almost ruined everything.

Mo took a deep drag of her cigarette. Normally she wasn't a smoker. These past few days had tested her. She winced ever so slightly, her arm tender from where the knife had pierced her skin. "You sure you're okay?" Vic asked.

"I told you I'm fine," Mo said. Now that Ash had been taken care of, Mo promised herself she wouldn't expend any more energy thinking about her. They'd done what they needed to do. She needed to focus all her attention on Nate's rehabilitation. "How's Nate doing?" she asked Vic.

"Same. Sitting there, staring into space like a zombie,"

Vic said gruffly. He was still holding a grudge, still pissed that Nate planned to leave. It would take time to heal these wounds, but Mo had faith it would happen.

She understood that it wasn't a done deal. This would be her most significant test yet—determining if Nate could be trusted again or...she hated thinking about the alternative. She didn't want to lose Nate, but if he wasn't willing to accept the Tribe's rules now that Ash was gone, they would have to reassess his place in this family. She stubbed out her cigarette and headed toward Nate's tent. Vic stood guard outside.

"I think I'll have a chat with Nate," Mo said.

Vic blocked her path. "I'm not sure that's a good idea," Vic said.

"Don't be silly. Nate and I are overdue for a little heart-to-heart," she said. "Go ahead and gather the others."

Vic opened the flap of the tent and obediently stepped aside. Mo slipped into the tent. Nate sat hunched in the corner, his face puffy and bloodstained. A strange sense of déjà vu came over her. She told herself that was silly. Nate wasn't Leslie. He was special. Worthy of her mercy. She handed him a bottle of water and a towel.

"For you. To clean up," she said. Nate ignored her kind gesture, refusing to take the items. "Nathaniel, don't be petulant."

"Is she dead?" he asked numbly, resisting the peace offering she brought. "Is Ash dead?"

Mo sighed and set the water and cloth down beside him. "I don't know, and I don't care. Neither should you."

Nate didn't respond, gazing vacantly into the distance.

"Ash was a liability. Leslie and Eli too. We're stronger without them. I need you to see that."

He gazed off into the distance. "I care about you, Nathaniel, and don't want to lose you. The thing is I'm facing a lot of opposition from the others. They aren't happy you brought Ash here. Or that you were going to leave us without a second thought. They aren't happy that I want you to have a second chance."

"Ash is good...and smart...and she loves me."

"If she loved you, she never would have tried to steal you away. Or threatened to tell the cops. That's not love, Nathaniel. That's not what you do to your family."

Mo's voice was sharp, her anger bubbling up. "I'm giving you a lifeline, Nate. A lifeline I've never offered to anyone. The second I saw you that day, playing your guitar, I knew there was something special about you."

Tears began to fall down her cheeks. Mo rarely cried, but she found it useful in convincing others that she was sincere. "You're a good boy. I've known that from the start. I love you. More than I've ever loved anyone, Nate. The others are angry, but they love you too. I want to show them what I see inside your heart. That's why I'm fighting for you. What happens next is your decision," Mo said.

She pulled out the blade from her pocket. It was Ash's

blade. She saw Nate eyeing it with concern. "So what's it going to be? You must prove to the Tribe that you're still one of us," Mo said.

She prided herself on knowing exactly what her kids were thinking. Not this time. Nate's blank expression was impossible to read. There was a chance that she'd misjudged him. God, she hoped she hadn't misjudged him. She sat in silence, wanting to give Nate the time he needed to make this important decision. She could see the wheels turning as he considered his choices. Life and the Tribe or his own reckoning. The minutes and seconds passed by, agonizingly slow.

"I choose the Tribe," Nate whispered.

It wasn't as enthusiastic as Mo would have liked, but it was a start. There would be more than enough time to rebuild their trust. First things first. Mo gestured to the knife. "Now we have to convince the others of your commitment. Are you ready?"

The Tribe tattoo signified loyalty. This was Nate's chance to convince everyone he was back and committed to the group. Mo took the knife and purposefully dug it into his flesh, piercing the skin in the center of the eye of his tattoo. Blood pooled, Nate's face a stoic mask in spite of the obvious pain she was causing.

"Good. Very good," she said. "Vic, we're ready," Mo called out.

The tent flap opened and Kelsey entered. She looked at

Mo with watchful eyes. Mo held out the knife. Kneeling down, she took it and dug it into the tattoo. "The Tribe endures," she said.

Then one by one the others filed in, taking their turn. This was Nate's opportunity for redemption, and everyone seemed on board. Mo leaned back, a shiver of pleasure flooding her body as she looked on. She couldn't have asked for a better end to the day. Ash and Leslie were gone, and Nate was back where he belonged. She hoped that he would prove his worth, but only time would tell.

BECCA

Becca had to stay focused. She hurried down Lincoln Boulevard, hoping to put some space between her and Wishard and Christian, her head pounding. She couldn't remember the last time she'd eaten, and the coffee had turned her stomach. She told herself not to worry about them. What mattered was the news she'd discovered, the news that serial murders were happening and Ash might be in the crosshairs. Becca needed to think. She remembered meeting a doctor from UC Irvine at a conference a few years back. He specialized in tracking serial killers. She would call him first thing in the morning and have a sit-down with him. Perhaps he could help Becca build a profile. There was also a reporter she knew from the *LA Times*, who would jump at an exclusive, the chance to expose an LAPD cover-up. If the department wasn't going to let the public know, Becca would have to.

"Get in the car, Becs," Christian barked. She turned to see him leaning out the window of his black SUV.

"I'm calling an Uber. Go home with Joanne," she said. She sounded like such a brat, but she couldn't help herself.

Christian gritted his teeth, climbing out of the car and storming over to Becca. "Cancel the Uber and get in the goddamn car. Or I swear to God, I will pick you up and put you in it myself," he said. She crossed her arms. She wasn't going to let him bully her. "I'm not your problem anymore, Christian. And neither is Ash."

He exhaled. "Jesus, don't you see that I'm worried? You might have been able to shut me out of your life, but I never stopped caring about you and Ash. Not to mention you just went through a major physical trauma. I know you better than anyone, and I can tell you're on the verge of collapsing. I just want to get you home. Make sure you're safe. Please, Becs," he said.

She wanted to argue, but Becca was exhausted and coming apart at the seams. The idea of a chatty Uber driver was too much to bear. As much as Becca didn't want to admit it, she needed a few hours of rest.

"Fine. But no lectures, Christian. I can't handle one of your lectures," she said. He nodded and moved over to the passenger-side door, opening it for her. She climbed in and leaned against the seat, her body aching. She waited for Christian to start driving. He sat motionless, tapping his hands against the steering wheel.

"You have to admit you acted like a total asshole," Christian said. "Joanne wasn't any better."

"I'm sorry. Was I unclear about not being in the mood for a lecture?" Becca said.

Christian raised his hands in surrender, and their no-talking policy was reinstated. His anger simmered just below the surface, his hands gripping the steering wheel, his jaw clenched tightly. Every so often, he'd let out a frustrated sigh. That sigh used to drive her crazy. She wasn't going to let it get to her tonight. Becca leaned her head against the window, the city flashing by in a blur.

Twenty-five minutes later, Christian pulled into the driveway. Becca had never been so relieved to be home. "Thank you for the ride," she said, wanting more than anything to not be in this car with him. He reached out to stop her.

"I know how hard all of this is on you. I really do. But lashing out at Joanne won't bring Ash home any sooner," he said.

So they were really going to do this. "Oh, I'm sorry. Did I hurt your girlfriend's feelings? Excuse me, I mean your fiancée?" Becca snapped, continuing her petty streak. Christian sighed.

"I tried to tell you earlier, and you said if it wasn't about Ash, you didn't want to discuss it. It wasn't like I could just blurt it out. 'Hey, sorry your kid is missing, but I've got good news,'" he said pointedly. Becca didn't speak.

Christian continued. "You were the one who said we couldn't be in each other's lives. You were the one who pushed me away. I'm sorry if this news blindsided you. I never wanted to hurt you, no matter what you may think. To answer your question, no, I'm not worried about Joanne.

She can handle herself. It's you I'm worried about. You and your single-minded obsessiveness."

Becca bristled. "Thank you so much for the analysis, Dr. Stevens."

"There you go with your sarcasm and deflection. You think just because you spent all those years studying that you've got it all figured out, but you don't. I see it. I always did. Watching you take on this job, watching how it consumed you."

"Your job was just as important," she interrupted.

"Not like yours. Never like that. I knew how to turn it off, to put it away. You let it worm its way in. Night and day these cases haunted you. Everyone you had to fix. Or save. The ones you couldn't. Then everything happened with our babies..." His voice caught.

Becca's eyes flared, a fury building inside of her. He'd never wanted to discuss it, insisting that they needed to keep moving forward. "You want to talk about it now? For months...no, years...I tried to get you to open up and to be a goddamn person about the miscarriages. I wanted you to tell me what you were feeling and thinking and you just...you shut down."

"You're really going to sit there and say it was all my fault? Yes, I wasn't honest with you, but Jesus Christ, Becs, you're the ultimate liar."

Becca hesitated before responding. "I lied? What the hell are you talking about?"

222

"About the last miscarriage. You went through that all alone. You got pregnant with our child, you lost it, and you never said a word to me."

Everything went quiet. All Becca could hear was the pounding of her heart. How did he know? The only people she ever told were the hospital staff. For two and a half months, she carried that baby, feeling her body change, feeling the pressure in her belly, thinking if she didn't say the words "I'm pregnant" out loud, the end result might somehow be different. That this one might survive. Christian was at work when the bleeding started. Becca drove straight to the ER, the doctors confirming what Becca already knew. Her pregnancy wasn't "viable." Her baby, their baby, was dead. She couldn't tell him then. What was the point?

"How did you—"

"You thought I wasn't paying attention? That I was so stupid or selfish I wouldn't notice? The tiredness, the nausea, your mood swings, I clocked them all. Each day, I told myself, today is the day she's going to tell me. When you didn't, when you went through that loss alone, it broke me. I imagined our lives if we stayed together, that quiet desperation, both of us gripping on so tightly until we ruined each other."

"So, you cheated? You broke all your promises and bailed," Becca said. The pain of his betrayal came roaring back. "No. I can't...I can't do this. Not now," Becca said. She climbed out of the car, racing inside, her home shrouded in darkness. She paused, the familiar aroma of her mother's famous *albondigas*, a traditional Mexican meatball soup, filling the air. Virginia had been here and she'd cooked for her, the way she used to do when Becca was young.

The silence was deafening. No Ash. No loud music or blaring TV. None of her laughter ringing out as she tossed Freud's toy, the dog happily barking. She remembered her father's text. He wanted her to come home, but her mother must have known she wouldn't. It was less than a five-minute drive, so she'd come here and made this food. For a second, Becca considered driving over to her parents' house, crawling back into the old twin bed with Freud, the walls covered with family photos from a happier time, when Robbie was still alive. Virginia would hover around her, peppering her with endless questions about Ash. Becca would have to lie to them, remembering her promise to Wishard to keep what she learned a secret. No. She was better off here.

Right now she had to lie down. She climbed the stairs, each step heavier than the last. She reached her bedroom, eyeing the king-sized mattress longingly. All she wanted to do was crawl into bed and throw the covers over her head, but she reeked, her body covered in a thin layer of dirt, sand, and sweat. Becca made it to the bathroom, stripped naked, and climbed into the shower, letting the hot water soak her body.

She couldn't stop thinking about the dead girl on the

beach. Who was she? Who killed her and why? Was it the tattooed man Hopper mentioned? Or the evil old broad? And if so, how were they all connected to Nate and Ash?

Becca stood in the shower for so long, the water turned cold. She finally climbed out and dried off, pulling on a pair of old jogging pants and a faded LAPD T-shirt. She sank down onto the bed, staring at the framed picture on her nightstand, the Disneyland selfie Becca and Ash took, both wearing Mickey Mouse ears and oversized grins.

Becca closed her eyes. What if Ash was dead? Her eyes popped open. *Don't do that. Don't let those terrible thoughts sneak in.* She heard footsteps on the landing.

"What do you want, Chris?" she said, recognizing his footsteps. He lingered awkwardly in the doorway.

"I didn't want to leave you. Not like this," he said.

"It's fine. We're fine. Please just go," she said.

"Becs, before you start spinning all sorts of terrible scenarios, remember Ash has all of us on her side. You've never given up on her. You can't start now."

His words triggered something deep inside her. She'd tried to keep it together, but the dam finally broke. Becca sobbed, the pain of this day, the magnitude of the loss, the fear of the unknown, pouring from her.

"Becs," Christian said softly.

"Please go," she pleaded through her tears.

"Becs, you will get through this. I promise you. You're so much stronger than you even realize," he said, moving

over to her. He said that so many times, and then he violated her trust and walked away. She wanted to shout at
him, to scream, *Get out*, but he was here now.

Christian sank down onto the bed and wrapped his arms
around her. They always fit together, and no matter how
much time passed, she knew they always would. It wasn't
right that he was here in her room, on her bed, but she let
him hold her. She cried until there were no more tears, the
two of them lying together, wrapped in each other's arms.

"I should have told you," she whispered.

"Yes, you should have. But I should've told you..."

"Told me what?

"That I wanted an escape from all the sadness and fighting. That I resented Ash. You said that once and it was true.
The more you fixated on her, the more resentment I felt.
I couldn't get over it. I punished you for loving Ash. I see
that now. It wasn't fair."

No, it wasn't. She'd always wondered if she were crazy,
making it all up in her head. But it was true.

"But you spent so much of your life thinking that if you
saved everyone, it would somehow make up for losing
Robbie. You gave so much to everyone else, and there was
nothing left when you got home. You never saw how much
I suffered. I'd failed Annie, and when we got together, I
told myself, 'I'll never let Becs down.' But I did. And yet
you never once acknowledged that. Not once. Hell, I
almost hoped when you'd discovered those pictures, the

texts from that trainer, that you'd ask me why. But you didn't. You just shut down and pushed me away, just like you did with the baby. I realized that would never change."

It was as if Christian had doused her in cold water, his words setting in. She'd been so selfish, making it all about her sorrow, her loss, her desire for a child. "I guess I didn't take you into account." She sighed. "I wish . . . I wish we'd done things differently. That we could go back and do it all again."

"I don't know about that. I mean, look at what you gained in the process. You wanted to be a mother and you are. Ash brought you back to life."

That was true, Becca thought. "And you fell in love again," she said.

Christian tensed ever so slightly, but he held on tight. "I wasn't looking for anything serious. Joanne and I were supposed to keep things casual. That's what we both agreed. Somehow things evolved and grew. I know it's hard for you to hear me say this, but I do love her. Joanne's not complicated."

Becca snorted. "I find that hard to believe."

He chuckled. It was so strange to be here, in this bed with him, laughing and talking as though they hadn't broken each other's hearts. "Okay, she's quite complicated, but it's different. You and I were so young when we met, but we'd already been through so much, and that baggage is hard to escape. Maybe this was how it was all meant to be.

227

Things would be different if I didn't think you were happy, but you are. I know you are."

Becca was happy. At least before Ash left, she was. In fact, she'd never been happier. She looked up at Christian, the streetlights through the window casting a shadow on his face. She remembered telling him how handsome he was. That hadn't changed either. She laid her head on his chest, his arms around her. She used to love doing this, lying in the "nook," as she called it, listening to the steady beat of his heart. "I wish we could've done this back then. Talked about everything. Laid it all out there," she said.

"I do too," Christian replied. She wasn't sure how long they stayed like that. Christian finally reached for his phone and sighed. "I should go."

The thought of him leaving her alone in this house was unbearable. The silence alone might actually kill her. "Could you stay? Just a bit longer," she said.

"Okay...but only if you try and sleep."

She'd spent all this time being angry at Christian, and now it was gone. "Can I ask you something?"

"Always," Christian said.

"Do you think Ash is alive? Do you think we're going to find her?"

This wasn't a fair question. Becca understood that. Cops were trained to never answer questions like this. You were setting yourself and the loved one up for heartbreak if things went south. His grip tightened and he pulled her in even closer.

"Hell yes. I know in my heart that Ash is coming home. You just have to keep the faith. We all do." She understood he couldn't make any guarantees, but his words soothed her. At last Becca's eyes flickered shut.

It was still dark outside when she jolted awake. A storm was brewing, angry clouds hovering in the distance. She wasn't sure how she'd wound up back on the beach. There wasn't anyone in sight for miles, only an endless horizon of water and sand. She blinked again, spotting a solitary figure in the distance, sitting in the sand, just inches from the sea. It was Ash. She tried running, the sand weighing her down, her body heavy and clumsy.

"Ash. Ash, it's me." The young girl's eyes showed no recognition. None at all. "Ash," Becca called out again, but this time her words were drowned out by the roaring of the ocean. Becca picked up her pace, watching as the tide changed in an instant, waves rushing in. Becca tried to run faster. With each step she sank deeper and deeper into the sand. She was so close. All Ash had to do was turn around, and Becca could reach out and grab her.

"Ash, it's me. It's Mom," Becca shouted, her voice heavy with emotion. Ash spun around, and Becca gasped. Ash's eyes were hollowed out, slashes on her neck, the same wounds as the dead girl on the beach.

"You're too late," she said with a bloody, toothless smile. Becca's breath caught. She woke up, gasping for air. Her eyes opened and she was back in her room. She tried to shake free of the image of Ash's mangled body. She stretched, searching for Christian. Disappointment flooded her. He was gone. It was almost like a dream, only the imprint of his body remaining beside her.

Becca glanced at the clock. It was almost six in the morning, a hint of sunlight peeking through. She heard the creak of the stairs and tensed for a moment. "Christian, you scared the hell out of me," she said.

"Who's Christian?" she heard a woman call out. Becca froze, the smell of cigarette wafting through the room. *You're still dreaming. It's just a dream.* She squeezed her eyes shut, hoping she would wake up. "Doc, you really need to improve your security system. Anyone could get in here."

This wasn't Christian, and this wasn't a dream. Becca jolted upright and scrambled out of bed, fumbling for the lamp switch. She gasped, stunned to find Raya, the homeless schizophrenic young woman from Skid Row, standing in the doorway of the bedroom, still clad in the same dirty T-shirt and jeans, a lit cigarette dangling from her mouth.

"What are you...Raya, what are you doing here?" Becca asked.

"You said if I remembered anything about your girl to let you know. So here I am."

BECCA

From Becca's vantage point, Raya didn't appear to have any weapons. That didn't mean she wasn't dangerous. Becca stilled, avoiding any quick movements that might trigger Raya if she were in the midst of a schizophrenic episode.

Becca quickly searched the young girl's face for any physical symptoms that indicated a mental break. A vacant gaze. Involuntary facial tics. Jerky movements. So far, aside from the breaking and entering, Raya seemed perfectly reasonable, her eyes bright and focused, her gaze steady.

"Are you okay, Doc?" Raya said.

Becca kept her voice calm and even. "Raya, you're in my home. You're in my bedroom. I'm not okay. I'm quite worried. About you. About this situation." Becca paused, weighing her words carefully. "About your current condition."

Raya's face fell. She stepped back, wrapping her arms around her waist in a protective manner. "I didn't, I mean, I'm not having an episode if that's what you think. Shit. I rang the bell and knocked. I knocked and knocked. No one answered. I went around back and the side door was open. I mean, I just turned the handle and walked right in. It wasn't like I broke into the place or anything," she said, her words coming out in a flurry. That was semantics. Walking into someone's house without permission was still breaking and entering, no matter what your intentions.

"Raya, I should probably call someone," Becca said, reaching for her purse in search of her phone. She scanned her texts. A message from Christian appeared. *Had to go to work. I'll check in with the task force. Please rest and call me when you're up.*

Becca should text him back and let him know Raya was here. Christian would help get her to the hospital, he would make sure she was examined by a doctor, while Becca resumed her search for Ash. For some reason though, she froze, knowing once she hit send, Raya would be back in the system.

Raya shifted back and forth like a child caught swiping candy from the teacher's desk. "You'll tell them I didn't come here to hurt you?"

"I will, Raya. It's just...how did you even find me?" Becca asked.

Raya shrugged. "I'm good with computers. I was a computer science major at Caltech before I got sick. The public library in downtown is free. All you need is an Internet connection. It's not hard to find someone if you know where to look," Raya said with an awkward laugh. Becca wasn't sure whether to be impressed or frightened at how easy it was for Raya to locate her. It was a good lesson in her need to improve her home security once all of this was over.

"Why come here? I don't understand," Becca said.

"You said your girl was in trouble and I knew I needed to talk to you."

Her girl. Raya's words created a physical ache deep inside Becca. Raya continued, pleading her case like she was on trial and Becca was judge and jury. "I was out walking, just thinking and smoking, when I saw the kid from the picture you showed me. I knew I recognized him from the neighborhood. I tried calling you from a friend's phone. You didn't answer."

Becca hadn't let her phone out of her sight since Ash left. She would've answered any call, but she didn't say anything, allowing Raya to continue talking.

"I could see what Ash meant to you, how important finding her was. I wanted to help. Do something good for a change."

Becca couldn't believe what she was hearing. Raya found Nate. *Don't get your hopes up. Manage your expectations.* "You found Nate? You know where he is?" Becca said.

"Yes, ma'am. Spotted him last night outside one of those tent cities over on Skid Row. He looks like he's been through some really bad shit."

"He's hurt?" Becca asked.

"Yeah, someone really messed him up. He's not alone though. Got a whole crew surrounding him. Once I knew he was down there, I began chatting up some folks in the neighborhood. Asking questions. I'm good at that. Mama always said I had a gift for gab. From what I hear that boy rolls with some fucking crazy people."

Becca took this in, Raya's words echoing Hopper's. Becca had to know more. "Raya, are you hungry?" she asked.

The young girl's eyes lit up. "Fucking famished."

Becca led Raya downstairs and heated a heaping bowl of her mother's *albondigas*. Raya leaned over the steaming bowl, slurping hungrily. "Doc, this is next level. I mean, this could be served in restaurants."

Becca smiled. "I'll pass the compliments along to my mother."

Raya's smile faded. "You're lucky you got family who cares. That's why I came here. 'Cuz you should never give up on the people you love."

"You said there's something going on downtown I should know about?" Becca asked.

"Yeah, there's this group that lives down there that my buddy Otis said is straight-up dangerous," Raya said. "Otis is a real solid dude. He's not a junkie or crazy or anything like that. He just fell on hard times and never found his footing. He's been on the streets for a few years now," Raya said, her spoon clanging against the bowl as she hungrily slurped at the broth.

"Can I talk to Otis?"

"He's not real fond of the five-oh," Raya said.

"I'm not police," Becca said.

Raya shrugged. "Close enough. And look, I'm telling

you exactly what Otis told me. Said a few weeks ago he was just chilling on the street, minding his own business, when this tattooed kid gets up in his face. Otis called him a kid, like nineteen or twenty. Anyway, the kid starts telling Otis he's trespassing. Otis was like, 'What the fuck are you talking about? This is a public street.' Next thing he knows this dude's coming at him with a blade. Now, you don't know my boy Otis, but he is not one to back down. Things were about to get ugly when this woman appears out of nowhere. Some middle-aged white chick, looking like she came from Burning Man or some shit, he said. She starts whispering to this tall freak, and all of a sudden, he's kind as can be, apologizing to Otis. He's saying he's sorry and they're cool! Otis said this dude just walked away and this woman smiles at him and says, 'I suggest you stay away from my family and we won't have any trouble.'"

"He hadn't seen this woman before?"

"Nah, and he said he wasn't interested in seeing her again. Told me there's something about this chick that scared him, and that's saying something. He said she's one crazy bitch, and Otis doesn't mess with crazy bitches." Raya paused, staring down at her empty bowl.

Becca caught her wistful gaze. "Would you like some more?" she asked.

Raya smiled sheepishly. "If you don't mind. Been a while since I've eaten."

Becca filled her bowl and sat back down. "This group,

do they have a name?" Becca asked. She waited, hoping to get a confirmation.

"Yeah. They call themselves the Tribe. Fucking stupid and kind of offensive if you ask me. I mean you have to admit the optics aren't great." Raya shrugged. "Otis said they even got matching tattoos, which is so fucking stupid. I mean the whole point behind a tattoo is to showcase one's unique and individual expression," Raya said, shaking her head.

Tattoos. Matching tattoos. This was it. This was the group Ash was caught up with. Becca was certain. "Raya, please tell me you know where they are?" Becca asked.

"Hell yeah. Why else would I come all this way if I wasn't going to show you?"

Becca needed to call Christian. Or maybe Nina. One of them could notify Wishard with this lead. That's what she *should* do. Then she had a thought—what if Raya's intel was false? What if this Otis person was full of shit? What if Otis didn't even exist? All of these things were possible considering Raya's condition. The last thing Becca wanted to do was sound the alarm. They already thought she was losing it. If she was wrong about this, she'd wind up looking like an idiot. It was best that she got solid evidence. Then she would call someone.

"Raya, what's the exact address?" Becca asked.

"It's tricky if you don't know where you're going. Lot of folks down there and lots of tents. Might be easier if I show you."

If Becca didn't know better, she would think Raya was enjoying this, like she was on some kind of adventure. "Raya, I don't think that's a good idea," Becca said. Involving one of her clients in a potentially dangerous personal matter was ethically questionable at best, illegal at worst.

"Why? You gonna call the cops? Have them haul me away?"

That's what Becca should do. She wouldn't though. She made the decision in an instant.

"We'll go down together. You'll show me and then I'm giving you money to go to a motel so you can get some rest. Okay?" Becca understood that physical stress, including exhaustion, could worsen Raya's condition.

Raya nodded.

"I just need to get dressed," Becca said. She paused, eyeing Raya's stained clothing and noticing the pungent odor emanating from her.

"I have some clothes you could wear, if you want to take a shower and change?"

Raya's eyes widened in surprise. "We have time for that?"

"If we're quick," Becca said. Raya looked away, swatting at the tears in her eyes so Becca wouldn't see. She led her upstairs toward Ash's bedroom.

"Hey, Doc, you might want to wear something a little less..." Raya trailed off.

"A little less what?" Becca asked.

"Less Ann Taylor. Actually, a lot less. The goal is not to draw attention to yourself."

"Message received," Becca said with a laugh. In less than twenty minutes, Raya and Becca were dressed and heading out of the house. At approximately seven forty-five in the morning, they arrived downtown. Becca parked in a small pay lot, paying seventeen dollars for the privilege. Raya gestured for Becca to follow her down an alleyway.

"Keep your eyes down and walk with purpose. Don't make eye contact and try not to walk like you own the sidewalk."

"I don't—"

"Yes, you do, which is fine in the real world. Down here people get nervous, and when they get nervous, bad shit happens."

"I can defend myself," Becca said. "It's not like they're gonna knife me right here."

Raya snorted. "That's what you think."

Her comment was enough to rattle Becca as she considered the reckless nature of what she was doing. If the Tribe or whatever the hell they called themselves really did those terrible things, there was no reason to think Becca and Raya weren't in danger. But she had come this far; there was no way she was backing out now.

They walked through a deserted industrial area filled with abandoned buildings, all waiting for a crafty developer to turn them into loft apartments and event spaces.

Becca was profoundly aware of the sound of their footsteps as Raya led her toward Alameda and Seventh. Rats skittered past them, unfazed by human interactions. The empty streets grew more and more crowded, now thick with dozens of homeless, many roaming the streets aimlessly, talking to themselves or huddled in groups, chain-smoking furiously. Others were fast asleep on the hard concrete or wrapped in sleeping bags.

"We're close," Raya said. They turned right and kept going down another alley and then a side street, past a produce wholesaler. Becca stepped around a single orange in a white plastic bag, noticing the sun bouncing off the yellow and green buildings, the unmistakable smell of McDonald's sausage wafting from the nearby corner.

"That's it. That's where they stay," Raya said, pointing to the street where a row of tents were arranged, backing up against a chain-link fence and covered with blue tarps. It was a makeshift village encompassing nearly an entire city block. The surrounding area appeared relatively free of trash, several brooms propped up nearby, a stark difference from the area across the street, practically bursting with garbage, the surrounding area empty and deserted, everyone still hibernating.

"Looks like they're all still sleeping," Raya said.

Murder wears you out, Becca thought. She glanced around, eyeing the McDonald's a few hundred feet from the encampment. "Are you still hungry?" Becca asked. The restaurant would provide the perfect vantage point to wait.

Raya's eyes lit up. "Hell yes. I would love one of them breakfast egg muffin things," Raya said excitedly. Becca ordered coffee and hash browns, knowing she needed to eat something. Raya ordered two Egg McMuffins, two orders of hash browns, and a Coke. They both took a seat at one of the colorful booths closest to the window. Raya unwrapped her first sandwich and ate greedily, her eyes never leaving Becca. "You must've been young when you had your kid?" Raya said.

Becca took a sip of coffee. "She's not my biological daughter. Ash is my foster kid."

"Foster kid, huh? I bet she's seen some shit."

"More than any girl her age ever should," Becca said.

"You think maybe that boy broke her heart and your girl said fuck it, and took off?" Raya asked.

"I considered that. Now I think she just got caught up in something and thought the only way out was to run," Becca said.

Raya took another big bite of her sandwich. "You're all about fixing wounded birds, aren't you?"

Confusion clouded Becca's face. "Wounded birds?"

"You know, broken people like me, and like your girl. You see one of us, we've fallen out of our tree. You rush over, pick us up, brush us off, do your best to make us whole again. Wash. Rinse. Repeat."

Becca tried not to think about all the money she spent on therapy when this young woman had summed up

Becca's entire existence in minutes. She imagined telling her colleagues all about this new diagnosis, "wounded bird syndrome."

"Guilty as charged," Becca said with a smile.

"So why are you so wounded, Doc? What's your damage?" Raya asked.

"What do you mean?" Becca said, shifting in her seat.

"What makes you tick? Why are you working with burnouts like me when you could be making a fortune in some Beverly Hills office?"

There was something about Raya's innate curiosity that allowed Becca to drop her guard. "When I was younger, my brother... he suffered a mental breakdown. That changed everything."

"I see that. So he was a wounded bird you couldn't save. Is he still in the nuthouse?" Raya asked.

"Hollywood Forever Cemetery."

Raya sucked in air through her teeth. "Shit, Doc, I didn't mean no disrespect."

"It's okay. It was a long time ago," Becca said, her party line delivered with a casual indifference to keep other people comfortable. No matter how much time passed, the loss of Robbie was the defining experience in Becca's life. At least until Ash came along.

Sometimes, Becca wondered whether the legend of her brother was a reality or something she'd built up as time went on. Four years older than Becca, Robbie was a star in every way. A gifted athlete, he landed a baseball scholarship at Stanford but decided not to continue playing. His goal was to work in the tech space and he wanted to focus completely. He used to joke that he was going to be a billionaire. She remembered the day Robbie left to go to school, her mother weeping in the kitchen, her father in the car outside, laying on the horn, eager to get on the road. Becca was the last to say good-bye, standing on the porch, trying not to cry, not wanting Robbie to tease her. Instead he grabbed her and hugged her tightly. "Don't worry, Becca. I'm only a few hours away. You can bug me anytime, day or night."

With Robbie gone, Becca set out to "win" high school, with that same single-minded determination she did everything with, joining all the clubs, landing a spot on the varsity cheerleading squad, and taking every AP class her schedule would allow. A few months into freshman year during a trip with her friends to the Grove, LA's attempt at a mall, complete with a musical fountain, a talent agent approached Becca and asked if she might be interested in auditioning for a deodorant commercial. Before long Becca had an agent, and Virginia was driving her to auditions. Becca's life was so full, she barely had time to miss Robbie. On the few occasions that they spoke, he confessed the academics were harder than he expected. He came home for Thanksgiving, bringing along his freshman roommate, Anthony, a computer whiz from New Jersey. Anthony made them all laugh with his spot-on *Sopranos* impressions and even entertained Becca with his close-up magic tricks.

Becca was thrilled when Robbie landed an internship at a tech start-up that summer. Each morning they'd wake up at dawn. Sometimes they'd hike Griffith Park; other days they'd walk around the Silver Lake Reservoir. There were times when Robbie seemed moody and distant. He always blamed work; the hours were long and the work was challenging. Looking back, there were endless signs he was struggling. She tried to tell herself she was just a kid. How could she have known what was going to happen to Robbie? When he returned to Stanford for his sophomore year, something shifted. He began calling Becca at all hours of the day and night. He confessed he wasn't sleeping, worried someone was trying to break into his apartment. "Don't let them know where you hid the crown jewels," Becca teased, not realizing there was something more serious at work.

As the weeks went by, Robbie began sending rambling e-mails, insisting his roommate Anthony didn't like Mexican people and that he was plotting to have him deported. Becca thought these e-mails were jokes and responded accordingly. When Robbie e-mailed her with elaborate tales about people following him, she told him to talk to their parents. Sometimes he would call and Becca didn't even pick up. She was too busy to get sucked into one of his rambling phone calls. It wasn't until she came home after school one day and found her parents in a full-blown argument that Becca realized there was real trouble.

"I don't care what you say, Rafi. Robbie hasn't called or e-mailed in days. Becca hasn't heard from him either. Call it intuition, I just can't shake this bad feeling," Virginia said.

Those were magic words in the Ortiz household. No one ever argued with Virginia's bad feelings. Once, she became convinced that something was wrong with her mother back in Mexico. She sent her brother over to check, and he found Becca's grandmother lying on the bedroom floor with a fractured hip.

Another time, the family booked a Caribbean vacation. Two days before they were scheduled to leave, Virginia canceled it. "Something awful is going to happen. I know it." A day later, a storm hit, leveling the entire resort and killing two tourists. After twenty years of marriage and countless examples, her father didn't argue with her mother. He went upstairs, packed up a bag, and said he was driving straight to Palo Alto.

There had to be a good reason why Becca went along and her mother stayed behind. They never spoke about it. Everything Becca saw and heard that day was hers to bear alone.

Becca remembered the long drive, sitting in her father's gray Mercedes, dread gnawing at her, remembering Robbie's e-mails, recognizing the growing paranoia and anguish. She didn't tell her father, reassuring herself it would all be okay once she saw Robbie again.

"We arrived at my brother's apartment in Menlo Park. My dad knocked and knocked on his door. No one answered, and he finally said to hell with it. He grabbed his tools from the car and picked the lock and we stepped inside." Becca could remember it all so clearly, following her father into the apartment. She saw the blood covering the walls, symbols and nonsensical words on what seemed like every surface. She remembered screaming, and her father, who was always so gentle, shoving her out the front door, shouting for her to go to the neighbors and call 911.

Becca took a deep breath. She wasn't supposed to be telling Raya all of this. But Ash's disappearance was bringing up so many memories. It was almost as if Becca couldn't stop herself. "I told the 911 operator something was wrong with my brother. A few seconds later, my dad stumbled outside, tears in his eyes. 'It's not Robbie. It's Anthony. He's dead.' He'd been sleeping and someone had stabbed him—over seventeen times. The desperate search to find Robbie began, everyone wondering what happened. Was he kidnapped? Dumped in the woods? A statewide manhunt unfolded, students at Stanford forming search parties, the entire community rallying together to find one of their own. A trucker discovered Robbie a day and a half later, sitting in his car, covered in Anthony's blood. He tearfully confessed that he'd stabbed his roommate. Robbie was transported to the local jail and booked. He was not allowed to phone us. He was not given any medical attention nor was he placed on suicide watch. At some point in the middle of the night, before he was even arraigned, my brother hung himself with the bedsheets in his cell. In the days and weeks that he had been e-mailing me, we discovered that Robbie was in the early stages of a psychological breakdown. From high school valedictorian to murderer to dead in less than two years."

Raya continued gently patting Becca on the hand. "Goddamn, Doc, that's some fucking sad shit. Though, and don't take this the wrong way, I envy your brother just a little bit."

Becca's eyes widened. Raya quickly interjected. "I mean, not the whole losing it and the murder part, just the idea that he's not suffering anymore, that he might actually be at peace," Raya said.

Becca's gaze narrowed. What the hell was she thinking? She'd already crossed boundaries by bringing Raya down here. Now she was sharing this story with Raya. The last thing Becca wanted to do was unleash some emotional trigger. "Is there something I should be concerned about?" Becca asked.

"You mean am I gonna off myself? Not anytime soon, but even if I was, you can't save all the wounded birds," Raya said matter-of-factly as she grabbed Becca's half-eaten hash brown.

"I can sure as hell try," Becca said. They shared a smile.

For this brief moment, they weren't all that different. Two people trying to survive in a world that tested them at every turn. Two people whose lives had gone off course and who were trying to find their way back. They grew quiet, Raya refilling her soda while Becca sipped her coffee and stared out the window. Watching and waiting. No one objected to their presence. As long as they could pay, they were welcome. McDonald's, the great equalizer.

By now Skid Row was springing to life, more and more people hurrying through the streets, men and women heading to the shelters for breakfast service, junkies on the hunt for their first fix of the day. "Hold up. I think I see someone coming out," Raya said, leaning forward, her nose pressing against the glass like a child peering in a storefront window.

Becca held her breath. She understood it was unlikely, but she hoped she might catch a glimpse of Ash. Two teenage girls exited the first tent, both reed thin, one with platinum blond shaggy hair that covered her eyes, the other with bright purple hair that hung down her back. Their mannerisms were affectionate, holding hands, sneaking looks at one another, obviously a couple. As if on cue, more kids emerged; teenagers, Becca thought, of varying ages and ethnicities, all of them smiling and joking with one another.

"Tattooed freak at six o'clock," Raya said. Becca's gaze darted over to a tent at the farthest end of the street, watching as a giant of a man unfolded himself and stepped out of the tent, his entire face and hands covered in blue and black ink. One of the girls in the group opened a plastic bag and began handing out Pop-Tarts and apples. How ordinary it all seemed, and yet so terribly sad, this ragtag group, banding together in a city that abandoned them.

Becca watched as the flap of another tent opened. A middle-aged woman appeared, a tie-dyed scarf wrapped around her hair. From Becca's vantage point, she appeared small, maybe five foot four, her mousy brown hair streaked with gray. She reminded Becca of a middle-aged secretary, someone who might ask how you did in school before offering you baked goods. Becca watched as the others registered her arrival, all of them offering up smiles, hugs, and handshakes. She demurely accepted their affection with the graciousness of a Hollywood star greeting her fans.

"Hundred bucks that's the crazy bitch right there," Raya said softly. It was a sucker's bet. The second Becca saw her, she was certain this woman called the shots. Call it gut instinct from a lifetime of analyzing people. Even from this distance, Becca could tell her vibe was toxic, darkness pulsating off her.

The woman's head swiveled toward the restaurant as though she were an animal sensing her prey lurking nearby. Becca shivered and fought the urge to look away. This was a street family. Street families were common, especially in communities with large homeless populations. They were often composed entirely of children or teenagers, with one or two adults taking on the parental role. Becca had no proof other than a gut feeling, but she was certain this woman was in charge.

"There he is," Raya gasped. "That's the boyfriend. That's him, isn't it?"

"That's him," Becca said softly, watching Nate emerge from one of the last tents.

"Damn, he looks rough," Raya said.

Even from this vantage point Becca could see both of Nate's eyes were blackened, his lip swollen. She took out her phone and opened the camera app. Becca zoomed in on each and every person in the group, making sure she had a clear and precise image. She took their photos and texted them to Christian with the message *Call me*.

Becca's phone rang seconds later. "Who is that?" Raya asked, anxiously shifting in her seat.

"A friend," Becca said, hoping that Christian would overlook Becca's lack of protocol and appreciate that she was doing this for Ash. Still she braced for Christian's wrath. He did not disappoint. "You went back downtown? Becs, for fuck's sake, what are you doing?"

"I found him, Christian. I found Nate, and the others. I'm pretty sure this is the Tribe," Becca said, her words spilling out. "I texted you their pictures."

"You know if these are the people we're looking for they're likely responsible for multiple murders?" Christian inhaled. "Joanne's already pissed about your involvement in this case. Hell, she could have you arrested for interfering in a goddamn murder investigation. Not to mention what that could mean for your work in the department."

"You think I care what happens to my job? You think any of that matters now?" Becca asked. "I called you because I trust you. And Ash trusted you. That's why I called you. You owe us."

There was a long pause on the other end of the line. "I'm putting in a call for the nearest available units. I'm heading to you as we speak. *Do not* leave the restaurant until I get—"

She hung up the phone before he could finish his sentence.

"So what now?" Raya asked.

"I see if they know anything," Becca said. She stood up, reached into her purse, and pulled out the hundred-dollar bill she kept for emergencies.

Raya's face fell. "You can't just go over there. You know they aren't right in the head."

"The cops are on their way. I'll be fine," Becca said. This might be her only chance to get close to Nate before the cops came. Her only chance to ask about Ash. Raya looked unconvinced. Becca held out the cash to Raya.

"Take this. Check yourself into a motel. I know you'll be safe there."

"Doc, I don't want your handouts, and I'm sure as hell not letting you go over there. Not alone," Raya said nervously. "You don't know these people."

She was wrong. Time was running out and Becca wasn't going to argue with Raya. She tossed the bill on the table and hurried out of the restaurant. As Becca fast walked across the street, toward Nate and the others, she unearthed her LAPD badge from her bag.

"Nate? You're Nate, right?" Becca said calmly, summoning all her courage. The entire group swiveled around, staring at Becca with wide, mistrustful eyes. She ignored them, devoting all her attention to Nate. Her gaze lingered on his arm where the tattoo would be, a bandage wrapped around it, blood seeping through his long-sleeved T-shirt.

"You remember me, don't you? I'm Becca Ortiz, Ash's foster mother, and I work with the LAPD. We met once before. I know you remember. I'm looking for Ash. Is she here? Have you seen her?"

Nate darted anxious glances at the woman Becca believed was calling the shots. "Nate, I need to find Ash. Please tell me where she is," Becca pleaded. Nate's eyes flitted from Becca and back to the woman. "Nate, we can help each other."

For a second, Becca thought she got through. Nate took a step forward. As if on cue, three of the other kids surrounded him, completely obscuring Nate from Becca's view. Out of the corner of her eye, she saw the big guy with the tats coming at her, his entire body tensed, his meaty hands clenched in fists. The "crazy bitch" stopped him with a gentle whisper Becca couldn't quite decipher.

Her eyes were drawn to their matching human eye tattoos. Just like the girl on the beach. Just like Ash.

"Vic does excellent work, doesn't he?" Mo said, her voice heavy with pride, holding up her arm so Becca could get a closer look. "You see, the dagger here represents the challenges in the world, worry, fear, and our determination to slice through all of that and find our pure truth. The eye reminds us all we're watching out for one another. It's quite profound, don't you think?"

Becca didn't answer, scanning the tents for any sign of Ash. "Sounds like a bunch of bullshit to me," Raya said. Becca swiveled around and saw Raya behind her. "Raya, I told you to go," Becca whispered, trying to keep the anger out of her voice.

Raya shrugged. "I ain't leaving you alone with these crazy fuckers," she said softly.

"I prefer 'Mo' to 'crazy fucker,'" the grinning woman said. Her smile was almost punishing in its intensity. Becca wagered that wasn't her real name. "And Raya, is it? We really should learn to mind our manners."

Raya opened her mouth to say something. "Not another word," Becca snapped, shielding Raya from Mo.

"I know my daughter was dating Nate. She's been gone almost two days. I need to find her," Becca said again.

"I'm afraid we haven't seen her. Isn't that right, Nate?" The others stepped aside, waiting for Nate to answer. He regarded Becca with empty, hollow eyes.

"Nate, please, if you know where she is..."

"He doesn't know," Mo said, putting a protective arm around Nate. He didn't react, didn't even blink. "This can be a dangerous place. I would suggest keeping better track of your child."

Her words were tossed off, though there was something sinister in Mo's delivery. Becca knew when people were lying. She'd learned the tells. Swallowing hard. No direct eye contact. Shifting or closed-off body language. This woman displayed none of them. Yet Becca knew without question that this woman was lying. Still, Mo held her ground. "You should leave. My family finds your presence unsettling," Mo said.

"That's interesting because I'm unsettled too. That happens when someone you love goes missing," Becca said.

Mo cocked her head. "Sometimes people get hurt because they do foolish things."

It took everything in Becca's power not to react, not to shout at her or lunge for her. *Remember your training. She's goading you. Testing you. Don't let her win.*

"What did Nate do? Must have been something really foolish," Becca said, gesturing to his wounds.

For an instant, the woman's carefully cultivated mask of Zen dropped, replaced by flared nostrils and squinty eyes. It was almost imperceptible, but Becca clocked it. Mo's smile was soon plastered back in place. "My family is none of your business," Mo said. There was a stillness to the group, all of them flanking her, an unnerving quiet, as though they were soldiers awaiting their general's orders.

"No, they aren't. Ash is. It won't be long before the police arrive."

The woman laughed. "You know what I've learned living on the streets? Law enforcement doesn't care about us. Do you know how long we've been out here? Two years. And in two years, not a single police officer has approached us or moved us from these dwellings; not one social worker or county official has done a wellness check. We're invisible, which is fine. We cultivate our own happiness in a place where misery abounds. Unfortunately, you're here now. You're here disrupting things and any disruption simply isn't tolerated."

She could see the others tensing. This was a threat. That much was clear. Becca could stay and risk angering Mo, give her the opportunity to cause Becca harm, but that wouldn't do Ash any good. It was time to retreat, at least for now.

"I didn't mean to disrupt your morning. Come on, Raya," Becca said, turning back toward the safety and security of the McDonald's.

She hated backing down, but she had no choice. In the distance, the sirens were wailing. The police were close. She would let them handle things from here. She led Raya back inside the McDonald's to wait for the officers. Becca could feel Mo's probing gaze on her, but she wasn't afraid. *They're coming for you*, she thought with a smile. *They're coming for all of you.*

MO

Mo couldn't believe that stupid woman came here, that she thought she would ruin their sacred space like that. This woman thought she could intimidate Mo. It took all her self-restraint not to tell her exactly what happened to Ash. "We made her beg for her life and left her to die in the streets."

God, there was nothing Mo wanted more than to wipe that smug, constipated look off Becca's face. As Becca walked away, Vic grumbled in Mo's ear. "We shouldn't let this bitch walk away. Let me take care of her."

Mo clocked Becca, rushing back toward the restaurant, her threat about the police lingering. This was definitely a hiccup in Mo's plan, but she saw things more clearly than Vic and the others. That was her gift. She understood that this woman worked in law enforcement. She wasn't stupid enough to challenge them without knowing the police were en route. There wasn't time to run, that much was clear. Mo already knew that everything was going to change—the Tribe as they knew it would cease to exist. The most important thing was preserving their legacy.

She eyed her kiddos, all of them, staring at her with wide, trusting eyes. Mo wasn't going to sugarcoat things. That wouldn't do anyone any good.

"We all know the things we did were righteous. Our daily struggles have challenged us, but we're stronger because we're in this together. The world is crumbling. It won't be long before the life we lead is the only way. Not everyone is strong enough to survive these hardships we've endured. All of you are. You've proven that. And every single one of us understands what's coming, but you know that change frightens people. That's why they want to stop us. Stop me. I may be locked up. Or even killed."

Her words activated everyone, a terrified murmur spreading through the group. "Then we leave. Let's go now. We can build our future somewhere else," Vic said.

"Let's do it," Kelsey chimed in.

"How about San Diego? Or Phoenix?" Andrea suggested.

They were talking over one another, making all kinds of plans. Mo whistled to silence them. "We don't have time for that. I need you all to listen and focus. I'm going to turn myself in. I'll take the burden off all of you and confess to everything."

Vic's eyes flashed with anger. "No way. That's not the plan and you know it," Vic said. It was true. The two of them had talked on several occasions about what might happen if the cops discovered their way of life. "If you go to jail, the Tribe falls apart."

The others murmured their agreement. "We talked about this, Mo. I'm ready. I'll do what needs to be done," Vic said confidently. Mo reached out and squeezed his hand. Of course Vic would have her back. Kelsey and Andrea volunteered next. God, she loved these kids. She reassured them that she would be with them for as long as possible, and then the next phase of their plan would unfold. Mo offered up hugs, whispering last-minute words of encouragement, reminding each one of them how special and unique they were. She went to Vic next.

"No tears," she warned Vic. She got a hint of a smile. In all the time she knew Vic he never cried, though she could see the sadness in his eyes, mirroring her own. "You were the first to believe in what I was building. You've been my most loyal and treasured soul," Mo said to him. She could hear the sirens growing louder by the second. Vic's Adam's apple quivered. Mo gently caressed his ink-covered cheek.

"Mo, I know already. You don't have to..."

"Let me finish. Meeting you on the beach was the greatest gift I could've been given, and I know you will represent this family with dignity and honor until the very end."

Vic's eyes were watering ever so slightly. "The Tribe endures."

Mo gently kissed him. "Yes indeed. This is temporary. One day we will all be reunited."

Out of the corner of her eye, Mo caught Nate, standing

frozen, eyeing the McDonald's as though he was considering making a run for it.

"Make sure the others are okay," she told Vic. "I need to counsel with Nate."

"Mo, you're sure about him? He could fuck it all up for us."

She patted Vic's arm. "He won't. Trust me." Vic gave her a curt nod and ambled over to the camper chair he'd set up outside his tent. He sank down and lit another cigarette, his posture carefree. If he was nervous about the way things were unfolding, he didn't show it. Such a good, sweet boy, she thought.

Mo hurried over to where Nate was standing, his eyes darting toward the restaurant. She grabbed him by the shoulders, watching as the squad cars sped down the street, sirens wailing. She had to talk to fast.

"Nathaniel, I need you to listen to me. That woman wants to ruin us. She wants to punish all of us for Ash's mistakes. I can make sure you're okay. I will make sure you're taken care of. First I need to know I can count on you."

She could see Nate trembling, a bead of sweat forming on his upper brow. She put a steady hand on his shoulders. He nodded. "You can count on me," he whispered.

She took Nate's hand and placed a handful of pills in it. Mo kept these for special cases. She'd only used them once or twice to get rid of the truly undesirables. As long as Nate received prompt medical attention, he would be fine.

"You have to trust me. Because even when we're apart, I'm always looking out for you."

Nate hesitated, eyeing the pills and Mo warily. "Go on. It's the only way for us to see this to the end."

Her words seemed to have a magical effect. Nate swallowed them quickly. "What happens now?" he said. Mo would have appreciated more enthusiasm on his part, but at least he was on board.

"This next part won't be pleasant, but it's necessary. They'll take you to the hospital, but, whatever you do, don't say a word about me or the Tribe. Not the doctors. Not the cops. When the time comes, you'll know what to do and where to find me. We have to make sure that woman pays for what she's done to our family. It's your job to make sure."

BECCA

For Becca, it seemed as though time were moving backward. From the secure confines of the McDonald's, Becca studied Mo and the others, watching as they milled about. She was convinced they might try to make a run for it. In fact, she expected some outward display of concern, but they were completely unfazed. They resumed their morning ritual of eating and talking and smoking as though it were any other day, barely even glancing at the two black-and-whites that had descended on the scene, lights and sirens flashing. Becca watched as the officers emerged from their car, surveying the Tribe's encampment. "Wait here and I'll be back in a few," Becca said to Raya.

The young woman shook her head. "Nah, Doc, I think it's time for me to bounce."

"Raya, if you can wait a few minutes, I can see about finding you a place to stay—"

"I'm good, Doc. Don't need a babysitter. You just keep your head up and don't lose hope. I'll be praying for your little bird."

She watched as Raya hurried out of the McDonald's, her head down, her own mistrust of cops obvious as she raced past the officers. Becca exited the restaurant behind her and beelined toward one of the officers, who was surveying the Tribe with studied indifference.

"Officer, I'm Dr. Becca Ortiz. I'm with MEU," she said.

The tall, middle-aged African American man reached out to shake her hand. "Lieutenant Stevens said you'd be here. I'm Officer Morris and my partner over there is Officer Ghazalian."

Becca saw the young Middle Eastern woman, clearly a "boot," the LAPD slang for training officer. She stood at attention by the cruiser, awaiting instructions from Officer Morris.

"The lieutenant said you reported these people as possible suspects in your daughter's disappearance?"

"They're persons of interest in at least one homicide," Becca said. "My daughter's boyfriend is one of them. The kid in the gray T-shirt with the bandaged wrist. Most of them appear to be minors," Becca said.

"Copy that. We'll get CPS out here. Detective Wishard, the lead detective, is en route. For your safety please wait here while my partner and I have a chat with them, see what we can find. The last thing we want is for them to feel like we're taking sides."

"I wager that it's too late for that, but I appreciate your optimism, Officer," Becca said.

"Only thing keeping me sane," he replied with a strained smile before heading across the street toward the Tribe's tent village. Becca watched as Mo greeted the officer, shaking his hand as though she were president of the neighborhood welcome wagon. If Becca were a civilian, it might look like Office Morris was a friendly officer simply making a welfare check. But Becca could see him shifting his torso to ensure his body camera captured a good view of everyone. While Officer Morris talked to Mo, the other officer began to wander the camp, inspecting the surroundings. Becca could see she was doing her best to stay out of the kids' line of sight, but Becca's heart raced when she saw her pulling the blue latex gloves from her pocket. This meant she'd found something, potential evidence that would allow them to search their dwelling.

"Alex, over here," the officer called out. Becca saw her holding up what looked like several designer handbags. This discovery instantly shifted the casual nature of the conversation.

She wasn't sure what was happening, but Officer Morris's voice took on a more authoritative tone. "All right, I need you all to stand where I can see you. Make sure I can see your hands." Becca didn't want to get too excited, but it seemed things were now in motion. They must have found something that gave them probable cause. Now they were legally within their rights to search the Tribe's belongings. There could be evidence in the tents, something that might lead them to Ash.

"Did you hear what I said? Hands up," Officer Morris said again.

The kids ignored his commands, watching Mo. Becca could see the officers tensing, their hands lingering on their Tasers as they prepared to be challenged. Seconds ticked by. Becca held her breath, waiting.

Mo smiled. "You heard the officers," she said, obediently holding her hands up in the air, ever the martyr. The others followed suit. Officer Ghazalian produced a stack of zip ties from the trunk of the cruiser, and they began their methodical search of the kids, separating them by gender. Boys on one side of the sidewalk, girls on the other. Becca watched as Officer Morris approached the tattooed man. She could see him balling up his fists again as though he were trying to keep from exploding. One look from Mo and he relented, allowing the officer to cuff him.

Once everyone was secured the officers began a more thorough inspection of their tent city, starting at the far end and working their way down. In a matter of minutes, they had recovered dozens of stolen purses, wallets, and bags, placing them in a pile near the cruiser.

Becca heard more sirens wailing, and she inhaled, bracing herself for Wishard's arrival. She watched as an unmarked LAPD cruiser pulled up, blocking the entire street. The driver flung the car into park, and Wishard emerged from the driver's seat. She didn't even acknowledge Becca, heading straight for Officer Morris.

"Becs!" She was so focused on Wishard she didn't notice Christian emerging from the passenger's seat and heading straight for her. His department-issue shades concealed his eyes, but Becca could tell by the tension that gripped the corners of his mouth that he wasn't happy. Fucking pissed might be more accurate. "Becs, I need you to come with me. Now," he said.

"Not yet, Chris," Becca said. She wasn't going anywhere until she knew for sure that Ash wasn't in one of those tents. She turned away from him, watching as the search continued.

"Becs, please, at least come with me so we can talk," Christian said.

His plea was interrupted by one of the officers. "Detective, I found something else," Officer Ghazalian shouted, a glimmer of excitement in her voice as she held something up in the air. "There's blood on it." For a young cop, finding evidence in a murder case could be a career-making break, and this woman knew it. Becca's gaze turned to where she was holding up a knife, the blade glinting in the sun. Becca rushed forward, determined to get a closer look. She could see the knife more clearly now, with its bright silver and ivory embellishments.

She gasped. "That's Ash's knife." She'd tried to take the knife away. It was the biggest fight they ever had. Ash explained this knife was the one thing that made her feel safe. The words echoed in her head. *There's blood on it. There's blood on it.* She wondered if by relenting she'd signed Ash's death certificate. Becca pointed at Vic. "That's his tent. I saw him come out of it earlier this morning." His eyes narrowed, a menacing look in his eyes as he glared back at her.

Wishard gave Becca a curt nod and directed her attention to the officer. "Bag it. I want this entire area sealed off. I want forensics here now. No one touches anything until they arrive," she barked.

"Becs, come on, we have to go," Christian said again, reaching for her.

She shook free from him. "I said I'm not going anywhere." Becca could feel her tears falling. Ash's knife was her most treasured possession, a gift from Nate. Becca and Ash had more than a few heated discussions about Ash's insistence on bringing it everywhere she went. If the Tribe had her knife, it meant something terrible had occurred. That was the only way Ash would ever relinquish it.

Nate. He knew something. He had to. Becca swiveled her gaze over to him, and that's when she saw Nate lying on the sidewalk, slumped over, his hands cuffed behind his back, head lolling to the side, drool pooling down the front of his shirt.

266

"Chris, there's something wrong with Nate. He needs help." She was shouting now, the panic setting in as the officers raced over to him. Becca took a step forward to assist.

Christian's hands wrapped around her waist. "I swear to God if you take another step, I will cuff you myself and throw you in the back of that goddamn squad car," he said.

She stood motionless, watching as Wishard and Officer Ghazalian removed Nate's restraints and laid him down on the concrete, while Officer Morris and another officer who had just arrived kept watch over the Mo and the Tribe.

"He's got a pulse, but he took something," Wishard shouted. "Get the medics out here now." Becca tried to break free from Christian.

"They've got it under control, Becs. Right now I need you to listen to me. Ash is alive. She's alive and she needs you."

His words didn't register at first. "Did you hear me, Becs? We found Ash."

The words she'd been waiting to hear. Ash was alive. Her girl was alive. "Where is she?" Becca said.

"Cedars-Sinai. Your parents are on their way too. We need to go. Right now."

"What happened? Where did they find her?" Becca asked, her entire body buzzing with relief and uncertainty of the unknown.

"Downtown. A few blocks from the Greyhound station. A shopkeeper spotted what looked like a brawl unfolding outside his store. He called 911 and then raced to break it up. By the time he got there the attackers were gone. He found Ash and waited with her 'til the medics arrived."

"She was beaten?" Becca asked.

"She was beaten and stabbed," Christian said softly.

She absorbed the words, the reality that someone had hurt Ash, that they'd wanted her to suffer. She thought about the wounds on Nate's face. Did he attack Ash and she fought back? Was the guilt too much to cope with and that's why he'd taken something?

"We need to go now. Ash's condition is critical," Christian said.

Becca thought about how she'd left Nate before. It felt cruel to leave him again, but she had to get to Ash.

"We'll take Joanne's car and she'll find her way back," Christian said. Becca numbly followed him. Ash would be okay. She had to be. As Becca hurried toward the squad car, she glanced back at the unfolding chaos. All the kids sat on the sidewalk. They were so young, looking much less intimidating with their hands tied behind their backs. They all seemed uninterested in Nate's distress, staring vacantly into the distance. The only person who watched intently was Mo. She sat up straight, her posture impeccable despite the restraints, a look of pure delight on her face as she watched the officers working to revive him.

It's over. It's all over now, Becca told herself. There was no way this woman could hurt her or Ash. As if she'd read

Becca's mind, Mo turned, and the two of them locked eyes. Mo's smile grew even wider, almost taunting. Becca didn't blink. She wasn't one of these helpless, vulnerable kids. She wasn't letting this terrible woman intimidate her. At least that's what she told herself. But as Becca climbed into the car, despite her best intentions, she couldn't shake the feeling that somehow Mo was still pulling the strings.

BECCA

The heavy stench of antiseptic cleaners invaded Becca's nose as she raced down the halls of Cedars-Sinai Hospital, Christian keeping pace beside her. It broke her heart that Ash had been here for almost eleven hours and she didn't have a clue. She'd ranted the entire drive over about not being notified. Christian patiently explained that Ash's condition was critical when they brought her to the ER. Doctors had to stabilize her before they could get Ash's fingerprints and make an ID. Becca tried not to obsess over the fact that Ash had been through all of that alone. She was here now. Becca burst into the ICU waiting room and spotted her mother first, though she almost didn't recognize her. Virginia never left home without a full face of makeup and something designer. Today she wore an old housedress, her hair a frizzy mess, no makeup, her face tearstained. Her father was still in his jogging pants, the ones he always slept in, his face unshaven, his mouth turned down in a grimace.

"How is she? How is Ash?" Becca asked. Christian stood beside her, both anxiously waiting for any news.

"*Mija*, they wouldn't tell us anything until you got here," Rafi said.

"I'll go find the doctor," Virginia said, turning on her heels and disappearing down the hallway toward the ICU.

Rafi wrapped Becca up in a giant bear hug. "I'm telling you no matter what happens we will get through this."

She wanted to believe him. She leaned into him and he wrapped his hands around her tightly. "I was supposed to protect her," Becca whispered. Her father gently patted her back, the way he always did when she had a bad dream.

"No matter how hard we try, things happen that are out of our control. None of this is your fault," Rafi whispered. Tears streamed down Becca's face, and she could see the tears in Rafi's eyes. This was a man who had buried his only son. He didn't have to say a word. He knew exactly what she was feeling. She hugged him again, wishing she could stay right here. She could hear her mother's footsteps and saw the doctor out of the corner of her eye. Becca broke away from Rafi and rushed forward. "I'm Becca Ortiz, Ash's mother. How is ... how is she?"

The doctor was in her mid-thirties, with red hair pulled up in a ponytail and kind hazel eyes that made you trust her instantly. "Dr. Ortiz, I'm Dr. Osterman, the trauma surgeon that treated your daughter. Ash suffered multiple rib fractures, a fractured wrist, as well as contusions and bruising to her body. The main causes for concern at the moment are her internal injuries. She suffered bleeding in

the lungs and has tubes on both sides of the chest, and a
liver laceration from a stab wound to the abdomen. Inter-
ventional radiology treated her shortly after she was admitted, and we managed to stop the bleeding, though Ash's
condition continues to be critical."

The doctor was kind, though her affect was flat, as she had
developed the same trait cops employed, a careful detachment. This wasn't one of those "she'll be fine" speeches. Ash
was in a fight for her life.

"Can I see her?" Becca asked.

"Of course. We ask that you keep visitors at a minimum.
No more than two at a time," Dr. Osterman said.

"I'll go with you," Christian said, stepping forward. She
raised her hand to stop him.

"No. I want to...I'd like a few minutes alone," Becca
said. It was always Becca and Ash against the world. It
should be just the two of them now. Becca was relieved
no one put up a fight. Rafi kissed her on the cheek, and
Virginia nodded obediently, silent for a change as she sank
into one of the waiting room chairs, tightly clutching her
rosary.

"We'll be waiting right here," Christian said. Becca
couldn't speak. She needed to stay strong for Ash.

She followed Dr. Osterman through the ICU double
doors, past the nurses' station, and into a small, dimly
lit hospital room. There she spotted Ash, her sweet girl
lying in the hospital bed, looking smaller than Becca

remembered. Ash's dark hair was splayed out against the pillow, her face a ghoulish shade of gray, so swollen she appeared otherworldly.

Becca clutched Ash's hand, her skin soft and warm. It was impossible to imagine how much Ash had suffered. She thought of Mo and the others, going about their lives like nothing was wrong. She thought about what they'd done, the sheer brutality of it, and she wanted to hurt each and every one of them.

"I'm so sorry, sweet girl," Becca whispered, clutching Ash's hand. "I didn't mean to let you down." All she wanted to do was crawl into the bed and wrap her arms around Ash. Her injuries made that impossible. She would have to settle for holding her hand.

Dr. Osterman cleared her throat, signaling that she was still there. "Ash is in and out of consciousness. She may not be able to speak, but she can hear you. Talking to her may help. If you need anything, let the nurses know and they'll page me," Dr. Osterman said.

As she headed out, Becca called after her. "Did Ash say anything when they brought her in? About who did this to her?'

"She was unconscious when they brought her in. She came to for a few minutes after surgery and kept asking for her mom."

Her mom. Ash asked for her mom. The revelation landed like emotional dynamite. Becca let out a cry, holding her hand up to her mouth as if she could somehow contain the sobs threatening to explode from her. Dr. Osterman gently patted Becca on the shoulder. "I'm sorry. Are you okay?"

The woman's kind, pitying stare only made it worse. Becca closed her eyes, willing the doctor to leave. After a few seconds, she heard the door close, and Becca lost it, weepily openly, not caring who heard her.

Ash was broken and battered, but she was alive. Ash was alive and fighting. The only sound in the room was the beeping of the monitors. Becca nervously eyed the monitors above Ash's bed. Her vitals were terribly low, which made her condition even more real.

"If you could hear me, you'd probably tell me I was being ridiculous," Becca said through her tears. The quiet was disconcerting. Becca scooted even closer, grabbing her phone and searching through Ash's country playlist.

Becca pressed shuffle. Garth Brooks's "Friends in Low Places" filled the room. This was Ash's go-to karaoke song. "You can't help but smile when it's on," Ash had once said, and it was true.

Becca reached out to stroke Ash's cheek. There were so many things left for Ash to do. She was supposed to graduate high school and backpack across Europe. She deserved a chance to go to college and make bad fashion choices and find a career that fulfilled her and fall in love with someone kind and decent. Becca envisioned her trips home for Thanksgiving and Christmas, Ash regaling her with stories about annoying coworkers and promotions. She imagined Ash having her own kids, complaining about how hard it was, while Becca lovingly reminded Ash of her own rebellious years. It was possible, Becca told herself. It wasn't over yet. Ash was still here, still fighting.

"We're gonna get through this," Becca said softly. Ash's hand twitched. Taking this as a sign, Becca squeezed her hand tighter.

"Ash, it's me," Becca whispered. Ash let out a soft moan, her fingers tightening around Becca's. Ash's eyes fluttered open. "I'm here. I'm right here," Becca said over and over again. "You're so brave. The bravest person I ever met. I just need you to hurry up and get better soon because Freud misses you. He said that things just aren't the same without you around."

"Mom . . . ," Ash croaked.

There it was. The word Becca longed to hear. Ash was awake. She was talking. Becca smiled through her tears as she leaned in closer. "We've been searching everywhere for you. All of us. Nina, Rafi, and Virginia. Even Christian. Hell, half the LAPD was looking for you."

"I'm sorry. So, so sorry," Ash mumbled.

"None of this is your fault. None of it. I know who did this," Becca said.

"The Tribe. Find the Tribe," she gasped.

"I know. I found them. I found the people who did this. They're going to answer for this. I promise."

"Mo," Ash mumbled. "It's Mo."

Becca sat up a little straighter. Ash was confessing something very important. "Mo did this to you? She's the one?"

"Crazy...she's crazy. Don't let her hurt Nate. Help... him," Ash pleaded, her eyes closing again, these final words stealing her last bit of energy.

"I will, sweet girl. I promise." Ash's hands were grasping for Becca. "And I promise she can't hurt you anymore. She can't hurt anyone. You're safe," Becca said. Ash drifted back to sleep, her breathing slow and labored.

Becca sat there, thinking about Ash's plea. She'd failed Nate once before; she couldn't do it again. She wasn't sure how long she sat there watching Ash, seeing the rise and fall of her chest. She wanted to stay there forever, but Becca had to know the status of Mo and the others.

Becca leaned down and kissed Ash's forehead. "Stay strong," Becca whispered.

She returned to the waiting room, empty except for Virginia, who sat in the same chair, her eyes closed, tightly clutching her rosary and murmuring prayers under her breath.

"Mama, where did Christian go?"

Virginia startled. "Oh dear, Rebecca, you can't sneak up on me like that." She took a ragged breath. "Your father and Christian went to grab coffee. They'll be right back."

Becca's entire body was buzzing as she anxiously paced back and forth. "I need to see Chris," she said. "I have to talk to him."

Virginia stood, gently taking Becca's arm. "Rebecca, sit down before you collapse. I told you they'll be back in a few minutes."

Unsteady on her feet, Becca reluctantly sank into the chair. Virginia took out a bottle of water from her purse. She loved that about her mother. Always prepared. "Drink this. I know you're dehydrated," she said. Becca wanted to laugh. Her mother's obsession with hydration was a long-running family joke, as though it might fix all that ailed them. Becca drank thirstily until she'd finished the bottle. Becca leaned back in her seat, her stomach gurgling.

"How is she?" Virginia asked.

"She's hanging in, Mama. The things they did to her... they...they tortured her."

"Rebecca, I am so very sorry," Virginia said.

Becca couldn't help herself. "Are you?"

Virginia flinched, jerking her hands back. "What does that mean?"

"You think I don't know how you felt about Ash?"

"I don't know what you're talking about."

"Don't play dumb. I saw how you treated her like she was a houseguest who overstayed her welcome. You think I didn't hear the snide comments you made under your breath when Ash was struggling to get clean? Or should we talk about how you never once introduced Ash as part of the family? You went out of your way to make sure everyone knew she wasn't an Ortiz."

Virginia took a breath. "Is that what you think?" Her voice trembled. Becca shrugged. That's exactly what she thought.

"Rebecca, I want you to listen to me. I want you to hear every word I say. I don't hate Ash. I never...I don't hate anyone. It was just so hard. I wanted to love her, I really did. It's just...Ash reminded me so much of Robbie, that same energy and intensity. But there was darkness there too. I missed it with Robbie, but I saw it so clearly with Ash and it terrified me. I failed you when Robbie died. I know I did. I thought with Ash, I could protect you, that it was my duty to make sure you didn't end up heartbroken again."

Becca wiped at her eyes, wondering if she would ever run out of tears. "You could've said that. You could've said something. Anything."

Virginia paused as though she was struggling to find the right words. "I'm not from your generation where we over-share every single thought and feeling. After Robbie died, I was lost, Rebecca. That's no excuse, but he was my baby boy, and it took me years to find my way back. By then I'd missed so much time with you, and we were always at odds, always so different. I should've said it before. You've got such a big heart, and you gave someone the gift of love and a home. I am so proud of you. I should've said that."

She reached out and hugged Becca. It startled her. Becca tried to pull away but Virginia held on. Becca's eyes closed, taking in the hint of vanilla, her mother's signature scent transporting Becca back to her childhood days when she would lie on one side of her mother, Robbie on the other, the three of them reading in bed. There was nothing better than being in her mother's arms. She wanted to say it was all okay, but a few kind words couldn't erase years of coldness, all those years when Becca desperately needed a mother. She couldn't show up now and expect Becca to forget about it.

Out of the corner of her eye, Becca spotted Christian and Rafi heading back toward them. She slowly untangled herself from Virginia, watching as her mother's shoulders slumped. She ignored it. She wasn't going to worry about managing her mother's feelings.

"How is Nate? Did you get an update on him? Or on Mo and the Tribe?" Becca said, focusing all her attention on Christian.

"Nate's stable. The doctor said he ingested a large dose of heroin. The paramedics gave him Narcan at the scene, and he was transported to Good Samaritan Hospital. The ER doc saw a cut on his wrist and combined with the drugs, they're concerned he was trying to commit suicide, so he's been placed on a 5150," Christian said.

"Did he say anything at all about Ash?"

"He's not talking. Hasn't said a word since they brought him in."

"Maybe I could speak to him. See if I can't get through to him. Get him to tell us something."

"No one is going to let that happen. It would interfere with the investigation."

She knew the answer before she ever asked the question.

"What about Mo and the others? Have they been arrested? Or charged?"

"Not yet. Joanne's processing everyone and then she's got to do interviews. It could be hours before we know anything else."

Becca's heart was racing, thinking about Ash's confession.

"Ash said Mo was responsible for her attack. I need to speak with Wishard and tell her what she said," Becca said.

"What are the odds I can convince you to stay here and let Joanne handle things?" Christian asked.

"Less than zero," Becca responded.

Virginia sighed. "Rebecca, you've been running yourself ragged. I don't usually agree with Christian, but he's right. Let the police handle this. You should focus on Ash."

There it was. Classic Virginia Ortiz. She couldn't simply say, "I understand. Do what you need to do." Even now, even after all they'd been through, she still wasn't on Becca's side.

"No one asked for your opinion," Becca snapped.

Virginia opened her mouth. Becca braced herself for some kind of argument. That's the way things usually went. Virginia stopped herself. "Your father and I will stay here with Ash. As long as it takes. Go do what you need to do."

She considered telling her mother to leave. She wasn't

part of their lives before. Now she wanted to barge in and act like nothing had happened. Then she thought about Ash; the last thing Becca wanted was for her to wake up and find herself all alone.

"Call me if anything changes," she said to her parents, the fight fading from her, and then she turned away and headed out, her promise to make things right for Ash spurring her on.

BECCA

Half an hour later, Becca and Christian arrived at the Rampart station of the LAPD. Rampart was one of the busiest police departments in the city and chaos was commonplace. A fat shirtless drunk sat cuffed on a bench, screaming obscenities at everyone who passed. On another bench, a teenage mother tried to console her wailing toddler, and Becca clocked a homeless "frequent flier" muttering to himself in the corner.

Becca's lack of sleep and food along with this complete sensory overload left her unsteady on her feet. Christian clocked it. "Easy, Becs," he said, gently taking her arm and leading her down a long corridor.

They stopped at a small office filled to the brim. On the messy desk covered in papers and case files, Becca spotted several pictures of Wishard, one with a beaming elderly couple, Wishard in her uniform at the police academy graduation, and the other with Christian, the two of them nestled close together on a boat, Marina del Rey in the background.

She glanced at Christian, her eyebrows raised. "This is Wishard's?"

"Yeah, don't worry, Joanne gave the green light. It's just her office. It's not like she's doing ritual sacrifices here."

"That you know of," Becca said.

Christian gave a little smile; then his expression turned serious. "I know I said it before, but this could take a while. If you insist on staying here, we both figured you should be as comfortable as possible. Just don't steal anything."

"I can't make any promises. I mean, the temptation is unreal," Becca said, gesturing to the mess spread out before her. Christian laughed again, and for a second, it was like old times. Except now she was sitting in his fiancée's office, waiting to discuss her daughter's attempted murder case.

"You need to slow down and take care of yourself. I know it feels like you're all alone in this, but your family is trying. Even your mom."

"Hold up. Did hell just freeze over? You're actually defending my mother."

"I'm as surprised as you are."

He was trying to be helpful, but Becca knew that, if she wasn't careful, she would wind up on the receiving end of one of Christian's well-intentioned lectures.

"What's the status on Mo and the others?" Becca asked, changing the subject. Christian thankfully took the hint.

"I'll go check and see where things are at. I may be a while. I'm also trying to see if I can get someone to cover my shift."

"You don't have to do that."

"You may be able to shut out your mom and dad, but after everything you've pulled so far, I'm keeping a close watch on you." Becca offered Christian her best attempt at a smile. "Text me if you need anything, okay?"

She nodded and he closed the door behind him. The silence was a welcome change after the intense noise of the precinct. Becca shifted in the office chair, trying to find a comfortable position, which she realized was a futile endeavor. The room was freezing, a vent blowing down on her. She trembled, her focus drifting back to the picture of Christian and Wishard. They looked blissfully happy together, almost carefree. It was positively annoying. She blinked, trying not to stare at it. God, it was as if they were watching her, judging her, their smiles almost mocking. Becca had enough. She grabbed the photo and shoved it in the desk drawer. She leaned forward and placed her head on the desk, her eyes flickering closed.

"Becca?"

She wasn't sure if minutes had passed or hours. Becca sat upright, wiping a small puddle of drool from her mouth. Nina stood over Becca, her sleek black LAPD uniform neatly pressed. She was carrying two cups of Intelligentsia coffee, Becca's drug of choice. She held out one to Becca, who took it, the warm cup soothing her.

"I can't believe I fell asleep. What time is it?" she asked.

"Seven thirty. My shift starts soon, but I brought good-ies," Nina said, digging around in her bag and emerging with a tasty treat. "Blueberry chocolate chip muffin. Your favorite."

"You're a goddess. You know that, don't you?" Becca said.

"I do. I really do," Nina said. Becca smiled and removed the lid, taking a small sip of the steaming hot coffee. The caffeine was a much-needed jolt. She tore into the muffin as Nina pulled up a chair and scooted next to Becca. "You hanging in there?" Nina asked.

"By the smallest of smallest threads." Becca took a ragged breath. "If you saw what they did to her..."

"Ash is alive, Becca. That's what matters."

Becca sipped her coffee. She told herself that was true, but what Becca wanted now was justice. She wanted reassurances that Ash's attackers would pay for what they did, and that they wouldn't hurt anyone else. She clocked Nina's knees bouncing up and down, nervous energy fueling her. "There's something else. What is it?" Nina hesitated. "Come on. We never bullshit each other. Don't start now."

Nina sighed. "I wanted you to hear this from me. Wishard reported you going down to Skid Row by yourself. The brass wasn't happy. Not after everything that happened yesterday."

"Nina, I didn't know these were the people we were looking for. Can you imagine if I was wrong? I swear I was careful..."

Nina raised her eyebrows. "Careful? Your definition of

'careful' is going to Skid Row by yourself and confronting potentially dangerous individuals about their extracurricular murdering and kidnapping activities?" Nina asked.

Becca took a sip of her coffee. It didn't sound great when Nina phrased it that way. "Okay, so you're here to tell me what? That I'm in deep shit at work," Becca asked.

"Trust me, everyone is sympathetic. They all understand the pressure you've been under the last few days. There are people in the LAPD and Department of Mental Health who have expressed serious concern for your well-being and state of mind. They believe a temporary leave of absence might be the best course of action. Just until everything blows over."

"Blows over? What does that mean exactly? Ash dies? Or she gets well? And then what? What *exactly* is their definition of 'blow over'?"

"Becca." Nina grabbed Becca's hand. She jerked free, pushing herself back in the chair. She couldn't believe Nina was springing this on her now.

"This is why you came here? To tell me this?"

"No. I wanted to check on you and make sure you were doing okay. I also didn't want you to hear about this from someone else."

"How kind of you. Tell me, Nina, what did you say when the department asked you for your assessment? I know they must have asked what you thought about my mental health status."

Nina didn't hesitate. "I told them I didn't think you were in the right frame of mind at this point to properly do your job. I said that you needed time off to process all the trauma you've been through."

It was like being punched in the gut. "You're really telling me if one of the twins went missing, if they were out there in the city, you wouldn't break every goddamn law in order to find them."

"I don't know, Becca. All I know is you're my friend and I'm worried. I want to make sure you're okay."

There were very few situations in which Becca didn't have something to say. Right now, she was speechless. Becca thought about pleading her case, defending herself and fighting her suspension. Nina clearly expected this, anxiously awaiting Becca's reaction. She expected her friend to put up a fight. It was part of Becca's DNA. The thing was, Becca simply didn't care. Not right now.

"Tell them I'm grateful for this time to be with my family, and I appreciate their continued support in bringing her attackers to justice," Becca said, adopting the tone of the department press releases.

"Becca..."

Nina was preparing to double down on the why of it all, insisting that she loved Becca and this was in her best interests. The same bullshit speeches Becca herself had delivered a hundred times before.

Thankfully the door swung open, Christian entering with his usual blistering intensity.

"Becs, Wishard needs to see you," he said. He paused, suddenly assessing the obvious tension in the room. "Unless you need a few minutes?"

"We're good. Nina was just leaving. Don't want her to be late for her shift," Becca said pointedly. Nina reluctantly stood. She leaned down and gave Becca a kiss on the cheek. "I'm just looking out for you. Like I always have."

She headed out, offering Christian a pat on the shoulder and what could almost count as a smile. How quickly tragedies transformed people, bringing them back together, erasing years of grudges in a matter of seconds.

"You okay?" Christian said.

"I'm fine. Where is Wishard?" she said.

"Interview room. Let's go," he said, turning and leading Becca down a long gray corridor, fluorescent lights flickering on and off. He headed through the bull pen at a clipped pace. Becca trailed behind, trying to shake off her anger at Nina, at the department, at the whole damn world.

As she headed across the bull pen, Becca's gaze landed on the bright tie-dyed colors of a scarf. She blinked, gasping as she took in Mo. The woman was tucked away in a corner, sitting at a desk, her hands cuffed behind her back, chatting with a middle-aged man. There was a hawkish, almost predatory look about him, and judging from his suit, he was an attorney. They were always easy to spot, in their custom-made Brioni suits and Ferragamo wing tips. The hawkish man said something to Mo, and she laughed, throwing her head back. Becca couldn't believe it. Ash was lying in that hospital bed, fighting for every last breath, and this woman was acting like she was on a goddamn Tinder date.

"You're a monster. You're a fucking monster," Becca shouted, rushing toward her, spittle flying. "She's just a child. Why would you do that to Ash? Why?"

"I'm terribly sorry. I have no idea what you're talking about," Mo said softly.

To the outside observer, her response was sincere, but Becca heard mocking in her tone. It was the smile that nearly broke her. All rational thought faded. In a matter of seconds, Becca crossed the distance between them, wrapping her hands around Mo's neck and squeezing, wanting to erase that smile from Mo's face. The lawyer stepped back, wildly gesticulating for help.

"Somebody stop this woman. She's attacking my client. For God's sake, somebody do something."

There was more shouting. Becca ignored it. All she wanted was for Mo to confess.

"Tell them what you did to her. Tell them," Becca shouted, her hands gripping even tighter. No matter how hard Becca squeezed, the godforsaken woman never blinked, never showed even a glimmer of fear.

She would have kept squeezing if Christian hadn't pulled her away. She could feel his arms around her, pinning her arms to her sides so she couldn't move. His grip was tight. The pain was nothing compared to the rage Becca felt.

"You have to calm down," she heard Christian whisper in her ear. "Do you hear me? You can't do this. Not now."

"This is unacceptable," the lawyer muttered, returning to Mo's side now that Becca had been contained.

"It's okay, Graham. This woman is clearly troubled. I understand that. I do," Mo said.

The look on her face and the taunting tone were unbearable. Becca strained against Christian. His voice was low, barely a whisper. "Stop it. Stop it right now. She's baiting you. This is what she wants."

She heard Christian's voice, like an echo. *This is what she wants. This is what she wants.* Like a balloon deflating, Becca's rage dissipated. She blinked, clocking the brightness in Mo's eyes, that glint of pleasure at triggering Becca's outburst.

Becca turned, now acutely aware the entire bull pen had ground to a halt. Every cop, the support staff, and even some of the suspects were regarding her with pity and concern, as though Becca were the crazy one. There was no denying it. Mo had just outsmarted her. Becca instantly stopped struggling, her body going slack.

"I'm okay," she said. The officers remained, Christian still restraining her so she couldn't move. "I swear to you, Chris, I won't do anything else."

He hesitated. "Let her go, Christian. Everyone else get back to work," Wishard demanded, her tone leaving no room for argument. On her orders, Christian released Becca. For the first time she saw pity on Wishard's face. Becca's face flushed, hating that Wishard had witnessed her meltdown.

"Come with me, Dr. Ortiz," she said. This time Becca resisted the urge to look back at Mo. She followed Wishard, Christian trailing them as they hurried down another hallway. Wishard led her into a small cramped room, complete with a large two-sided mirror.

"I want to explain what happened," Becca began.

"I know what happened. Your kid is hurting and that woman pushed all your buttons. Am I right?"

Becca nodded, surprised by Wishard's understanding. "Ash woke up. She said Mo was the one who hurt her. She said it," Becca said. It felt so good to say it out loud. She would make sure Ash was heard.

"I know. Christian briefed me earlier. I'll want to get a full statement from Ash once she's awake. Right now though, I have an interview to do, and I wanted to loop you in. You're not here in an official capacity; I want to make that clear. I'm doing this because I believe you might have insight into this kid and what his damage is," Wishard said.

Becca thought about Wishard reporting her, and she wondered if this was because she felt guilty. She nodded in gratitude, watching as Wishard raised the shades covering the window to reveal Vic, "the tattooed freak" as Raya called him, sitting on the other side of the two-way glass. He was sipping a Dr Pepper and munching on chili cheese Fritos. If his surroundings intimidated him, he didn't show it.

"I'll be back," Wishard said. She slipped out of their room.

"What's going on?" Becca whispered to Christian, even though it was just the two of them.

Christian was staring at the window, watching as Wishard settled herself across from Vic.

"We got a profile on this kid. Name is Victor Zamora. He's nineteen. No parents. Spent time in over twenty foster homes. At fifteen, in his last placement, he assaulted his foster father with a hammer and disappeared onto the streets of LA. Social workers said he displayed signs of aggression and self-harm. They also said he had a low IQ, which means he could be easily manipulated. So far he's the first person in the group that's willing to talk. He even agreed to waive his rights to counsel. Said he's ready to confess."

Becca's breath caught, thinking of Ash's broken body lying in the hospital bed, the young woman on the beach. "Confess to what?" she said.

Christian leaned forward, all his attention focused on Wishard and Vic. "That's what we're about to find out."

BECCA

The air conditioner was on the fritz, a humid staleness filling the room. Becca wiped away beads of sweat, watching as Wishard sat across from Vic, holding up a piece of paper.

"Just to clarify, for the record you've agreed to waive your rights to counsel. Correct?" she said.

"Yeah, I already said it twice. Can I sign the damn form and get on with this?" he asked, wiping chip dust on his T-shirt. There was something childlike in his mannerisms and the way he spoke, a lack of awareness about others around him. Wishard placed the form in front of him. He gave it a cursory glance, scrawling his name and shoving it back toward her.

"Okay, first things first. Tell me, how long have you known Maureen Wilson, a.k.a. Mo?" Wishard asked.

"Long enough," Vic said flatly.

Wishard sighed, clasping her hands in front of her. "The condition of the agreement you just signed is that you cooperate. That means answering all our questions in full."

Vic rolled his eyes, like a petulant teenager. "I met Mo

295

two years ago. We looked out for one another. There's no law against that," Vic said.

"There is, actually. A very serious law preventing adults from cohabiting with unrelated minors," Wishard said.

"I'm nineteen. Not a minor," he said matter-of-factly.

"You were a minor when you met Mo."

Vic's eyes widened, sensing he'd just walked into a trap, but he shrugged. "Can't prove anything."

"That's true. Let me ask you this. Was your relationship with Mo sexual in nature?"

Vic leaned forward, a menacing expression in his eyes. "Say that shit again…"

Wishard was a skilled interrogator. There was no doubt about it. Her question warranted a strong reaction and she got one. She held up her hands in polite surrender. "Would you care to tell me about your relationship with the other people in your group?"

She glanced down at a file in front of her. "Kelsey, Andrea, Eli, Nate, and Leslie. Would you say you were all close?"

"Sure. Streets are a fucking war zone. You've gotta have people looking out for you."

"Is that why you all got the same tattoo? So people would know you were all together?"

"Not sure what you're talking about. I got a lot of tats," Vic asked.

"I'm talking about that one," Wishard said, pointing to the sword-and-eye combo on Vic's forearm.

"We thought it was cool. Not everything has to have some kind of deeper meaning," he said. Becca thought back to Mo's analysis of the tattoo. No way that Vic was going to admit that the tattoo was some kind of gang symbol.

"Let's talk a little about how you all survived out on the streets. I'm guessing the stolen bags and wallets we found in your possession are related."

"People lose things. If you pay attention, you can find them."

Wishard pulled out Ash's knife sealed up in an evidence bag and set it on the table. "So this weapon we found on you? Who lost this?" she asked.

"Nate gave it to me. Said he didn't need it anymore."

"And the blood we found on it, the blood that our lab is currently testing, you don't know whose blood that is?"

Vic shrugged. "Nope. Not my knife. Gotta ask Nate."

There was a quivering in his voice, and he didn't quite meet Wishard's eyes when he spoke. He was lying. Quite badly, in fact.

"Okay, you're the one who said you wanted to talk. We ID'd the body of the woman in Venice Beach. Her name is Leslie Doyle, but I'm sure you know that. You said that there were things you needed to, and I quote, 'get off your chest.' So start talking."

"Yeah, I knew her. I'm the one that beat on her. Then I slit her throat and dumped her body near the toilets."

The tiny hairs on the back of Becca's neck stood up. She was shocked by the sheer casualness with which Vic spoke about killing someone. Leslie. Her name was Leslie.

Becca couldn't begin to imagine what Leslie's parents were going through. She wondered how long she'd been missing, couldn't bear thinking about that horrible moment when the phone rang and they learned their daughter was never coming home. If Wishard was shocked by Vic's callousness, she didn't let on. She calmly reached into her folder and pulled out several autopsy photos. She placed them in front of him.

"Is this Leslie?" Wishard asked.

"Yeah, that's her," he said with a shrug.

"Did you know that Leslie had a family back in Ohio who reported her missing eleven months ago? Two parents and a ten-year-old brother who loved her very much and never stopped looking for her."

Vic shrugged like it was no big deal. Becca wanted to tell Wishard she was wasting time playing the empathy card. It wouldn't work. Vic believed in something much greater than himself. Whatever Mo wanted, Vic was willing to do.

"Why did you kill Leslie? Were you in a relationship? Did she do something to provoke the attack?" Wishard asked, gesturing to the photos.

"She got on my nerves."

"And Eli Naylor?"

Wishard laid out more photos. Becca looked away, the disturbing images of the young boy's naked body, every inch covered in bruises, his face bashed in, rendering him unrecognizable. She had seen her share of dead bodies, but she could tell this boy had suffered.

"Eli Naylor was so badly beaten the coroner initially believed his fatal wound was caused by a gunshot. Did he get on your nerves too?"

"Yeah. He was a troublemaker. So I sent him a message."

"And you did all of this by yourself, without anyone knowing or asking where Leslie and Eli went?"

"That's right. It was me. All me. You think I can't fuck someone up on my own?" Vic asked menacingly. Wishard didn't bat an eye. Becca admired how well Wishard held her own. She looked over at Christian, who was still watching Wishard intently. He clearly felt the same.

"Do I believe you're capable of committing these crimes on your own? Of course. Do I think that's what happened here? No, I do not."

"Too bad, because I did it. I killed Leslie and Eli."

"What about Ash?"

"What about her?" Vic said.

"You didn't hurt her? You weren't one of the people our witness saw beating her until she was half-dead?"

"Yeah, so what if I was. She was a nosy little bitch who got what she deserved," Vic said.

Becca swallowed hard, bile rising in her throat. The thought of this massive man kicking and punching Ash, no possible way to defend herself, left Becca sick to her stomach. Christian must have sensed she was struggling, listening to all of this. He reached out and squeezed her hand. Becca was relieved when he didn't let go.

"Would you care to elaborate? Why you felt the need to assault Ash?" Wishard asked.

Vic gazed back at her sullenly. "Okay," Wishard said, shifting in her seat, ready to try a different tactic. "Let's get back to Mo."

"I told you she's got nothing to do with any of this."

"I know that's what you said. I am actually curious; how much do you know about Mo?"

For the first time, Becca saw a glimmer of uneasiness. He shifted in his seat. "What do you mean?" he said. She saw his eyes narrowing, looking back and forth nervously as though he sensed something bad was coming.

"Where she's from? What was her life like before she wound up on the streets?"

"She said something about growing up near New York. Had a bad marriage and needed to get out."

"So she never told you her net worth is close to eleven million dollars? Did she mention she walked away from her trust fund and multimillion-dollar Malibu home to live on the streets?"

Vic's eyes widened. Becca's did too. She glanced at Christian. "Is that true?"

"Family money. A ton of family money it seems," Christian said.

Vic was still processing this news. He shook his head emphatically. "You're full of shit," he finally said.

Wishard leaned back in her chair, her hands clasped together. "I can understand this might be upsetting, but this is the truth. She had a child as well. An eleven-year-old boy she left behind," Wishard said.

Becca saw Vic's mask drop again, saw the damaged little boy trapped inside this man-sized frame, a little boy who never knew love, who was passed from home to home, used and abused, who wanted nothing more than someone to care for him.

Wishard pushed a few pieces of paper toward Vic. Glossy slips of paper straight out of a magazine. "Go on. Read all about her. The mansion she lived in, the private schools she attended. Her fancy Ivy League degrees."

Vic's body stiffened as he flipped through the clippings. "She lied to you—to all of you. For years, it seems. I understand you care about her, but she hasn't been honest. We want to help you. First you need to come clean. Tell us what role Mo played in all of this."

Vic's gaze hadn't left the paper, though Becca could see his body tensing, the muscles in his chest and arms flexed as though he were gearing up for a fight.

"Did she use you? Sleep with you and convince you that it was love?" Wishard asked.

"I told you it wasn't fucking like that," Vic said through gritted teeth. "You wouldn't understand."

"You mean she's not a sexual deviant? She's not a socio-path who uses young kids to do her bidding? You sure about that? Because the way I see it, Mo is a woman who gets kids to do terrible things and she gets off on it."

Vic's hands were trembling. Becca could see it from here. Vic was shaking his head furiously, his mask of tattoos seeming to tremble along with him.

"Here's the deal. If you tell me what happened to Ash, if you come clean about the others' involvement, including Mo's involvement in these other murders, you might actually get out of prison one day. If not, you're looking at life, possibly even death row. Do you really want to be put to death because some rich psycho conned you into killing for her?"

Becca prided herself on recognizing body language and nonverbal expressions and energy shifts. Wishard had done her job, digging in deep and pushing Vic's buttons, triggering his loyalty and devotion for Mo. Her final words were like tossing a match into gasoline.

"Chris... he's going to..." Becca was too late. They watched in horror as Vic leapt across the table and grabbed Wishard. He let out a primal scream as he slammed her against the wall, watching with a triumphant smile as she crumpled into a heap on the floor.

BECCA

In a matter of seconds, Christian was out the door, racing toward the interview room. Frozen in place, Becca watched as Vic picked Wishard up, his hands wrapped around her throat. Becca felt a strange sense of déjà vu, remembering her hands around Mo's neck. Wishard was flailing against him, trying to break free, but Vic's superhuman strength and single-minded determination spurred him forward.

The door swung open and Christian charged at Vic, knocking him off balance, forcing him to release Wishard. She dropped to the floor, scrambling to stand, leaning against the table, coughing and gasping for breath.

Christian and Vic were grappling, arms and legs everywhere, each getting off a punch. An alarm blared as two officers joined Christian, all three of them struggling to subdue Vic. He was a formidable opponent, his body a weapon he wielded with maximum efficiency, punching and kicking, thrashing on the ground. The officers were shouting and cursing, their words indecipherable. It took seconds, but it felt like ages until they were finally able to flip him onto his stomach, pinning his hands behind his back. Cuffs snapped around his wrists and he was pulled to his feet, his eyes darting around the room. He spotted Wishard, who was leaning against the table, still woozy from her assault. He lunged again. "You lying fucking bitch. Mo said you would lie. She said you would make up all kinds of lies. She's innocent. She didn't do anything. Do you hear me?"

This was his last gasp at defending the only mother he ever knew. As the two officers dragged him out of the room, he spat on the floor, his final fuck-you to Wishard.

An uneasy silence lingered once he was gone. Becca on one side of the glass, Wishard, Christian, and another officer on the other. Someone had switched off the sound. Becca could see Wishard wasn't pleased with the attention she was receiving, waving off their attempts to sit her down. She motioned for the other officer to leave and he relented. Wishard bent over, picking up her files, which were scattered across the room. Becca watched as Christian reached out for her, his hands gently inspecting her neck and face to make sure she wasn't injured. His hands caressed her face, Wishard's expression softening. She leaned into him and let him hold her.

Becca suddenly felt very uncomfortable watching this intensely personal moment. She forced herself to look away. Now that Wishard was okay, Becca focused on what Vic had said.

He'd exonerated Mo, which meant they'd still need proof she was guilty. Ash's testimony would be crucial.

Becca's mind drifted to the worst-case scenario, and what might happen if Ash didn't pull through. She shook away the thought. She wouldn't underestimate Ash.

The door slowly opened, and Becca turned to see Wishard returning, carrying her file folder, acting as though it were business as usual.

"Joanne, don't walk away from me. First, you need to see a doctor. Then you need to file a report. This assault has to be on the record," Christian said, almost shouting. He didn't even acknowledge Becca, his focus solely on Wishard.

"I told you I don't want you micromanaging this. I said I'm fine. Now, you can have a seat while Dr. Ortiz and I talk, or you can leave."

Becca admired Wishard for standing up to Christian, but she also knew that Wishard had just suffered a serious trauma. Becca could see hand-shaped bluish bruises beginning to form on her neck. "Are you sure you're okay? That guy went at you pretty hard," Becca said, her therapist training kicking in.

"It was a calculated risk. Now I know how committed he is to his lies."

"I can say without question that nothing will shake his faith in Mo," Becca said.

"I'm glad we agree. I'm convinced Maureen Wilson was calling the shots, and those kids were her pawns, but I can't prove it yet."

Maureen Wilson. The name rolled around in Becca's head. It was a name befitting an East Coast Ivy Leaguer. "What's she saying?" Becca asked.

"Nothing. First thing she did when she was arrested was lawyer up. Made one phone call and within thirty minutes, the top defense attorney in the state and his minions arrived."

"So it's true? Mo's rich?" Becca asked.

"Old East Coast money. Her grandfather started a hedge fund in the 1920s; her father, Francis Forrester Jr., took it over and turned it into a billion-dollar empire. According to *Forbes*, Mr. Forrester is the three hundredth richest man in the world and very politically active. He's donated to political causes, including our very own mayor's reelection."

"Who you won't be surprised to hear is now very interested in this investigation," Christian interjected. Becca's stomach turned, thinking about all those kids who had gone missing, the runaways vanishing onto the streets of LA, and how no one gave a shit.

"Old money talks," Wishard said, a hint of bitterness in her voice.

"What brought Maureen to LA?" Becca asked.

"Apparently, while attending grad school at Columbia, she met her future husband, a man by the name of Paul Wilson. A Malibu local, he was attending law school in New York. They relocated shortly after he graduated."

She handed Becca the same file she'd shown Vic. On top was a printout from an old issue of *Los Angeles Magazine*. "LA's Biggest Heart," the headline read, complete with a full-length color picture of Maureen Wilson. The picture was at least fifteen years old. Maureen was late twenties, wearing a Ralph Lauren white silk blouse and black linen trousers, looking out over the balcony of a massive Malibu estate, the Pacific Ocean sparkling in the background, her hair perfectly blown out. The caption under her picture read "Maureen Wilson at home in Malibu." If it weren't for that unmistakable smile, Becca might not have even recognized her. That goddamn smile.

Becca scanned the article, the writer waxing poetic about Maureen's dedication and commitment to helping others. Over the years, Maureen worked for half a dozen nonprofits, using her financial connections to raise millions. She earned money for health care and education programs for teenagers and low-income mothers. In an effort to break the cycle of incarceration, she created a nonprofit that helped connect fatherless young men to male mentors.

Mrs. Wilson could be content with organizing galas or hobnobbing with celebrities. Instead, she spends her days in run-down classrooms and fading downtown office buildings working alongside students, young mothers, and ex-cons. "My goal is to make an impact; to be on the ground floor, working with the kids and their families, getting to know who they are, learning about their hopes and dreams, and doing everything in my power to make them come true."

"Mrs. Wilson is our hero," said sixteen-year-old Gustavo Trevino, from South Central Los Angeles. "All of us love coming to the center. I'm learning how to code, and Mrs. Wilson helped me land a summer internship in Silicon Valley. Without her, none of this would be possible."

Becca scanned the pages in the file. Nothing indicated why Mo had ended up on the streets. But there was always a trigger in someone's life, something pivotal that caused their downward spiral. "Any arrests? Or psychiatric episodes?" Becca asked.

Wishard tossed down more pieces of paper. "It appears Maureen didn't play well with others. There was a roommate in college who filed a complaint with the university charging her with harassment and intimidation. A few weeks later it was dismissed. A year after that, a colleague at a start-up in Brooklyn filed harassment charges with the NYPD, which coincided with Maureen's relocation to the West Coast. From what I've gathered, she was on her best behavior for years. Nothing unusual. She got married, worked various jobs. Had her son."

"I can't believe she left him behind," Becca said.

"Yeah, he was eleven when she left. He's thirteen now," Wishard said, not pleased with the interruption. Becca kept quiet. This was important. If Mo cared for this child, bonded with him and their relationship were threatened, it could be enough to cause her to snap.

Wishard continued. "It was around that time her coworker, a woman named Aura Vasquez, filed a harassment claim with the human resources department of the nonprofit Maureen worked at. She said their relationship started out friendly. Maureen even mentored her in the beginning. But as the young woman began to receive promotions, Maureen suddenly turned on her. She kept sending her e-mails and texts criticizing her work, insisting she wasn't pulling her weight, going behind her back and slandering her to her fellow employees. Aura filed a complaint with HR and said it got worse. That Maureen started making veiled threats, and Aura was convinced she'd been following her. When HR refused to take further action, Aura filed a restraining order with the LAPD. A verbal altercation occurred outside their place of work resulting in Mo's termination. The court ordered that Maureen receive a psychological evaluation. Unfortunately, the therapist determined there was no threat."

"Who was the therapist?" Becca asked.

Wishard checked the file. "Dr. Carlton Stowers. He's on staff…"

"At UCLA," Becca interjected. Dr. Stowers was one of Becca's first professors in grad school, a man who adored the sound of his own voice. He was well sought after, appearing all over the country as a mental health expert. Defense lawyers loved him because for the right price, you could purchase whatever diagnosis you wanted.

"According to Dr. Stowers's report, Maureen Wilson had anger management issues, but he stated, 'Mrs. Wilson poses no threat to the victim nor does she meet the criteria for inpatient treatment.' He called the victim's claims 'a sincere misunderstanding.'"

Becca shook her head. "I'm assuming Dr. Stowers's assessment proved incorrect," Becca said.

"I would say so. A few weeks after Maureen's evaluation, Aura was brutally beaten outside her apartment. The attack nearly crippled her. A few days after that, a fire broke out at Maureen's home. Her husband and kid barely made it out alive."

"Hold up, she set fire to her own home? Tried to kill her own family?" Christian asked.

Becca could hear the disgust in his voice, the sense of disbelief. It was a rhetorical question, of course. Plenty of people did terrible things to those they loved.

"Witnesses at both scenes identified a sixteen-year-old boy, Carlos Ochoa, one of the interns Maureen mentored at her nonprofit. The kid took the fall for the assault, arson, and attempted murder. But the detectives assigned to the case were convinced Maureen put him up to it. They couldn't prove it, and then Maureen vanished. Until today."

If Becca allowed herself to think about the damage Mo

inflicted on others, not just Ash, it would paralyze her. What she had to do was focus on the science, the question everyone always wanted to know when crimes like this were committed. Why? What made someone like Mo do such terrible things?

"I haven't been able to examine Mo...Maureen extensively, so this is all based on what I've heard and seen so far. We know Maureen comes from privilege. Let's say she didn't have a lot of love and support in her life. She doesn't understand give-and-take. For her everything was transactional. She wanted to call the shots, be in charge, be the person people looked up to. Over the years, she sought out people she could control. When they resisted her efforts or fought to gain independence, she lashed out, determined to hurt them before they hurt her. Something triggers her, and she walks away from this life, and the pattern continues, only this time it's with these vulnerable kids. Kids like Vic and Nate, with no family or support system and zero self-esteem. She gives them what they need. At first it's the basics, food and shelter; then it's emotional support. She builds them up, makes them feel loved. She becomes this motherly figure who fills the void in their lives."

"Okay. What motivates them to start killing?" Wishard asked.

"People like this, their delicate sense of self-worth relies on no one ever challenging them or second-guessing them. When something goes wrong, when she's slighted or

311

perceives some kind of slight, she loses it. She wants revenge. She doesn't strike me as the type who likes getting her hands dirty. I bet Vic is telling the truth that he did the killings, but I can almost guarantee she ordered it, and even watched. I don't believe Mo was having sex with these kids. She was fucking with their minds, which is even more powerful. I believe she sanctioned these crimes and was at times an enthusiastic observer. These kids become her proxy, willing to steal, kill, go to prison for her. There's nothing she can't convince them of once she's earned their love."

Wishard sighed and took off her glasses, rubbing her tired, bloodshot eyes. "It's a solid theory. Trouble is we have zero evidence to hold her. I was hoping Nate would say something to implicate her, but the detective I sent over said it's no use. Kid's gone mute. We've got nothing but theories, which won't hold up in court."

"What about the kid who attacked the coworker and Maureen's family?" Christian asked.

"He turned eighteen last year and was moved from the juvenile facility to big-boy prison. I've got someone heading out to Victorville to speak to him, but it's a long shot. He never wavered in his story. He said the attacks were all his idea."

"And Mo's husband?" Becca asked, hearing the desperation in her voice.

"Won't even speak to us. His lawyer said he wants nothing to do with Maureen or this investigation."

Wishard leaned against the door, her arms crossed, a

defensive posture that told Becca she was preparing herself to deliver bad news. God, she wasn't sure she could handle bad news. "Dr. Ortiz, I need you to understand all we've got on Maureen is criminal trespassing, identity theft for the stolen IDs we found, and cohabitating with minors. Her lawyer is a real shark. Unless I can find something incriminating to hold her on, I'm afraid she will make bail."

Becca shook her head. "You have Ash's confession. I heard it. She told me Mo was the one. Mo was responsible. That has to be enough."

Wishard rubbed her neck, an angry bruise beginning to form. Wishard shot Christian a pointed look. "I wish it was. You wanna explain this to her?"

"Explain what?"

"Becca, your recent actions, the hostage situation in Hollywood, you going down to Skid Row today, that outburst in the bull pen, compounded with your family's history and what happened with Robbie, means your statement might not hold much weight," Christian said gently.

Of course. Becca understood instantly. They would paint Becca as the crazy person. Everything she'd done to this point, all the risks she took, were about ensuring Mo was arrested for her crimes. Now it was all backfiring. They were just going to let Mo walk away, no justice for her and all those other kids. Becca thought about relenting. Heading back to the hospital and sitting with Ash. But that wouldn't do her any good. Ash was in good hands. It was up to Becca to keep her promise. She stood up quickly, her legs giving out. She nearly tumbled to the ground. Christian and Wishard moved in unison to catch her before she fell.

"Dr. Ortiz, are you okay?"

"Becs, what is it? What's wrong?"

She didn't speak for a second, sucking in air. "It's my blood sugar. I haven't eaten anything...," she said, trailing off.

"Stay here. I'll grab you something from the vending machine," Christian said.

Wishard eased Becca back into the chair, reaching over and switching on a fan, cool air filtering through the humid room.

"I'm afraid I have to get back. I want to assure you none of us are giving up. We're going to get them all. We just need to be patient and do things by the book."

"I understand," Becca said. She put her head in her hands, doing her best to look as pitiful as possible, hoping it would motivate Wishard to go. She waited until the door was closed and then sprang to her feet. She hated playing the damsel in distress, but her ruse worked. She rushed over to the computer tucked into the corner. As a member of the LAPD, Becca was granted access to the department's database. This allowed her to search a variety of records, ranging from DMV records to arrest reports. Becca typed in her password.

"ACCESS DENIED" appeared on the screen. The LAPD

certainly didn't waste any time removing her security clearance. Nervously eyeing the door, Becca weighed her options. She could wait for Christian to return with snacks and an offer to drive her back to the hospital, or she could say, "Screw it." Becca took a deep breath, knowing she was crossing a line if she did this, but she did it anyway. She entered Nina's password, her son and daughter's birthday, hoping Nina hadn't changed it.

The search screen popped up. Becca typed in the name *Paul Wilson*. Within seconds, she located his driver's license photo and address. She snapped a picture with her phone and logged off. She remembered Christian's promise not to let Becca out of his sight. She had to get out of here before he came back. Becca grabbed her bag and slowly opened the door.

She took a quick glance, relieved that the hallway was empty, and then fast walked out, heading toward the front of the station, holding her breath and praying they wouldn't see her. Wishard said she needed more concrete evidence, something that might connect Mo to these crimes. If anyone could fill in the blanks about Mo, it was her ex-husband. Becca didn't care what rules or laws she had to break. All that mattered was stopping this woman before she hurt anyone else.

BECCA

Thirty miles west of Los Angeles sits the coastal paradise of Malibu. At one time a coveted Spanish land grant, Malibu was passed down to a succession of wealthy Los Angeles families. In the 1950s, surfers discovered these beaches. Today, Malibu was home to a few devoted locals and celebrities who could afford to pay millions of dollars for their piece of paradise.

Becca sat perched on the hood of her car, sipping the worst cup of 7-Eleven coffee she'd ever tasted. Today the skies were a bluish gray, the beaches empty apart from the locals and the hard-core surfers refusing to let a little bad weather ruin the quest for the perfect wave. She envied their freedom, longed for her own escape from this nightmare she was trapped in. Becca used to hate going to the beach, and then she met Ash. There was something magical about seeing this place through Ash's eyes. Somehow Becca didn't mind the endless traffic jams she had to endure to get there, or the overpriced parking or jockeying for the best spot on the beach. It was all worth it, seeing the sheer joy on Ash's face as she launched herself into the waves over and over again, laughing as Freud barked and splashed along-side her.

Becca's phone buzzed. A steady stream of texts from Christian poured in, saying that he was worried, that she needed to check in so he would know that she was okay.

Ignoring the pang of guilt, she switched off her phone and focused her attention on a middle-aged man in a wet suit emerging from the water, a surfboard under his arm. She watched as he grabbed his things and jogged down the beach. Becca recognized Paul Wilson instantly. He was six feet tall, with a deep golden tan and a lean athlete's body. His nose was a bit too large for his face and just slightly off-center, which made him slightly less handsome, instead giving him an air of approachability. There was something guarded in his movements though, as if he were constantly analyzing any and all situations.

"Mr. Wilson? Paul Wilson?" she called out, rushing to catch up to him.

His eyes darted over, sizing up Becca. "I'm Paul," he said, the mistrust etched in his defensive stance and clenched hands.

"My name is Dr. Becca Ortiz. I'm with the LAPD. I'd like to speak with you about Maureen." Becca wasn't here in an official capacity, but Paul didn't need to know that.

Paul's lips tightened, and he scanned the area as though someone were watching them. "How did you find me here? Who told you I was here?" he snapped.

"Your neighbor at the trailer park," Becca said.

"I've told that nosy woman to mind her goddamn business," Paul said, shaking his head angrily. He turned away, his pace quickening as he hurried away from Becca, heading back toward the trailer park he now called home. Most people didn't even know there were trailer parks in Malibu though this wasn't your typical trailer park. It was designed for maximum visibility and eye-pleasing aesthetics. With some of the trailers priced at over a million dollars, the *New York Times* once called it "America's most glamorous trailer park."

"Please, I have to speak with you," Becca pleaded, practically jogging to keep up.

He avoided looking at her as he spoke. "You people need to learn to communicate. My lawyer spoke to the detectives already. I told them I don't care what Maureen did. Unless you came to tell me she's dead, I don't care about her at all. So whatever it is you're looking for, whatever terrible unspeakable thing she's done, I'm not interested," he spat out.

"Mr. Wilson, I'm here to talk about my daughter. She's in the ICU at Cedars-Sinai, fighting for her life right now, and I believe..." She was almost shouting at Paul, trying to get him to hear her. He never broke his stride. In fact, he was moving even faster, darting through parked cars, until he reached an Airstream, a sleek and shiny metallic contraption. Out front was a small herb garden with a Buddha statue and meditation bench tucked into the corner. Less than seven hundred square feet, Becca estimated. A far cry from his multimillion-dollar mansion. Paul reached for the door.

"I'm begging you for five minutes of your time," Becca pleaded, reaching out to grab him. She could see his hands were shaking, his eyes darting toward the trailer.

"I said I don't want to talk to you," he shouted, shoving Becca away. This was an act born out of frustration, not malice. Unfortunately, Becca was operating on very little sleep, and her reflexes were slow. She went tumbling backward, landing hard on a small bed of rocks. Unable to stop herself, she let out a cry.

"Dad?" a voice called out. The door to the trailer swung open, revealing a teenage boy. He had his father's tall, athletic build, but he was unmistakably Maureen's son, with her same brown hair and piercing blue eyes. He was handsome by any definition, even with the deep red burns, angry thick scars that marred the entire right side of his face. Becca remembered Wishard's words. "There was a fire." She recalled Christian's horror that this woman had wanted her own son dead. She hadn't gotten her wish, but this boy was forever scarred.

"Aidan, get back in the house."

"What's wrong? Is everything okay? Are you okay?" the young man said, eyeing Becca, confusion and suspicion all rolled into one. She hated coming here, intruding in this peaceful world they'd created, bringing Maureen Wilson back into their lives. It wasn't fair to him, but Becca was out of options.

"Get back inside, and do not open the door again," Paul Wilson said. He waited until his son shut the door, and then knelt down beside Becca to inspect her injuries.

"I didn't mean to . . . I wasn't trying to hurt you."

"I'm okay," she said. "I just need to catch my breath."

He gestured to a cut on her arm from the rocks, a small bit of blood beginning to form.

"Sit tight for one second. I'll grab a first aid kit."

"That's not necessary. I don't need it," she said.

He hesitated, still kneeling beside her. "You don't understand what it was like. I can't go through this. Not again. If you don't go, I'll have no choice but to—"

"Call the cops? I work for the LAPD. They'll send me away with a warning and I'll come back here. I'll keep coming back until you talk to me."

Becca held his gaze, wanting him to see she wasn't giving up. Hell, she would set up camp in this goddam garden if she had to. Paul sighed heavily and placed his hand in hers, lifting her up off the ground. He gestured to the small garden table tucked in the corner. She took a seat in one of the wrought-iron chairs.

"The last thing I want is to upset you. I came here today because I believe your wife was responsible for assaulting my daughter, and I need answers."

She reached into her pocket and held out her phone, Ash's face appearing on the home screen. "Ash is in the ICU. She was beaten and stabbed and left for dead on a street in downtown LA. It's not just Ash. There have been a series of murders, and we believe she orchestrated them. Right now we can't prove it. I'm here because if she goes free, she will hurt other people."

"Jesus Christ, it never ends," Paul said, his shoulders slumping, the posture of a defeated man. He looked away from Ash's picture as though the image physically pained him. She tucked her phone back into her pocket and waited for him to speak.

"Aidan just turned thirteen. Your daughter, how old is she?" Paul asked.

"Sixteen and a half. Ash is…she's my foster daughter. The things she's been through in her life, the things she's overcome. She's a remarkable person." Becca's voice broke. She paused. "I promised I would protect her."

"I made my son the same promise," Paul said.

They sat in silence. Becca could sense he was waging a war with himself. "It's not your fault. None of this is your fault," Becca said.

"That's in the shrink handbook. My own therapist used to say it once a session before I fired him."

Becca didn't disagree. It *was* in the shrink handbook. In all her years as a clinician, she never found a more appropriate phrase. "Afraid it's all I've got right now. I'm all tapped out on forgiveness and understanding when it comes to what's happened these last few days. I can't imagine what it's been like for you and your son."

"We've learned to manage," he said, reaching under the table and pulling out a small wooden box. From inside, he unearthed a tightly rolled joint and a lighter. He lit the tip and took a deep inhale. He closed his eyes, allowing the high to wash over him. He offered the joint to Becca. "No, thanks," Becca said. She needed to be as clearheaded as possible.

"I saw half a dozen shrinks who had all kinds of well-meaning advice. At some point, I couldn't talk about Maureen anymore. Couldn't analyze or discuss or second-guess everything. I had to focus on Aidan."

"I understand. I'm just here because I want to stop her. To do that I need to understand her. Who is she? What makes her tick? What broke her?" Becca said.

"You think I have any clue? I don't know who the hell she is. I never did."

"You were together for a long time. There had to be signs, something that signaled Maureen wasn't well, that she was capable of doing the terrible things she's done," Becca said.

"Of course there were signs. Not ones that hinted at a violent streak, but there were signs something was wrong. I see it all now. When we first met it was so subtle, kind of like LA weather. You get so used to the endless sunny days, you forget about the power of the storms. Maureen and I met in college. She was like this—this powerhouse, with all these ideas and optimism. I met her at a frat party, watched everyone, men and women, orbit around her. I told my buddy I thought she was cute and he said, 'Go for it, man. You'll be set for life.' Turns out her family was loaded. I didn't really care about her money. I grew up in Santa Monica. Raised by a single mom in a one-bedroom apartment, but I got a scholarship to Harvard-Westlake so I went to school with millionaires. I wasn't worried. I told myself I'd make my own way. I ended up in New York for law school. I wanted to play around, enjoy the new city, have some fun. I definitely wasn't looking to get serious. I guess Maureen saw something in me. Her first project," he said bitterly.

"Her project? What does that mean?" Becca asked. In her head, she could hear Ash's voice. "Stop acting like a TV shrink," she would say. Paul didn't seem to notice.

"Maureen always found a way to tap into what you needed. One evening after we began dating, I casually mentioned that when I was a kid I loved watching shows where good things happened to people. You know, like when Oprah gave all those people a car, or some TV show paid off someone's medical bills. A week later, Maureen shows up at my apartment and says we're going on an adventure. She takes me to the Times Square subway station and hands me a stack of pre-loaded MetroCards. It must have been ten thousand dollars in cards. 'Hand them out to whoever you want,' she said. I couldn't get over it. Another time she hosted a party for these kids at this cancer charity she volunteered with. Brought in rescue puppies to play with the kids. God, you should've seen the smiles on their faces. She lived and breathed joy and excitement, and I knew six months in I was going to marry her. She seemed so good and pure and unconcerned with labels. She married a nobody with less than ten thousand dollars to his name. It wasn't until later I discovered that Maureen fed off that stuff. She loved the underdog. She targeted them. She was relentless in her approach. Flattery along with a steady stream of presents and all kinds of adventures she'd planned. What I like to call a full-blown charm offensive. It was intoxicating. The trouble began when someone resisted her efforts. It made her even more determined to win them over. The more they resisted, the harder she worked to bend them to her will."

"And if they didn't bend?" Becca asked, though she already knew the answer.

"She broke them," Paul said matter-of-factly.

"Is that why you left New York?" Becca asked.

Paul took another hit from the joint. "Yeah, only I thought we were moving here to keep her safe. You see, a few days after I'd taken the bar exam, Maureen comes home in tears and explains that a girl from work had become obsessed with her. She said she was making trouble at work.

I understood how someone could become obsessed with Maureen. I know I was. There was talk of the police getting involved. Maureen's father's eventually intervened and that talk ended, but she was so on edge. My mom's health wasn't great, and we'd talked about starting a family. I suggested we move back to LA, and Maureen agreed. It seemed like the right move for both of us."

"And it was?"

"For a while things were good."

"Mr. Wilson, I'm trying to understand Maureen's mental state. What were those early years with Aidan like?"

"She took to motherhood with the same intensity she did everything. I was a new lawyer trying to prove myself at a cutthroat firm, so I wasn't always the most consistent presence, but I didn't see any red flags. It wasn't until Aidan got older that it all began to crumble. When he was little, Maureen loved Aidan. I mean, she was literally the definition of helicopter parent, practically smothering him with love and affection. As he got older, she wanted him to stay her sweet, malleable baby, and he wanted his independence. He didn't worship her the way she needed, and it triggered something. I came home from work one day when he was ten, and Maureen told me, 'I got a job.' I always supported her working. This job was different. It became Mo's obsession. She would leave at dawn. Return home at midnight or later. She barely saw Aidan, and when she did, she had no interest in him whatsoever. I didn't know what the hell was happening. Whenever I would broach the subject, she shut me down, telling me her work required her ultimate focus. 'He's fine without me,' she used to say."

Paul snorted. "Can you imagine saying that a child is perfectly fine without his mother? The kid suffered. He wanted and needed her. As time went by, Maureen grew more and more annoyed by minor things at work. Let's say a coworker received praise for something. She would stew about it, analyzing the slight, agonizing over why she wasn't getting credit for all she'd done. We'd be at dinner days later, or at one of Aidan's soccer games, and all Maureen could talk about was work. Ranting and raving about this woman, Aura, and how she was sabotaging everything Maureen did. She always took her work seriously, always needed to be valued and appreciated. I chalked it up as a product of her environment. Growing up in that kind of wealth is…"

"Exhausting?" Becca said. Some of her most privileged were also the most depressed, anxious, and unfulfilled.

A sad smile escaped from Paul. "It is exhausting. Which is why I left it all behind. Legally I was entitled to half of Maureen's assets. I didn't want a dime. There's a trust fund set up in Aidan's name. When he turns twenty-one, he can do what he wants with it, but as far as I'm concerned her money is poison."

"I understand. I do," Becca said.

Paul took a final drag of the joint and stubbed it out. "About six months before she disappeared, Aura accused

Maureen of violating the nonprofit's policy by spending time with the teenagers outside of designated hours. Rumors were going around that Maureen was taking these kids to dinners and on shopping sprees. Many staff members thought these relationships were inappropriate."

"Were they?" Becca asked.

"Not in the way you might think. I was never under the impression sex was involved. Was Maureen manipulating those kids? Hell yes."

"She was grooming them," Becca said. It was the same behavior a pedophile used trying to lure a child into a van.

"Exactly. But this accusation that she was being inappropriate enraged Maureen. Of course she didn't walk away. That wasn't her style. She doubled down. She wasn't even subtle about it, taking the kids to Lakers games, shopping trips to Rodeo, renting them rooms at the Four Seasons. Aura was pissed. Maureen's disregard for the rules became her hill to die on. She wanted Maureen to admit her wrongdoing and step down. Maureen said no fucking way. It went back and forth. Eventually the board worried that a potential scandal could affect the organization's fundraising efforts, and asked for Maureen's resignation. In exchange they would provide her with a reference. When she refused, they fired her. After that things went downhill fast. She kept going on and on about there being a conspiracy to destroy her and ruin her good name."

"Clearly at this point, you knew this was some kind of mental health issue?"

"Hell yes. I was aware of that for at least a year before all this went down. I tried to get Maureen to see a therapist, and she turned on me. She said I was like everyone else, I wanted her to fail, I'd turned my back on her and ruined Aidan in the process. Next thing I know she's moved into the guest room. She started staying up all night, sending threatening e-mails to Aura and the organization. The harassment got so bad, several of her former coworkers called me, insisting if I didn't stop her, they would go to the police."

"So Maureen never was never diagnosed with anything?"

"Not that I know of. Maureen's mother died of cancer when she was nine, and she was raised by her father. Excuse me, raised by her father's staff of nannies. He was staunchly against psychotherapy. Called it fake science. As far as he was concerned, his daughter could do no wrong, and there was nothing wrong with her. I finally got so desperate I called him..."

Becca was used to skepticism when it came to mental health issues, especially among the megarich and the very poor. "Let me guess, he suggested Maureen needed rest?"

"Offered to send her to a spa in Switzerland, a place her mother loved. Said it would help her 'clear all that nonsense up.'" Paul scoffed. "Next thing I know the police show up and start asking all these questions, like if we know anything about Aura being assaulted. Maureen said she didn't know anything about it, but a few days later, our home is set on fire, and my kid is in the hospital fighting for his life. They said the main suspect was a sixteen-year-old kid, one of Maureen's students at the nonprofit. Maureen was insistent that she didn't know anything, and then she vanished. Gone just like that," Paul said, snapping his fingers.

"But they caught the kid?"

"He wasn't exactly a criminal mastermind. He was at his mother's house when the cops busted him. They found bloody clothes, lighter fluid in his bedroom. He took the fall for everything. The attack. The fire. He told the cops that people were 'hurting Maureen, and they needed to pay.'"

"So now this kid is locked up for twenty-five years for something Maureen made him do?" Becca asked.

"It's fucked up, isn't it?" Paul replied. Becca nodded in agreement. The more she witnessed what people did to one another, the more screwed up everything seemed.

"I keep telling myself she's insane. It's easier to cope if I believe that. Then I think about everything she's done and it's all so calculated. I can't seem to reconcile the two."

Becca had dedicated her whole life to trying to understand what made people tick, why they reacted to things the way they did. "Ted Bundy was insane. He also knew exactly what he was doing when he murdered those women. If he hadn't been caught he would've kept doing it. Same with Jim Jones before he ordered the assassination of a congressman and the mass death of his hundreds of followers. Crazy people can also be highly functional, rational even. Do I think Maureen's capable of being rehabilitated? From what I've seen, no," Becca said. "Which means she's a danger to anyone who gets in her way. That's why if you can think of anything you didn't tell the cops…"

"Hold up. I never said I would speak to the cops."

Becca leaned back, stunned that she hadn't made herself clear, that she assumed they were on the same side. "Mr. Wilson, the police need your help. Detective Wishard is the lead investigator in this case. If you went to her, asked to speak to Maureen, you might be able to reach her…"

Paul cut her off. "You think I would ever step foot in the same room with that woman after what she did to us?" He shook his head, and she clocked a slight tremor in his hand.

"Do you know what it's like to wake up to the sound of your son screaming in agony? I swear to you at least once a week I wake up in the middle of the night to that scream. It sounds so real. I relive that night over and over again. Even after I grabbed Aidan and got him out of the house, even after I managed to cover his body with my own, lying there on the grass, I had to wait for the medics, watching as he writhed in agony, his screams growing louder and louder, as part of his goddamn face melted off. I knew his mother was responsible for this. I knew it. She wanted us both dead. I live with that every single day. That is my reality. Enough time has passed that Maureen has forgotten about us. That's all I wanted. I know I might sound callous or selfish, but my job is looking after Aidan. Let's say I get involved, and Maureen finds out. Who do you think she's targeting next?"

"We can protect you. The police will protect you."

He scoffed. "Like they protected your daughter? You work for the goddamn police and she still got to her." He shook his head, his hands trembling again as he fumbled with the lighter. "I'll say it again, there's no fucking way I'm getting near any of this."

Becca could feel tears forming, the sense of failure returning. "You're going to turn your back on my daughter? On all the other kids Maureen hurt, on the families she's destroyed?"

"If it means keeping Aidan safe, hell yes," Paul said. He moved quickly, standing up and crossing the distance from the patio table to the door of the Airstream in a matter of seconds. Becca followed, but it was too late. He slammed the door in her face, effectively shutting her out.

Becca stood there in disbelief. She thought about pounding on the door, screaming until he returned or the neighbors complained. It was clear he'd made up his mind. Even if he had a smoking gun to implicate Mo, he wasn't talking. Becca didn't agree with him, but she understood. A parent has an obligation to protect their child at all costs.

She headed out of the trailer park and made her way back to her car. The beach was desolate, only a few sightseers with cameras, and wayward seagulls searching for food. Becca climbed inside the car and yawned. She was exhausted and still had no leads for Wishard. For once, she was out of ideas. Becca leaned her head on the steering wheel.

A tapping on the window startled her. She jerked upright and saw Aidan Wilson staring back at her. Surprised, Becca wiped away her tears, trying to seem put together, and opened the door. She scanned the beach for any sign of Paul.

"My dad...he wouldn't want me to be here, but I had to talk to you." His voice wavered. Becca hesitated. The last thing she wanted to do was piss off Paul Wilson. She wasn't sure Aidan could help.

"I don't know if that's a good idea," Becca said.

"I heard you talking about my mom. She hurt someone else, hasn't she?"

"She hurt a lot of people. But we don't have any proof."

Aidan gestured to his scarred face. "I'm the proof, don't you think?" Becca couldn't imagine what it was like to wake up every day and see them—a permanent reminder of his mother's cruelty. She wished they were proof.

"I wish that were enough. The only witness that knows what Mo...Maureen...did is my daughter, Ash, and she's in the ICU, unconscious and fighting for her life. I know what you've been through, but without eyewitness testimony, or a confession, the police don't have enough to build a case. They need something to establish a pattern, something that says Maureen's responsible."

Aidan shifted from foot to foot, nervously kicking at the sand with his flip-flops. "Dad's not a bad person. He's pretty awesome. Gave up his career, all the money and stuff so we could have a simpler life. He's just scared. I'm not. Not anymore. I just don't want her to hurt anyone else." Becca was impressed. He was so matter-of-fact, so resilient in spite of everything he'd been through. Aidan opened his backpack and pulled out a manila envelope.

"What's this?" Becca asked, reaching for it. She opened it up to find a stack of letters inside.

"It's the proof you need to show everyone that my mom is a total fucking psycho."

BECCA

Becca studied the envelope, Aidan's gaze watchful and a little uneasy. "I don't understand. What is this?" He sighed, twisting his hands nervously, darting glances across the parking lot as though any minute his father might come racing over and rip the envelope from her hands.

"They're letters. Tons of 'em. From Carlos, the kid that attacked my mom's coworker. The one who set the fire that nearly killed us. That kid wrote her hundreds of letters. They're all about how much he cared about my mom, and how sad he was people were out to get her. He talks about their 'plan.' Setting the fire. Beating up that woman. He said he trusted her and would do anything to help her out. She promised him all kinds of things if he did what she asked. Money. An apartment. Even a Camaro. He wanted a red Camaro. All he had to do was get rid of her... her problems," Aidan said. He stumbled over the word, a reminder that he was the problem she wanted to get rid of.

"How did you... I mean, where did you find these?"

"My mom's office safe. I knew it was off-limits, but I

had this dumb idea..." He stopped, furiously kicking at the sand beneath his feet.

"What is it, Aidan?" Becca said.

"I used to think I might find something, like some kind of clue that would explain why she didn't love me anymore." Aidan ran a hand through his mop of hair. "She left her safe open one day. It was never open, and that's when I found the letters. All I could think about was how she loved this other kid more than me."

Becca's heart broke for him. "Whatever was going on with your mom, it had nothing to do with you. You know that, don't you?"

He shrugged, clearly not believing a word Becca said.

"Why didn't you tell your dad? If you knew she was planning something?"

Aidan's eyes filled with tears. *Wow, Becca, way to blame the victim.* "Aidan, this wasn't your fault. I just want to understand why you didn't think you could ask for help."

"I guess I thought it was all talk. I didn't really think she'd hurt us. And I was scared of what might happen if my mom found out I took her stuff. I wanted to tell Dad. I kept the letters in my locker at school, and every day I'd tell myself I was going to bring them home and show him," Aidan said.

"You didn't tell him after the attack either? Were you still scared of her?" Becca said. She could hear the therapist voice creeping in.

"I was really sick after the fire. My lungs were damaged and the burns were... it took a while to heal. Afterward, Dad was so angry. He wanted us to forget about Mom; he didn't even like talking about her. I guess I also thought if I hid the letters away, I could tell myself it wasn't real."

This time his voice broke. "That makes me like her, doesn't it? Because I kept this secret for so long, and she kept hurting more people."

"Aidan, don't you dare put this on yourself. You went through something unimaginable. What matters is this... it's so very brave. I'm so sorry you had to go through all of this. I'm so very sorry."

"Me too," he said. He shuffled his feet and turned to go, all his teenage self-consciousness returning now that he had unburdened himself. He turned back around, staring at Becca, his blue eyes laser focused.

"Dad and I have a nice life. We surf every day, play soccer, we grill, and we watch movies. It's different than before, but it's cool. I don't want to mess anything up. Since I gave you all those letters, can I ask you to do something for me?"

"Of course," Becca said gripping the envelope tightly, already feeling like she owed this boy more than she could ever say.

"Promise my mom won't ever come back. That they'll lock her up so she can't ruin things again?" Aidan said softly.

Becca clutched the letters even tighter, thinking of her promise to Ash that she'd stop Mo. Becca wasn't a detective building the case against Mo. In all likelihood, once Wishard found out she was here, Becca might not even have a job with the LAPD. The correct answer to this fragile boy's plea would have been something diplomatic, something along the lines of "I'll do everything in my power to make sure that doesn't happen." Aidan was putting his trust, his faith, in Becca's ability to make things right. "You have my word."

MO

Maureen Wilson?" Mo grimaced at the guard's shrill voice and the use of her given name. She hated that name and all it represented. This wasn't the time to bring that up. Mo needed to play the game. She stood up from the bench she was camped out on and dutifully made her way over to the front of the jail cell.

"That would be me," Mo said agreeably, offering the visibly bored guard her winningest smile. In Mo's experience, a little kindness went a long way, especially with people who rarely received it.

"You made bail. Congratulations," he said with zero affect, unlocking the jail cell door and leading Mo down a long gray corridor toward the processing area. She spotted her attorney, Graham Langham, the soulless ghoul with a bad tan and slick custom Brioni suit. He saw her, and his face lit up, a practiced expression, not an ounce of sincerity in his eyes.

"I'm so pleased I was able to secure your release with such expedience," he said with a giddy smile. *What a fool*, Mo thought. This moron was patting himself on the back for his impeccable legal skills. She would bet his yearly salary that it was her father and one well-placed phone call that secured her freedom. He paused as though he were waiting for some kind of ticker tape parade. Her hatred for lawyers was reignited. Useless just like her ex-husband. She had to force herself to focus on what he was saying. "Mrs. Wilson, just a reminder your bail stipulates you must not leave the LA proper area. There is an ongoing investigation into some of the more . . . serious allegations."

"I am sure they will realize those charges are completely bogus. Of course, I am at the detective's disposal," Mo said.

"That is good to hear. I understand your living situation is . . . in flux," he said diplomatically.

"I live on the streets, Graham. It's nothing to be ashamed of," she said. She enjoyed the discomfort flashing across his face, the nervous way he adjusted his overpriced Rolex. Men like that didn't think about people like her and the kids. She enjoyed providing him with a much-needed reminder.

"Yes, I am aware. You'll be happy to hear your father has secured a suite for you at the Beverly Hills Hotel and some additional funds for necessities." He handed over a thick envelope filled with cash. If he thought any of this situation was odd, he didn't show it. She imagined a distasteful man like this did all sorts of unusual things for his clients.

"What about the young man I mentioned? Nate Sutton? Were you able to secure his release? The boy has suffered so much. I wanted to look after him."

"I'm afraid he's currently under medical supervision, which is all the information I was able to obtain," Graham said.

Mo wanted to tell him this was bullshit. Her father was probably paying him three thousand dollars an hour; he could do his fucking job and locate Nate. She couldn't get flustered, not when there was so much left to do. "Well, Graham, I appreciate you trying. He's a good kid," Mo said.

"At least he's off the streets," the ghoul said dismissively. Mo smiled, imagining how miserable this man's life was, the endless obsession with billable hours, the antacids he downed when he thought he wouldn't meet his quota, the backstabbing partners and associates, all hoping they could usurp him. Mo considered educating him on the meaning-less nature of his life, but she stopped herself. It was a waste of the gifts she had been given. The sooner she got out of this place, the better. The ghoul seemed to sense it was time for good-byes.

"I should get going. I have a car waiting. If you'd like, we could drop you off at the hotel," he said half-heartedly.

Mo shook his hand firmly. "That won't be necessary, Graham. I certainly appreciate all your help."

"Of course, Mrs. Wilson. You and I will talk soon," he promised. Mo turned and beelined for the exit. No way in hell would she be talking to or seeing that awful man again. She would do her best to avoid any more encounters with the authorities.

Mo headed toward the exit, feeling the intense glare of that lady detective. She offered the woman a friendly wave good-bye and stepped outside, taking in the spectacular horizon, bluish pinks and grays cascading over the city. The fresh evening air gave her a second wind, erasing all the negativity of the last few hours.

Mo began walking, heading away from the police station, turning onto residential streets and busy intersections, darting down alleys. Every so often she would stop and do a quick check to make sure she wasn't being followed, not convinced the police weren't monitoring her.

Mo always did her best thinking on the move. Somehow this walk didn't feel the same without Vic by her side. The longing was natural, she reminded herself. She needed to live in the discomfort and allow it to fuel her. From the start, when the Tribe formed, she told her kids there would be an end game, a final reckoning. Now they were here. Mo needed to be ready.

She spotted a taxi idling on the corner, and raised her hand. Might as well put some of her father's "spending money," to use. Mo climbed inside. "Seventh and Alameda," she said.

The driver hesitated. "You sure that's where you want to go? Nothing but junkies and lowlifes down there. It's a goddamn nightmare."

Mo offered him a smile. "That's where I'm going," she said. It was hard not to pity his lack of awareness. He was just like that ghoulish lawyer, a cog in a wheel he could never escape. Despite today's unexpected events, Mo had never been happier. She was reveling in that moment when Becca came at her, hands around Mo's throat, her eyes practically on fire.

You get me. You see how good this feels. One day very soon Becca would understand that they were one and the same. Mo would make sure of it. She smiled and leaned back against the headrest. There was no reason the Tribe had to fall apart. It simply needed to evolve. A smile enveloped Mo's face as her plan came into focus. It wouldn't be long before she was reunited with Nate, and she could settle the score with Becca. Then she would start over. She could hardly wait. It would be a rebirth, a new day for them all.

BECCA

The letters were laid out on the passenger's seat of Becca's car, organized by date. She was careful not to bend or wrinkle them. She knew she should take them straight to the police, they were evidence after all, but this was Becca's chance to gain a deeper understanding of Mo and what made her tick.

Each letter was written in neat block letters, as though every word were agonized over. The early ones were filled with teenage ramblings, Carlos complaining about his family, especially his abusive stepfather. As the letters continued, the young teen grew more effusive, thanking Mo for the money she'd given him so he could attend soccer camp, and how much he appreciated being able to crash in her office when his stepdad went on a bender. He would tell her how grateful he was for her friendship.

You make me feel like things will get better. That all of this is temporary, he wrote. Toward the end of the stack, they grew more and more desperate. Carlos didn't understand why Mo was fired, and he was even more upset that they couldn't see one another.

*They've got things twisted, making it seem all sordid and shit.
I keep telling them we're just friends, but no one ever listens to
me. Except you. I feel like you really get me.*

Carlos struggled to understand why he wasn't allowed
to accept rides or gifts from Mo. He didn't care about rules
or optics. All he cared about was the future Mo promised
him, a future in which she would care for him, finance his
education, help him find a life away from his abusive stepfather and indifferent mother. A future in jeopardy because
the people in Mo's life objected to their relationship.

The last letter in the bunch left a lump in Becca's throat.

*That's it. I'm tired of this. I'm ready to handle that stupid
bitch that got you fired. And your family has turned their back
on you too. You deserve better. It's time for them to go. I won't
do anything until I hear from you. Whatever happens, I want
to thank you for never giving up on me. You're the only one
that hasn't. I've always got your back. Love Carlos.*

Becca swallowed hard, fighting back the bile. As far as
she was concerned, these letters were proof Mo was responsible for the fire and the assault against her coworker, and
could establish a pattern of behavior. Becca needed to get
this to the police. She sent a text to Christian and Wishard.
Found something on Mo. Heading to hospital now.

Of course traffic in LA was horrid and it took almost an

hour and twenty minutes to get back to the hospital. She beelined for the ICU waiting room and spotted Christian, his massive frame crammed into one of the plastic chairs, his face a mask of calculated concern. Seated beside him were Nina and Wishard, drinking coffees, the two of them laughing. A pang of jealousy bubbled to the surface. It wasn't rational, but as far as Becca was concerned, Wishard was supposed to be the enemy. Why was Nina laughing and talking like they were old friends?

"Becs?" Christian said. She shook off the annoyance and moved toward them. Nina's and Wishard's smiles faded. Becca could see that something was wrong, all three of them regarding her with identical expressions of concern.

She ignored it, thrusting the stack of letters at Wishard. "You need to read these. Mo's son gave them to me. They're letters from the kid at the nonprofit. He talks all about Mo. How she manipulated him like she manipulated all the others. How she orchestrated the attack on her colleague, the fire he set that nearly killed her family. This should establish a pattern. At the very least, it will give you something to hold her on."

There was a long pause as Christian, Wishard, and Nina exchanged glances. "What is it? What's going on?"

Wishard sighed. "These letters may prove useful in the future, and I still want to speak to Ash, but she's unconscious. I'm here because you should know that Vic exonerated Maureen of any and all culpability in the murder of

Eli and Leslie as well as Ash's assault. We were only able to charge her with several misdemeanors. Based on Maureen's family's connections, she was released two hours ago."

"You let her go? You let Mo go?" Becca said softly. "What about Ash? What about her testimony?"

"Like I said before, Ash has to wake up first. Then we can get her statement and amend the charges. Until then, Mo walks," Wishard said.

"Please tell me you've got eyes on Mo. That someone is watching her," Becca said.

Wishard's jaw tightened. "I requested surveillance, and my request was denied. Like I said before, Maureen Wilson has some very powerful, and very wealthy, allies."

A red-hot fury surged through Becca. She clenched her fists, gritting her teeth as she summoned every ounce of control.

"That woman is a goddamn sociopath and you just let her go?" Becca repeated.

Joanne's eyes widened in disbelief. "You think I wanted this to happen?" she snapped. "You think I looked at how that awful woman manipulated those kids, and I said, 'Yeah, sure, let her walk'? You think I wouldn't like to break all the rules? Just say fuck it and go off the reservation like you? Of course I would, but there are rules. I had no choice but to follow those rules. I'm not finished with this. Not by a long shot. I'm going to do everything I can to build a case against her, with Ash's help. That's how this works, Dr. Ortiz, in case you've forgotten." Becca saw the strain on Wishard's face, her eyes bloodshot and lined with deep, heavy circles. If Becca weren't so angry, she might have felt sorry for her.

Christian laid a hand on Wishard's shoulder. "Joanne, ease up."

"Yes, let's all take a beat," Nina said.

Wishard softened, shaking her head as though she were disappointed in herself for losing her temper. "We will get her. It's just going to take time." She sighed, then stood up. "I have to get back to the station. Christian, you can handle the rest," she said, giving him a curt nod as she strode down the hall toward the elevators.

Becca clocked the tension between them and watched her go, her mind spinning. There had to be something else they could do. She zeroed in on Christian. "Handle the rest? What the hell does that mean?"

He ran a hand through his hair. She knew Christian's non-verbal cues inside and out. This one meant he was about to deliver bad news.

"Becca, Vic was found hanging in his cell at county. He hung himself with his bedsheets. Left a message in blood. It read, 'The Tribe endures.'"

"He killed himself?" Becca said, but it was a rhetorical question. She remembered Vic's rage and the deep sadness that clung to him, his loyalty and devotion to Mo, and it made complete sense. Becca took a deep breath, not wanting to know the answer to her next question, but asking it anyway. "What about the others?"

"I'm afraid it's not looking good. Over the course of the last two hours, three other Tribe members who were taken into protective custody also attempted suicide."

Becca leaned forward, her eyes filling with tears. "They're dead? All of them?"

"Two were pronounced on site. One is in critical condition," Christian replied.

Becca closed her eyes, thinking about those kids laughing, talking, eating, and enjoying life just a few hours before. They believed in Mo until the very end, even when she'd turned her back on them and walked away.

Becca thought about her promise to Aidan, and Ash. "You're safe. She can't hurt you. I won't let her hurt you." It was such bullshit. All of it was a lie. If anything, she'd made things worse. Becca's legs wobbled ever so slightly. Lack of sleep and food and this news were all too much. Christian reached for her. "Becs."

Becca held up a hand to stop him. "I'm okay. I'm okay," she said, as though she was trying to convince herself. She took a breath to steady herself. She wanted to feel every bit of this pain and sorrow. She wanted it to fuel her. "I should go check on Ash," Becca said. That wasn't entirely true. She needed to think about what she was going to do next.

"Becca, wait," Nina said, reaching out to stop her. "There's something else. Something that's very important." Becca inhaled. She knew the question was coming before

Nina ever even asked it. "Did you use my security code to access the LAPD database?" Nina asked.

Becca could have said no, denied it, played dumb, but she wanted them to understand. "I had to do something. I didn't want Mo to get away with all of this. I thought this would be enough to keep her locked up."

"Nina is here because we're both very concerned. We're hoping that you might be willing to talk to someone, someone who can make sure you're coping with all the stress and trauma…"

God, Christian was turning the tables, trying to therapize her. She stared at him, took in the pitying gaze, the almost patronizing tone in his voice. She let out a gasp. He knew. About the pills. About her good-bye notes. However lackluster her suicide attempt was, she'd still done it.

"Nina told you?" Becca asked, her voice barely a whisper. The shame of that day came flooding back, the sense of hopelessness she felt when she grabbed the bottle of sleeping pills, wanting an escape from the ache of losing Christian, and all her worries that she might fail Ash.

Becca glared at Nina. "You promised you wouldn't say anything," Becca said, her eyes blurring as she swiped at the falling tears.

Nina shrugged. "I'm not sorry, Becca. Your behavior is troubling. You're barely hanging on, and you don't even know it." Becca's face flushed. She couldn't speak, she was so furious.

She could try to defend herself, explain it away, but what did it matter? They weren't here to help her find Mo, or to help get justice. They were here because they didn't trust Becca.

"So what is this? My intervention?" she asked.

Christian's eyes flashed with surprise. "No. Of course not."

"You're sure? I'm not about to find myself in some padded cell, with a therapist asking all sorts of questions about whether I've considered harming myself?"

Nina sighed. "No, that's what why we're here. We're here because we care about you and we're concerned."

"Fantastic. Your concerns have been heard. Now that you've done your civic duty, Officers, you're both free to go," Becca said.

Becca's harsh tone didn't faze Nina. She turned to Christian, their alliance in full effect.

"This is what I was talking about, Christian. She's nearly gotten herself killed twice. She needs to see someone."

Becca wanted to shout at Nina, "My daughter was nearly murdered. How would you handle it? How?" But losing her temper would only prove Nina's point, make her seem unstable. "Tell me, Chris, do you think I'm losing it? That I need help?"

Christian didn't answer, as he shifted from one foot to the other. Nina threw her hands in the air. "Why am I not surprised? Like Christian would ever make the hard choice. It's easier to just walk away."

Christian flinched, but that was Nina. She always went for the jugular. "If something goes wrong, if she gets hurt, it's on you," she said to him.

She snatched her purse off the chair. "You know that I love you, Becca. You're like family, which is why I won't sit around and watch you self-destruct," Nina said. She hurried back down the hall, leaving Becca and Christian alone.

"You can go too," Becca said, shooing him away. After tiptoeing around everyone, saying to hell with everyone felt good.

Christian reached for her again. Becca tried to pull away. He held on tight. She hated how familiar and comforting his embrace was. "I hate that I hurt you. I thought you were fine after I left. You moved on so quickly, focusing all your energy on Ash. The idea you'd do something to hurt yourself... That I didn't even know..." He trailed off.

"That was the past," she whispered. She wanted to push him away, but she stayed there, letting him hold her.

"Is it? I want to believe you. I want you to be okay, Becs. I don't think you are," he said softly.

"I'm not crazy," Becca whispered.

"I know you're not. You are hurting, and you should be. What happened to Ash is tragic and unfair. But you know as well as I do what happens when you don't talk about what's going on. You can't run from it." She heard his voice catch, thought about what he'd said in her room that night, all the pain he'd been through, that she'd put him through.

Becca closed her eyes, leaning her head on Christian's chest, finally letting her tears fall. She thought about Robbie and how he was never able to ask for help and that eventually the darkness consumed him. She didn't want that to happen to her.

"You were never this wise when we were married," Becca said through her tears.

"What can I say? I found a good therapist."

Becca laughed, looking up at Christian's slight smile. She wanted to push him away, but everything he said made sense. This was the same thing she would tell her own patients. She didn't want to fight with him anymore. She just wanted to stop hurting and being angry and feeling so goddamn helpless. "I could reach out to Dr. Atterman. I saw him after... after everything happened," Becca said reluctantly. After the incident with the pills, Nina insisted she find a therapist. She spent almost a year and a half with him, sitting in his Silver Lake office, telling him everything, about her divorce and Ash and all the rest. She knew he would be able to help her through this.

"Give me his number. I'll call him. See when he might be able to get you in."

She thought about putting it off. She could see him later, once things with Ash were more stable. Of course, stable was relative. Ash would need therapy and counseling, and emotional support. She wasn't waiting for the right moment. She was deflecting. If she really wanted to be there for Ash, she had to show up for herself. Becca reached for her phone. "I'm sending you his number," Becca said, forwarding the contact to Christian. "While you do that, I'd like to see Ash."

"Sure thing. I'll be here for as long as you need me," Christian said.

Becca nodded gratefully and headed toward the ICU entrance. Christian called after her.

"Keep the faith, Becs. This isn't over."

She wanted his words to comfort her, but he was wrong. It *was* over. Ash and Nate were hospitalized; most of the Tribe was dead. After all the terrible pain and suffering she'd inflicted, Mo was still free. It wasn't fair or just, but even Becca understood when it was time to walk away. As she made her way to Ash's room, the chorus of their favorite country song played in her head. *You've got to know when to hold 'em, know when to fold 'em.*

BECCA

Becca hovered at the entrance of Ash's room, relieved to find her sleeping peacefully, her father dozing in the chair beside Ash's bed. She glanced at the monitors and was pleased to see Ash's vitals were improving. Rafi sensed Becca's arrival and stirred, offering her a tired smile.

"There you are. I was starting to worry. Did Nina and Christian find you?" Rafi asked.

"They did," Becca replied, quickly changing the subject. "Where's Mama?" she asked.

"She felt one of her migraines coming on so I sent her home. Ash and I've been having a nice chat," he said with a smile. Becca did her best to hide her relief. She didn't have the emotional bandwidth to deal with her mother. "Becca, what's going on? Are you okay?" Rafi said.

"Not really. I..." She trailed off.

"Would rather not talk about it?"

She gave him a curt nod. Rafi always knew how to read a situation, though she hated how much he kept bottled up inside. The only time he ever opened up about losing Robbie was the night before Becca's wedding. After the rehearsal dinner, Christian took his parents and her mother to the hotel, while Becca and Rafi decided to have some father-daughter bonding time. The Cuba libres and Rafi's emotions over his little girl getting married got the best of him, and he admitted Robbie's breakdown was the greatest failure of his life. Staring down at Ash, Becca felt his pain now in a way she never could before. She placed a gentle kiss on Ash's forehead, her skin warm to the touch. "She looks better, doesn't she?" Becca asked.

"She looks so much better," Rafi said. "Dr. Osterman came by and said Ash is doing great. A real fighter," Rafi said.

"She is, isn't she?" Becca said proudly.

"You look so tired, *mija*. I'm worried about you," he said.

Join the club. She didn't say that, forcing a smile instead. "Papa, I'll be okay. You know how strong I am," she said, wanting it to be true.

"That's what worries me. Sometimes the strongest people break the worst. I know you love Ash, and that love is a beautiful thing, but if it destroys you, what's it really worth?"

"Everything. That's what it's worth, Papa. Everything and then some."

There was a moment of silence and then he nodded. He understood that better than anyone. "You know I don't mind staying. Your mother hasn't stopped cooking since Ash disappeared. She'll heat you up something and you can take a nap. I won't leave Ash's side, and if anything changes, I'll call you."

His offer was so tempting. Becca was exhausted, and she'd barely had anything to eat in the last few days. The downside was having to see her mother. They hadn't spoken since the other night at the hospital, and Becca knew her mother well enough to know that she wasn't going to let their conversation go.

"Thanks, Papa, but I want to spend time with my girl."

He relented, reaching for his jacket and Dodgers cap. "I'll be back later with breakfast tacos. If you need anything, call me." He leaned down and kissed her gently on the head. "Trust me, the worst is over," he said as he slipped out of the room.

Rafi couldn't know how wrong he was. The worst was still out there, lurking, plotting, manipulating, ruining lives with every breath she took. Becca collapsed into the chair beside Ash and carefully adjusted the railing on the hospital bed. She held Ash's hand, feeling the warmth, willing her to open her eyes. The hum of the machines and the warmth of the room were like a sedative, Becca's eyes flickering closed. Her cell phone buzzed and she jolted awake, fumbling through her purse. She eyed the unknown number on the caller ID, praying it was Wishard calling with news. "Hello, this is Dr. Ortiz," Becca said.

She heard sobbing on the other end, almost a desperate wail. "Hello? Who is this? Hello?" she called out.

"Doc, I fucked up. I'm so sorry," Raya whimpered.

"Raya, what is it? What's wrong?" Becca asked.

Raya was silent and then: "I'm afraid Raya's a bit incapacitated right now."

Becca froze. Mo. It was Mo on the other end, her voice unmistakable, that lilting, taunting voice. "I told Raya she should be more careful with the company she keeps."

"I could say the same about you," Becca snapped, instantly regretting the knee-jerk reaction. *Keep it together. Don't push her buttons. Don't give her a reason to hurt Raya.*

"I'm sorry, Mo. I really am. Is she okay? Is Raya okay?"

"For now. It's a shame it came to this. The good news is you have the opportunity to fix the mess you've made."

The mess I made. Becca counted to five, biting back the fury she felt. "What do you want?" she asked.

"I was expecting a little more back-and-forth. I do appreciate a direct approach. Here's the deal. You bring Nate to me, and we can make a trade."

Of course she wanted Nate. This was all a game to Mo, these kids were her chess pieces, and she moved them about as she saw fit. "Don't you think Nate's suffered enough? What more could you possibly want from him?" Becca asked.

"He's my family, Dr. Ortiz. You don't walk away from family. Now, this isn't a negotiation. Nate knows where to find me. I'm sure this goes without saying, but no police. Raya and I will be here waiting," Mo said.

Then the line went dead.

BECCA

All of Becca's training and experience clicked into place, and she knew exactly what she had to do. First things first, she needed to pull herself together. Becca grabbed her purse and hurried into the bathroom, shutting the door behind her. She barely recognized the ravaged woman in the mirror. The bloodshot eyes, the deep bags settled under them, the worry lines that seemed to have multiplied overnight. She grabbed her makeup bag and went to work, carefully applying her foundation with precision and care. She applied blush, eye shadow, and lipstick and braided her hair. In a matter of minutes, she had transformed herself from distraught mother to trustworthy and reliable therapist. A text suddenly appeared on her phone. *Dr. Atterman can see you in an hour.*

Damn it. Becca forgot all about Christian and her promise to see her therapist. Now she had a decision to make: tell him about Mo and her threats or go it alone. Becca knew once she told him, she would have no control over the outcome. Law enforcement had to follow rules and regulations. It could be hours before they were able to interrogate

Nate. Even if he told them where to find Mo, it might be too late for Raya. She texted Christian back, hating herself for lying. *Be there in ten.*

She returned to Ash's bedside and squeezed her hand. "Sleep well, sweet girl. I'll be back soon."

She slowly opened the door, heading toward the exit sign at the end of the hall. By the time Christian came to check on her, Becca would be long gone.

She hurried across the street, toward the parking lot, a light rain falling, the night sky starless and clear. Becca made her way back downtown toward Good Samaritan Hospital, Nate's current place of residence, which was less than ten minutes from Skid Row.

She understood the risks. There was a good chance Becca's plan would fall apart, but she was going to do whatever she could to make sure no one else got hurt.

Becca approached the security desk, where a young woman with smoky eyes and bright pink lips was busy flirting with a security guard. Becca clocked her name tag and approached the desk. "Hi, Cheryl, I'm Dr. Ortiz with the LAPD. I'm looking for Nate Sutton's room," Becca said, channeling every ounce of confidence she possessed. The woman glanced down at her computer screen, her nails clacking loudly on the keys as she typed. Something caught her attention, probably a notation that Nate was on a mental health hold. The young girl sat up straighter, eyeing Becca curiously. "You're LAPD?"

"Dr. Ortiz with the Mental Evaluation Unit. I've been ordered to evaluate Mr. Sutton," Becca said. She took out her badge and handed it over to the woman, not blinking.

Cheryl studied Becca's badge for what seemed like an eternity, and then motioned Becca toward the bank of elevators. "Room 1209. Take the elevators to the twelfth floor, make a right, and it's the last door on the left," she said. Becca smiled in approval, saying a silent thank-you. She reached the twelfth floor and headed down a long corridor.

At the end of the hall, Becca spotted a police officer sitting outside Nate's door. This was game time. She strode toward the officer, a young cop, early twenties, tall and lanky, with an unfortunate buzz cut. He stood the second he saw her, an intense kind of enthusiasm, like a puppy, all legs and arms, eager to impress.

"Can I help you, ma'am?" he asked.

The lies were effortless as she repeated the same story she told the receptionist, holding out her badge, her gaze focused and measured. The officer's brow furrowed. "No one said anything about him having visitors," he said.

"It's standard procedure for me to assess him. If you'd like to place a call to my supervisor, I'm happy to provide you with her home number," Becca said, hoping the thought of disturbing a superior would deter him.

The cop looked uneasy. "I mean if it's standard protocol, there's no need to bother anyone," he said as though trying to convince himself. He stood to follow Becca inside the room.

"Actually, our conversations are privileged." From her vantage point, she could see Nate was restrained, so she wouldn't need to worry about him getting physical.

Another nod. "Yeah. Good luck getting him to talk. That kid is not saying anything."

"That's what I was told. Orders are orders. Gotta at least try."

"I hear that. Mind if I go grab a coffee? They've got me working a double tonight," he said.

Leaving his post was actually completely against protocol and very much a fireable offense. Becca was relieved she wasn't the only one breaking the rules.

"Take all the time you need," she said. He smiled and hurried down the hall. Becca took a deep breath and opened the door. Nate lay awake in bed, gazing up at the ceiling. His hands were held down with soft restraints, his left eye swollen, shades of blue and yellow forming. He was so pale, he appeared almost ghostlike, as though he weren't quite there.

"Nate," Becca said softly. His gaze swiveled over to her. He blinked furiously as though not quite believing she was here.

"Get the fuck out," he said through clenched teeth.

"Nate, I don't have much time. I need to find Mo, and she said you would know where she was staying."

Nate shifted in the bed, his mouth turned upward in a sneer. "You want me to help you? Like you helped me?" he spat. Becca's face flushed. He remembered their meeting.

"Oh yeah, I remember. One of the first times Ash and I are hanging, she gets a call and your picture pops up on her phone screen. I couldn't believe it. You were the fucking 'Saint of Silver Lake' Ash kept going on and on about. This amazing woman who took her in, this mansion she lived in, the private school she went to. All I could think about was how you sat across from me, all prim and fucking proper, asking all those questions about Ash, and how we knew each other. I couldn't believe it when you said that Ash was safe and you said she was happy. That's all I wanted. Then you started asking about my case, promising you'd try and get someone to look at it, saying maybe Ash could visit. I was used to people lying to me, but you, you seemed different." Nate snorted.

"You never told Ash? About our meeting?" Becca said. It was selfish to ask, but she did it anyway.

"Why would I tell her? She thought you were the shit. You think I wanted to be the one to ruin that? It's not Ash's fault you're a liar." He spoke with almost no affect, though his eyes told a different story. Becca deserved every bit of his derision.

"I'm sorry, Nate. If I could go back and do things differently, I would. All I wanted to do was to protect Ash."

"Guess we both failed her," Nate said dispassionately.

He didn't know about Ash. God, he didn't know. Becca inched closer. "Nate, she's alive. Ash is alive."

Nate tried his best to sit up straight in his bed. "No. No. No. She can't be. Mo said…I mean, I was sure they…" Nate couldn't finish the sentence.

"They tried their damnedest to kill her, but she's fighting like hell."

"She's alive. Ash is alive," Nate said, repeating the words over and over again. This revelation transformed him, the spark returning to Nate's eyes, color staining his cheeks. He began to pull against the restraints. "And the others?" Nate asked softly.

The last thing Becca wanted to do was to tell Nate his friends were dead. She owed him the truth. "Nate, I'm sorry. They're gone."

Nate shrugged as though this were inevitable. "Mo promised the afterlife would be better than this shit. For their sake, I hope she's right," he said. He tried to act as though it didn't matter. He wasn't that good of an actor. She saw the depth of despair in his expression, and then Nate began pulling at his restraints. "If Ash is still alive, then she's not safe. I have to get to her. Mo isn't going to stop. I have to make sure she can't hurt her."

Nate's voice was rising, his entire body flailing, as if he might be able to levitate off the bed. It wouldn't be long before a well-meaning nurse or the officer returned to check on him. Becca needed to take control of the situation.

"Nate, listen to me, please listen. There's no way anyone is going to let you visit Ash. She's in the ICU at another hospital. But I swear to you she's safe. I'm here because Mo is threatening to hurt another girl. She's using her to get to me. This girl didn't do anything to anyone. In fact, all she's tried to do is help. I can't let anything bad happen to her. Please just tell me where I can find Mo," Becca pleaded.

It took a second for Becca's words to register. Nate leaned back against the pillows.

"Mo wants something, doesn't she? That's why you're here. She always wants something," Nate said, understanding Mo's psychology better than Becca ever could.

"She wants me to bring you to her. That won't happen, of course. You just have to tell me where she is," Becca said.

"Oh yeah, and then what happens?"

Becca didn't hesitate. "I get her to confess. Tell me everything she did to Ash and Leslie and the others. How she hurt all of you."

"Won't work. Mo's too fucking smart. She always gets her way. Always."

"Not this time."

Nate closed his eyes. She didn't blame him for not trusting her. Becca shifted anxiously, eyeing the door, knowing time was running out. *Don't rush him, Becca. Don't rush him.*

"I want to go with you."

"There's no way. You're recovering from an overdose, not to mention you're in police custody," Becca said.

"I thought you worked with the cops. Can't you pull some strings?" Nate asked. Even before Becca's suspension this would have been difficult. At this point it was impossible.

"I'm so sorry. I can't, Nate. It's too dangerous."

"Now you're worried about my safety?"

She winced. "If you tell me where she is, I promise no one else will get hurt."

Nate sighed heavily, weighing his options. "There's a motel on Temple called the Boulevard Inn. It's where Mo would go every now and then to shower or recharge. She always stays in the last room near the back of the motel. She says it's the quietest."

You can take the woman out of Malibu, but you can't take Malibu out of the woman, Becca thought. She wished she could find the right thing to say to take away Nate's pain. Only time would ease that.

"I have to go, Nate. But you don't deserve any of this. I hope you know that."

She saw the tears welling in his eyes. He closed them, as if to stem the tide of emotion. Becca ignored the feeling that she was abandoning him yet again, and slipped out of the room.

Becca paid the parking attendant and sped out of the lot, the hospital growing smaller and smaller. She understood how dangerous Mo was. If she was going to face off with her, she had to be prepared. *Hang on just a little longer, Raya.*

Just a little longer. Becca made a quick right and headed home, the traffic cooperating for a change.

She didn't bother going into the house, heading straight for the garage. She dragged the ladder over to the storage cabinet tucked into the corner of the garage and stood on her tiptoes, unearthing the lockbox she'd stored on the top shelf when Ash moved in. Tucking the box under her arm, she climbed down from the ladder. She used the key and removed a small .40-caliber pistol from inside the box. When Christian moved out, Becca told him to take it with him.

He refused. "Becs, do me this one damn favor and keep it. It'll help me sleep better knowing you have it." Now she was relieved that she had relented. Becca gently cradled the gun in her hands, ensuring that the safety was in place. She quickly loaded the clip in the chamber and held it, reorienting herself with the weight and feel. *Last resort. That's all this is.*

"Rebecca, what are you doing?"

Startled, Becca shoved the gun in her purse. Of course her mother was here. Of course. She spun around and saw Virginia leaning against the garage door, her arms crossed, watching Becca warily. "Rebecca, Christian said you left the hospital suddenly and that you weren't answering your phone. He sounded quite concerned. What is going on?"

She needed to think fast. It was almost two hours since Mo's call. She had to get to Raya.

"It's nothing, Mama. I needed to run a quick errand for a client. I'll text Chris and let him know." Virginia's brow furrowed. Becca held her breath, wondering if her mother knew about her suspension or the therapist she was supposed to meet.

"This late? Maybe I should go with you?"

For the first time in a long time, Becca really saw her mother. The bloodshot eyes, the pinched mouth, the uneasiness, the pure, unabashed love reflected back in her eyes. Her mother loved her, just as much as Becca loved Ash. Deep down Becca always knew that, but it was even clearer now. Robbie's death should have brought them closer together instead of tearing them apart. It wasn't anyone's fault. No one was to blame. It's just the way it was.

"I'll be fine. It's . . . a confidential matter," Becca said, doing her best to slip past Virginia. She wasn't quick enough. Virginia grabbed her wrist. "I'll wait here until you get back. You need to eat."

Her mother's obsession with feeding her was so comfortably predictable, Becca wanted to laugh. "That sounds good, Mama," Becca said, hoping everything would go well, and she would have the opportunity to sit across from her mother and eat her food, and just talk, allowing all the bitterness and blame to fade away. She reached out and hugged Virginia. Her mother tensed, surprised by the gesture. It would be so nice to stay right here, but Raya was counting on her.

"I'll see you soon." Becca pulled away and headed to her car, refusing to look back, afraid she'd lose her nerve entirely.

She headed downtown, the city lights twinkling in the distance. Her phone buzzed, the Bluetooth ringing loudly in the car, startling her. She saw Christian's name flash across the caller ID on her dashboard. There was no logical reason why she should answer, but she'd never been logical when it came to Christian. His voice boomed through the speakers. "What in the hell were you thinking? Going to see that kid was insane. Do you realize how much shit you're in?" Christian said.

"You wouldn't understand," Becca said.

"You're right. I don't understand. Jesus Christ, Becs, this isn't about you. Did you think even for one second how your visit might affect this emotionally unstable kid?"

She'd considered it, but went anyway. Some therapist she was. Becca's voice wobbled. "He's the only person who can lead us to Mo."

"Nate *was* the only person, and now he's in the wind. Faked a seizure. When the medical staff intervened, he attacked them. Do you understand what I'm saying? Nate escaped. He's out there somewhere, Becca, and he's very dangerous."

A shiver ran through Becca. She thought of Mo's demand, insisting Becca bring Nate to her. Nate had given up Mo's location fairly easily. Maybe this was another part of Mo's plan? It didn't make sense that Nate would go along with it. Not if he really loved Ash. Maybe she underestimated Nate's devotion and commitment to Mo. She could see all the red flags, how her plan might backfire, but she could see the Boulevard Inn looming in the distance. She couldn't give up now. "I'll be okay, Chris."

"Becs, you don't know that. Tell me where you are and I'll come and get you."

She could hear his desperation. "I'm sorry. I know it won't make sense to you, but I have to end this. I can't let her hurt anyone else."

"Jesus, Becs...what are you talking about? What the hell is going on?" She heard an inhalation of air on the other end of the phone, and then whispering as though he were talking to someone. "Nina put a GPS tracker on your car. We're going to find you," Christian said.

Becca had no way of knowing if this was true or not. And she didn't care. Hopefully, by the time they located her, she would have Raya. "You're a good man, Chris. I didn't say that enough. I neglected you and your feelings, took up so much space in the relationship. I know so much of what happened was my fault too. It just made things easier if I turned you into the bad guy. I see that now," Becca said. She didn't mean to make things sound so final, but he needed to know that she was sorry too.

"Becs, I'm begging you not to do—" She hit disconnect, cutting him off as she pulled into the parking lot of the seedy pay-by-the-hour motel, a crash pad for junkies and working girls.

Becca headed toward Mo's motel room at the end of the property, checking her bag one more time, the gun tucked inside. If things went wrong, she could still protect herself. She reached the motel room, opened the recording app on her phone and hit record, then placed it in the front pocket of her purse. She could do this. Becca knocked softly. "Mo, it's Dr. Ortiz," she said, hearing the tremble in her voice.

Steady. Don't let her see your weakness. She will exploit it at all costs.

"Come in," Mo said calmly, as though she were inviting Becca in for tea. She slowly opened the door. The mirror was shattered, furniture overturned, and in the corner, Raya sat on a plastic motel chair, her hands bound behind her with a thick cord, a towel stuffed in her mouth, her face bruised and swollen. She wasn't the only injured party. Mo's lip was busted and blood stained her T-shirt. Becca felt a surge of pride knowing Raya had put up a fight.

"I'm sorry I didn't have time to tidy. There was a bit of a misunderstanding. Things have been sorted now. Isn't that right, Raya?" Mo said. Becca caught sight of the large butcher knife glinting in Mo's hand, the blade so close to Raya's neck it would take only seconds to pierce her skin.

Raya's eyes widened, her head nodding frantically as though she were trying to warn Becca. Her gaze darted behind her, but she was too late, feeling large hands shoving her forward. Becca stumbled, the bed catching her fall. She turned and saw Nate looming over her, clad in a pair of oversized sweatpants and T-shirt two sizes too small. His hair stood up straight, a terrifyingly blank expression on his face. She fumbled for her bag. She needed the gun. If she could just get the gun.

"Nate, if you don't mind..." Mo waved the knife toward Becca's bag. He obeyed, snatching it from her.

"Don't... please," Becca said, her voice barely a whisper, her entire body trembling. She watched Nate dig through her purse. She held her breath, waiting for him to retrieve the gun.

"We're good," Nate said. He held on to the bag but didn't reveal the weapon. Becca's eyes widened. She wasn't sure what Nate was doing. All Becca could do was play along.

Mo seemed to revel in this drama. There was nothing Becca hated more than this woman's goddamn smile. "I hope you know this is not at all how I wanted this to turn out," Mo said.

Becca didn't believe her for a second. "Mo, let Raya go. She's got nothing to do with this. She's innocent..."

"No one is innocent, and she's going to stay put until we finish our chat."

Becca gritted her teeth. "Okay, let's talk, Maureen," Becca said, hoping to get a reaction. Her reward was instantaneous. Mo's eyes narrowed, and she grew very still, clutching the knife tighter in her hands.

"Maureen is dead and buried. That woman was an empty vessel," Mo said, her clipped diction revealing her Ivy League roots. "I assume you know all about the pathetic weasel I married."

"Paul seemed like a very decent man. He certainly didn't deserve what happened to him."

Mo's ruddy face twisted in an angry sneer. "You don't know what the hell you're talking about. Sure he's handsome, but soulless. Paul loved me when we were getting invites to cocktail parties and political functions, when he got to hobnob with Oprah and Spielberg, but he never cared about my work. All he cared about was what people were saying about him. 'There goes Paul Wilson. Isn't he a fucking catch because he's got washboard abs and can balance on a goddamn surfboard?' He never cared about anyone but himself. When things got hard, he tried to ruin me. I showed him and my father. Nothing can trap me. Not the money or the houses…"

"Even your own child," Becca said.

"Save your judgment," Mo snipped. "Your kid was hanging on the streets with us, and you didn't have a clue. Maybe you don't like our methods, but we changed lives. Right, Nate?"

Nate hadn't said a word. Becca could see something behind his eyes. He was planning something. If he were on Mo's side, he would've given up Becca's gun. The unknown was unbearable. She could barely think with Mo's nonstop rambling.

"You therapists are all alike. All that training and schooling and you don't know a single thing about human nature. I've dedicated my entire life to helping children and families. The things I did for those kids, the time and effort I spent, really listening to them, making them feel cared for and comforted. No one else did that. Then they all looked down on me for it, acted like I was some kind of deviant. Next thing I know these nosy busybodies start spreading lies about me. I showed them how wrong they were. I've been living my truth. All those kids I've helped...they couldn't do that. They didn't have the ability. You must be truly special to help these kids. I worked miracles."

Mo fluttered her hand as if gesturing to Nate. "Take Nathaniel. Do you know what he was like when I met him? Desperate. Lost and hopeless. But I saw his potential. His capacity for love, his desire for connection. That's what I gave him. I did that."

"So you were helping Nate? Helping all the other kids? That's what you were doing?" Becca asked.

"Yes. Yes. How many times do I have to say that? I have a gift. The things I did, the things we did, were crucial in their evolution."

"What things?" Becca asked. "Hurting children? Killing them?"

"They were already damaged," Mo insisted. "Whoring themselves out, using drugs, failing to connect with anyone. They did those things because they were betrayed by their families, cast out by people who claimed to love them. I know what that feels like. That's why I rescued them, gave them a safe place to call home. I gave them hope. Some of them were redeemed. The others were damaged. They couldn't be saved."

"You mean, Ash and Leslie and Eli?" Becca asked.

Mo's eyes flashed. "You expect me to believe that your life wasn't easier without that girl? That she wasn't weighing you down?"

"No. She wasn't. She wasn't." Becca insisted. She could feel her temper growing and had to fight to maintain composure.

"They were failures. There are always failures. It's a flaw in the design. The way some babies are born blind. You can't function as a family unit if you're lying and betraying one another, breaking rules right and left. That's how my own family fell apart. I swore I wouldn't let that happen. These children needed to understand rules were imposed for a reason. To restore order. The ones we discarded, they could not, or would not, change. They would always be flawed. It is very rare for a baby born blind to ever see."

It was all such garbage, a woman's twisted psychology. Becca thought about the hundreds of times she sat across from the mentally ill and how easy it was to distance herself. This time it was personal. *Flawed. Failures. Discarded.* These were children, kids who'd been abused and neglected. Kids like Ash.

"And your own kid, Maureen? What about him? What about Aidan?"

Mo shrugged as though Aidan were inconsequential. "My greatest failure. I didn't let it break me. I endured. I reinvented. Love isn't biological, as you know," Mo said.

He was your child, Becca wanted to scream. Mo kept blathering on. "The Tribe made me whole again, and in turn I made them whole." Mo's hands trembled from the weight of the blade. Raya whimpered again. Becca wanted to reach out and hug her. *Hang on just a little longer*, she thought.

"It was all fine, everything was fine until that bitch showed up," Mo said. The knife hovered closer to Raya, the blade pointed downward. "We'd have continued living our lives. On our terms."

"Enough," Nate screamed. Becca didn't even have time to look at him when she heard the unmistakable sound of a bullet exploding from the gun's chamber. She instinctively ducked, the noise deafening in the cramped space. The bullet soared past Becca, bypassing Raya and Mo and exploding into the wall behind them.

Mo's survival instincts finally kicked in. She dropped the knife and raised her hands in surrender. "Don't hurt me. Please don't hurt me," she begged.

Becca turned to see Nate pointing the gun at them, his fury unleashed. "Nobody say another fucking word, or I'll fucking kill you both."

BECCA

Nate gripped the gun, his stance strong and assured, daring anyone to challenge him. The only sounds were Raya's pained whimpers as she tried to free herself. He aimed the gun at Mo, who was crouching in the corner. "Get up and sit over there," he barked, gesturing to a chair shoved into another corner.

"Nathaniel, I can see you're confused and need counsel," Mo said, taking a few steps forward.

"Shut up. I don't want your fucking counsel." His finger hovered over the trigger as he moved closer, the gun inches from her face. "You've done enough talking. It's my turn. Open your mouth again and I'll put a bullet in it."

Mo's mouth closed instantly. She sank back onto the seat, her posture erect, hands clasped across her lap. Nate kicked the knife away from her and waved the gun at Becca. "Untie her. Do it now," he said, eyeing Raya.

In the distance, Becca thought she heard the faint sound of sirens. She thought about trying to disarm him, but in these cramped quarters, with Nate's level of fury, it was dangerous to gamble. If she miscalculated, she could cost

Raya her life. She prayed that someone heard the shot or that Christian was telling the truth and they were on their way.

"I said fucking untie her," Nate growled. Becca knelt down beside Raya and gently removed the gag. Raya coughed, greedily sucking in air.

"I'm so sorry," Becca whispered, moving over to undo the bindings.

"Why are you sorry? It's this crazy bitch's fault. Still can't believe I let her get the jump on me," Raya said. Becca was relieved to see Raya keeping it together. Becca wasn't. Her hands were trembling so hard she could barely undo the cords. "Take your time. I don't think he wants to hurt you," Raya mumbled.

Becca wasn't sure about that. She'd turned her back on Nate, again and again, chose Ash over him. In his eyes, Becca probably wasn't any better than Mo, picking and choosing what kids were worthy.

"What the hell is taking so long? Hurry up," Nate barked.

Becca unhooked the last of Raya's bindings. Raya rubbed her raw wrists. "Go on and shoot the bitch," she dared Nate. "Or if you don't have the balls, give me the gun, and I'll do it for you."

"Raya, stop talking," Becca ordered. The last thing Nate needed was encouragement.

Nate didn't blink. "Get out," he shouted. Becca was stunned. He was letting Raya go?

"Fuck that. I'm not leaving Dr. Ortiz with you psychos."

"Raya, do what he said. Go. Please!"

"Jesus Christ, I said go," Nate said, grabbing Raya by the arm and yanking her toward the door. He opened it and shoved her outside, slamming and locking it. He spun around before Becca or Mo could make a move. By then Mo's smile had vanished, her hands balled up in fists. There was something strangely satisfying about seeing Mo afraid.

"Wanna know why we're really here, Mo?"

Mo's eyes widened. She shook her head. "Nate..."

"This is *your* reckoning. Unfortunately, Ash is unavailable, but the good news is Dr. Ortiz can fill in," Nate said. The reckoning? What the hell was a reckoning? Nate glanced over at Becca.

"Oh, she's not familiar with the reckoning. Mo, why don't you educate her?" Nate demanded. Mo didn't speak. Nate stepped forward, the gun inches from her head. She swallowed hard.

"The reckoning was how we kept things functioning. When you joined the Tribe, you promised to uphold the standards of the group. If you violated our trust, you were punished."

"By death. That's what Mo and Vic fucking left out. Somehow it wasn't in the goddamn fine print," Nate said through gritted teeth.

"Vic and I were trying to maintain order. Things were good for so long. You have to understand—"

381

"Shut up," Nate said, his movements sharp and precise as he backhanded Mo with the butt of the gun. Her head flopped backward as if on springs. It took at least thirty seconds before it returned to its normal position. Mo raised her hand to assess the damage, blood trickling down the side of her face. Becca could see the raw hurt in Nate's eyes. He had been pushed too far, his suffering was too much, and he had snapped.

"Nate, I know you're hurting. I know. I am too. But Mo confessed. We can end this now. We can make sure she gets justice," Becca said.

Nate shook his head emphatically. "We don't need the cops for that," Nate said. He grabbed the discarded knife from the floor and held it out. "Take it," he said. "Go on. Take it." He placed the knife in Becca's hand. "Today is your lucky day. You get the first cut, Doc. Go on. Cut her," Nate said.

Everything was happening so fast, it took Becca a second to realize what Nate was asking. Kill Mo? He wanted her to kill Mo.

"Go on. You saw what she did to Ash, and the others. It's only fair," Nate said.

"Mo, tell him to stop. Let's end this," Becca said softly, locking eyes with Mo.

"If Nathaniel feels like this is a fitting end to everything we've built, then who am I to argue?" Mo said. Becca couldn't believe it. This woman was endorsing her own murder. Nate nudged Becca with the tip of the pistol.

"See there, she's ready. Fucking do it already."

Mo regarded Becca with a stoicism that belied the seriousness of the situation. "C'mon, you can do it. You tell yourself you're better than I am, but you've got that part deep inside you, the part of yourself that you never acknowledge. You don't understand it yet, how good it feels, watching someone die, that feeling, the jolt of pleasure that courses through you when the light fades from someone's eyes, knowing that they can never hurt you or betray you. I felt that with Ash. That moment she cried out was like poetry in motion."

She was baiting Becca now. On the deepest primal level, Becca understood that. The more Mo talked, the angrier Becca got. She closed her eyes, trying to shut out Mo's words.

"Don't be a fucking pussy. Do it," Nate screamed.

Mo was still talking, her words running together. "We're one and the same, you and me. We're all animals just waiting for our taste of blood. You can't resist."

Something shifted, Mo's words and Nate's blending together, like some kind of twisted chant. It was as though Becca were standing outside of her body, watching everything from a distance. She clutched the knife tighter, placing the blade at the edge of Mo's collarbone.

For the first time, Becca understood Mo and the things

she'd done. She liked watching Mo's eyes flicker with fear, liked the way her breath quickened, her entire body tensing as the blade pierced her flesh. A tiny trickle of blood dripped down onto Mo's shirt. Mo wasn't sorry for the things she'd done. She wasn't going to beg for forgiveness or ask for mercy. She was incapable of feeling any kind of empathy.

Becca could do this. She could kill Mo. That would be a fitting end. All she had to do was keep digging the blade in. A rush of pleasure coursed through her body. In that rapid-fire way the mind works, another murder invaded Becca's thoughts, Robbie's apartment stained red with blood, her father's ravaged expression as they waited for the police, the devastated wail Rafi made when he learned that his son was dead. She imagined Christian on her parents' doorstep, delivering the news. "Becca snapped."

The media would have a field day. Headlines blaring "Murder Runs in the Family." She could already see her parents, totally and completely ruined. Becca would go to prison or, if she got a lucky break, a mental hospital, which was a fancy version of a prison. Ash would wake up from the worst moment of her life and find herself all alone again, tossed back in the system. She couldn't do that to her girl. She shook free from the haze that gripped her, and stepped back. She didn't care what Nate did to her. Becca wasn't a killer. She wouldn't let either of them turn her into one. She dropped the knife at Nate's feet. "I can't. I'm sorry. It's not what Ash would want. You know that."

Mo snickered. "I knew you were weak. Like mother, like daughter."

The second those words were out of Mo's mouth, Nate raised the gun, his finger on the trigger. Becca could see it now. This would be Mo's greatest victory, turning Nate against her, going out in a blaze of glory. A true martyr.

Becca couldn't let that happen. "Stop this, Nate. Stop it now," Becca said, reaching for the gun, all her training going out the window.

"No," Nate shouted. He shoved Becca so hard, she almost flew across the room. She felt herself falling, heard a sharp thud as her head slammed into the edge of a worn dresser. The pain radiated from the top of her skull all the way down to her toes, a ringing in her head. Nate's words were muffled, though she could hear him shouting at Mo.

Get up, Becca. Get up. She fought through the pain, lifting her head as another bullet exploded from the chamber. Everything seemed to slow down as Becca watched in horror as the bullet struck Mo, a flurry of red spreading across her chest. She pulled herself onto her knees, blinking furiously as she watched Mo topple to the ground, her shit-eating grin erased.

Becca staggered to her feet, struggling to keep her balance. She watched as Mo writhed and whimpered in agony.

She heard a sob, and she turned to see Nate still holding the gun. "I loved her. I loved Mo."

"I know, Nate. I know," Becca whispered over and over again, her heart breaking for this poor, damaged child.

"Tell Ash I'm sorry. Tell her it's better this way." Nate raised the gun to his temple.

"No!" Becca screamed, summoning her last bit of strength as she lunged for him. They both went flying, landing on the bed as Becca wrestled for control of the gun. She was certain she'd fired it, the entire room seeming to explode, smoke filling her nostrils, her eyes burning.

"Breach! Breach!" She realized suddenly that it wasn't the gun, but the police. Through the smoke, she could make out a half dozen men in their SWAT uniforms, surrounding her and Nate with their guns drawn. Becca's vision began to blur, a pain unlike anything she had ever experienced drowning out all sound. She wondered if she'd been poisoned again, but this felt different, more intense and all-consuming. She wanted nothing more than to close her eyes and drift off to sleep, but she forced herself to stay awake, clutching Nate tightly. The officers were trying to untangle them, shouting orders at her, but Becca ignored them, kept holding on tight. She'd turned her back on him before, but this time she wasn't letting go. "I'm right here, Nate. You're not alone. Do you hear me? You're not alone."

BECCA

In an instant all the pain and suffering Mo and the Tribe unleashed vanished, a warm, hot heat enveloping Becca. In the deep recesses of her mind, she heard the paramedics' urgent shouts, the doctors barking orders as they worked on her. She couldn't believe she was back in this place, at the mercy of doctors and nurses. Becca wanted to get up and go to Ash, but the pain kept drawing her further away from them. "Dr. Ortiz, you suffered a serious brain injury. Can you hear me? Squeeze my hand if you can hear me."

Becca didn't want to squeeze the doctor's hand. She wanted to escape and it was easy to do, the warm, peaceful place where nothing bad could touch her. It wasn't easy though. Nurses were constantly prodding and poking, and people wouldn't shut up. Her mother was unsurprisingly relentless. "I'm here, Rebecca. I'm going to give you a real piece of my mind when you wake up, but I'm not letting you go. Are you listening? I lost Robbie and I will not lose you too. Do you hear me?"

Becca was certain astronauts in space could hear her mother. The worst was when she began weeping. Virginia never cried, not even at Robbie's funeral. She'd remained stoic and immovable. Becca wanted to reach out and say she was sorry, but the warmth kept pulling her back under.

There was no sense of time or place. No sunsets or moonlight. The warmth somehow made up for it. She could feel herself wanting to let go. If she let herself, she could sink deeper and deeper into the warmth until it enveloped her completely. She was so tempted. Until she heard a familiar voice.

"C'mon, Becca, enough is enough. You've got to wake up."

Ash. Was it really Ash? Becca wasn't sure at first. Her voice was so soft and a little raspy. It could be her mind playing tricks. Wishful thinking. "Freud's here too. They gave me such a hard time about seeing you, I had to throw a total fit to make it happen. Told them he was a licensed therapy dog. Hope they don't call me on my bullshit."

Becca wanted to laugh, and cry, but more than anything she had to see Ash. She fought the warmth, a jolt of pain rushing through her body.

"I am here, Becca. I'm right here. I told the doctors you wouldn't bail on me, not when we've come so far. They don't seem convinced. That's why you've got to wake up. We can prove them wrong together," Ash said.

Ash wasn't just awake and talking; she was making jokes. This was enough to fuel Becca. She fought through that warmth, a sensation not all that different from swimming upstream.

Becca's eyes flickered open, the fluorescent lights blaring down, the awful hospital death scent filling her nose as Ash slowly came into focus. Sitting in a wheelchair, an IV pumping antibiotics, her skin a ghostly pallor, the bruises that were once black transitioning into an angry shade of blue, Ash gazed back at her, a smile lighting up her battered face.

"Freud, look who's awake." Freud let out an enthusiastic bark, his tail wagging furiously. Becca tried to speak, but no words would come. She panicked, grabbing at her throat. Ash's hands wrapped around hers, pulling them down by her side.

"Becca, don't. They put in a tube. It's helping you breathe. The doctors said once you woke up they'd remove it. It'll be a little bit longer," Ash said.

Becca blinked back tears, her breath still coming out in quick spurts. "It's okay. You're okay, Becca," Ash said over and over again. Becca nodded in agreement. She was okay. They both were. They'd survived Mo and the Tribe. They'd survived and were here together. Tears streamed down Becca's face. Ash gently wiped them away, and just like that their roles were reversed.

Ash leaned down close and whispered in Becca's ear, "Thank you for never giving up on me."

Becca didn't need words to tell Ash what she was thinking. She squeezed her hand tightly. *And I never will.*

BECCA

For three more days Becca floated in and out of conscious-ness. At one point, she managed to stay awake and she was finally able to speak with Dr. Osterman. She explained that Becca's fall at the motel caused significant trauma. "You suffered a bleed known as an epidural hematoma. We per-formed emergency surgery to relieve the pressure on your brain. We'll continue to monitor your condition. You must be patient. It will take you time to get back on your feet."

She wanted to tell the doctor she was fine, but her body had other ideas. The days rushed by, a revolving door of tests, shift changes, and endless medications.

On the sixth day, Becca woke with a pounding head-ache, a constant these days. She opened her eyes, expecting to find Ash camped out beside her. To Becca's surprise, she found Wishard, sitting cross-legged in the chair beside her bed. Dressed in jeans and a T-shirt, she seemed less intense off-duty, a notebook open on her lap. The clicking of her pen told another story.

"That's not exactly therapeutic," Becca said, gesturing to her pen.

Wishard smiled and clicked it one more time before placing it and the notebook her bag. "Oh good, you're awake," she said, as though Becca had taken a long nap instead of suffering a severe brain injury.

Becca slowly sat up, scanning the room for Christian. "Afraid Chris is working, so it's just the two of us. I figured I should stop by and pay my respects to LA's conquering hero," Wishard said.

Wincing, Becca leaned forward, fumbling for the nearby water pitcher, her throat dry, her voice raspy from the breathing tube. "I'm not a hero," Becca said.

"Tell that to the media camped outside," Wishard replied, grabbing the glass and filling it in one swift motion.

"Is this the part where you inform me of my rights and I demand to speak to a lawyer?"

"If I had any say in the matter, it would definitely have crossed my mind. Trust me, there are plenty of charges. Obstruction of justice, interfering with an investigation, impersonating an officer, the list goes on and on. The thing is, when someone is instrumental in apprehending a ritual serial murderer, the LAPD isn't as motivated to make an arrest. Go figure. Though I imagine there may be issues with your current state of employment."

Wishard's words cut deep. Becca devoted everything to her career and now there was a pretty good chance it was over. Her head ached even thinking about it. So she wouldn't.

"How is Nate? Is he . . . ," she asked.

"Fucked up? You bet. Maureen did a number on him, and you didn't help things," Wishard said. Becca flinched. She didn't seem to notice, or if she did, she didn't care. "Nate's currently on suicide watch and undergoing intensive counseling at Patton State Hospital. Hopefully he can make it through to the other side. It's going to take time."

"You're not pressing charges?" Becca asked. Wishard stared blankly back at Becca. "For Mo's murder?"

Wishard laughed. "Oh yeah, like cockroaches surviving nuclear war, Maureen Wilson is very much alive."

Becca shook her head. She must have heard Wishard wrong. "Nate shot her. Point-blank in the chest. I saw it. I saw the bullet hit her..."

"Missed her heart by two centimeters. Fucking one in a million. Doctors anticipate a full recovery."

This news stunned Becca. She leaned forward, her chest constricting. She hadn't thought to ask if Mo was alive, but of course she'd survived. Over and over again, Mo defied all the odds.

"I taped her." Becca glanced over at the new iPhone her father bought her, a memory returning. "Mo admitted to everything," Becca said, her words slurring together. Dr. Osterman warned her these were potential side effects, especially if she got emotional. Becca's panic grew, worried that Mo could go free. "It was all on my phone. She confessed to it all."

"I know. I know. We located your phone at the scene,

and our techs were able to preserve the recording. Pretty damning stuff. With Mo's pattern of harassment, the letters from Carlos, as well as Raya's, Nate's, and Ash's testimony, it's likely she'll spend the rest of her life locked up."

Becca hoped that was true. She couldn't dwell on Mo right now. "What about Raya? How is she coping?" Becca asked.

"Your colleague Officer Stanton's been looking after her. Trying to secure housing and get her counseling for possible PTSD."

Nina for the win, Becca thought, hating that they hadn't spoken since everything happened. Becca sank back onto her pillow, their conversation sapping her strength, the pressure growing in her temples, a deep exhaustion hovering like storm clouds. "I appreciate the update," she said, hoping Wishard would get the hint.

"I should let you get some rest," she said. She stood to leave. "It doesn't always happen, but I'm relieved this case had a satisfying conclusion." Becca wasn't sure she would call any of this satisfying.

"Thank you, Detective. I appreciate everything you did for us," Becca said, her eyes flickering shut. It took a few seconds to realize Wishard was still standing there.

"Is there something else?" Becca asked.

Wishard cleared her throat, and for the first time, Becca could tell the woman was flustered, maybe even a little nervous. "I realize I'm overstepping here by saying this, and I'm not one of those ridiculous women who is going to tell you to stay away from my man. Christian's a grown-up. He makes his own choices. All I ask is if there's something going on between the two of you, you don't make me look like an asshole," Wishard said.

Becca's cheeks flushed. She could still remember learning about the personal trainer, and screaming at Christian, "What kind of a pathetic person goes after a married man?" The last thing Becca wanted was to be on the other side of the equation.

"All I want is for Christian to be happy," she said.

Wishard offered Becca an honest-to-goodness smile. "Good. We're finally on the same page."

Becca watched as Wishard headed out. In a perfect world, she would say to hell with Wishard. She would fight for him. She could fight. Maybe it would be enough. Near-death experiences changed people. What if they'd gone through all of this to find their way back to one another? It would be the silver lining to everything. Her husband back. Her daughter home. She wanted it to be that easy, but she knew it wasn't realistic. She meant what she said to Wishard though. She texted Christian. *I need to see you.*

Visiting hours were over when he arrived, still in uniform. "If it isn't Sleeping Beauty," he said with a wry smile. Becca clocked the edge in his voice. She didn't blame him for being pissed. She would be too if the roles were reversed and he did something so reckless. He reluctantly sank into the chair beside Becca's bed.

"I heard that Ash is making a remarkable recovery," he

said. His words seemed a bit too formal, his manner uneasy. Becca forced a smile.

"The doctors say if we behave ourselves and our progress continues, we could both be out of here next week."

"That's good, Becs. That's really good," Christian said. He was quiet, his eyes wandering to the TV in the corner. An awkward silence lingered. Christian finally spoke. "You said you needed to see me. I'm here. What do you want?"

Christian wasn't going to make this easy for her. She probably deserved that.

"I owe you an apology. What I did...the situation I put you and Nina, even Wishard...Joanne in, it wasn't fair, and I wanted to tell you that in person."

"I appreciate that. Is that it?" he asked.

Becca's breath caught in her throat. "I didn't have a choice. I need you to see that."

"That's where you're wrong. There's always a choice. You could've let Wishard do her job. You could've trusted me with what was going on. You didn't do any of that."

"You're right. I didn't. I guess that's it, then," Becca said, hating the empty feeling she experienced. She wasn't sure what she expected, but she could already see what would happen. Christian would go back to his life. Becca to hers.

"I don't know. We could try being friends. See how that goes," he finally said.

Becca couldn't hide her shock. "I'm sure Joanne will be thrilled."

Christian laughed. Becca joined in. "She'll warm up to you eventually. I'll deny I ever said it if you tell her, but Joanne was quite impressed with your determination. I mean, she also thought what you did was incredibly fucking stupid."

"She would be right," Becca said.

"Hold up, Becca Ortiz not arguing? You're sure your head is okay?" Christian asked. She laughed again. There was no going back, or erasing the past, but Becca could finally let go of all that anger and resentment she'd clung to. It was time to move on.

A week later, Becca and Ash were discharged from the hospital. Becca couldn't wait to get home, back to Freud, to her own bed, to food that actually tasted like food. Her mother and father arrived to pick them up, cheerfully packing up the mountain of flowers and get-well gifts. Virginia was in her element, bossing all the nurses around and insisting that Becca stop micromanaging.

"I am my mother's daughter," Becca teased. Virginia wasn't amused, directing her attention to the waiting nurse.

"Why don't you take my daughter downstairs. I'm going to get Ash and we'll meet you there."

Becca tried to walk out on her own. The no-nonsense nurse wasn't having it. "Sorry, Dr. Ortiz. Hospital policy dictates all patients leave in a wheelchair. Even hotshot heroes like yourself."

Becca fought the urge to explain that she wasn't a hero. All those stories were simply exaggerated to sell papers.

Instead she sat in the chair and allowed the nurse to wheel her outside. She waited at the curb, scanning the parking lot for her father's Mercedes.

"Please tell me that blow to the head knocked some sense into you." Becca swiveled around and saw Nina leaning against her father's SUV, carrying a giant teddy bear, the words "Get well soon" scrawled across its chest. The last time Becca spoke to Nina was that night at the hospital when they fought. Becca wanted to reach out, but she was too embarrassed. Without warning, tears streamed down Becca's face. Nina held up her hand. "Come on, Ortiz, what's with the waterworks?" she said.

"It's a side effect of the injury…it makes me…," Becca began.

"An even bigger softie," Nina said.

Becca laughed through her tears, easing herself out of the wheelchair. She wrapped her arms around Nina and the massive bear. "I missed you so much. I have a whole apology prepared. I've practiced it so many times. It might be the best apology ever written."

"I'm sure it's exceptional, but I don't need an apology. All I wanted was for you to be okay." Nina regarded her curiously. "Are you?"

"I got a little lost," Becca said softly.

"It happens. The good news is you always find your way back," Nina said. Becca spotted Ash and her mother heading their way, and she smiled. There was a long road ahead, but Becca was already on her way.

BECCA

All Becca wanted was for things to return to normal for her and Ash, or as normal as possible after surviving a near-death experience. She tried to convince her mother that they'd be fine on their own.

Virginia wasn't having it. "Save the martyr act, Rebecca. If I can't help you girls during your recovery, what good am I?" Becca was so used to doing things on her own, this was an adjustment. Some days Becca wasn't sure if Virginia was their nurse or their jailer. Even Ash was struggling with this new arrangement. "I swear, the other day she actually followed me into the bathroom," Ash said.

After a few days though, things stabilized, and Becca found herself comforted by her mother's constant presence. She'd taken over the kitchen, preparing her famous *migas* for breakfast and what seemed like an endless supply of casseroles, pies, and cakes.

Ash and Becca spent their days camped out on the sofa, binging on Netflix and napping. Their bodies were healing at an impressive pace. Becca knew that the emotional recovery would take much longer. They had weekly appointments with therapists that began immediately. Becca and Ash were undergoing counseling together and on their own to process all they'd been through. It was painful work, but important for their healing. At least that's what Becca told herself. On more than one occasion, she was jolted awake, the sound of Ash's screams sending her running. On those nights, Becca would crawl into bed, holding on to Ash, Freud nestling beside them.

"You're safe. No one's going to hurt you. You're safe," she would whisper over and over again, until they both drifted off to sleep. Becca wanted to believe that. They both did. Mo didn't make that easy. In a perfect world, she would be a nonentity in their lives, locked away where she couldn't hurt them anymore. Unfortunately, the story of a Malibu millionaire, a former philanthropist, a wife and mother, ordering homeless kids to kill for her made for some seriously spectacular headlines. Overnight, Maureen "Mo" Wilson became infamous. There were endless episodes of *Dateline* and *48 Hours* that seemed to air nonstop, not to mention the relentless blogs and vlogs dedicated to Mo. There were *People* magazine covers and a podcast that had millions of hits and talk of a TV adaptation. Everyone was so obsessed with Mo's story, but they seemed to have very little interest in the children whose lives she'd destroyed. Becca remembered the officer's comment on the beach: "just some dumb runaway." These poor kids were as easily discarded and dismissed in death as they were in life. No one would ever know who they really were, what they dreamt about, or how they'd gotten caught up in Mo's web.

Not surprisingly, Becca's career was in the toilet. Placed on paid administrative leave, she considered walking away from the department. When she told her union lawyer that she planned to resign, the woman suggested a more cautious approach. "Lie low, continue your therapy, don't talk to the press, and maybe, just maybe, you'll get your job back."

Becca expressed her doubts. "After all the rules I broke, that seems unlikely."

The lawyer laughed. "You should see the shit they let people get away with. Just be patient, and we'll see what happens." Becca agreed, promising herself she wouldn't make any big decisions.

Once she was back on her feet though, Becca became obsessed with tracking down Raya. Despite Nina's best efforts to secure housing, Raya didn't last long. Two weeks in, she clashed with one of the residents and wound up back on the streets. Becca couldn't stand the thought of Raya out there all alone. It consumed her thoughts, Raya's face invading Becca's dreams, or during her physical therapy. Becca expressed her concern to her mother, then spent the next hour listening to Virginia's outraged objections, insisting that Becca focus on her own rehabilitation.

Becca knew it would eat away at her, so she waited until Virginia and Ash left for therapy; then she called an Uber and headed down to Skid Row.

Becca started at the Downtown Mission and spent the next hour wandering the streets. She finally reached the Tribe's campsite. It was prime Skid Row real estate, and new tenants had moved in. Becca eyed the tents that had been erected, a half dozen men and women sprawled out in camper chairs. Her vision began to blur, another side effect that hadn't faded. Becca grabbed a cup of coffee and sat down, needing a few minutes' rest. She was sitting, staring out the window, when she spotted Raya hurrying past the McDonald's, a cigarette in her hand. Becca rushed out of the restaurant.

"Raya," Becca shouted from across the street.

The young woman was disheveled, her hair uncombed, face streaked with dirt, but the moment she saw Becca, Raya's face lit up. She raced over to Becca and flung her arms around her. "Holy shit, Doc. You're alive and kicking. What the hell are you doing down here?"

Her mannerisms were overly exaggerated, her speech frenzied. "I came down to check on you. I'm sorry I didn't do it sooner."

"Shit, I'm so glad you're better. You and me will always be cool. That bitch was crazy and sometimes crazy can't be contained." She chuckled, stubbing out her cigarette and lighting a new one.

"Where are you staying? Do you have someplace you can go?"

Raya nodded a little too enthusiastically. "Sure thing,

Doc. I'm cool. I mean, I appreciated your cop friend help-ing me out. Couldn't stay there though. They were fucking psychos. I tell you, Doc, they were plotting to take my kid-neys. I heard 'em whispering about it late at night."

Raya must have stopped taking her meds, which meant her delusions had returned. "Can I buy you lunch? I've got some cash if you need a little..."

Raya laughed. "Doc, this wounded bird is doing fine on her own. Don't you worry about me. Focus on getting healthy. Your girl needs her mama."

Becca hugged Raya and held on tight. "You need any-thing, you can always call me. Don't stop by for a visit though. Call first."

Raya burst out laughing again. She returned the hug; then she was on the move, already lighting another ciga-rette. "Gotta bounce, Doc. Take it easy."

Becca wished she could stop her. That she could convince Raya to check herself into a hospital and get back on her meds before her condition worsened. Or that Becca could pay a visit to Mrs. Parsons and convince her to take her daughter back. Though she wasn't sure Raya would even go for that. No matter how well intentioned Becca's efforts might be, Raya was free to make her own choices, even if it meant living right on the edge. As much as Becca didn't want to admit it, Raya was right. There were some wounded birds she just couldn't save.

ASH

Ash grimaced as she slowly pulled on the simple purple sheath dress. It had been almost three months since she'd been discharged from the hospital, but the wound on her abdomen was still healing. All her doctors tried to get her to take pain meds, but Ash wasn't interested. She didn't care how hard the recovery was, Ash wasn't relapsing. Not again.

The good news was Becca was there with her every step of the way. They were quite the pair, with their non-stop physical therapy appointments and twice-weekly sessions with their psychotherapists. All that talking about Mo and Nate and Vic and Leslie and Eli and her own mistakes weighed on her. Sometimes, after a particularly grueling session, Ash thought about running away again, escaping to someplace where she didn't have to think and feel all the time.

Those thoughts were fleeting. Today running was the furthest thing from Ash's mind. Today was adoption day. She remembered when she landed in foster care, one of the older kids told her how it worked. "You'll live with a bunch of shitty people looking to make a few bucks, and when you're eighteen they'll dump your ass back on the streets. No one's ever gonna take a reject teenager."

That girl was wrong. Ash couldn't believe it when Becca told her they had a court date. "All we have to do is show up, and the judge will make it official."

"Wow, you look beautiful," Becca said. Ash turned to see her leaning against the doorframe, wearing a simple white blouse and lilac slacks. "You wore my color," Becca said, her voice trembling with emotion.

When Becca suggested color coordinating, Ash couldn't stop laughing. "Sorry. Not happening," she said. She'd always thought it was lame when families wore matching colors. It wasn't until she saw the purple lace dress on the rack at the Goodwill that Ash said to hell with it. She was glad she had. The look on Becca's face made it all worthwhile.

"You all set? We don't want to be late," Becca said.

"Let's do it," Ash said.

On their way out of the house, Ash knelt beside Freud, throwing her arms around his neck, his tail wagging excitedly as he licked her face. "Sorry, bud, they don't allow pups at the courthouse. We'll celebrate later. All the steak you can eat."

She climbed into the car with Becca, the two of them heading to the Edmund D. Edelman Children's Court in Monterey Park. They were quiet, the anticipation building.

Ash stared out the window, her thoughts turning to Nate. No matter how good things were, and things were really good, he was never far from her thoughts. In the beginning, Ash pleaded with Becca to let her visit. "It'll help him get better if he can see me. He'll see I'm okay, and that I still love him. It'll make him work harder to get well."

Becca wanted Ash to understand that Nate had suffered a serious psychological break.

"We have to give him the best opportunity for recovery. He's learning a lot of coping skills, and he's learning how to trust again. As much as he loves you, the doctors are worried a visit might set him back."

That was the last thing Ash wanted. Becca swore they weren't abandoning Nate. "He's not alone, Ash. He still has us. Right now he needs the doctors and nurses to see him through."

When Ash first learned that Becca knew where Nate was and had lied about it, she was pissed. They spent hours in therapy discussing this betrayal. As more time passed, Ash finally came to realize that Becca's decision was misguided, but she meant well. It wasn't like Ash hadn't told her share of lies.

Still, she hated that he wasn't part of her daily life. Some days Ash's whole body ached, she missed Nate so much. She comforted herself by writing to him. Once a week, she handwrote a letter, since he wasn't allowed access to the Internet. Some of it was boring stuff, like how she was doing in school, or stories about Zoe and Allison, the friends she'd made when she joined the school newspaper.

She couldn't believe she'd actually joined the paper. Ash wasn't big on extracurriculars, but she wanted an opportunity to put her photography experience to practical use. She was surprised by how much she enjoyed taking pictures of her classmates, the feeling of accomplishment when the paper went to print each week, seeing her name in color underneath the photo. Sometimes she sent Nate copies of the paper in her letters. More than anything she wanted him to know she hadn't forgotten him. She ended every letter with a promise. "I'll wait for you. As long as it takes."

She never talked about Mo or Vic or the others. Even if the subject weren't off-limits, Ash wanted to forget them all. Every time she opened Twitter or Instagram, she was confronted with it all over again. Ash hated that people were treating Mo like she was some misunderstood hero. The worst were the private messages from people who thought Ash was to blame and that she should have died. Ash didn't tell Becca about those. They were just bored losers who spewed shit to feel important. Mo's son, Aidan, had sent her an Instagram message and they'd talk a lot about how hard it was.

They both hoped it would all go away once Mo went to trial. She was facing three counts of murder for Leslie, Eli, and a third victim, sixteen-year-old Rachel Whiteman, two counts of conspiracy to commit murder for Ash and

Becca, one count of kidnapping for Raya, and four counts of advising and encouraging suicide. Ash couldn't wait to stand in front of a judge and jury and tell them everything. She wanted the whole world to know who Mo really was.

Unfortunately, Mo decided to make their lives even more hellish and represent herself. Arguments over whether Mo was competent to act as her own attorney were now dragging on. Ash wasn't surprised. Mo thought she was smarter than everyone else. Of course she thought she could win this case. Becca wasn't worried, or at least that's how she acted. "This case may drag on, but she's not going anywhere. The best thing you can do is forget about her."

It was good advice. No way was Ash letting Mo ruin things, especially not today. Becca pulled into the parking lot and they hurried through the courthouse, both of them a bundle of nerves. As they headed toward the courtroom, Ash saw Virginia, Rafi, and Nina waiting outside of it, all wearing various shades of purple. It was totally cheesy, and Ash would never say it out loud, but she kind of liked it. No one had ever done something like this for her.

"You both look gorgeous," Virginia said. She reached out and gave Ash a hug. Virginia had always been a bit of a cold fish, but she was starting to display actual human emotions. Ash was happy for Becca, who seemed to like having her mother around.

Ash's social worker, a very patient woman named Louise, echoed Virginia's sentiment. "You two are like a couple of supermodels," she said, hugging Ash so tightly she practically crushed her in the process.

"We're up in just a few minutes," Louise said. Ash glanced down at her phone anxiously. There was one more person she wanted here, but they were running out of time. There was always a chance he wouldn't come.

"Hey, what is it? Is something wrong?" Becca asked, following Ash's gaze to the bank of elevators at the end of the hall.

"It's nothing," Ash said, trying to hide her disappointment. She was about to send a text when she spotted Christian stepping off the elevator. He wore a fitted gray suit and purple tie as requested, and he carried two yellow roses. Ash watched Becca's eyes widen.

"I can't believe it," she said softly.

Christian joined them, handing one rose to Becca and the other to Ash. "I don't understand. How did you know it was today?" she asked.

"I got a phone call that my presence was requested, so here I am."

Becca turned to Ash. "*You* called him?"

"You said it was a family thing." Ash saw Becca getting all misty-eyed and this was Ash's cue to step away. It was just way too early for the waterworks. "I'm going to take a few photos," Ash said, digging into her bag. She began to shoot, loving the feel of the camera in her hands, the way the world suddenly made sense when she was surveying it through her lens. Nina was the one who'd let it slip about Christian's breakup. Ash had always been kind of shitty to Christian. She couldn't admit it back then, but she'd wanted Becca to herself. She knew their relationship was complicated, and that too much time might have passed for a second chance, but Ash figured it couldn't hurt to give them a little push.

A few minutes later Rafi commandeered the camera. "No hiding out. This is your day."

He took charge, ordering everyone to gather together for a group photo, their laughter ringing out as he struggled to operate Ash's high-tech camera. They all posed, laughing and smiling. Louise finally reappeared and said, "It's time."

This was it. Becca took Ash's hand and they all filed into the courtroom. Becca and Ash sat at the front table, Ash's lawyer by her side. The judge, a gruff-looking elderly man with an unruly head of white hair, quickly entered, banging his gavel and ordering the court into session. He regarded Becca with a probing gaze.

"Ma'am, can you verify your name and confirm you are able to support and provide for the minor child?"

Becca spoke, her voice clear and steady. "My name is Dr. Becca Ortiz, and I am more than able to provide and care for Ash."

He nodded. "Can you tell me why you would like to adopt Ash? Why you want to make her a part of your family?"

Becca smiled down at Ash, tears welling in her eyes. *Of course Becca was already crying*, Ash thought. "The luckiest day of my life was when I met this remarkable young woman. Ash has changed my life. She has taught me so many things, how to appreciate Malibu at sunset, the culinary pleasure that is putting salt on watermelon, a Southern thing I urge you all to try. She even turned me into a country music fan, which I would have said was impossible. I watched her grow as well, overcoming things most people couldn't begin to imagine, developing her photography talent, and learning how to love. Ash has made me better in every way possible. I already feel like her mother, but I would love to make it official. It would be my greatest honor to have her as my daughter."

Ash bit her lip, promising herself she wasn't going to cry in front of all these people. She could see the judge peering down, the courtroom's attention focused on her.

"Young lady, would you mind telling the court why you would like Dr. Ortiz to adopt you?"

Ash paused. The lawyer told her the judge sometimes asked questions, so this wasn't coming out of nowhere. Ash wanted to take her time and answer the question the right way. She nervously adjusted her watch, catching sight of the Tribe tattoo. Becca offered to pay for laser removal, or she suggested they find a tattoo artist who could transform the current tattoo into something new. Ash considered both options, but in the end she decided to keep it. This tattoo was a reminder above all else that she was a survivor.

With that in mind, Ash addressed the judge, her voice trembling slightly. "I wasn't very nice to Becca the first time we met. If I'm being honest, I was kind of awful. At first, I was just using her. I knew it wasn't right, but using people is all I knew. Use them before they used me. Becca would take me to all these nice dinners and buy me clothes and makeup. Only Becca wasn't most people. She kept coming back. Again and again, she came back. Even when I screwed up. Even when I almost ruined everything." Ash's voice trembled. She took a deep breath. "She never gave up on me. That's why I want her to be my mom. Because no matter what happens, she'll always be there."

The judge nodded, a lazy smile appearing on his face. "Young lady, tell me, what would you like your legal name to be?"

Ash didn't hesitate. "Ash Ortiz," she said

His smile never wavered. "Ordinarily my courtroom is a very serious place where deeply sad things occur. I cannot tell you how much happiness and joy it brings me to see you and your family here today. It is with great pleasure I finalize this adoption and officially welcome Ash Ortiz to her new family. Congratulations!"

The judge banged his gavel, and the courtroom exploded with applause and cheers. Ash looked around at Christian and Nina, Rafi and Virginia. Her new family. All the bad stuff, her mother's abuse, those endless days and weeks and months on the streets worrying about her safety, were replaced with the warmest feeling that she finally belonged. She hated that Leslie and Eli and Vic and all the others were denied this happiness, denied a future of their own. She hated that Nate was waging a war with his own mind. But like her therapist reminded her again and again, Ash wasn't responsible for any of that. She deserved happiness. She told herself that when things got hard again—and Ash wasn't naive enough to think they wouldn't—she would force herself to remember today. Ash turned and saw Becca smiling back at her, but this time Ash was the one with tears in her eyes. Without hesitating, she hugged Becca, holding on tight, just like she'd been taught. After all the years of searching and seeking, all the years of running, Ash was finally home.

MO

Jail wasn't nearly as terrible as Mo anticipated. If she were being truthful, her accommodations were actually quite comfortable, a significant improvement over the Tribe's previous dwellings. Mo had a bed, three square meals, and space for contemplation. Her lodgings at the county jail were more than adequate.

Of course, Mo's recovery wasn't without struggles. The first few months she spent on the medical ward. After Nate shot her in cold blood, Mo's condition was quite critical. The staff didn't say it outright, but Mo could sense they were impressed with her miraculous recovery.

"Very few patients survive an injury of this magnitude," the surgeon said in awe.

Mo wanted to tell him that she had to survive. She was the chosen one, after all. Unfortunately, there were too many naysayers and doubters, so Mo kept those thoughts to herself.

Once her wounds healed, she was transferred to a special unit for high-profile inmates and kept in isolation, the guards monitoring her 24-7. Vic and the others had gone ahead with the original plan, and they were concerned Mo intended to join them and end it all. There were moments after her brutal attack when Mo considered that alternative. After all, she'd made a promise to Vic and the others that she would join them in the afterlife. She hated breaking their trust, but she wasn't sure that was her destiny. At least not yet.

Fortunately, after a month, the authorities agreed that Mo wasn't a suicide risk, and she was released into the general population. She preferred this to being sent to a mental hospital. The last thing Mo wanted was to be drugged up and shuffling around like some kind of mindless zombie. She made that clear when the ghoulish lawyer turned up.

"I won't let them poison my body and mind with their toxic chemicals. I won't allow them to alter my thinking."

"I have to disagree with you, Mrs. Wilson. One of these facilities would be the best possible place. You would be able to get specialized, individualized care."

Mo wasn't budging. "I'm not pleading insanity, Graham, so shut up and find a new defense."

"Maureen, I need you to work with me. I am trying to ensure you don't get the goddamn death penalty."

She'd already lost faith in this idiot before he even stepped into the room. The charges against her were bogus. If this man possessed an ounce of intelligence, he would see that. His incompetence was quite astounding, something she felt compelled to share when she fired him. She watched him sputter and spin, his chiseled, overly spray-tanned features contorting. "If you do this, your father won't continue to fund your defense. As it is, you have caused him great embarrassment. I'm your last chance, Maureen."

Mo laughed. She wasn't interested in his threats. She decided the best course of action was to defend herself. The courts weren't making this easy, but Mo wasn't in any rush. In her short time in jail, she'd come across some truly bright souls, girls who were desperately in need of guidance and mentorship.

Of course, she missed the Tribe. Mo's family played such a huge role in her growth and development over the years. Losing them was unfortunate. Still, she firmly believed one must not dwell on the past. It wasn't as if everyone had died in vain. Mo and the Tribe's message was out there.

Mo wasn't sure at first. She was worried Nate and Ash and Becca would somehow pervert Mo and the Tribe's mission. It wasn't until the letters began to arrive that she recognized this might be different. People sent her letters from all over the world. Many of them were from angry pathetic souls, people who called Mo a monster, and a sick bitch, and all kinds of horrifying names. But there were hundreds of others who offered encouragement, understanding, and prayers. People pleaded with her to write them, wanting to know more about her way of living.

This was a big moment. If Mo wanted to maintain integrity and loyalty, a response was required. She couldn't ignore these troubled souls. That's when Mo recruited several of the girls from her unit to help. Three times a week, after lunch, they responded to each and every letter. In them, Mo poured out her heart, offering gratitude to the people who showed her kindness and doing her best to explain herself to those who misinterpreted her message. They needed to understand that the end of days was coming. It was up to Mo to prepare these lost souls for when it happened. This work was therapeutic for Mo, and it provided the girls with a deeper understanding of what she was all about. Her excitement only grew when she heard from Corey, one of the guards, a sweet twenty-two-year-old girl from Tujunga who worked the evening shift.

"You're all over the news and Twitter, and, like, your pictures are in *People* and *US Weekly*. On the *Today* show, they were talking about making your story into a movie," Corey said.

Corey continued rambling, but Mo stopped listening, thinking about all the possibilities. For so long she'd shunned the spotlight, convinced her message wouldn't translate. This news was a revelation. People cared. They wanted to hear from her. It took a bit of digging and some outside help from Corey, who did some Internet research for her. Mo was able to track down a former classmate who worked at one of the big Hollywood agencies.

It didn't take long before the agent showed up with all kinds of ideas about how to get the word out about her story. There were some legal issues, something about criminals not profiting off their crimes or some nonsense like that. Mo wasn't concerned, and neither was the agent. "I see a film. Maybe even a series. It's a star vehicle. Actresses will be lining up to play this role. It's award caliber for sure."

Mo didn't care about fame and fortune. It was her vision for the Tribe that she was focused on; all the Hollywood nonsense was simply a means to an end. Mo's visions were no longer a pipe dream. She was slowly rebuilding. Once she was exonerated for her crimes and set free, the sky was the limit. Mo couldn't help but smile. This was just the beginning. *The Tribe endures.*

ACKNOWLEDGMENTS

As I was writing *The Runaway*, I often joked it was like my troubled third child. Fortunately, my wonderful editors, Anne Clarke at Redhook, and Emily Griffin and Sonny Marr at Penguin Random House were there to co-parent. Thank you for your laser-focused notes and incredible patience, and for believing I could and would get it right. There are so many people who helped bring this book to life as well. I'm so thankful to the talented marketing and PR teams at PRH and Redhook, especially Ellen Wright. Special thanks as well to cover designers Glenn O'Neil and Lisa Marie Pompilio. To my lovely, hardworking agents at WME, Eve Atterman, Matilda Watson, and Janine Kamouh, thank you for doing all you do so I can focus on doing what I love.

This book tackles highly sensitive subjects that include homelessness, infertility, and mental health issues. To accurately portray these topics, I relied on countless experts. My tireless search to find someone with Becca's professional experience led me to Dr. Ryan Solomon, a clinical psychologist who spent years working with the LAPD's Mental Evaluation Unit. Ryan's unique experience, as well as his understanding of storytelling, helped bring Becca to life and truly enriched her character. Thanks to Jonathan Thiele at the Denver Health Medical Center and Dr. Jessica Lange Osterman for providing their own expertise. To Javen Smith, thank you for your courage and for entrusting me with your foster care experiences.

I'm grateful as well to Scott Madden, a retired captain with the Riverside County Sheriff's Department, for sharing his expertise and laying the groundwork for this story. I'm also lucky that one of my longtime high school friends, Matt McArthur, is an expert in all things police related. Thanks, Matt, for responding to nightly e-mails and phone calls with random questions, and for knowing how to fill those annoying plot holes. Thanks also to Travis Ivie, Taylor Howerton, and Halley Massey-Felt for reenacting what has to be the most entertaining weapons demonstration I have ever seen.

Thank you, Mem Kennedy, Rebekah Faubion, Liza Sandoval, Zoe Broad, Adam Czartoryski, Nick Chapa, and Adesuwa McCalla for being such amazing friends and creative champions.

To Edward Santiago, my creative guru, they say the third time's a charm, but I feel lucky each and every time we go on this journey. Dedi Felman, you're a rock star, who with a few targeted questions helped break this book wide open.

Allison Rymer, thanks for coming to my rescue and acting as though reading several drafts of an entire novel was no big deal. You're my hero.

Zac Hug, I am so grateful for your LA field trips, your wordsmithery, and of course your friendship. Elena Zaretsky, whenever I sounded the alarm, you were there with an encouraging word and a creative fix for whatever was ailing me.

Giselle Jones, there's a bit of you in Becca, and I couldn't love her or you more. I am in awe of all you do to encourage, support, and nurture those around you. The world is a better place with you in it.

To my sister, Heather Overton, nothing I write is done until it receives your seal of approval. Thank you for your patience and for reading hundreds if not thousands of pages. Your notes would be annoying if they weren't spot-on. You're one of the most talented people I know, and I can't wait to see what you do next.

I am so grateful to my amazing, handsome husband, David Boyd, who told me on our first date, "I don't get stressed," and then married a very stressed-out writer. Thanks for accepting my messy nature (and forever tidying up around me), making me laugh, and reminding me no matter how hard things are to keep fighting. I am so lucky I get to live out my dreams with you by my side.

Finally, to all the readers who bought my books, checked them out at their local libraries, passed them along to friends, and took the time to blog, e-mail, or share on social media, thank you for your unwavering support. While *The Runaway* is a work of fiction, it is by far my most personal book. I've experienced many of these issues firsthand, from mental health struggles to ongoing infertility issues. Writing what you know comes with its own pitfalls, and I sometimes questioned why I wrote a book that was so close to home. Some days your messages were all that kept me going. I hope wherever you are, whatever challenges or struggles you may be going through, you know you're not alone. Keep going, keep fighting, and remember to breathe.